LARGE
PRINT
EDITION

RANDOM
HOUSE

THE
COBRA
EVENT

A NOVEL

Richard Preston

Published by Random House Large Print
in association with Random House, Inc.
New York 1997

Copyright © 1997 by Urania, Inc.

All rights reserved under International and
Pan-American Copyright Conventions.
Published in the United States of America
by Random House Large Print
in association with Random House, Inc.,
New York, and simultaneously in Canada
by Random House of Canada Limited, Toronto.
Distributed by Random House, Inc., New York.

Library of Congress Cataloging-in-Publication Data

Preston, Richard, 1954–
The cobra event / Richard Preston.
p.   cm.
ISBN 0-679-77447-5 (PB)   1. Large type books.   I. Title.
[PS3566.R4126C63   1997]
813'.54—dc21   97-16258   CIP

Random House Web Address: http://www.randomhouse.com/

Printed in the United States of America

FIRST LARGE PRINT EDITION

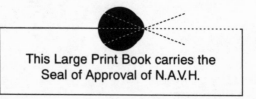

This book is dedicated to my brother
David G. Preston, M.D.,
and to
all public health professionals,
wherever they may be

*It is the greatest art of the devil
to convince us he does not exist.*

—Baudelaire

The Reality Behind
The Cobra Event

This book is about biological weapons—the modern version of what were once known as germ-warfare weapons. The creation of advanced biological weapons using methods of genetic engineering and biotechnology is sometimes called "black biology." My previous book, *The Hot Zone,* which was about the threat of emerging viruses, particularly the Ebola virus, led me naturally to biological weapons: What is a bioweapon? Who has them? What can these weapons do? The characters and story developed here are fictional, not based on any real persons or contemporary events, but the historical background *is* real, the government structures are real, and the science is real or based on what is possible.

The Cobra Event is also about forensics, which is the science of looking at physical evidence to analyze a crime and identify its perpetrator. I call the particular forensic operation in this book a "Reachdeep operation." *Reachdeep* is a term invented by me, but it is in fact a special type of criminal investigation, and it is defined by a partly classified presidential order known as National Security Directive 7. If a biologic terror attack were to occur in the United States, there are organizations that would implement an operation similar to Reachdeep. My sources include people at the Federal Bureau of Investigation, in the U.S. military, and elsewhere in the government who have been given the task of preparing for a Directive 7 emergency. At one point I was at the F.B.I. Academy in Quantico, Virginia, where I heard an F.B.I. scientist who knows a lot about biological weapons describe them to a class of agents in training. He said in a simple way, "You will be dealing with this during your careers." The room became very quiet. You could have heard a pin drop. I would say they believed him.

I pursued the subject of biological weapons with the same reporting methods I've used for my previous books, which were nonfiction. The nonfiction roots of this book run deep. I conducted numerous interviews with experts, some of whom did not wish to go on the record by name but were willing to give detailed factual information on condition of anonymity. My sources include eyewitnesses who have seen a variety of biological-weapons installations in different countries, and people who have developed and tested strategic bioweapons. They are scientists, medical doctors, and technical people, both military and nonmilitary. They understand what they have seen, and they describe it with precision.

As I drafted this story, I re-interviewed people, telling them the story as it developed, asking them, "Could this happen? Is this how the U.S. government would work? How would you respond to *this*?"

The transparent substance I call "viral glass" in this book is an actual material. I have chosen not to give its technical name or describe it too precisely. I have deliberately distorted and blurred certain key aspects of the bioweapons-making process so as not to publish a deployable recipe.

The biosensor technology that I call "Felix" does not presently exist but is in development. Biosensor research is often classified, so I have had to make educated guesses as to what may be possible. What I call the "hand-held Boink" biosensors actually do exist now in prototype form. (I call them Boinks because I imagine them giving off a chiming tone when they detect a biological weapon.) They have been partly developed by the United States Navy.

The natural strain of the virus in this book is real, and engineered strains of it have been developed with a broadened host range. They are capable of infecting but not necessarily replicating in the cells of mammals, including humans. The virus has great peaceful potential because it is so versatile. Its versatility also makes it a potential weapon. I have imagined the engineered form of the virus that appears here as Cobra, but it should be taken as one example of a wide range of possibilities that actually exist for the construction of advanced bioweapons. The knowledge is public, the techniques are commonplace. The dark apple hangs on the tree.

□

For many years the scientific community told itself and the public that biological weapons were not much of a problem, but recently there has been a painful shift in thinking. Many scientists have come to believe that biological weapons are a serious threat that has not been reckoned with. People close to this process have described it to me as an opening of the eyes. Even so, some experts are reluctant to talk too freely about biological weapons, for fear that the information could spark bioterrorism or might encourage countries to cross the threshold into biological weaponry. Other experts say that the problem has become so bad that the public simply must be told. I say that problems that aren't moved into the light of general public discussion become less manageable as time goes by. Public awareness can help shape a constructive response from governments and scientists around the world far more effectively than the lone warnings of a few experts.

In case anyone should accuse me of being "anti-science," let me say that I am exactly the opposite of that. Open, peer-reviewed biological research can reap great benefits. Genetic engineering is a process, like metallurgy. Steel can be used for ploughshares or swords. What is dangerous is human intent. The next emerging virus may not come from a tropical rain forest; it may come from a bioreactor. In a deeper sense it will come from the human mind. To think that the power of the genetic code is not being bent toward weapons is to ignore the growing body of evidence, the lessons of history, and the reality of human nature. As Thucydides pointed out, hope is an expensive commodity. It makes better sense to be prepared.

RICHARD PRESTON
September 1997

Contents

Part One

TRIAL

Arc of the Circle

Kate Moran was an only child. She was seventeen years old and lived with her parents in a loft apartment on the top floor of a handsome old building to the west of Union Square, just on the edge of Greenwich Village. One Wednesday morning in late April, Kate was slow getting up. She had woken in the middle of the night in a sweat, but it went away, and she fell back asleep, into bad dreams that she could not remember. She came awake with a fresh cold, and she could feel her period coming on.

"Kate!" It was Nanette, the housekeeper, calling to her from the kitchen. "Katie!"

"Okay." She didn't like being called Katie.

She sat up and found a Kleenex and blew her nose, and went into the bathroom. She brushed her teeth, then went back into the bedroom and dressed in a flowered dress that she had found in a flea market. The mornings could be chilly this time of year, so she put on a sweater.

Kate had wavy russet hair, beautiful hair with natural pale highlights, which she wore medium length. Her eyes were grayish blue or bluish gray, depending on the light and the weather and her mood (or so she liked to think); complicated eyes. Her face was changing fast. She could almost see the bones of the woman emerging, yet she had found that the more she stared at her face in a mirror the less she understood it. She thought about this as she brushed her hair, pushing it back so that the two platinum earrings in her left ear were visible.

Kate's mother called her the Packrat, because she accumulated things. The worktable in the corner of her room was littered with old cigar boxes covered with their original illustrations, plastic boxes, metal containers, purses, bags, puzzles. Things that opened and closed. There was an old dollhouse that she had found in a junk shop in Brooklyn and had been taking apart, cannibalizing it for a project. She reached into the dollhouse and pulled out a prism made of glass, and the smooth white skull of a vole, with tiny yellow teeth, that she had bought at a bone shop in SoHo. She held the prism up to the light falling through the skylight of her bedroom, and just to see what it would look like, she held the vole's head behind the prism. No colors appeared; you needed direct sunlight. She stuffed the objects into her knapsack. They were going to become part of the Box that she was constructing in Mr. Talides's art room at the Mater School, a private girls' school on the Upper East Side.

"Katie!" Nanette was calling.

"Okay, okay." She sighed and threw her knapsack over her shoulder and went out into the living area—a large open space with polished wood floors and antique furniture and rugs. Her parents had both already left for work. Her father was a partner in a Wall Street investment house, and her mother was an attorney at a midtown law firm.

In the kitchen, Nanette had poured orange juice and toasted a bagel.

Kate shook her head. She wasn't hungry. She sneezed.

Nanette tore off a paper towel and handed it to her. "Do you want to stay home?" "Uh-uh." Kate was already out the door and into the elevator.

It was a glorious morning. She hurried along Fifteenth Street to Union Square, striding on long legs, heading for the subway entrance. The ash trees in the square were threatening to break bud. Puffy white clouds drifted in a blue sky over the city, winds whipping in from the southwest, bringing a warmer day than Kate had expected. The daffodils were mostly gone and the tulips were blown and flopping their petals. Spring was beginning to give way to summer. A homeless man passed Kate going in the other direction, leaning into the warm wind as he pushed a shopping cart piled high with plastic garbage bags full of his possessions. She threaded through the stalls of the farmer's market that filled up the northern and western sides of the square, and at the subway kiosk she ran down the stairs and caught the uptown Lexington Avenue express.

The train was crowded, and Kate found herself crushed in a corner of the first car by the front window. It was where she had liked to stand when she was a girl riding with her mother and father, back when they had more time to take her places. You could look out the window and see the steel columns marching by under the car's headlights, and the track extending out into seemingly infinite darkness. Switches and branches whirled past, and if you were on an express train that caught up with a local on the adjacent track, there would be a moment when the two trains were locked together in a shuddering rush forward.

She didn't like it. The lights flashing in the tunnel made her feel sick. She turned away. Then she found herself looking at the faces in the subway car. The faces bothered her. If you look at too many faces jammed together, every face begins to look alien. People in the subway can look . . . humanoid.

The Mater School was only a few blocks from the Eighty-sixth Street subway station. Kate was still running a little late, and by the time she got to the stone parish building that housed the school, the younger girls had mostly gone inside, although some of the upper-school girls were hanging around on the steps.

"Kates, I have to tell you something." It was her friend Jennifer Ramosa. They walked in together, with Jennifer talking about something that Kate didn't follow. Kate felt strange, as if a feather had brushed across her face. . . .

A gong rang . . . and there was the headmistress, Sister Anne Threader, going by. . . . For a moment Kate had a feeling of vertigo, as if she were staring into a black pit with no bottom, and she dropped her knapsack. It hit the floor with a smack. There was a sound of breaking glass.

"Kate? You moron. What's the matter with you?" Jennifer said.

Kate shook her head. It seemed to clear. She was going to be late for homeroom.

"What's going on, Kates?" Jennifer asked.

"I'm fine." She picked up her knapsack. It slushed and rattled. "Something broke. Damn, I broke my prism." She headed into class, annoyed with herself.

□

At about ten o'clock in the morning, Kate went to the nurse's office and got some Tylenol. It didn't help her cold, which was getting worse and worse. It was a real sinus cold. Her mouth was hurting a lot; it felt bumpy and it stung. She was debating whether or not to go home. She decided to go to art class and leave after that.

The art teacher, Peter Talides, was a balding, middle-aged painter, likable and disorganized, and his art room was a satisfying place. Students hung out there during the day and after school hours. Kate settled herself at a table in the corner of the room, near the window, where her assembled Box was taking shape. It was an ambitious construction, a kind of a house, made of pieces of dollhouses and all kinds of found objects. Kate felt dizzy and weak. She tried to work on the house but couldn't remember what she had planned to do with it. She felt as if she had never seen it before and as if some other person had built it.

"I want to go home," she said out loud.

The students looked at her. She started to stand up—she intended to go back to the nurse's office—when suddenly she felt really dizzy. "Oh, no," she said. She got partway to her feet, and found she couldn't stand. She sat down heavily on her work stool.

"What's the matter, Kates?" Jennifer asked.

There was a crash. Kate had slid off the stool and landed on the floor beside her worktable.

Peter Talides came hurrying over. "Are you all right?"

"I'm sick," Kate said in a thick voice. She began to tremble. She was sitting on the floor with her legs out straight. "My mouth hurts."

Talides bent over her. "We need to get you to the nurse," he said.

She didn't answer. Her teeth were chattering and her face was flushed and feverish.

Peter Talides was frightened. Kate's nose was running with clear mucus that flowed down over her lips. It was gushing out, as if she had a very bad cold. Her eyes flicked over his face without seeming to see him.

"Someone tell the nurse," he said. "Go on! Go!" To Kate he said, "Just sit still, okay?"

Kate said, "I think I'm going to throw up."

"Can you stand up?"

"No. Yes."

He helped her to her feet. "Jennifer. Prasaya. Please take Kate to the bathroom, will you?"

The two girls helped Kate out of the room and into the bathroom, while Peter Talides waited in the hallway.

Kate stood in front of the sink, hanging on to it, wondering if she was going to throw up. Something moved inside her mind, as if some being that was not Kate but *was* Kate was in agony. There was a mirror over the sink. For a moment, she couldn't bring herself to look. Then she opened her mouth. The inside of the mouth reflected in the mirror was dotted with black blood blisters. They looked like shining ticks feeding there.

She screamed and hung on to the sink, and screamed again. She lost her balance and crumpled to her knees.

Peter Talides ran into the bathroom.

He found Kate Moran sitting on the floor, looking at him with glassy eyes. The clear mucus was running out of her nose and mouth, and she was weeping. She said in a thick voice, "I don't know what to do."

Kate's expression went blank. The left side of her face rippled in a series of twitches that moved in a wave. The twitches were marching jacksonian seizures. Suddenly she uttered a fierce, guttural cry. She toppled backward. Her knees straightened out and her body seized and froze hard in a clonic jerk. Her head hit the tiled floor with a crack. The stiffness lasted for a few seconds. Then her arms and legs began to tremble and jerk rhythmically. She lost control of her bladder. A puddle formed under her.

Talides tried to hold her arms still. "My God!" he cried.

Her legs lashed out in a clonus, knocking over a wastebasket, kicking Talides backward. She was very strong. Then her body began to scissor back and forth. Her teeth clicked together repeatedly. Her mouth was working. Her lips moved and rippled. Her tongue stuck out and was withdrawn again. Her eyes were half open.

He thought Kate was looking at him and trying to say something to him. She moaned but no language came out.

Then her teeth sank into her lower lip, cutting through the lip, and a run of blood went down her chin and neck. She bit her lip again, hard, with ferocity, and she made a groaning animal sound. This time, the lip detached and hung down. She pulled her lip in, sucked it into her mouth, and swallowed. Now she was chewing again. Eating the inside of her mouth, chewing her lips, the insides of her cheeks. The movement of her teeth was insectile, like the feeding movements of an insect larva chewing on its food: intense, greedy, automatic—a kind of repetitive yanking at the tissues of her mouth. Her tongue suddenly protruded. It was coated with blood and bits of bloody skin. She was eating her mouth from the inside.

"She's biting herself!" he yelled. "Help!"

He got his hands around her head and tried to hold her chin steady, but he couldn't stop her teeth from gnawing. He could see her tongue curling and moving behind her teeth. He was begging for help at the top of his lungs. Jennifer was next to him, weeping, crying for help, too. The bathroom door was open, and students were standing in the hallway, looking in, stunned with fright. Most were crying. Several of them had run to call 911.

The girl's body went into a back-and-forth thrashing movement. Then she began to writhe. It was a type of writhing associated with damage to the base of the brain, the midbrain, a knot of structures at the top of the spinal cord. The movements were what is known as basal writhing.

Kate opened her mouth and a hoarse croak came out. She was lying on her back now. Her spine began to bend backward. Her body arched into the air. Her stomach lifted up higher and higher. Her teeth clacked together in a spasm. Her spine re-curved impossibly far, lifting off the floor, until only the back of her head and her heels were touching the floor, her stomach raised up. Her body formed the shape of a C. Her head and heels were supporting her weight.

Her body remained poised in the air, writhing slowly, squirming, as if it were being driven by some force trying to escape from within. Her eyes opened wide. They were pure white. There were no pupils. The pupils had rolled up into the eye sockets. Her lips drew back from her teeth and she smiled, and a dark, bright liquid flowed from her nose. It was a nosebleed, a heavy epistaxis. With each heartbeat, a pulse of blood came from both nostrils. The epistaxis stained Talides's shirt and ran across the floor, where the blood tangled with the urine on the tiles and swirled down a drain in the center. She drew a rasp-ing breath, inhaling blood—the nosebleed was pour-ing back down her airway now, running into her lungs. Her body was as hard as a piece of timber. Cracking sounds came from her spine.

The nosebleed died down.

The bleeding stopped. It stopped completely.

Her spine relaxed. She sank to the floor. She coughed once, lurching up blood mixed with sputum.

Peter Talides was on top of her, his face to her face, crying, "Kate! Kate! Hang on!" He had taken a CPR class with the Red Cross years earlier, but he couldn't remember what to do.

□

Inside, deep in her mind, Kate came awake, fully aware. She heard Mr. Talides's voice begging her to hang on. There was an absolute peace, no feeling of pain, and she couldn't see anything. It was not possible to hang on. She thought: Oh. She fell away.

Part Two

1969

Forbidden Zone

JOHNSTON ATOLL

Looking into history is like shining a flashlight into a cave. You can't see the whole cave, but as you play the flashlight around, a hidden shape is revealed.

□

One evening late in July 1969, a thousand miles southwest of Hawaii, the waters of the Pacific Ocean had calmed to a liquefaction of blue. A moderate swell rocked the deck of a fishing boat that was heading slowly across the prevailing wind, and the boat's radio masts and weather sensors swung gently. The sun had descended to a handsbreadth above the horizon. Mare's-tail clouds fingered in veils across the sky, but you could see the moon, a gibbous moon, as pale as a spirit. Somewhere on that sphere the Americans had been walking.

Captain Gennadi Yevlikov held his binoculars on the moon, wondering which of its dark areas was the Sea of Tranquility, but he couldn't remember. Then he focused on the horizon toward the north. He could not see Johnston Atoll, but he knew it was there, and that the Americans were there, too.

All around Yevlikov on the deck, the scientific men from the Ministry of Health hurried to put out petri dishes and to set up their bubblers and glassware. They moved among equipment racks, intense, disquieted, trying not to break anything. Fishing nets, unused and in perfect condition, hung from winches above them.

A sailor standing near the bow shouted, and Yevlikov turned and saw that the man was pointing to the north, in the direction of the atoll. Yevlikov looked with his naked eyes, then snapped up his binoculars. He saw a tiny brown dot on the horizon, above the water. It was not moving. There was no sound. For a moment he thought the dot must be a seabird.

It was not moving. But it grew larger.

Then he saw the wings. They were greenish brown.

It was an American Phantom jet with Marine Corps coloration. The reason it seemed not to be moving was that it was heading straight for the fishing boat. It was perhaps a hundred meters off the water. It gave no sound, which meant that it was traveling at supersonic speed. Yevlikov saw a pop-flash around the tail: the pilot had just fired his afterburner. The Phantom, already traveling close to Mach 1, was still accelerating toward the boat. It came lower, skimming the surface of the sea. They saw a V-shaped shock wave tearing up the water behind the Phantom. There was total silence.

"Down!" Yevlikov shouted.

With a thudding of bodies, everyone hurled himself to the deck. They stabbed their fingers into their ears and opened their mouths wide.

They all did this, except for one scientist from the Ministry of Health, a thin man wearing spectacles. He stood by an assembly of laboratory glassware, his mouth hanging open, his eyes fixed on the incoming Phantom like a man before a firing squad.

The Phantom went over the Russian trawler going Mach 1.4. It passed exactly ten feet above the boat's foredeck, flicking by in silence.

An instant later, the sonic boom blew over them like a bomb. Yevlikov felt his body bounce on the deck. The breath was knocked from his lungs. Every window and port, every gauge, the petri dishes, all of the laboratory glassware, everything made of glass exploded, and Yevlikov felt glass showering over his back. The air was filled with falling glass and the roar of the departing Phantom, its afterburner glowing as it climbed to get off the water. Two more trailing sonic booms passed over the boat, echoes of the Phantom's passage.

The Ministry of Health scientist was left standing in a heap of glass. His eyeglasses had cracked. He touched one finger to his ear. His finger came away with blood on it. His eardrum had broken.

Yevlikov stood up. "Clean up, please."

"Captain! There's another one out there!"

"What's he doing?"

The second Marine Corps Phantom was flying easily, almost languidly, turning at an angle to the boat. There was a playful quality in its movements that seemed incredibly dangerous.

One of the sailors muttered, "American *gav-nuki*." Shitheads.

Now the Phantom's wings tipped, and it banked, and it began to close with the Russian trawler. This time, they heard the Phantom coming. It was traveling slower than the speed of sound.

There was a clattering noise mixed with a slushy sound of bodies moving through broken glass as the crew and scientists fell to the deck. This time Yevlikov remained standing. I will not bow to these people again, he said to himself.

The incoming Phantom cocked its wings slightly as the pilot made fine adjustments to his aim. He was targeting the boat.

He won't open, Yevlikov said to himself.

The Phantom opened.

He saw the cannon tracers coming straight in. Whanging explosions tore through the bow where the shells hit, and white towers ripped the water. The Phantom floated by with a metallic whine, the pilot holding up his middle finger at them, and then there was a *whomp* and a flash as he kicked his afterburner in their faces, a gesture of contempt.

"Razebi ego dushu!" Yevlikov yelled. Fuck his soul.

The man from the Ministry of Health was kneeling now by his broken glassware, in complete paralysis. His eyeglasses were gone. Streams of blood were threading from both ears down his neck, and a wet stain had coursed down his trousers. They took him below, and Yevlikov set a course for the east, moving his trawler along the edge of the forbidden zone. "Try to find some dishes that aren't broken," he said to the scientists.

□

Seventy miles north of Yevlikov's boat, Lieutenant Commander Mark Littleberry, M.D., stood with his colleagues on the beach at Johnston Atoll, the monkey labs at their backs, the Pacific Ocean moving gently at their feet, a mild surf rushing and sliding over coral sand. The sun had touched the horizon. The mare's tails of clouds feathered slowly, ice crystals moving in the upper air. The inversion had occurred. The winds had smoothed. The moon was rising. Conditions were perfect for a laydown.

"I feel sorry for those guys on the tugboats," one of the scientists remarked.

"I feel even sorrier for the monkeys," another scientist said.

Each person on the beach was holding a gas mask, in case the wind shifted unexpectedly.

"The men will be all right," Littleberry said. Mark Littleberry was a medical doctor in the United States Navy, a tall, handsome African-American with a crewcut and gold-rimmed spectacles. He was a medical officer for the Johnston Atoll Field Trials, and he was regarded as brilliant by the other scientists in the program, but perhaps too ambitious, a man who seemed determined to rise high and do it at a young age. Littleberry had a degree from Harvard University and a medical degree from Tulane University. His Harvard degree did not make him very popular among the military people, but they listened to him because he knew the science. He had made valuable contributions toward explaining the exact ways in which the weapons they were testing entered the lungs, and he was bringing in crucial data from monkey dissections. But Mark Littleberry was becoming unhappy with his success. He had begun to ask himself what, exactly, he was doing.

"Here it comes," someone said.

All heads turned to the left. They saw a Marine Corps Phantom flying low and straight, about two hundred meters above the water, traveling just under the speed of sound. It flew parallel to the beach, heading west toward the setting sun. It carried no stores underwing except for a small, strange-looking pod. They watched. In the evening light they saw it: something bleeding into the air from the wing pod. The wing pod was known as a dry line-source disseminator, and the way it worked was highly classified. What was coming out of the pod was a living weapon in the form of a dry powder.

It was a whitish haze that almost instantly dissipated and became invisible. The particles were very small, and they had been treated with a special plastic to make them last longer in the air. They were between one micron and five microns across, the ideal size for a weaponized bioparticle. It is the size particle that can be inhaled deep into the human lung, a particle that will stick naturally to the membrane of the lung. To get an idea of the size of such a particle, you can think of it this way: about fifty particles lined up in a row would span the thickness of a human hair. One or two such particles trapped in the lung, if they are a weapon, can cause a fatal infection that kills in three days. Particles this small do not fall out of the air. They stay aloft. You can't smell them, you can't see them, you don't know they are there until you start to get sick. Not even rain can wash them out of the sky—they don't get caught by raindrops. Rain actually improves the effectiveness of a bioweapon in the air, because rain clouds block sunlight. Bio-aerosols don't do well in sunlight. It destroys their genetic material and kills them. Biological laydowns are best done at night.

The jet shrank and seemed to vanish into the disc of the sun, leaving a departing rumble. It was doing a streakout across the Pacific Ocean. The streakout line was fifty miles long.

"Beautiful," someone said.

"Incredible."

The talk among the watchers grew technical.

"What's the dissemination rate?"

"One gram per meter."

"That's all?"

"A gram per meter! Holy Christ! That's *nothing*." The jet was spraying only one kilogram of hot agent per kilometer of flight.

"If it was anthrax," one of the scientists remarked, "they'd have to shovel it from a dump truck to have any effect on the monkeys."

"There's only about eighty kilos of agent in that pod." Less than two hundred pounds.

"Yow. And he's laying it for fifty miles."

"What *is* the agent?"

"It's the Utah cocktail. You didn't hear me say that." The identity of the material was classified.

"The Utah cocktail? That's *Utah* he's laying down? Man, a fifty-mile laydown."

The streakout line was downwind of Johnston Atoll. The hot agent would drift away from the island. As the line of particles left by the jet moved along with the wind, it would sweep across a huge area of sea. The laydown worked along the same principle as a windshield wiper making a stroke across an area of window, except that the line of bioparticles moved straight across the sea, without turning.

"That could create, what—two thousand square miles of hot zone?" one of the scientists said.

"If the stuff works. It won't work."

"Two thousand square miles of hot zone with just two hundred pounds of agent. Jesus. That's two ounces of weapon per square mile. That will never work."

"That's a laydown the size of Los Angeles!"

"I wonder what it'll do to our Russian friends out there?"

"Poor saps."

"Ask the doctor here what he thinks."

"I think it's going to work," Mark Littleberry said.

He went off by himself and walked along the beach. He was thinking about the monkeys, thinking about what he had seen recently at Pine Bluff, Arkansas, at the Biological Directorate X-201 plant, thinking about who he was. But Littleberry had work to do, people to worry about. He stayed up all night, maintaining radio contact with the Navy crews on board the tugboats. The tugboats were pulling barges full of monkeys.

The monkey barges with their tugboats were stationed at intervals downwind. The monkeys were rhesus monkeys housed in metal cages. Some of the cages sat on the decks of the barges; some of them were in closed rooms in the holds of the barges. The scientists were interested in knowing if closing yourself in a room might provide some protection against a biological weapon drifting in the open air.

Littleberry stayed by a radio set in the command center on the island. "Tugboat Charlie. Come in. This is Littleberry. How are you guys doing? Y'all hanging in there?"

Fifty miles downwind, at the far end of the test zone, a tugboat captain was standing at the wheel of his boat. He was wearing a heavy rubber space suit with an Army gas mask that was equipped with special biological filters, HEPA filters. HEPA stands for *h*igh-*e*fficiency *p*article *a*rrestor. A HEPA filter will trap a virus or a bacterial particle before it can get into the lungs.

"We're dying of the heat here," the captain said. "The heat's gonna kill us before the bugs do."

"Copy, I hear you. Wind direction is south-southwest. Holding steady at eight knots. They're going to call you in as soon as possible," Littleberry said. He was watching the weather reports coming from the ships stationed around the test zone. Judging from the speed of the wind, he could guess where the wave of hot agent was as it moved southwest with the trades.

It was a soft night in the South Pacific, and a pod of sperm whales played in the forbidden zone. One of the techs on the last tugboat was sure he had seen white jets in the moonlight, whales rising and blowing. The waves flashed with phosphorescence as they slopped against the hull of the monkey barge. The men inside the rubber suits were drenched with sweat, and they worried constantly about getting a rip, a crack in their masks. The tugboat's engines rumbled gently, pulling the monkey barge, keeping the boat on location. The captain could hear the monkeys hooting and calling. The animals were nervous. Something was up. Something bad. The humans were doing experiments again. It was enough to make any monkey a nervous wreck.

On the tugboat's deck, two Army technicians in space suits were tending the bubbler and the blood clock. The bubbler was sucking air through a glass tank full of oil. The oil would collect particles that were in the air. The blood clock was a rotating dish that held a circular slab of blood agar. Agar is a jelly on which bacteria grow easily. Blood agar has blood mixed into it, and it has a dark red color. Biological weapons often grow better in the presence of blood.

The blood clock turned slowly, moving the blood jelly past a slit exposed to the open air. As particles of hot agent touched the jelly, they would bind to it and begin taking nutrients out of the blood, and they would multiply, forming streaks and spots. Later, the face of the blood clock would show the rise and fall of hot agent in the air.

The Army techs had to shout to each other to be heard through their space suits. "I hear Nixon's gonna use this shit in Vietnam," one of them yelled, his voice muffled by his mask.

"Yeah, they're probably thinking about it," the other tech shouted back.

"Think what a laydown would do to the Ho Chi Minh Trail. If you did a few line laydowns from north to south, you know, right along the trail?"

"Shit. Half the North Vietnamese Army would just disappear. They'd melt away in the jungle. Nobody would know what happened."

"We could say it was a plague."

"And it was."

They both laughed.

Downwind, the Russian trawler moved along the edge of the forbidden zone. Most of the glassware had been broken, but a few petri dishes full of blood jelly sat in the racks, open to the air. Captain Yevlikov steered right on, wearing his green rubber suit, looking through the eyeholes and sweating like a man in a mine. He couldn't see any U.S. Navy vessels, and he kept his radar turned off, but he knew there was a fleet of steel shadows out there. Logistics and transport. Surveillance. Perimeter safety. Air support. Come daylight, he was going to have more trouble, and he knew it.

□

The activity around Johnston Atoll in 1969 was officially a "joint naval exercise," but that was a cover for the fact that what was going on were hot field trials for the strategic use of biological weapons over large areas of territory. The trials had been gradually increasing in scope since 1964. At the peak of the trials there were enough ships involved to make up the fifth-largest navy in the world. This was as large a fleet as the naval forces used in the air tests of hydrogen bombs in the Pacific Ocean during the 1950s—a fact not lost on the Russians. Captain Yevlikov threaded his little vessel along the outskirts of a formidable naval force, wondering if he would get out alive.

The wave of bioparticles—the bio-aerosol—moved all night. It passed the monkey barges one by one, and later it passed over the Russian trawler. At four o'clock in the morning, the order came to bring the last barge home. All the monkeys had breathed the particles by then. The last tugboat's engines roared, and the crew drove the boat at full speed for the atoll. They wanted to get out of there in the worst way.

The monkeys were placed in cages in the monkey labs on Johnston Atoll. During the next three days, Mark Littleberry and the other scientists saw the effects of the hot agent called the Utah cocktail.

Half of the monkeys became sick and died. They coughed and coughed with Utah until their lungs burned up, but no moisture came out. The other half of the monkeys lived, and remained healthy. They were fine. No problems.

The infected monkeys always died. Once a monkey showed any signs of Utah, the animal was doomed. Not a single monkey became sick and recovered. In other words, the case-fatality rate for Utah in untreated primates was 100 percent. As to whether a primate became infected or not, it seemed to be random chance. Those animals that got one or two particles of Utah lodged in their lungs ended up dead. Those animals that got no particles in their lungs, or those animals that, for some reason, were able to resist one or two particles of Utah in the lungs, were fine. There was no such thing as a mild case of Utah.

This is typical of biological weapons. It is essentially impossible to completely exterminate a population with a biological weapon. On the other hand, it is quite easy to crash a population, reducing it by half or more in a few days.

The animals that had been in closed rooms belowdecks experienced the same death rate as the animals in the open air. Being in a closed room did not help. A bio-aerosol behaves like a gas. Bioparticles are not like nuclear fallout, which falls out, hence its name. The particles of a bioweapon are light and fluffy. Organic. They float in the air. They dance through the smallest cracks. You can't hide from a living hot agent in the air.

Day after day, Mark Littleberry walked along the monkey cages, looking in at the sick animals. They were hunched over, lethargic, broken. Some were deranged: the Utah had gone to the brain. The animals wheezed and coughed, but nothing came up, or they were curled up in the fetal position, having crashed and died.

The doctors took some of the animals away and killed them and opened them up to see what was going on inside them. Littleberry himself opened up many monkeys. He was most impressed with the fact that the animals looked fairly healthy inside. But if you tested a dead monkey's blood, you found that it was radiantly hot with Utah. This scared him. Later he would write in a classified report: *"Well-trained physicians might not recognize the signs of infection by a military weapon in a patient, especially if it is a mixed combination. Physicians should be warned that the effects of a weaponized organism on the human body may be very different from natural disease caused by the same organism."*

Then Littleberry began to see that the monkeys from the farthest barge were dying at the same rate as the monkeys in the barge nearest the release line. The hot agent was just as strong and deadly fifty miles downwind. After fifty miles of drift, the killing power of Utah had not diminished. This was completely unlike a chemical weapon. Sarin and Tabun, chemical nerve gases, lose killing power rapidly as they spread out. Utah was alive. Utah stayed alive. Utah needed to find blood. It needed to find a host. If it could find a host, it would make copies of itself explosively inside the host.

The tests had rendered an area of the Pacific Ocean larger than Los Angeles as hot as hell, in a biological sense. The scientists never found out how far the agent spread during that test, only that it went beyond the test area and kept going. It passed over the last barge and moved on through the night, undiminished in strength. It did not kill any fish or marine organisms, because they don't have lungs. If any sperm whales crashed and died, no one noticed.

Captain Yevlikov and his crew survived, all but the shocked man from the Ministry of Health, who had refused to wear a mask; his lungs shriveled, and they buried him at sea. The Utah grew up in little spots and colonies on the Soviet petri dishes. They froze some samples and carried them back to Vladivostok. It is believed that the frozen samples of Utah were flown by jet transport to a closed military facility known as the Institute of Applied Microbiology at Obolensk, south of Moscow, where the weapon was analyzed and Russian scientists began growing it in their laboratories. This may be how Russia obtained the American weapons-grade strain of Utah for its own arsenal of strategic life forms. Captain Gennadi Yevlikov was given a medal for bravery and service to his country.

The rising sun over the Pacific Ocean on the morning following the test began to neutralize the Utah, killing its genetic material. Eventually it biodegraded, and no trace of it remained in the sea or in the air. It was totally gone, and all that was left was knowledge.

Invisible History (I.)

President Richard Nixon's prepared statement was very brief, and he took no questions from the press. Sticking to the text, he said that the United States was renouncing the first use of chemical weapons. Then he went on to what was clearly the more important subject to him: biological weapons. "Second, biological warfare, which is commonly called *germ* warfare—" He shook the word *germ* with Nixonian emphasis, as if he shuddered to his jowls at the thought of germs. "*Germ* warfare: this has massive, unpredictable, and potentially uncontrollable consequences. It may produce global epidemics and profoundly affect the health of future generations."

He said that after consulting with experts he had decided that the United States of America would renounce the use of any form of biological weapons, and he was ordering the disposal of existing stocks of the weapons. "Mankind already carries in its own hands too many of the seeds of its own destruction," he said. "By the examples that we set today, we hope to contribute to an atmosphere of peace and understanding between all nations. Thank you." He walked off the podium without another word.

The next day, in an analysis of "What Nixon Gave Up," *The New York Times* noted rather skeptically that the president was repudiating only "a few horrible and probably unusable weapons in the American arsenal to gain possible advantages of security for the nation and prestige for himself." "Informed sources" said that the chemical weapons given up by Nixon were expensive and unreliable. As for biological weapons, "experts" said that the United States would have been unable to use them. "In the first place, the germs and toxins (the dead but poisonous products of bacteria) stockpiled in refrigerated igloos at the Pine Bluff arsenal in Arkansas have never been tested; it is not clear what effect they would have on enemy forces or population."

Of course the experts had it wrong. Either that or they lied to the *Times*. Nevertheless, their position prevailed. The idea that bioweapons were never fully tested, were never made to work, or are unusable is a myth that persists to this day. The existence of the Johnston Atoll field trials was not reported publicly and is unknown to most civilian scientists.

The trials, which went on steadily from 1964 to 1969, were successful far beyond the expectations of even the scientists involved. The results were clear. Biological weapons are strategic weapons that can be used to destroy an army or a city, or a nation. ("Tactical" weapons, as opposed to strategic weapons, are used in a more limited way, on a battlefield. Chemical weapons are tactical, not strategic, since it takes a large quantity of a chemical weapon to destroy a small number of enemies. There are only two kinds of strategic weapons in the world: nuclear and biological.)

The reasons for Richard Nixon's decision to end the American biological-weapons program were complicated. His intelligence people were telling him that the Russians were getting ready to embark on a crash biological program, and he hoped to encourage them not to do it. The Vietnam War protests were going on, and some protesters had focused on chemical and biological weapons. Not only did the protesters not want the weapons used on anyone by their government, they also did not want them stored near where they lived, or transported across the country. Nixon had apparently considered using biological weapons in Vietnam, but military planners couldn't figure out how to deploy them without sickening or killing vast numbers of civilians. Even so, the Pentagon was furious with Nixon for taking away a new strategic weapon.

The success of the Pacific trials was also a factor in Nixon's decision, for the trials had surprised everyone. The problem with bioweapons was not that they didn't work, it was that they worked too well. They were remarkably powerful. They were difficult to defend against. They were easy and cheap to make, and while they depended on weather for their effectiveness, they were a good or even superior alternative to nuclear weapons, especially for countries that could not afford nuclear weapons.

The meaning of the Pacific trials was not lost on the supreme leader of the Soviet Union, Leonid Brezhnev, or on his advisers. Brezhnev was reportedly furious at his scientific people for having fallen behind the Americans. The Soviets believed that Nixon was lying, that he never really canceled the American bioweapons program. They thought he had hidden it away. So Brezhnev did exactly what Nixon was trying to head off. He ordered a secret crash acceleration of the Soviet bioweapons program in response to a perceived threat from the United States.

In 1972, the United States signed the Convention on the Prohibition of the Development, Production, and Stockpiling of Bacteriological (Biological) and Toxin Weapons and on Their Destruction, commonly known as the Biological Weapons Convention. Soviet diplomats helped to write much of the language of the treaty, and the Soviet Union became one of three so-called depository states for the treaty; the other two were the United States and Great Britain. By making themselves depository states, the three nations offered themselves as an example to be followed. It was believed that the resources of the intelligence community and the vigilance and concern of the scientific community would serve to sound the alert to any violations of the treaty.

But that belief turned out to be only a belief in the years following the treaty. For there was no way to verify whether or not violations were taking place, and the truth is that much progress was made in the development and engineering of bioweapons in various places around the world. This was not noticed for a long time. It was an invisible history.

Part Three

DIAGNOSIS

Monkey Room

The weather in Atlanta had turned glorious, blue, sunny, and hot. The late April air was filled with a drifting scent of loblolly pines. Northeast of the city center, Clifton Road winds through hilly wooded neighborhoods and goes past the headquarters of the Centers for Disease Control, a warren of buildings made of brick and concrete. Some of the C.D.C. buildings are new, but many are old and deteriorating and stained with age, offering visible evidence of years of neglect by Congress and the White House.

Building 6 is a stained brick monolith, almost without windows, that sits in the middle of the C.D.C. complex. It was once an animal-holding facility that stored populations of mice, rabbits, and monkeys used for medical research. The C.D.C. grew and became so short of space that eventually the animals were moved elsewhere, and the animal rooms were converted to offices. They are the least desirable offices at the C.D.C., and therefore they are occupied by the youngest people. Many of these people are in the C.D.C.'s Epidemic Intelligence Service—the E.I.S., everyone calls it. About seventy officers enroll in the E.I.S. every year. During a two-year fellowship, they investigate outbreaks of diseases all over the United

States and, indeed, the world. The Epidemic Intelligence Service is a training program for people who want to go into public health as a career.

On the third floor of Building 6, inside a windowless former monkey room, Alice Austen, M.D., a twenty-nine-year-old E.I.S. officer, was on phone duty. She was taking calls, listening to people talk about their diseases.

"I got something bad," a man was saying to her. He was calling from Baton Rouge, Louisiana. "And I know where I got it, too. From a pizza."

"What makes you think that?" she said.

"It was a ham and onion. My girlfriend got the disease, too."

"What do you think you have?" she asked.

"I don't want to, like, get too specific. Let's just say I got a V.D."

"Have you seen a doctor?" she asked.

"I'm installing Sheetrock for this guy, and he don't give us no medical," the man said. "That's why I have to call the C.D.C." The man went on to describe how he had been eating a pizza at a local restaurant with his girlfriend when he'd found himself chewing on a piece of plastic. He'd pulled it out of his mouth and discovered it was a bandage strip stained with yellow pus. He was convinced that it had given both him and his girlfriend certain symptoms that he was reluctant to describe.

"You could not get a sexually transmitted disease from eating a bandage," Austen said. "You should go to an emergency room and get an exam, and your girlfriend, too. If it turns out you have gonorrhea, we recommend treatment with Cipro."

The man wanted to talk, and Austen couldn't get him off the phone. She was a slender woman of medium height, with wavy auburn hair, a fine-boned face, and a pointed chin. She was a medical pathologist by training—her specialty was death. Her eyes were gray-blue and thoughtful, and seemed to absorb the light, considering the world in a careful way. Her hands were slender but very strong. She used her hands to probe among organs, bone, and skin. She wore no rings on her fingers, and her fingernails were cut short, so as not to break surgical gloves. It was Wednesday, uniform day at the C.D.C., and Austen was wearing a Public Health Service uniform—pants and a short-sleeved khaki shirt, with the gold oak leaf of a lieutenant commander on the right shoulder. It looked like a Navy uniform. The U.S. Public Health Service is an unarmed branch of the U.S. military.

One would not describe Alice Austen as a lonely person, or a person incapable of love, for she had many friends, and she had had her lovers, including a man who had wanted to marry her, but there always seemed to be a distance between her and the world. Like many pathologists, she was a loner by temperament, independent minded, curious about how things worked. She was the daughter of a retired chief of police in the town of Ashland, New Hampshire.

"We got a lawyer. We're gonna sue over that pizza," the man was saying.

"The bandage would have been sterilized by heat in the oven. It couldn't hurt you," Austen explained.

"Yeah, but what if the pus didn't get cooked?"

"Those ovens are pretty hot. I think the pus was probably cooked," she answered.

An older man walked into Austen's office. He raised an eyebrow. "Since when has the C.D.C. been advising people on how to cook pus?"

She pushed the mute button. "Be done in a minute."

"A minute? The C.D.C. advises people to cook pus for a minimum of five minutes. Tell the guy to use a meat thermometer. The pus is done when it says 'pork.' "

Austen smiled.

The man sat down at an empty desk. He was holding a file folder, slapping it against his hand restlessly. His name was Walter Mellis. He was a public-health doctor in his late fifties, and he had worked at the C.D.C. for most of his career.

Meanwhile, on the phone: "I got the pizza in my freezer. You folks want to check it out in your hot zone?"

When she hung up she said, "Wow."

"You burned up a lot of time with that guy," Mellis remarked.

Austen did not know Walter Mellis very well, but she knew that something was up. He wanted something from her.

"Anyway," he went on. "I'm looking for someone to observe at an autopsy. You're the only E.I.S. officer trained in pathology."

"I'm pretty busy writing up my last outbreak," she said.

"I just had a call from Lex Nathanson, the medical examiner of New York," he went on, seeming to ignore her. "They've had two cases of something pretty unusual. He asked me if we had anyone to send up there to help him out. Quietly."

"Why don't they use the city health department?"

"I don't know why." He looked a little annoyed. "I know Lex from way back, so he called me."

Walter Mellis had a pot belly, gray frizzy hair, and a mustache. He refused to wear his Public Health Service uniform on Wednesdays, and today he had on a shirt the color of mud, with frayed cuffs. She found herself imagining Mellis as a younger man, grooving at a Peter, Paul, and Mary concert, believing the world was about to change. Now he was getting close to retirement. He had become an aging federal official, stuck at the same government pay scale forever, while the world had changed far more than his generation had expected.

"This *could* be something good," he said. "You never know. It could be a John Snow case."

Dr. John Snow was one of the first great disease detectives, a founder of the science of modern epidemiology. He was a physician in London in 1853 when there was an outbreak of cholera. Snow found a cluster of cases. He began interviewing the victims and their families, carefully tracing their activities during the days just before they became sick. He discovered that the sick people had been using the same public water pump on Broad Street. The paths of the victims crossed at the water pump. Something in the water from that pump was causing the disease. Snow did not know what substance in the water was making people sick, because the microorganism that

causes cholera had not been discovered, but he removed the handle from the water pump. It stopped
the outbreak. He did not need to know what was in
the water. This is the classic story of epidemiology.

The C.D.C. has a coveted award called the John
Snow Award. It is presented each year to the E.I.S.
officer who is judged to have done the best case investigation. Walter Mellis was suggesting to Alice
Austen that there was a possibility that the New York
case could lead to a John Snow Award.

She did not buy it. "Is this case part of your
project?" she asked. Mellis had some kind of a mysterious project going, a project that no one at the
C.D.C. wanted to be involved with, or so she'd heard.

"My project? The Stealth Virus Project? Yes—it
is. My idea is that there may be unknown viruses out
there. They don't cause obvious outbreaks. They
sneak around. They're not very contagious, so they
just hit one person here and one person there.
They're Jack the Ripper viruses, serial killers—
stealth viruses. Lex Nathanson knows a little bit
about the Stealth Virus Project, and I've asked him to
keep an eye out for anything like this."

She noticed that he was wearing a beeper on his
belt. She wondered why he needed a beeper.

"Are you telling me everything?"

Mellis put his hand up. He sighed. He was accustomed to people ducking his project. It didn't
seem to be going anywhere. "Look," he said, "if you
don't want to do this, I'll call Lex and tell him we just
don't have anyone available right now. He'll understand. It's no big deal."

"No. I'll go."

Mellis looked a little surprised. He opened up his file folder and pulled out a Delta Air Lines ticket and a government expense sheet. He put them on her desk. "I appreciate this," he said.

Vision

Alice Austen drove her Volkswagen Jetta back to her rented condominium in Decatur, a few miles from the C.D.C. She changed out of her uniform and put on a blue silk-and-wool skirt and a silk blouse.

She put some extra clothing into a travel bag, along with a book to read, although she knew she'd never read it. A big chunk of space in the bag was taken up by her leather work boots, which were encased in a white plastic garbage bag tied with a twist tie. The boots were Mighty-Tuff boots, the kind construction workers wear, with steel toes and nonskid waffle soles. They were her autopsy boots. She put her laptop computer, a cellular telephone, and a green federal-issue cloth-covered notebook—an epi notebook, they called it—into her briefcase. The green epi notebook was for keeping all her data and records of the investigation. She packed a small digital electronic camera. It took color photographs and stored them in memory cards. The memory cards could be plugged into her laptop computer, and she could review the images on the screen.

She placed a leather folder containing her autopsy knife and sharpening tools on top of the things in her travel bag. The knife is a pathologist's main piece of professional equipment. She also threw in a Boy Scout knife, fork, and spoon set, for eating meals in a rented room. She would not be staying in a hotel. The C.D.C. travel allowance was ninety dollars a day for accommodations in New York City. You can't get much in the way of a hotel room in New York for ninety dollars, so she would be staying in a bed-and-breakfast.

□

Her flight took off in clear weather. The moon was down, and the stars were bright in the dark sky. Austen watched North America move slowly below the aircraft, a cobweb of lights imposed on blackness. Cities approached and fell behind—Charlotte, Richmond, then Washington, D.C. The Mall was visible from thirty thousand feet, a luminous rectangle against the Potomac River. The federal government looked small and helpless from up here, like something you could step on with your foot.

They went into a holding pattern around Newark Airport, and when they turned and prepared to land, coming in from the north, they passed close to Manhattan. Looking out her window, Austen unexpectedly saw the organism called New York City. The beauty of it almost took her breath away. The core of the city seemed to emerge from the black waters that surrounded it in a lacework of light and structure, like a coral reef that glowed. She saw the buildings of midtown Manhattan shimmering in the Hudson River, so remote and strange as to seem almost imaginary. The Empire State Building was a spike washed with floodlights. Beyond Manhattan lay expanses of Brooklyn and Queens. To the south she recognized the luminous bulge of Staten Island, and the lights of the Verrazano Bridge hanging in a chain. Closer to the airplane, the waters of Upper New York Bay spread out like an inky rug, devoid of light, except for the sparkling hulls of ships at anchor, their bows pointed to sea with an incoming tide.

Austen thought of a city as a colony of cells. The cells were people. Individually the cells lived for a while and were programmed to die, but they replaced themselves with their progeny, and the organism continued its existence. The organism grew, changed, and reacted, adapting to the biological conditions of life on the planet. Austen's patient, for the moment, was the city of New York. A couple of cells inside the patient had winked out in a mysterious way. This might be a sign of illness in the patient, or it might be nothing.

□

The bed-and-breakfast apartment where the C.D.C. had rented a room for Alice Austen was in Kips Bay, on East Thirty-third Street, between Second and First avenues. Kips Bay is a seventies-era development of blocklike concrete buildings surrounded by gardens, nestled up against a huge complex of hospitals. Her hostess was a German widow named Gerda Heilig, who rented out a room looking toward the New York University Medical Center and the East River. It was a pleasant room with a desk and an antique carved German bed that squeaked when Austen sat on it. The room was full of books in German. There was no telephone.

Austen placed her knife pack on the desk and opened it. Inside the leather folder were two short knives and a long knife. They were her autopsy blades. The short knives were like fish-fillet knives. The long one was a prosector's knife. It had a straight, heavy, carbon-steel blade. The knife was two and a half feet long. It was almost like a short sword. It had a comfortable handle made of ash wood, the same wood used in axe handles. She kept a diamond sharpening stone in her prosection pack and a round edging steel. In case they asked her to participate in the autopsy, she wanted to be ready with her own knife. She wet the stone with water under the bathroom faucet, and ground her knife on it, testing its edge on her thumbnail. When you touch the edge of a prosector's knife to your thumbnail, you want it to stick, to grab the nail, the way a razor grabs. If the edge slides or bounces over your thumbnail, it is not sharp.

The long knife made a whisking sound as it passed over the diamond block. Then she refined its edge on the steel rod—*zing, zing, zing.*

West of Babylon

April in Iraq is normally dry and blue, but a cool front had moved down from the north, bringing an overcast sky. The United Nations Special Commission Biological Weapons Inspection Team Number 247—UNSCOM 247, it was called—was traveling along a narrow paved highway at the edge of the desert to the west of the Euphrates River, with its headlights on, moving slowly. The convoy consisted of a dozen four-wheel-drive vehicles. They were painted white, and they displayed large black letters, "UN," stenciled on their doors. The vehicles were plastered with glue-like dust.

The convoy arrived at a crossroads and slowed to a crawl. All the vehicles' turn signals went on at the same time, blinking to the right. Vehicle by vehicle, the UNSCOM 247 convoy turned to the northeast. Its destination was the Habbaniyah Air Base, near the Euphrates River, where a United Nations transport aircraft waited to fly the inspectors out of the country to Bahrain. There they would split up and go their separate ways.

A white Nissan Pathfinder 4 × 4 in the middle of the convoy slowed when it came to the crossroads. Its right turn signal came on, like the others. Then, suddenly, with a roar and a whipping whirl of tires, the Nissan broke out of line. It swung left onto a ribbon of cracked tar heading west, and departed at high speed into the desert.

A hard voice broke over the radio: "Snap inspection!"

It was the voice of Commander Mark Littleberry, M.D., U.S. Navy (Retired). Littleberry was in his sixties. He was a tough-looking man ("the indestructible Littleberry," his colleagues called him), but his age showed in the gold-rimmed half-glasses perched on his nose and in the silver at his temples. Littleberry worked as a paid consultant to various U.S. government agencies, most especially to the Navy. He had top security clearances. Through his Navy connections, he had been appointed an UNSCOM biological-weapons inspector. Now he was sitting in the passenger seat of the breakaway Nissan, with a military map of Iraq draped across his knees. He was holding a small electronic screen in his hands.

The Iraqi minders had been traveling behind the UNSCOM convoy in a rattletrap column of vehicles— beat-up Toyota pickup trucks, smoking dysfunctional Renaults, hubcapless Chevrolets, and a black Mercedes-Benz sedan with tinted windows and shiny mag wheels. Most of these vehicles had been seized in Kuwait by Iraq during the Gulf War, and they had seen constant use by the Iraqi government in the years afterward. Some of the cars had been cannibalized from junk parts, and they had body panels of differing colors.

When the Nissan broke away and Mark Littleberry's words "snap inspection" crackled over the radio, it created confusion among the Iraqi minders.

Their vehicles came to a grinding halt, and they started yelling into hand-held radios. They were reporting the breakaway to their superiors at the National Monitoring Center in Baghdad, which is the Iraqi intelligence office that supplies minders to U.N. weapons-inspection teams. There was a pause. The minders were waiting for orders, since no minder who valued his life would do anything without orders.

A snap inspection is a surprise weapons inspection. Inspectors suddenly change their itinerary and go somewhere without giving advance notice. But this time there was a problem. Commander Mark Littleberry did not have permission from the chief inspector, a French biologist named Pascal Arriet, to do a snap inspection. This was a rogue snap.

Suddenly four Iraqi vehicles detached from the column and took off after the Nissan, which had picked up considerable speed. Its engine howled. The Nissan hit sand drifts that covered the road in places, flinging out boiling yellow-brown puffs of dust. It seemed to leap out through the dust with its headlights glowing, surfing waves in the road, nearly becoming airborne.

"Damn it, Hopkins! We're going to roll over!" Mark Littleberry said to the man driving, Supervisory Special Agent William Hopkins, Jr., of the Federal Bureau of Investigation.

Will Hopkins was a rangy man in his early thirties. He had brown hair, a square face, and a seven-day beard. He wore baggy khaki trousers and a formerly white shirt (now streaked with dust), and Teva sandals with green socks. There was a plastic pocket protector in his shirt pocket. It was jammed with pens and pencils and bits of junk. The belt that held up his trousers was a length of nylon webbing. Slung on the webbing was a Leatherman Super Tool, a combination pliers and screwdriver and knife and various other tools. The Leatherman on his belt identified Hopkins as a "tech agent"—an F.B.I. agent who deals with gadgets. Anything secret, especially if it's high-tech, is guaranteed to break down, and a tech agent never goes anywhere without a Leatherman tool.

Hopkins had earned a Ph.D. in molecular biology from the California Institute of Technology, where he had become adept with the machines and gadgets that are used in biology. He was a Caltech gadgeteer. His current job title was Manager of Scientific Operations—Biology, Hazardous Materials Response Unit, Quantico.

As the vehicle lurched and bounced, Littleberry watched the screen mapper in his hands, and he compared it to the military map on his knees. The mapper was a glowing panel that showed a changing outline of the terrain. It was linked to some Global Positioning Satellites overhead. The current location of the car appeared on the screen.

The Nissan hit a dip in the road. Two black metal Halliburton suitcases sitting on the back seat went bouncing into the air.

"Watch it!" Littleberry yelled.

"Are you sure this is the right road?"

"I'm sure."

Hopkins mushed his foot on the accelerator and the Nissan moaned, the tires whomping over cracks in the road. The engine was running hot and hard,

just under the redline. He looked in the rearview mirror. Nothing. He could almost hear the satellite calls
to New York and Washington, Paris, Baghdad,
Moscow: two UNSCOM inspectors had just gone out
of control in Iraq.

A long line of vehicles stretched behind the Nissan. First came the four Iraqi chase vehicles, which
seemed to be losing hubcaps and bits of metal every
time they hit a bump. Next came the entire UNSCOM
247 convoy, lumbering at a more dignified pace. Pascal Arriet had given orders for the rest of the convoy
to follow Littleberry and Hopkins, and now he was
speaking in French and English to various relay contacts on his shortwave radio, telling them there was a
problem. As the leader of the convoy, Pascal Arriet
had the same authority as the captain of a ship. He
was supposed to be obeyed without question. Behind
the U.N. convoy came yet more Iraqi vehicles. In all,
there must have been at least twenty vehicles following them.

In the Nissan, a hand-held shortwave radio
beeped; it was sliding around on the dashboard.

Hopkins picked it up. "Hello?"

A crackly voice came out. "This is Arriet, your
commander! Turn back! What are you doing?" He
was speaking on a secure radio channel. The Iraqis
couldn't hear him.

"We're taking a shortcut to Habbaniyah Air
Base," Hopkins said.

"I command you to turn back. You have not permission to leave the group."

"We're not leaving. It's a temporary detach-
ment," Hopkins said.

"Nonsense! Turn back!" Arriet said.

"Tell him we're lost," Littleberry said, staring at the electronic mapping screen.

"We got lost," Hopkins said to the radio.

"Turn back!" Pascal Arriet shouted.

"It's impossible," Hopkins said.

"Turn back!"

Driving with one hand, Hopkins popped a panel from the shortwave radio with his thumb. He fiddled with some wires. His fingers moved rapidly, with precision. Abruptly some grunting shrieks came out of the radio.

"You're breaking up," Hopkins said to the radio. "We've got trouble with the ionosphere."

"L'ionosphere? Crétin! Idiot!"

Hopkins placed the radio on the dashboard, wires dangling out of it. It continued to squawk and squeal. He reached into the radio with his fingertips and yanked out a part the size of a sunflower seed. It was a resistor. The squeals were transformed into a weird rubbery sound. The car swayed as he worked on the radio.

"I hope you can fix that," Littleberry said.

The French voice was sounding more and more hysterical on the shortwave radio.

"Our Iraqi friends can't hear our radios," Littleberry said to Hopkins, "so they don't know Pascal is ordering us to turn back. If I know Pascal, he won't dare tell the Iraqis we've gone AWOL. He'll follow us, because he's under orders to keep the group together at all costs. So the Iraqis are gonna think this is an authorized inspection, since Arriet is following behind us. They may let us in."

"Are we going to wear any safety gear?"

Littleberry turned around and reached into the back seat, next to the black suitcases, and pulled out a full-face biohazard mask, equipped with purple HEPA filters. He gave it to Hopkins to clip on his belt.

"We're not interested in the whole building," Littleberry went on. "There is a *door* I want to have a peek at. The folks at the National Security Agency have some information on that door."

"You're sure you know how to get to the door?"

Littleberry pushed a button and held up the screen mapper. It showed a detailed diagram of a building. "We pretend to stumble into the door by accident. Don't follow me in there, Will. Give me a minute and I'll come out."

"Then what?"

"Big apology. We rejoin Pascal. He will be furious, but he'll have to pretend the thing was authorized. We'll be in Bahrain by tonight."

Hopkins didn't ask Littleberry what they were looking for, but he knew it was not a chemical weapon. He assumed it was bacteria or a virus. A bacteriological weapon is grown in a fermenter tank, and it gives off a yeasty smell, somewhat like beer, or sometimes a meaty smell, like a meat broth. Virus weapons are not grown in fermenter tanks, because a virus doesn't cause fermentation when it grows. A virus converts a population of living cells into more virus. What happens is called amplification of the virus. The machine that amplifies a virus is called a bioreactor. Nothing ferments inside the tank, and no gases are let off, so there is no odor.

A bioreactor is a rather small tank with a sometimes complicated interior. The tank contains a warm liquid bath that is saturated with living cells. The cells are infected with a virus that is replicating. The cells leak virus particles, and the bioreactor becomes charged with them. A virus particle is a tiny nugget of protein (sometimes with a membrane) that surrounds a core of genetic material, which consists of strands of DNA or RNA, the ribbonlike molecules that carry the master software code that directs the activities of life. A typical virus particle is a thousand times smaller than a cell. If a virus particle were an object about an inch across, a human hair would be a thousand feet across. Viruses use their software code to take over a cell and direct the cell's own machinery to make more virus particles. A virus keeps a cell alive until the cell is full of copies of virus particles, and then the cell explodes and releases hundreds or even thousands of copies of the virus.

A wide variety of viruses are made into weapons. Hopkins understood that there were many possibilities as to what they might find in the building they were headed for. Keeping track of what strains of weapons the Iraqis were working with in their laboratories was exceedingly difficult. Some of the possibilities included VEE and EEE (brain viruses), Congo-Crimean hemorrhagic fever, Ebola virus (highly infective in the lungs when it's freeze-dried), Marburg, Machupo, Rift Valley fever, Lassa, Junin, Sabia, enterovirus 17, camelpox, monkeypox, and smallpox. And there was always the possibility

that you would run into a virus that no one had
thought could be used as a weapon. You could also
run into a virus that you had never heard of before.

□

The Nissan was a speck moving fast, trailing dust, on
a road that went straight over a landscape of browns
and grays. The road bent north now. It went through
scattered patches of desert brush, and it crossed pans
of chalk-white earth. In the distance ahead of them, a
line of date palms appeared and passed at an angle.
Hopkins noticed headlights behind them, shining
through dust in the Nissan's wake. The Iraqi vehicles
were closing the gap.

Hopkins realized that he had just driven past a
single-lane service road. It was unmarked. He spun
the wheel and pulled the emergency hand brake at
the same time. The Nissan went off the road into
some dry flats and spun around in a boil of dust. It
disappeared in its own cloud. Suddenly it popped out
of the cloud going in the opposite direction, headlights shining, bouncing over open land. With a
lurch, the Nissan veered onto the service road. Hopkins gunned the engine. The road headed east.

"Go left, Will, God damn it!"

Will swung onto another road. It passed among
cotton fields. The plants were green, the cotton bolls
ripening in the gray desert air.

A metal prefabricated building loomed at the
end of the road. It was windowless, about forty feet
tall. It looked like a warehouse. Silvery vent pipes
stuck up from the roof. The structure was surrounded
by a barbed-wire fence, and there was a gate and a
very strong-looking guard post.

Hopkins removed his foot from the gas pedal and began to slow down.

"Don't!" Littleberry said sharply. "Come up to the perimeter like you are not prepared to stop."

Hopkins floored the gas. Suddenly, up ahead, there were flashes of light at the guard post. The guards had opened fire in their direction.

Hopkins gasped. He ducked sideways on the seat. The Nissan slid down the road, out of control.

Littleberry stared straight ahead into the gunfire, holding the steering wheel for Hopkins. "Get your face out of my lap. They aren't going to pop a U.N. vehicle."

Hopkins peered over the dashboard and took the wheel again. The car was going very fast.

"The brakes, Will."

He jammed on the brakes. Too late. The Nissan spun around backward and slid into the gate, ballooning the wire mesh, punching out both taillights. The gate broke open wide. An instant later, the Iraqi chase cars came screeching and sliding in behind the Nissan in a great cloud of dust.

A rear door of the Mercedes opened, and a thin young man wearing acid-washed blue jeans and a white short-sleeved polo shirt stepped out. He was wearing an ostentatious gold wristwatch, and he had an anxious expression on his face.

"Wow, you are really scaring us, Mark," the young man in jeans said. His name was Dr. Azri Fehdak, but the U.N. inspectors referred to him as the Kid. He was a molecular biologist educated in California. He was believed to be one of the top scientists in Iraq's bioweapons program.

"It's a snap inspection," Littleberry said to the Kid. "Our chief inspector ordered it."

"But there is nothing here," Azri Fehdak said.

"What's this building?"

"I believe this is the Al Ghar Agricultural Facility."

A door to the building stood wide open. Inside, in the dim shadows, the inspectors could see ultramodern, gleaming stainless-steel biological production equipment.

A woman came scurrying out of the door, wearing a white lab coat. She was accompanied by several men. "What is this?" she demanded sharply. Under her lab coat she had on an expensive-looking dress. She wore cat-eye designer glasses, and her wavy brown hair was tied back in a loose roll.

"United Nations weapons-inspection team, ma'am," Will Hopkins said.

"We're on a snap inspection," Littleberry added. "Who are you?"

"I am Dr. Mariana Vestof. I am the consulting engineer. This is the *manager-générale,* Dr. Hamaq."

Dr. Hamaq was a short, stubby man who apparently spoke no English. His eyes moved searchingly across their faces, but he said not a word.

She protested: "We have already been inspected here."

"We're just doing a quick follow-up," Littleberry said. "What are you making here, currently?"

"These are virus vaccines," she said, waving her arm.

"Oh, good, okay. What kind, exactly?"

The Kid said, "I will check."

"Does Dr. Vestof know?"

"Our work is medical!" she said.

"Let's go," Littleberry said. He reached into the car and grabbed one of the black metal suitcases and took off running for the building. The minders parted to let him by. Everyone seemed thoroughly confused.

"Mark! What about our biohazard suits?" Hopkins called after him.

"Never mind the goddamned space suits!" Littleberry yelled back. "Come on, move it, Will! On the Q.T.!" Littleberry wanted to get what he was after before the minders went berserk and shot someone.

Hopkins grabbed his suitcase and the shortwave radio and ran after Littleberry, a motorized Nikon camera slopping around his neck, a face mask dangling by a hook on his belt. A crowd of people followed them into the stainless-steel jungle. There was no smell in the air.

The building, which was windowless, was lit with fluorescent lights. The floor was a kind of pebbled terrazzo. All around them were stainless-steel tanks and tangles of pipes and hoses. The tanks were bioreactors, and they were on wheels. Workers reached them by standing on movable catwalks. The equipment in the Iraqi plant was portable. The entire plant could be moved.

Dozens of workers were tending the equipment. They were wearing surgical masks and white coats and latex rubber gloves, but no other safety equipment. When they saw the inspectors, they drew back and stood around in groups, staring.

Littleberry hurried toward one of the larger bioreactors. He snapped on a pair of rubber surgical gloves. Hopkins also put on a pair of rubber gloves.

"Has this equipment been tagged?" Littleberry said. He addressed his question to Dr. Vestof.

"Yes. Of course!" She showed him the big U.N. tags with identifying information on them. UNSCOM was attempting to put tags on all pieces of biological-production equipment in Iraq, so that the equipment could be traced, its movements and locations known.

Littleberry studied a tag. "Interesting," he said. There was a warmth coming out of the tanks, a warmth of body heat. "Nice equipment you have here," he said to Dr. Vestof.

She stood very primly, her feet close together, her hair neatly arranged. Her calm was in marked contrast to the agitation of the Iraqi minders.

"We'll just take a couple of samples and we'll be out of here," Littleberry said. He opened a plastic box and pulled out a wooden stick about four inches long with an absorbent pad on the end, like an over-sized Q-Tip. It was a swab stick. He popped open the flip-top lid of a plastic test tube that was half-filled with sterile water. He dunked the soft tip of the swab stick in the tube to wet it, and then rubbed the tip— scrubbed it hard—on a valve on one of the warm bioreactors, trying to pick up dirt. Then he jammed the swab back into the test tube, snapped off the wooden stick, and closed the flip-top lid. He handed the tube to Hopkins. It contained a broken-off swab tip and a few particles of dirt sloshing around in the water. "That's Al Ghar large tank sample number one," he said.

With a laundry pen, Hopkins wrote "Al Ghar large tank #1" on the tube. He dated it and wrote down the tag number of the tank as well. He then photographed the tank with his Nikon camera.

In a low voice, Littleberry said to him, "Stay close."

Littleberry moved fast. He was heading deeper into the building, quickly, purposefully. Littleberry wasn't taking many samples, but he seemed to know his way around.

"Who built this plant?" Hopkins asked Dr. Vestof.

"BioArk. A respected concern."

"Is that a French company?" Hopkins asked.

"We are headquartered near Geneva."

"I see. But you personally, are you French?" Hopkins asked.

"I am from Geneva."

"So, you are a Swiss citizen, Dr. Vestof, is that correct?"

"What are you—the police? I am born in St. Petersburg! I live in Geneva."

Littleberry had almost gotten away during this exchange. His figure was nearly lost among the tanks and pipes. He was moving through the middle part of the building now, heading somewhere. He stopped at a metal door with no markings on it.

"Don't go in there!" Mariana Vestof called.

Littleberry pulled open the door.

Everything happened fast. Hopkins saw a hallway beyond Littleberry. In the hallway there were stainless-steel shower stalls—they looked like biohazard decon showers. The decon showers would be for decontaminating biohazard suits and equipment. It looked like a Level 3 staging room, an entry chamber leading to a Level 4 biocontainment zone. "Mark, don't!" he said.

Littleberry ignored him. He unclipped his mask from his belt and fitted it over his head, and suddenly he had gone into the staging room.

"Stop!" Dr. Mariana Vestof said. "This is not permitted!"

The far door of the staging room had a circular handle on it, like the handle on a pressure door on a submarine. Littleberry reached the door and spun the handle. There was a sucking sound of rubber seals giving way. It opened to reveal a narrow set of rooms, jammed with equipment, and two people wearing biohazard space suits. It was a Level 4 hot zone, and Littleberry had just opened it wide.

"United Nations!" Littleberry yelled. He hurled himself toward the hot zone, a swab stick held in front of him. He was like a terrier going into a rathole.

Frantic activity exploded in the hot zone. The space-suited researchers must have had some advance warning that a U.N. inspection team was in the area, and just as Littleberry started to cross the threshold into the zone, there was a rumbling roar, the sound of a diesel engine revving up.

A crack of gray desert sky opened up over Littleberry's head. It widened.

The hot lab was inside a truck. It was a mobile hot zone, and it was beginning to pull away from the building.

Littleberry slipped and fell to the ground. Hopkins saw him go down, and he ran for the newly opened space in the wall as if he were in a dream, dragging the suitcases. His camera was banging wildly around his neck. The truck was beginning to move away, and a rear door was swinging. A gloved hand was pulling the door shut. Hopkins jumped to the ground and dropped the suitcases near Littleberry. He fitted his mask over his face and vaulted into the moving truck.

He was standing inside the truck. He saw gleaming equipment, dim lights. There was a clap of rubber seals coming together. One of the men had shut the back door of the truck. Hopkins was shut inside a Level 4 virus-weapons lab, wearing only a mask, and the lab was moving.

There were two men inside the truck, both of them wearing green space suits of a type he had never seen before. They backed away from Hopkins. He could hear the dull hissing sound of air circulating. The older of the two men had tangled gray hair and a lined face and blue eyes. The younger man— who seemed to be an Iraqi—began to circle around behind Hopkins, his suit making shuffling sounds.

Hopkins had to get a sample fast. From his pocket protector he removed a swab stick. He ripped the wrapper off it and looked around for something to swab. His gaze took in control consoles, computer screens. At the far end of the hot zone there was a small cylindrical glass vessel about two feet high. It had a heavy stainless-steel top that looked like a hat. The metal hat had steel and plastic tubes coming out of it that ran in all directions. He recognized it as a virus bioreactor. A very small one. Inside the reactor vessel there was a translucent core shaped like an hourglass. The reactor was full of a reddish-pink liquid that looked like watery blood. The core would be producing some kind of virus.

The bioreactor was too far away to reach. But next to him stood a safety cabinet—a piece of equipment you'd find in any biological laboratory. It was designed for handling infective materials. It had a wide opening in it. Inside the safety cabinet he saw trays full of clear hexagons—six-sided flat crystals, like coins. The hexagons shimmered with rainbow colors.

He touched the swab to one of the crystals.

The younger man had circled around behind him. He grabbed Hopkins, pinning Hopkins's arms at his sides.

The older man, the blue-eyed man, wagged his finger at Hopkins and said, *"Nyet trogaite!"* He suddenly reached up with one hand and tore off Hopkins's mask—and with his other hand hit Hopkins in the stomach. Not very hard. Just hard enough to make him lose his breath.

The air flew out of Hopkins's lungs with a whoosh. He doubled over and threw himself against the rear doors of the truck, one hand flailing for the handle. There was a *thunk* and a burst of sunlight, and Hopkins was flying through the open air.

He landed in the dirt and rolled, gasping, taking in huge breaths of fresh air. He ended up lying on his back, coughing, keeping his body curled around the swab stick to protect it. He had not had time to take a photograph, but the swab might be the bearer of important DNA. The doors of the truck slammed shut, and it roared off down the road.

Morgue

The sun had risen by the time Alice Austen finished a cup of coffee and a sweet roll in Gerda Heilig's kitchen. She put her boots and her knife pack into a knapsack and went out onto First Avenue and turned south, walking quickly. She was entering a complex of hospitals lined up on the eastern side of Manhattan, overlooking the East River, like ships at dry dock—New York University Medical Center, with a number of research institutes; Bellevue Hospital; the Veterans Administration Hospital; and other medical institutions. At the northeast corner of First Avenue and Thirtieth Street, she turned up the steps of a gray building, number 520. It was six stories tall—small for this part of Manhattan. It had dirty aluminum-framed windows. The first story of the building was covered with blue glazed bricks, the color muted by dirt and dust. The building was the Office of the Chief Medical Examiner of New York City. The front door was locked, and she pushed the night buzzer.

A tall, somewhat overweight man in his sixties let her in. He had curly white hair at the temples and was going bald on top. He was dressed in a green surgical scrub suit. "I'm Lex Nathanson," he said. "Welcome to the O.C.M.E.—the ugliest building in New

York." The marble walls of the lobby had a peculiar brownish, mottled, streaky color. It reminded her of a cancerous liver, sliced open for inspection. On the liverish wall ran a motto, in Latin, in metal letters:

TACEANT COLLOQUIA EFFUGIAT RISUS HIC LOCUS
EST UBI MORS GAUDET SUCCURRERE VITAE

"How's your Latin, Dr. Austen?" Nathanson said.

"Hmm. Let's see . . . 'Speech quiets the place where Death is happy . . .'? That can't be right."

He smiled. "It means, 'Let conversation cease, let the smile flee, for this is the place where Death delights to help Life.' "

" 'Where Death delights to help Life,' " she murmured as she followed Nathanson into his office, a big, uncluttered room located near the front door.

A man stood up to greet her. "Glenn Dudley," he said. "Deputy chief medical examiner." He shook Austen's hand. Dr. Dudley had a massive grip and a tight mouth. He was a handsome, muscular man of about fifty. He had black hair and a square face, and he wore square metal-framed eyeglasses.

Austen opened up her green federal notebook, her epi notebook. She wrote Nathanson's and Dudley's names on the first page. "Could I have contact phone numbers for you?"

"Are you a forensic pathologist?" Glenn Dudley asked.

"No. I'm a medical pathologist," she said.

"You're not trained in forensics?"

"I *have* worked on forensic autopsies," she said. "I know basically how it's done."

"Where?" Dudley asked.

"In the Fulton County medical examiner's office, in Georgia. The C.D.C. has a relationship with them."

"Are you board certified?"

"Not yet," she said.

Dudley turned to Nathanson and said in a flinty voice, "They don't even send us a certified pathologist."

"I'll be taking my boards next year." She concentrated on her green notebook.

Nathanson said, "Well—as I imagine Dr. Mellis told you, we've had two very unusual deaths. The girl who died yesterday, and a similar incident five days ago. The first case we noticed—"

"I noticed," Dudley said.

"—Glenn noticed, was an unidentified homeless man. He was known locally as Harmonica Man. He was about sixty years old, and he used to ride the subway cars playing a harmonica. He had a cup and he asked for handouts. He went all over the city. I live on the East Side, and I actually remember seeing him riding the Lexington Avenue local. He died a week ago at the Times Square subway station, on the southbound platform of the Broadway line, if you know where that is."

"I don't know New York very well," Austen said.

"It doesn't matter. He died in grand mal seizures," Nathanson said.

"It was a spectacular death," Dudley said. "The guy seized in the middle of a crowd, he's screaming, he bit off his tongue, he bit his hands, and he had a hemorrhage. He was D.O.A. at Bellevue. I did the

autopsy, and found his tongue in his stomach. The
Fire Department E.M.T. squad reported that he
arched his back and froze and died on the platform
that way, having eaten his tongue, and with a massive
bleed from the mouth. He was with a friend of his—
another homeless guy named..." He flipped
through the case folder, glancing over the file.
"Named Lem. No last name given. When I did the
autopsy, I found that this Harmonica Man was an al-
coholic with cirrhosis of the liver, and he had vari-
cose veins in the esophagus. A vein had burst in his
esophagus. That was the source of the bleed from the
mouth, that plus bleeding from the tongue stump. He
had brain swelling and brain damage, with hemorrhage in the midbrain. It could be a poison, a toxin.
But nothing came up with the toxicology."

"What got my attention," Nathanson said, "was
the form of the seizure—that curvature of the spine."

"That's less important, I think, Lex," Dudley
said.

"It's known as an *arc de circle* seizure,"
Nathanson went on, in a thoughtful way. "I looked
into this. The *arc de circle* seizure was identified by
the nineteenth-century French neurologist Jean-
Marie Charcot. It's a fake seizure. A real seizure
doesn't make the spine curve. But the two decedents
weren't faking—they were dying." He turned to
Austen. "This second case has gotten into the news
media, and we're under some pressure to come up
with answers."

"So you called the C.D.C., Lex—and you listened to Walt Mellis with his theories. He's a nut,"
Dudley said.

Nathanson shrugged and flashed a smile at Austen. "You're not a nut, are you, Doctor?"

"I hope not," she said.

Dudley stood up suddenly. "Let's get going." He picked up a manila file folder that had been sitting on an empty chair. "We can talk in the morgue."

They stepped into a freight elevator. It went to the basement of the O.C.M.E. On the way down, Nathanson turned to her. "How old are you?"

"Twenty-nine."

"Kind of young for a fed," Glenn Dudley remarked, standing behind them.

"It's a training job," she said.

□

The morgue was in the first basement level, next to the receiving garage. A mortuary van had just pulled in, and a couple of dieners, or morgue attendants, were unloading a body covered with a sheet of blue paper. The attendants transferred the body to a mortuary gurney known as a pan, which is a sort of metal trough on wheels. The pan was shaped like a trough so that fluids would not drip out of bodies onto the floor.

The receiving garage was crowded with bright red Dumpsters marked with biohazard symbols, spiky three-lobed flowers. A sign on the wall said:

PLEASE DO NOT THROW LOOSE CLOTH OR
BLOODY SHEETS ON THE DUMPSTERS.

Nathanson approached a man dressed in a green scrub suit. "We're ready, Ben," he said. "Let me introduce you to our C.D.C. investigator. This is Dr. Alice Austen. And this is Ben Kly. He'll be the attendant. Ben, we're keeping quiet about Dr. Austen's presence here."

"Sure," Kly said, and smiled. His name rhymed with "fly." He and Austen shook hands.

Ben Kly was a slender man of medium height, an Asian-American with dark, creamy skin. He had a quiet voice. "I'll be with you in a second," he said. He wheeled the pan with the body on it into the hallway.

They pushed through a pair of battered swinging doors into the morgue, where they were enveloped by a thick smell, sour and penetrating—a smell as old as the world. It hung in the air like a liquescent fog, and seemed to coat the back of one's mouth. It was the smell of bacteria converting meat into energy. The bacteria were liquefying human meat and giving off gases. In the Manhattan morgue, this smell rose and fell and changed day by day, depending on the weather and events around the city, but it never went away. The Manhattan morgue emitted an endless Gregorian chant of smell.

It was Charles Darwin who first understood that evolution is caused by natural selection, and that natural selection is death. He also understood that vast amounts of death (vast amounts of natural selection) are required to effect a small permanent change in the shape or behavior of an organism. Without huge amounts of death, organisms do not change over time. Without death, life would never have become more complex than the simplest self-copying molecules. The arms of a starfish could not have happened without countless repetitions of death. Death is the mother of structure. It took four billion years of death—a third of the age of the universe—for death to invent the human mind. Given another four billion years of death, or perhaps a hundred billion years of death, who can say that death will not create a mind so effective and subtle that it will reverse the fate of the universe and become God? The smell in the Manhattan morgue is not the smell of death; it is the smell of life changing its form. It is evidence that life is indestructible.

□

The morgue was ring-shaped, with a central rectangular core where bodies were stored inside crypts. You circled around the core to gain access to a particular crypt. The walls were made of bricks painted a pale green. The crypt doors were made of stainless steel. Various smaller rooms led off from the main room. Some of these smaller rooms were for holding severely putrefied bodies, so that the smell would not fill the morgue area.

"There's the ladies' room," Nathanson said, pointing to a door off the morgue. "You can change in there."

It was cleaner than most rest rooms in morgues. Austen found a shelf holding fresh surgical scrub suits. She removed her street shoes and took off her blouse and skirt and changed into the scrubs. Then she put on her Mighty-Tuff boots, and laced them up.

She found Nathanson, Dudley, and Kly in a storage room on the other side of the morgue, putting on the next layer of clothing. The storage room was full of metal shelves holding biosafety equipment. They put on disposable surgical gowns over their scrub suits. Over the surgical gowns they tied heavy plastic waterproof aprons. They put surgical covers on their shoes, surgical caps on their heads.

Glenn Dudley pulled a disposable button mask down over his nose and mouth. It was a soft cup made of biofilter material, like a surgeon's mask. It had a blue button in the center. His voice came out of the mask. "Hey, Dr. Austen, where's your space suit? I thought you guys from the C.D.C. have to work in space suits." He laughed behind his mask.

"I've never worn one," she said.

They put on plastic safety glasses, to prevent blood or fluid from splashing into their eyes. Dudley didn't need safety glasses, since he was already wearing eyeglasses.

They put on rubber surgical gloves.

Then Glenn Dudley fitted a glove made of stainless-steel chain mail over his left hand. The chain-mail glove indicated that he was going to be the prosector—the leader of the autopsy, the person who did the cutting. In the New York O.C.M.E. the prosector wears a metal glove on one hand; it is a sign of medical authority and, more important, a safety measure. Most accidental knife cuts during autopsy occur on the pathologist's nondominant hand. In most people that's the left hand. You hold the knife in your dominant hand, so accidental cuts usually occur on the nondominant hand. You wear a chain-mail glove on your nondominant hand.

They put on heavy yellow rubber dishwashing gloves over their surgical gloves. Dudley drew a rubber glove over his metal glove.

"The decedent is in 102," Ben Kly said.

They followed Kly through the morgue as he wheeled an empty pan around the ring-shaped room to a stainless-steel door, crypt number 102. Inside, lying on a tray, was a white body pouch. A stale odor came out of the crypt.

"Dr. Austen, the smell doesn't affect you?" Nathanson asked.

"It's a little stronger than what I'm used to."

"They do them fresh in hospitals," Ben Kly remarked, rolling out the tray. A human form gave shape to the white pouch.

Nathanson said, "Manhattan is not like other places. People come to Manhattan to live alone. It means they often die alone. We handle a surprising number of putrefied bodies. What you are smelling is the stench of loneliness, Dr. Austen."

Kly took the shoulders, grasping them through the pouch, while Dudley took the feet. In one expert motion they lifted up the body and transferred it to the pan. Kly wheeled it over to a floor scale and read the dial. "A hundred and eighteen pounds," he said, writing it on a clipboard.

He pushed the gurney through a pair of doors into the autopsy room.

"Welcome to the Pit," Kly said.

The autopsy room was seventy feet long, and was partly underground. In it stood eight stainless-steel autopsy tables, lined up in a row. This was autopsy central for Manhattan, one of the busiest autopsy rooms in the world. Four of the tables had pathologists working at them; they were in the process of laying out bodies, preparing to go to work;

some had begun cutting. The Pit was a gray zone, a place neither definitely hot nor definitely safe. It was somewhere in between. An ultraviolet light on the wall shed rays into the room that were supposed to kill airborne pathogens, viruses and bacteria. On the floor, air-filtering machines hummed, cleaning the air of infective particles that might get into the lungs of the pathologists.

Ben Kly halted the pan next to an autopsy table and set the brake. He unzipped the white bag.

Kate

Her eyes were closed, the eyelids puffy. She had had a streaming bloody nose, and the blood had run over her chin and pooled in the hollow of her throat. Someone, probably a busy nurse, had attempted to wash her face, but the washing had not been thorough.

People are fastidious by nature, and have a hundred ways of grooming their bodies and keeping order about their persons. When a person dies, the ways of grooming vanish. The first impression one has of a dead person is of disorder—unkempt hair, purposeless limbs, blotchy moist skin with specks of dirt on it, eyes half open, a faint meaty unwashed smell.

Her teeth were visible in a grimace behind shredded lips. The teeth were stained with brownish blood. Her hair was russet, shining and beautiful, wavy hair. With a start, Austen saw that the girl's hair was the same color and texture as her own hair. There were two rings in her left ear.

"Her name is Catherine Moran," Nathanson said. "Our medicolegal investigator talked to some of her teachers yesterday. They called her Kate."

Ben Kly unzipped the pouch completely. The dead girl was wearing a short hospital gown, as if for modesty.

Dudley opened the investigator's report, a collection of sheets of paper in a manila folder.

"Case number 98-M-12698," Dudley said, reading from the file. "She collapsed in a school classroom." His eyes glanced rapidly over the report. "Mater School, on Seventy-ninth Street. She became extremely ill in class. Yesterday. About ten-thirty in the morning. She fell to the floor. She was grimacing and biting her lips—biting herself, chewing her lips and swallowing them—grand mal seizures—heavy nosebleed—sudden unexplained death. Yeah, and they reported she went into a hard tonic seizure at the end. Superficially, the case looks like Harmonica Man—you've got the wild seizures, the hard clonic tensing of the spine, the bleed, the chewing. She was D.O.A. at New York Hospital. It made the news last night."

"You've got a homeless man and a young woman from a well-to-do background," Nathanson remarked. "That in itself stands out. There's no obvious connection between them."

"Drugs," Dudley said.

"It's almost like there was a demon inside them," Ben Kly whispered.

"Want to call in a priest, Kly?" Dudley said.

"I'm a Presbyterian," Kly answered.

"The hospital did a blood and spinal workup?" Austen asked.

"They didn't run any tests—she was pronounced dead," Dudley replied.

Dudley and Kly lifted the girl out of the pouch and transferred her to the autopsy table. The inside surfaces of the pouch glistened with droplets of black blood. They stretched her out on her back, on the heavy steel mesh of the table, with water running underneath the mesh. They removed the gown. Her breasts were small. Her body was young.

The appearance of Kate's body disturbed Austen. The truth was that the girl looked very much like her. She could be my younger sister, Austen thought, if I had a younger sister. She reached out and took the left hand of the girl in her gloved hand. She lifted the hand up gently and looked at it. The fingernails were delicate.

"Someone could have given her a hot load, Lex," Dudley said.

Austen frowned, puzzled.

Nathanson explained, "A lethal dose of bad drugs, Dr. Austen. A hot load. Dealers do it when they want to get rid of a customer."

"That would make it a homicide, but it would be hard to prove," Dudley said.

Nathanson suddenly said, "Dr. Austen—I'd like you to be the prosector for this one. You can do the autopsy."

"But I came here to observe."

"I think your insights into this case could be interesting," Nathanson said. "Ben, she'll need a chain-mail glove. You'll use your own knife, I assume."

She nodded.

Kly got her a chain-mail glove. She put it on her left hand and replaced the yellow rubber glove. She opened her prosection pack and removed her steel knife.

"Glenn will help you with the forensics, and he'll sign the documents," Nathanson said.

Nathanson left to make his rounds in the Pit. He passed by the autopsy tables one by one, stopping to chat with pathologists, having a look at each of the day's cases. As she watched him walk away, Austen felt that he had been sizing her up from the moment they met. From the beginning, he had been thinking of turning the autopsy over to her, but he had held off making the decision until the last possible moment. She watched him out of the corner of her eye.

Dudley said to Austen in a low voice, "I never saw the point of Lex's calling the C.D.C. It was something he wanted to do, not me. You will follow my direction. Is that clear?"

"Yes."

"The last thing we need around here is a C.D.C. trainee who's carrying on her education in public."

Ben Kly pretended not to hear a word of this. He took up a rubber hose and rinsed the girl's body gently with running water.

Across the tables, the day's work had gotten under way. A flash went off on the other side of the room. A photographer was standing on a ladder, taking pictures of a shooting victim, a young Hispanic man who had been caught in a heroin deal gone bad. They had peeled off his bloody clothes and hung them to dry on a hat stand, and a pathologist was writing on tags with a Magic Marker and tying the tags to the clothes, while a New York City homicide detective stood by and watched. Another table was getting a lot of attention. On it lay a naked woman. She was marked with bruises about the chest and head, she appeared to have a fractured skull, and there were deep stab wounds in her belly, which was very large. Eight months pregnant, she had been beaten and stabbed to death by her husband. A fetus had apparently died of stab wounds inside her. Someone at another table said, "Who's got the loppers?" A hot smell of intestinal contents filled the air, a smell that resembled the foulest diarrhea. There was the murmur of voices, as pathologists chatted with one another across the tables. The Pit was one of the beating centers of life in New York City, essential to its daily existence, yet unseen and unimagined by most people who lived in the city. The case of the girl who had collapsed in school was not getting much attention from the other pathologists.

Dudley called over the photographer, who took a few pictures of Kate Moran. Then Austen and Dudley together did an external examination.

In the bright fluorescent light, they looked at the skin. They rolled the body sideways and examined the girl's back, then rolled her so that she was resting on her back again. When a baby is born, the attending pediatrician examines the baby's genitalia, to check for malformation. At the other end of life, the pathologist performs a similar examination. Austen parted the girl's legs and looked carefully there. She saw a string and some blood. The girl had been having her menstrual period. Pulling the string, she removed the tampon and looked at it, turning it over in her gloved hands. It bore a few spots of bright red blood.

An experienced morgue attendant, or diener, can help find things. Ben Kly pointed to the girl's nose. "Lot of mucus there."

Austen looked. Coming out of the girl's nose, along with the blood, was a slick watery fluid, a fair amount of it. "You're right," she said. "It looks like she had a cold."

"She *has* a cold," Kly commented.

"What?" Alice said, looking at him.

"You know how a cold survives in a dead body?" Kly said. "I've caught colds from bodies. Cadaver colds are the worst. I think that cold gets mean sitting in that body, saying, 'This guy is dead. *Get* me out of here.' "

"I wonder what else you guys catch," Dudley said to him.

"Hey, I've worked in the morgue for seven years," Kly replied, "and my immune system is like a rock by now. Nothing can get past it. Except every October I get my cadaver cold, as regular as an alarm clock."

Austen wanted to inspect the girl's mouth and tongue. She opened the mouth and grasped the tongue firmly with a forceps, and pulled the tongue partway out of the mouth.

Her mouth was stained with partly coagulated blood. Austen moved the tongue sideways. "She bit her tongue and lips," she said. "There are molar cuts toward the back of the tongue." She had shredded her lips with her front teeth, it seemed, and a portion of lip was missing. But that was not all. The inside of the mouth had the wrong texture and color, but the blood obscured it. Austen bent over and looked very closely, and now she saw something. The inside of the mouth was shining with blisters. They were very dark. They were blood blisters, it seemed.

Next came the examination of the eyes. Gripping the eyelids delicately with a small forceps, Austen rolled them back one at a time.

The inside of the eyelid was peppered with small red dots.

"She's got inflammation of the conjunctiva," Austen said.

Now she looked at the eye. The iris was blue-gray, but with a hint of golden yellow. Austen bent down until her face was inches from Kate's, and she stared into the pupils, left and right. In the cornea was reflected the blue glare of the overhead fluorescent lights and her own face, with the mask over her mouth and nose, and the safety glasses over her eyes. Pathology, above all, is the act of seeing. Seeing with understanding leads to diagnosis. Austen continued to stare into Kate's eyes, trying to understand what she was seeing, trying to recognize a pattern. Her eyes had an abnormal color, she thought. There seemed to be a ring of yellowish shiny pigment inside each iris—a pupillary ring, with flamelike offshoots. It had formed a kind of iridescent circle fringing the black dot of the pupil. The ring had a metallic sheen, like the wing of a tropical butterfly, with a predominantly yellowish cast, and it made the pupil look as if it had caught fire.

"These eyes seem unusual, Dr. Dudley. What do you think of the color in the iris?"

"Huh." Dudley bent over to look. "It's natural color. The conjunctiva's inflamed."

"But she has pupillary rings in the iris. Like some kind of crystalline or metallic deposit. I wonder if this is copper. She could have copper poisoning. These rings in the iris could be Kayser-Fleischer rings. That's a copper deposit in the eyes. It's a sign of Wilson's disease—"

"I *know* what that is," he said, looking at her. "Nope—no way. Rings from copper poisoning, Dr. Austen, would appear on the *outside rim* of the iris. This golden coloration is on the *inside* of the iris, near the pupil. It's normal eye color."

The girl had had a bloody nose. Austen decided that she wanted to look inside the nose. "Do you have an exam light?"

Kly found a standard examination light and handed it to Austen. She pointed the light into Kate's nostril and looked.

The nasopharynx is like a cave inside the head. This cave was clogged with congealed blood. Then Austen saw it: blood blisters in the cavity. They gleamed in the light.

"Wow," Austen said. "There's a blistering process." She thought: the bloody nose could be a broken blister.

"Let me look," Dudley said. He took the light. "Yeah. What the hell is that?"

"She has similar blisters in her mouth. This looks like an infectious-disease process, I think."

"Yeah. Or hemorrhages. This could be a toxin, a poison of some kind. Go ahead and open her," Dudley said to Austen.

Ben Kly prepared a fresh scalpel, snapping a clean blade onto the handle, and he handed it to Austen. She inserted the scalpel into Kate Moran's right shoulder. With a quick, careful, deft motion she ran the scalpel down from the shoulder and underneath the young woman's breast, then across her rib cage, bumping over the ribs. She reached the point of the sternum, where the ribs come together at the top of the abdomen, and from that point she cut straight down the abdomen, heading for the navel. She made a detour around the navel, still cutting. She stopped the cut when it reached the pubic bones of the pelvis, at the top of the pubic hair. As the skin of the abdomen parted, a strong whiff of feces filled the air.

Now Austen made a second cut, starting at Kate's other shoulder and running down and across her chest to her sternum, where the cut joined the first cut. The two cuts thus formed a Y. The points of the Y were in the shoulders and the joint of the Y was at the bottom of the rib cage. The shaft of the Y ran down over the abdomen to the pubis. Her skin gaped open, the yellow body fat revealed.

"*Ephphatha,*" Ben Kly said softly.

"What was that?" Austen said, glancing at him.

"*Ephphatha.* It's a good-luck word. It's what Jesus said when he threw a demon out of a deaf-and-dumb man. He stuck his finger into the guy's ear, and he put a dab of his spit on the guy's tongue. Then he said, '*Ephphatha.*' It means, 'Be opened.' And the demon came out."

"The Lord guides our diener's hand," Dudley remarked.

"He guides our prosector's hand," Kly said quietly.

Using the scalpel to cut away fat and tissue, Alice Austen gently pulled back the underlying tissue of the girl's chest. She reflected (laid back) the large flaps of skin, exposing her rib cage. She laid the skin of the chest backward and inside out, like a blanket, over the girl's face. The breasts were turned inside out, the breast tissue seen from the inside,

white and milky in color, while the outside of the
breasts lay upon Kate's face.

Kly handed Austen a pair of lopping shears—
the kind gardeners use to trim branches—and she cut
the girl's ribs. The ribs gave off cracking sounds as
they broke. Then she lifted away the chest plate, the
central section of the rib cage. She laid the chest
plate on the table.

Austen reached into the chest cavity with her
fingers and gently pulled the lungs away from the
heart, which was encased in a membrane. "I want to
get a blood sample," she said.

"You're going to take a blood sample from the
heart?" Dudley said sharply. "If you're testing for infective agents, you'll want to take blood from the leg,
not the heart. Don't you know that?" He went on to
say that the heart would be contaminated with many
kinds of bacteria, and thus it would not give a reliable
biological sample of blood.

Austen turned red. "Okay," she said.

Dudley had a look of satisfaction on his face.
He handed Austen a syringe. She slid it into the
femoral vein of the girl's leg in the groin area. She
found the vein on the second try and withdrew a
small amount of blood and squirted it into two jars of
blood-culture fluid, which is the color of beer. Any
bacteria in Kate's blood would grow in the liquid and
could be observed and tested.

Then she lifted out the heart and lungs. She laid
them on a white plastic cutting board. She sliced
open both lungs with her knife. The lungs were
heavy and dark. Kate had inhaled blood from her
nosebleed. But the blood in her lungs was not

enough, Austen thought, to be the cause of death. Not enough blood to drown the lungs.

With blunt scissors, she cut open the heart and examined the chambers, and she snipped open the coronary arteries. Kate Moran's coronaries and heart were normal, unremarkable.

She cut away one-inch chunks of heart tissue and lung tissue, and dropped them into a large glass jar full of formalin preservative, a clear, poisonous fluid that looks like water. This jar was known as the stock jar. It would be sent to the O.C.M.E. histology lab, where slices of the tissue in the jar would be prepared for viewing through a microscope. Austen also prepared a separate toxicology container, a plastic container with no preservative in it. The O.C.M.E.'s toxicology lab would test the samples in this container for toxins and drugs. She dropped raw pieces of lung into the tox container.

Now Austen reached into the abdomen, feeling around among the intestines. She removed the small intestine, pulling it out like rope, foot by foot, cutting the membranes that held the masses of intestines together. There was a sour reek, and a quantity of chyme squeezed out of the small intestine, like toothpaste coming out of a tube. Chyme is a soft gray paste that looks like oatmeal. It is partly digested food from the upper intestine, food that has not yet met the bile and darkened. She placed the small intestine in a cylindrical steel wash tank full of running water that sat at the end of the autopsy table. The tissue seemed healthy and normal.

She found the liver and pulled it up to look at it. The liver appeared normal in color: dark reddish brown. She removed the liver and weighed it on a scale over the table. "Liver's thirteen hundred and fifty grams." She put it down on the cutting board and sliced it quickly, then dropped a sample of liver into the stock jar, and another piece of liver into the tox container. She cut open the stomach and looked inside at the contents. Kate Moran had not eaten in a while.

Austen lifted the bowel out, holding it in both hands, loosely folded. This she handed to Ben Kly. He placed the bowel in the wash container and squeezed it and rinsed it, like hand laundry. Masses of feces floated away in the wash water and swirled down the drain. A stench of feces filled the air.

The body cavity was open and almost empty now, a red gaping cave of ribs. The girl's face was not visible. It was still covered with the blanket of chest skin.

Kly was standing close to Austen, looking into the body cavity.

"Find her soul, Ben?" Dudley said.

"It's gone to a better place, Doctor," Kly answered.

There were still the pelvic organs to remove. These are the organs that are tucked inside the pelvis (the hip bones). The pelvic organs open out through the natural openings between the legs.

Austen reached down through the abdomen, low inside the girl's pelvis, and grasped the vagina and rectum with her left hand (her chain-mail hand). With her right hand, she inserted a scalpel deep down into the pelvic area. Working delicately, by sense of touch, she cut through the base of the rectum, through the vagina, and she cut away the bladder at the base of the urethra. As she was cutting, she pulled steadily. Nothing happened. She pulled harder. The bundle of organs were suddenly freed, and they came out of the body with a bubbling squelch. The sound is known as the pelvic slurp, and it is caused by a suction drawing air inward as the organs are pulled out of the pelvis.

Austen lifted out the block of pelvic organs: the rectum, vagina and uterus with the ovaries, and the bladder. They hung together in a single baglike unit, a sac of organs that weighed about five pounds and wobbled and pendulated in her gloved hand. She placed the mass on the cutting board. It was soft, and spread out like jelly.

She began to feel cold. She wished they didn't keep the air quite so cool in here. She cut the pelvic organs apart from one another with scissors. She opened the bladder. It was empty.

Austen turned her attention to the kidneys. They were lying on the cutting board. She trimmed the kidney fat off them, and then she sectioned a kidney with her knife.

The kidney fell in half.

It was unusual.

She saw delicate golden-yellow streaks of color in the renal pyramid, in the center of the kidney. This was abnormal. The kidney should be a dark reddish-brown color, not golden and streaky. So often in an autopsy, color carries meaning. A golden kidney, that was unusual.

"Look at this, Dr. Dudley."

The two pathologists bent over the kidney. Austen sectioned the other kidney, and found golden streaks in it, too. She cut chunks out of both kidneys and put the chunks in the stock jar and in the tox container.

"That yellow tissue is dead," he said. "Those are uric acid infarcts, looks like to me. That tissue was killed by deposits of uric acid crystals."

"She seems healthy. Why would she have a lot of uric acid in her blood?"

"Maybe it's not uric acid. It could be a toxin. That would cause the blistering in the kid's mouth. Maybe she was getting chemotherapy for cancer. That would blast the kidneys."

"But there's no sign of cancer."

Austen turned her attention to the rest of the pelvic organs. She separated the rectum from the uterus, snipping through the membrane that joined them. She placed the rectum on the cutting board and split it with scissors, opened it up, and flattened it out, smoothing the rectum with her fingers.

She placed the vagina, uterus, and ovaries on the cutting board. She split the vagina with a knife. The inside of the vagina was speckled with a few blood blisters. Several had broken; perhaps that was what had stained the tampon. She snipped open the uterus with scissors. The tissues were in an early menstrual stage.

Austen sectioned one ovary with a scalpel. The girl's ovary fell apart under her blade. Cells in the ovary can become an adult human being. Looking at Kate's ovary gave Austen a deep feeling, and made her conscious of her own pelvic organs, her unknown future, the probability or hope that someday she would become a mother. This was the girl's motherhood being laid apart under the knife, a future that had ended like a door slamming shut. The tissues of the ovary were unremarkable.

She caught Ben Kly's eye. "Cranial contents," she said.

"Okay." He lifted up the girl's head and placed it on a hard rubber head block. The head block is an H-shaped chunk of black vulcanized rubber. It is used in autopsies to hold up the head and get it off the table, so that the skull can be cut open. He removed the chest skin from her face.

Austen took up a scalpel. She bent down to the level of the table and looked at the side of the girl's head, judging the best place to start the incision. With one hand, she lifted up the russet hair to get it out of the way. She put the scalpel on the skin just above the ear, pushing the tip straight in until it touched bone. Then, slitting the skin rapidly, she made an incision over the top of the head, a coronal incision running from ear to ear, cutting through the scalp. The scalp tissue parted with a slurping sound. It looked like the lips of a mouth opening across the top of the head. Some blood dripped onto the table, forming red puddles on the steel.

Now she gripped the scalp and pulled it forward, peeling it off the skull. There was a faint ripping sound as she pulled. The scalp lifted away very easily. She pulled the scalp and hair forward and then down over the face. As she did this, the whole face was compressed like a piece of rubber. Kate's eyes opened and sagged downward, and her face collapsed, creating an expression that seemed as if she were experiencing the deepest grief in the world.

The scalp was now reversed and hanging down from her bare forehead bone, covering her eyes, so the wet, glistening, red inner layer of the scalp was on the outside, like a hat pulled down low. Her hair was underneath it, like a rug turned upside down and lying on her face. A brush of matted hair stuck out from underneath the reversed scalp. This hair hung down and covered her nose and mouth. Then Austen pulled the scalp down off the back part of the skull, down almost to the top of the neck. This revealed the glistening-wet ivory-colored dome of her skull.

It is the task of the morgue attendant to open the skull. Ben Kly took up a Stryker saw and plugged the cord into a socket under the table. A Stryker saw is a power tool with a cutting blade that moves back and forth, rather than spinning around. Kly switched the saw on, and it gave off a chattering whine. He adjusted his safety glasses—you want to make sure your eyes are protected if you are using power tools that throw blood and particles around. The Stryker saw dug into the skull.

A cloud of mist appeared in the air around the girl's head. It drifted and coiled and snaked up from the blade of the Stryker saw, moving like cigarette smoke, and there was a sudden, sharp smell of bone. The "smoke" was bone dust. It had a piercing odor, strong and unpleasant. It resembled the smell that occurs in a dentist's office when a high-speed drill is cutting into a tooth—a smoky, bony, warm, bloody, wet stench.

Kly grimaced, bearing down hard on the Stryker saw. The cut circled the head. He finished the cut at an angle, making a V notch in the forehead. The notch was so that he could fit the skull bone back on properly afterward, matching the shape of the cut.

Then he took up a steel T-shaped bone chisel. He inserted it into the saw cut, and twisted the chisel. There was a cracking sound. He put it in another place and pried again. More cracking sounds came from the skull. He pried gently, here and there. Then he lifted off the top of the skull. It was a section of bone known as the calvarium. He held it in his hands, upside down. The calvarium was a dish of bone the size and shape of a soup bowl. It was the top of the girl's skull. A pool of blood had collected in the bottom of the calvarium. It was a bowl of blood.

"Calvary," Kly said in a dreamy way. "The Place of the Skull." He placed the bone on the autopsy table, where it rotated slowly.

"You read the Bible too much," Dudley remarked.

"I don't read it enough," Kly answered.

He had exposed a gray, leathery membrane that covers the brain, a membrane called the dura mater.

Austen continued from that point. She ran her hand over the dura, feeling the membrane. It seemed tight and swollen to her, but that was hard to tell. She took up blunt scissors and carefully cut the dura mater, snipping it away. She peeled it back. The folds of the brain came into view.

The brain was swollen, bulging like a strange forest mushroom. It had an eerie, abnormal, pearlescent color. It was a color that neither pathologist had ever seen in brain tissue before.

"Whoa," Dudley said.

Austen's heart thudded in her chest. This is a destroyed brain, she thought. She felt a mixture of fear and excitement.

"Flattened folds," Dudley said.

The folds of the human brain are ordinarily deep and sharply grooved. This brain had turned a silvery color and had puffed up like a balloon. The folds of the brain had been smashed up and pressed flat into the dura mater. The brain was smoothed, swollen, and flattened—as if the wrinkles had been pressed with an iron. This was a technical term, an ironed brain. It was almost as if the brain had exploded, bursting against the inside of the skull.

Austen touched the brain surface. It was very, very soft, like gelatin that had not set properly. The brain was a destroyed mess, almost liquefying. How to remove it? It could fall apart.

Gently, Austen pushed the fingers of her left hand, the chain-mail hand, in around the frontal lobes of Kate Moran's exploded brain. She was feeling her way behind the bones of the forehead, trying not to tear the brain. She pulled the brain back slightly with her left hand, and then, with her right hand, working entirely by sense of touch, she slid a scalpel down low under the front of the skull. With the blade she began probing for the optic nerves, the nerves that connected the brain to the eyes. She couldn't see the scalpel blade, and so she felt around with it, using her sense of touch. She found the optic nerves and cut them. She wiggled the brain and it loosened.

The removal of a person's brain seemed to Austen more of a violation of the person's dignity and privacy than any other procedure in the autopsy, because the brain is the most personal part of the body; the only body part that studies itself. Alice Austen felt that the life of a human being has a sacred quality. She did not know if she believed in the soul; that seemed a difficult question to answer. But she believed in the sacredness of human life. One very important way to honor life is to try to find out how it ended.

Austen pulled the brain backward, rolling it and lifting it. This brain is impossibly soft, she thought. Finally she had lifted the brain enough to gain access to the top of the spinal cord. With a quick angling slice of the scalpel she cut the spinal cord, and the brain fell into her hands.

Cradling the organ in her cupped hands—it was hugely, abnormally heavy, engorged with fluid, and so jellylike it threatened to slop apart—she placed the brain in the scale pan and weighed it.

"Oh, wow. Sixteen hundred and twenty-five grams," she said. It was a superfat brain.

Keeping her hands cupped around the brain, she lowered it to the cutting board. Then she turned the brain over, upside down. She let it go, and it spread out under its own weight, like a blob. It flowed over the cutting board like a bag of water, it was so soft.

It was a spotted blob.

The underside of the brain was speckled with tiny red spots.

She stared at the spots. They were small red speckles, tiny, less than a millimeter across. They were starlike hemorrhages. Yet there had been no general bleeding in this brain, no massive hemorrhage. It was a glassy, swollen brain speckled with red spots.

When a person gets measles, the skin erupts with red spots. The brain, when infected with a virus, also can become spotty.

She became aware of the fact that she was alive and this brain was not alive. But it might have something alive in it. "I see a lot of small bleeds," she said to Dudley.

Austen began trying to make a diagnosis. The word *diagnosis* in Greek means "knowing through." In a successful diagnosis, you search through possibilities, casting them aside, ruling things out, until at last there comes a sensation of a click, a locking in place, and the fragments of a puzzle snap into a clear picture.

She was missing something. What was it? She moved around the table, to reposition herself for further examination of the brain. In doing so, she brushed against the calvarium—the top of the skull—which was lying upside down on the table, with the pool of blood in it. It was getting in the way, so she picked it up in order to move it to a different place, and it slipped from her already slippery fingers. It hit the blood-covered metal of the table with a clang, and a fine spray of blood droplets went into the air.

"Damn!" Dudley said, drawing back.

There were tiny spots of blood on his eyeglasses.

"Good technique," he said.

"I'm sorry. I'm very sorry." A wave of nervousness swept over her, and her stomach clenched. "Did you get any in your eyes?"

"No. Fortunately. That's why we wear eye protection." He had a cold look on his face.

There was nothing to do but keep going. Looking at the brain, she saw the effects of brain swelling. The brain is encased in a hard skull, and when it swells, through injury or infection, it has nowhere to go. So it destroys itself. The brain puffs up with fluid—in the way any injured tissue does—and it crushes itself.

The swelling brain pushes downward on the deep structures at the top of the brain stem, especially on the midbrain. The midbrain is an old brain, a primitive brain. It contains nerve branches that control basic functions such as breathing and heartbeat, and it contains the nerves of the face; it also contains the nerves that govern the action of the irises of the eyes in response to light. If you crush the midbrain, these nerves are destroyed. The pupils dilate and become fixed, breathing ceases, and the heart stops beating.

Austen saw deep grooves in the underside of the brain. These grooves were a sign of rupture of the brain: the brain had almost literally burst. It had changed shape as it puffed up and died. The moving finger had written its message on Kate Moran's mind: she could not have been saved by any medical procedure. This was a hopeless case. By the time the girl collapsed, she was doomed.

As the brain crushes itself, the blood pressure can shoot sky high. This is a shock response known as the Cushing reflex. It happens in the moments before death. The brain must have blood, and as the swelling begins to close off the arteries that supply blood to the brain, and as pressure in the brain rises, the body drives up its own blood pressure to meet the rise in brain pressure. The body is trying to drive blood into the brain at all costs, because if the blood supply to the brain is lost, the brain stops functioning in a matter of a few seconds. Thus there can be a tremendous terminal spike of blood pressure. As the patient approaches death, the systolic blood pressure soars as high as 300. Normal systolic pressure is about 120. The sudden spike in blood pressure during a Cushing reflex can trigger hemorrhages, sudden bleeds anywhere in the body. The pressure soars, the pipes burst. The patient starts to bleed, the patient dies. That, Austen thought, was the cause of the girl's bloody nose. Her blood pressure had spiked, causing a hemorrhagic nosebleed at the point of death.

"This could be a virus infection of the brain. It led to brain swelling, which was the immediate cause of death," Austen said. "It triggered a Cushing reflex with a bleed from the nasopharynx."

Dudley looked at her. "Fine. We have an unknown brain virus that caused a nosebleed. Is that what you're trying to tell me?"

"This scares me. I've never seen anything like it. I want to section this brain," she said.

"The brain's a mess," Dudley said.

"I want to try."

"Go ahead."

She dipped her knife in the water of the rinsing tank, to wet it and make it slippery. She laid the edge across the brain, in a coronal section, as if going from ear to ear, and she sliced downward crisply in a smooth motion. She sliced again and again, her knife moving quickly, making slices that were about the thickness of slices of bread.

The brain slimed apart. As her knife hit it, it slumped into a kind of glassy, red-gray mush. Austen ended up with a slippery jumble of bloody-wet brain tissue that seemed to gleam with a pearlescent color under the lights. It spread out in a soupy mess on the cutting board.

"You've ruined it!" Dudley said.

Austen said nothing. She was tempted to warn him to back off.

"You've turned the kid's brain into roadkill!"

"I'm sorry, I'm doing my best." She sliced through the deep brain structures. Again, the tissue almost melted under the knife. Inside the girl's midbrain and pons medulla, she found what she was looking for: small weeping hemorrhages. These secondary weeping bleeds were areas of bloody discoloration, the result of tearing and crushing of the brain structures as the brain squeezed down upon them.

Ben Kly carried a glass jar over to the table. It was full of formalin. Using her knife as a paddle, she scraped and scooped the pulpy brain off the cutting board while Kly held the jar under it. The brain coddle plopped and splashed into the liquid, and floated in distorted fragments.

"Something destroyed the girl's central nervous system," she said.

The Chief

"So how did it go?" Lex Nathanson asked, half an hour later. Austen had found him in the death-reporting area, reviewing some new cases.

"It was bad," she said. She had changed out of her scrubs and back into her street clothes, but she noticed—in a vague kind of way—that she smelled like Kate Moran. That would last for hours, unless she took a shower, and she did not have time for a shower.

They went into Nathanson's office, and he slid open a drawer of his desk and took a cigar from a box and put it in his mouth, and then rummaged around for something. "Where in the hell is my cutter?" He held up a second cigar. "You want one?" he said.

Austen grinned. "No, thanks."

"Yeah? You're sure? These are twenty-buck cigars. If this vice of mine bothers you, please say so, okay?"

"It's not a problem."

He had found his cutter, and he notched the end of the cigar. He struck a wooden match, and, not holding the cigar in his mouth, but in his fingers, he toasted the end, rolling it gently in the match flame until the end of the cigar turned gray. "I'm afraid I am not an example to young people. Not only are these cigars a vice, but I have too much yellow abdominal fat. When they autopsy me—and I will insist on it—they will find a rat's nest of problems, I'm sure. It is true that pathologists do not always learn from the lifestyle disasters they see on the autopsy table." He drew on the cigar. A soft and mellow tobacco smoke infused the room. "Anyway, Winston Churchill smoked approximately sixty thousand cigars during his lifetime, and he lived to be ninety-one. Tell me what you found."

Austen described the findings: blood blistering in the external openings of the body, including the mouth, nasopharynx, and eyelids. Golden streaky damage to the kidneys. Fatal brain swelling.

Nathanson looked at her quizzically. "Go on. Tell me about the C.N.S." The central nervous system.

"The destruction was massive."

"How so?" he asked.

"The brain was devastated." She tried to summarize it. "The brain was puffed and swollen and had lost its physical integrity. It almost literally collapsed when I sectioned it. It had a shiny, glassy, reflective coloration that I've never seen before. The brain had turned into a kind of—how can I describe it?—like some kind of glassy pudding. She had a severe nosebleed, and she bit her tongue and mouth and lips very severely. She also showed signs of a common cold—streaming mucus exudate from the sinuses. There were golden pupillary rings in the irises of the eyes, with flamelike offshoots. It made the pupils look as if they were on fire. The total effect was—well—frightening. It made me think of a virus infection involving the central nervous system and possibly the tissues of the mouth and eyes and other openings of the body."

"We don't have the capability to test for a virus here."

"You don't have a lab for that?"

"No. We send biosamples over to the city health department's lab. They test for *bacteria.* They don't test for viruses."

"We can do it," Austen said. "May I send some samples down to C.D.C.?"

"Sure. Give them to Walt with my regards." He gave her a sharp look. "How are you getting along with Glenn?"

Austen took a moment to reply, and she framed her answer carefully. "He's straightforward in his views."

"Boy—you're quite a diplomat." Nathanson drew on his cigar. "Glenn's being a pain in the neck. If he gets to be too much of a pain, let me know and I'll kick his ass for you. But I imagine you can handle yourself, Dr. Austen."

She nodded and said nothing.

He went on, "Glenn's having a bad time in his personal life. His wife recently left him. She took the children with her. He had been having an affair with a younger woman. But Glenn is a colleague and a valued member of my staff."

"Of course."

"Do you want to continue with this investigation?"

"Yes, I do."

"Really, I don't want to impose on you. I could turn this over to the health department."

"You're not imposing on me, Dr. Nathanson."

He smiled broadly. "All right, enough of this 'my dear Alphonse.' Whaddaya need?"

"Well—I'd like to look at all your recent case files."

"Sure. What else?"

"I'll need a telephone. Also a map of New York City."

There was a pause while he smoked his cigar. "That's all you need?"

"Epi work is pretty simple," she said. She looked out the window of his office. There wasn't much to see, only the brick wall of the next building, but she observed that it had begun to rain. "I forgot to bring a raincoat."

"I'll get you one of our slickers. And you'll need an office, won't you?"

"I guess so."

☐

They gave her a tiny office, almost a closet, on the third floor. Someone brought her a bright yellow rain slicker. Across the back in black letters it said, "OF-FICE OF CHIEF MEDICAL EXAMINER." It was a disaster raincoat, meant for protecting workers from blood and body fluid splashed around a disaster site, as well as from rain. It smelled of sweat.

The room was the office of a staff pathologist, a woman who was away on maternity leave. The office's one window looked out on the blank wall of a parking garage some feet away. It was a nicer room than her digs in the C.D.C., anyway. She wondered why epidemiologists inhabited the world's worst offices. She taped a map of New York City to the wall.

With a pencil she marked an X on the map: at the location of the Mater School on Seventy-ninth Street, where Kate Moran had died. She marked another X on Times Square, where Harmonica Man had collapsed. The marks showed the *location* of death. They did not show where the victims had been exposed. If indeed they had been exposed to anything. If this was an outbreak of an infectious disease or a rash of poisoning, Harmonica Man was the first identified case. He was therefore what was known as the index case. Kate Moran, who died less than a week later, was the second case. There was no obvious connection between the two cases. It was not necessary for Austen to know what had killed them in order for her to begin an investigation. As Dr. John Snow knew, epidemiology can proceed without any knowledge of the nature of the disease-causing agent.

Deeper

Kate Moran's tissues were being processed in the
O.C.M.E. histology lab, and they would not be ready
for viewing for about a day. In the meantime, Harmonica Man's tissues could be examined, and
Austen called for samples, giving the case number to
a technician. "Those slides have been checked out by
Dr. Dudley," he said. So she went down to Glenn
Dudley's office on the third floor and found Dudley
sitting at a small table, staring into the eyepieces of a
doubleheaded microscope. This is a microscope with
two sets of binocular eyepieces, so that two people
can look at a specimen at the same time.

"What do you want?" Dudley said without
looking up.

"I wanted to take a look at the tissues of the first
case."

He grunted and kept staring into his microscope.

Austen sat down across from Dudley, facing
him, and looked into the other set of binocular eyepieces. She saw a field of brain cells. It was a thin
slice of Harmonica Man's brain tissue.

"It's from the underside of the temporal lobe,"
Dudley said. "The area of the hippocampus. It seems
damaged."

She let her gaze relax. She wandered through
fields of cells. She saw threadlike neurons, which are

the nerve cells that send signals in the brain. She saw other types of brain cells, and she saw white matter, which is a fatty substance in the brain. She came to a damaged area, where she began finding red blood cells. "I think I'm getting into a bleeding spot."

"Nothing else? Okay, I'm zooming."

The scene jumped. The cells were magnified more strongly. "Look at these cells," he said. "Zooming again." The scene jumped forward. They were on a voyage, running deep into the brain of Harmonica Man.

There was something wrong with the cells. A neuron, a nerve cell, is a long thread with branches. Somewhere in the middle of the thread there is a bulge. Inside the bulge there is a dot. The dot is the cell's nucleus, where the cell's genetic material is stored, its DNA. The nucleus of a cell looks like the yolk of a fried egg. It contains the chromosomes, which are pods of coiled protein that hold the cell's DNA intact. Austen did not like the way these brain-cell nuclei looked.

"The cell nuclei are abnormal," she said. "Would you zoom again, please?"

The scene jumped. The nuclei were bigger.

"That's the highest magnification," Dudley said.

It was hard to know what you were looking at. Life at the cellular level is complicated. There seemed to be structure in the cell nuclei—structure that didn't belong there. Then she saw something. It was something she had never seen before, not even in a textbook. There were *objects* sitting in the cell nucleus. *Things.* Maybe this was something normal.

Maybe the stain in the cells had brought out some feature that was explainable. It was hard to tell.

"What is this, Dr. Dudley?"

He grunted. He didn't have any answers either.

The objects in the nucleus were shiny, glittery, angular crystals. They had a mathematical shape. They were bulging with many facets, like angular soccer balls. They were far too large to be virus particles. Virus particles are invisible in a regular microscope.

The light broke apart in the crystals and seemed to shimmer.

"This is like nothing I've ever seen before, Dr. Dudley," Austen said.

"It's weird," Dudley replied, sounding unsure of himself. "This must be some kind of chemical compound. There's some new drug hitting the street."

"Maybe these crystals are lumps of virus in a crystallized form," Austen said.

"Lumps! *Lumps of virus.* Don't be an idiot," he snapped. And he continued to stare into the microscope in silence.

Union Square

A cool and gentle April rain was passing over New York City. Alice Austen stared out the window of her office at the O.C.M.E., watching water run down the blank wall. Then she put on the yellow disaster raincoat, shouldered her knapsack, and took a taxi to Union Square.

A television van from Fox Channel 5 was double-parked on the street in front of the Morans' building. A young woman reporter spotted Austen's yellow raincoat as she rang the buzzer. "You're from the medical examiner's office? What happened to Kate Moran? Was she poisoned? Was it a murder? Can you tell us anything?" Behind her trailed a video man.

"I'm sorry, but you'll have to talk to the chief medical examiner," Austen said. The buzzer sounded, and she slipped inside.

The girl's parents, Jim and Eunice Moran, sat holding each other's hands on a couch in the living room. They seemed devastated. A large black-and-white photograph in a steel frame—a portrait of Eunice Moran by Robert Mapplethorpe—leaned against the wall across from the couch. In the photograph Mrs. Moran was wearing a soft white wool turtleneck sweater, and she looked thoughtful and elegant. In real life she was haggard, her eyes red from crying.

The housekeeper, an older Irish woman, retired to the kitchen, her footsteps padding on the oak floor. Austen heard sounds of her weeping.

Austen knew that people who are in the throes of grief can have unpredictable reactions to an epidemiologist asking questions, and she very gently identified herself as a doctor with the Centers for Disease Control in Atlanta, working with the city medical examiner's office. When Kate's parents understood that Austen had been dispatched to New York to investigate the death of their daughter, they spoke freely with her. The conversation was difficult, because at times Jim and Eunice Moran lost their ability to speak. Kate had been an only child. The parents' life stretched ahead of them into a future that was more empty than they could have imagined.

They knew there had been an autopsy—in a case of sudden unexpected death an autopsy is required by law, and they had been notified. Austen chose not to tell them that she had performed the autopsy. "Your daughter's body was released to the funeral home an hour ago," she said. "However, because of the risk of possible infection, the city has ordered a cremation. The funeral home was instructed to take universal biohazard precautions. I called them myself and spoke with them, and they know how to do that."

"What do you mean, biohazard precautions?" Eunice Moran said. Her voice sounded like breaking glass.

"I'm sorry. Your daughter may have had a contagious disease."

"What kind of disease?" Mr. Moran asked.

"We don't know. We don't even know if it was contagious. What I'm here to do right now—I know it's hard—is, I need to ask you some questions about what your daughter did and where she went during the past days and perhaps weeks, while your memory is fresh. We want to try to find out if she was exposed to something."

Mrs. Moran held her husband tighter. Finally she said, "We'll try to help you." She nodded at a chair. "Please sit down."

Austen sat on the edge of the chair. "Can you think of anything Kate did lately that might have exposed her to something infective or toxic? Did she travel in a foreign country recently?"

"No," Mrs. Moran said.

"Was she receiving chemotherapy for cancer?"

"Kate? No!"

"Was she taking any strong or potentially toxic medications?"

"No," Mrs. Moran said.

"Did she receive any vaccinations recently?"

"No."

"Did she eat any shellfish or unusual foods? Visit any unusual places?"

"Not that I can think of," Mrs. Moran said.

There was silence.

"Had she been outdoors in the woods, hiking or camping, where she could have been bitten by a tick?"

"No."

"Did Kate have a boyfriend?"

They weren't sure. They said that Kate had been going out with someone her age, a boy named Ter Salmonson.

Austen wrote the name down in her green epi notebook and got his phone number from Mrs. Moran.

"She broke up with Ter, I think," Kate's mother said.

Austen asked if they could carefully review Kate's movements over the past two weeks. The parents were vague. Kate's life had been quiet. She had friends, but she wasn't a heavy socializer. She was a fan of rock music, and her parents had forbidden her to go to certain music clubs, but there had been no real trouble over that.

"There's another question. This is hard for me to ask. Do you know if Kate used drugs?"

"Absolutely not," Mr. Moran said.

"She didn't smoke pot or anything?"

"I don't know—I don't think so, no," Eunice Moran said.

Kate took the subway to school every day. She would come home late in the afternoon. She'd go into her room, listen to music, talk with friends on the telephone, do her homework, have supper, do more homework, sometimes surf the Web and send e-mail, go to bed.

"I've been very busy with my work," Jim Moran said. "We haven't done much as a family together lately."

"Did she go *anywhere* recently?"

"The only thing I can think of is her art project for Mr. Talides, her teacher." Mrs. Moran answered. "It's a construction thing or something, and Kate was going around buying her boxes and things—when?" She turned to her husband.

"I don't know," Mr. Moran said.

"Last weekend, I think. She was buying things in SoHo and on Broadway and at the Sixth Avenue flea market, I guess. Mr. Talides was—" Mrs. Moran's voice cracked. "I can't stop thinking—I'm sorry—he tried to save her."

"Do you know, did he attempt C.P.R.?"

"He had forgotten what to do, that's—that's what he told me when he called. He was very upset."

Austen made a note to herself to interview the art teacher right away. He might have been exposed. On the other hand, she was beginning to get an uncomfortable feeling that this could turn out to be a wild-goose chase, that she had been pushed into some kind of hopeless problem by Walt Mellis. An unsolved outbreak. One of those blips that never gets explained.

The telephone rang. The housekeeper, whose name was Nanette, answered. It was a priest calling about the funeral arrangements. Austen could hear Nanette saying, "There won't be a wake, Father, no, no, the health authorities have forbidden . . ."

"Do you mind if I look around the house just a little?"

The parents didn't answer.

"Sometimes looking can be helpful. Also, would you mind if I took some photographs?" She removed her electronic camera from her knapsack. "May I look in the kitchen, and in Kate's bedroom?"

They nodded, somewhat reluctantly.

She went into the kitchen first. Nanette hurried out as soon as Austen entered, almost hiding her face from her. It was a pleasant kitchen, with gray

stone counters and a huge stove. She opened the refrigerator.

Austen did not think this was a food-borne illness, but she could not be sure, and there was, too,
the issue of whether Kate had consumed a poison.
She moved a few things around in the refrigerator.
She photographed as much of the food as she could.
Milk, some fish in paper. She opened the paper. It
was salmon; it smelled fresh. Red-tipped lettuce. A
bottle of French white wine, half finished. She
sniffed at the wine. It seemed okay.

Then she went into a hallway. Down the hall
was a door standing half open. It led to Kate's bedroom.

It was a beautiful room, with bare brick walls,
illuminated by a skylight. It was cluttered with a
teenager's life. There was an unmade bed, a poster
for Phish on the wall—the drummer Jon Fishman
strutting onstage wearing a dress. There was a poster
of a Vermeer painting: a young woman playing the
clavichord. In the closet she found baggy jeans, tight
silk tops, little strap dresses, a short leather jacket.
Kate must have been sensitive and hip, somewhat
arty. There was an old bureau. A maple box containing odd bits of junky jewelry. There was a desk with
a computer, and a table piled with bric-a-brac. There
were joke dolls, a row of flutes and pennywhistles
lined up next to each other, made of wood, plastic,
reed, and steel. In the center of the table stood a dollhouse. This had to be Kate's art table. There were
small antique boxes, large new metal boxes. Small
metal cans and tubes. A can that said, "Twinings Earl
Grey Tea." Plastic containers of all shapes and col-

ors. Delicate boxes made of wood. Everything was well organized and ordered.

Austen had been wondering about the issue of drugs. She opened the drawers in the desk and opened some of the boxes, looking for drug paraphernalia. There was nothing like that to be found. She began to rule out Dr. Dudley's hypothesis that Kate might have been a drug user. This was not the bedroom of a druggie.

Kate had had quirky taste and an unusual sense of color and shape. Austen switched on her electronic camera and began to take photographs of the room. The light from the skylight gave everything a cool radiance. Momentarily she felt as if Kate were standing in the room with her; it could not be so, but she felt the existence of a world next to ours. That world was real, in a sense, for Kate was present in the arrangement of the objects, which had not been moved or touched since her death.

Austen opened up a box. Inside it was a mechanical toy beetle. It stared at her with sad green jeweled eyes. She put it down in the spot where she had found it, reluctant to move Kate's arrangements. In another box was a miniature cast-metal car. The camera focused automatically. She began shooting everything. There was a box full of bird feathers: from blue jays, a cardinal, a crow, and a banded feather that she thought might have come from a red-tailed hawk, but she wasn't sure. There was a box made of wood with a polygon painted on it. She tried to open it but it had a puzzle catch she couldn't figure out, so she took a picture of it. She photographed a sharp-looking jagged metal spring. She photographed a chunk of green malachite. An old skeleton key in a padlock. The skull of some small bird, maybe a sparrow. An amethyst geode. Then there was the dollhouse. Kate seemed to be taking it apart. She stepped back and took a picture of the dollhouse. She took a picture of the whole room. She wondered if she would ever look at these pictures again. They might hold information. Or maybe not. She jotted a few notes in her green epi notebook.

Tracking

Austen followed the same route to school that Kate had taken every morning: she walked to Union Square and then took the subway to the Upper East Side, trying to get a feel for Kate's world. The Mater School was situated in a quiet, wealthy neighborhood, among town houses. Austen arrived there at three o'clock in the afternoon. The headmistress, Sister Anne Threader, had ordered a morning assembly and chapel, and then had canceled classes but had kept the students in school for a day of reflection and prayer. She had dismissed school shortly before Austen arrived, but some of the students had elected to stay, and Sister Threader had seen no way to argue with that. She was a tiny woman in late middle age, with straight white hair and piercing eyes. She wore a pale blue dress rather than a nun's habit. "Kate was a much loved person here," she said to Austen. She led her to the art room. Three students were there, sitting around, doing nothing. They were subdued, in shock, and had been crying.

"Where is Mr. Talides?" Sister Anne asked them.

"He went home," one of the students said. "He was feeling really bad."

"I'm so *angry,* Anne," another young woman said to the headmistress. It was Jennifer Ramosa. She had been crying with rage about that which she could not change.

"God understands your feelings," Sister Anne said. "He loves Kate as you love her, and he understands your being angry."

"I saw her die," Jennifer said. Her voice trembled.

Sister Anne took Jennifer's hands. "Life is a mystery, and death is a mystery when it occurs. When you are reunited with Kate you will have answers, but for now what we need to be asking is what Kate would want us to do."

Austen felt the question herself. What would Kate want of her?

"Kate never got a chance," Jennifer said.

"We don't know that," Sister Anne said. She suggested that they all pray.

Finally the headmistress said, "This is Dr. Alice Austen. She is here to try to find out what happened to Kate."

"I'm a doctor working with the City of New York," Austen said.

"Kates was one of my best friends," Jennifer Ramosa said. "I can't believe she's gone."

"I think she would want us to find out what happened," Austen said. Then she said, "May I look around the room?"

She poked around the art room while the girls watched her, and Sister Anne spoke quietly with them. Nothing seemed unusual. There were coffee cans gobbed with paints. Tubes of gesso, canvas on stretchers. Kate's project area had been a table in the corner. On it stood more of Kate's things and a very large construction that looked like a house, sort of a dollhouse, but larger and more complicated.

Austen turned and faced the students. "Did the art teacher, Mr. Talides, get close to Kate when she was ill?"

Two of the girls nodded.

She turned to the headmistress. "Do you have his home telephone number?"

□

It was late afternoon on Thursday now, still the first day of Austen's investigation, and rush hour was beginning. It was about thirty hours since Kate Moran had died, thirty hours since Peter Talides had been in close proximity to Kate during the agonal phase of her illness. If Talides had been infected with something, he would probably still be in the incubation period, and he might well be asymptomatic, showing no signs of illness. Austen did not think that an infectious agent would cause any but the most subtle sign of illness during thirty hours or so. But she wanted to get in touch with Talides, have a look a him, and to keep track of him.

She got on the N train headed for Queens. Twenty minutes later she stepped off the train at the elevated station at Grand Avenue. A set of dilapidated iron stairs debouched into a bustling neighborhood of small markets, dry-cleaning shops, hair parlors, a Greek restaurant, a gas station. She tried to figure out where to go. She walked a few blocks into a quieter neighborhood and found herself in a small park. There were some Doric columns and a bronze statue of a man in a robe. Curious, she went over to the statue. It was Socrates—him all right, with his misshapen face and bushy beard. Under him were

engraved the words "Know thy self." The name Talides—she realized that this must be a Greek neighborhood. It began to dawn on her just how
exquisitely local are the neighborhoods of New York
City. She was looking at a biological system of be-
wildering complexity.

She kept going, turning up a side street. Peter
Talides lived in half of a small duplex house made of
brown brick. She rang the front doorbell.

Talides opened the door immediately. He was a
pudgy man, with a kindly, sad face. His living room
was also his studio. There were canvases stretched on
frames, coffee cans holding paint and water, paint-
ings piled up against the wall. The colors were bold
and vibrant.

"I apologize for the mess," he said. "Please sit
down."

She sat in a threadbare easy chair. He sat on a
swiveling stool. He sighed a deep sigh. He seemed
on the edge of tears.

"I'm very sorry about what happened," she said.

Peter Talides thanked her for her concern. "My
life is the school and my painting. I live alone. I have
no illusions about my talent. But—" He pulled out a
handkerchief and wiped his nose. "I try to make a
small difference with the kids."

"Can you describe what you did to try to save
Kate?"

"I—" He sighed. Long pause. "I tried to remember how to give rescue breaths. I couldn't remember . . . how . . . I had the lessons, but I couldn't
remember—I'm sorry, this is very difficult for me."

"Did you put your mouth to her mouth?"

"Very briefly, yes."

"Was there blood?"

"She had a—bloody nose."

"Did any of the blood get on you?"

His voice trembled. "I had to throw away my shirt."

"Could I look at your face more closely?"

He sat on the stool, uncomfortable and embarrassed. She looked at him carefully.

"Do you have a cold?" she asked.

"Yes. Runny nose. Stopped-up sinuses."

Austen took a deep breath. "Have your eyes been bothering you?"

"Yes. They bother me when I have a cold or allergies. I have frequent allergies."

"Can you describe the sensation in your eyes?"

"It's nothing. Just itchy, runny. Like an allergy."

"I'm concerned."

"About me? I feel okay."

"I can't give you an exam—I'm not a clinician." She did not mention to him that she also did not have a license to practice medicine in New York, and so she was barred by law from doing a patient exam. "I'd like for you to go to a hospital emergency room with me. We'll get a medical team to work you up."

He looked startled.

"But it's probably nothing," she said.

"I really don't want to go to the hospital. I feel okay."

"If you don't mind—may I just look at your tongue?"

She didn't have a tongue depressor. But she reached into her knapsack, felt around, and found a small case. From it she removed a penlight. She switched it on and asked him to say "ah."

"Ahhh."

"Well, your tonsils are a little reddened. It looks like you have a cold," she said. "Could I—I'm sorry—could I just look at your eyes?" He was reluctant. He seemed very nervous now.

She went around the room, closing the venetian blinds. Then she did what was called a swinging flashlight test. She pointed the beam of light first into one pupil and then into the other. The color of the irises seemed completely normal. He had deep brown eyes. She watched the responses of his pupils to the beam of light. She thought she saw a delayed response. That *might* be a subtle indication of brain damage.

This is ridiculous. I'm overreacting, she told herself. There's no clear evidence that Kate had an infective disease. There's been no human-to-human transmission.

She said, "If your cold changes in any way, would you please call me?" And she gave him her cellular-phone number and the number at Kips Bay. "Call me anytime, day or night. I'm a doctor. I expect calls."

On her way back to the subway station, she wondered if she had done the right thing. As a lieutenant commander in the United States Public Health Service, Alice Austen had the legal power to order a person into quarantine. Even so, officers with the

C.D.C. virtually never invoke this power. It is C.D.C. policy for field medical officers to work quietly, to avoid drawing attention to themselves, and to refrain from doing anything that might create a climate of fear in the public. She glanced at Socrates. He had no advice to give, except that she know herself.

Unknown

Back at Kips Bay that night, Alice Austen felt exhausted, and also ravenously hungry. You forget to eat during investigations. She found a Thai take-out restaurant and brought back boxes of food to her room. Mrs. Heilig gave her a disapproving look as she carried them into her bedroom. She sat at a desk and ate noodles and lemongrass chicken with her Boy Scout knife, fork, and spoon set. Meanwhile, she telephoned Walter Mellis at home on her cellular phone. She did not want Mrs. Heilig to overhear the conversation, and she had a feeling that Mrs. Heilig would try to listen if she could.

"So what's up?" Mellis said.

"Walt—this thing has me scared. It could be an unknown infective agent that destroys the brain. It would be a virus, not a bacterial infection. I think—" She stopped. She put her hand to her forehead. It was covered with sweat.

He was silent on the other end of the line.

"I think we may have done a hot autopsy this morning. Without strong biosafety containment."

There was a pause. "Good Lord!" he said. He hadn't really expected anything like this.

"I'm going on observation, Walt." She explained her findings, the rings in the eyes, the swollen, glassy brain covered with red spots, the blood blisters in the mouth and nasopharynx. She mentioned the unidentified lumps of material that seemed visible in the brain cells of the index case, Harmonica Man. "If it's an infectious agent, it's really bad," she said.

"No lab results from the second case, the girl?" he asked.

"It'll be another day."

"What lab is doing the work?" he asked.

"I wanted to talk with you about that. The city health department's lab is testing for bacteria. But it can't test for viruses—they just can't do that."

"Look, if you think this is serious, then we need to get samples here to C.D.C. so we can start doing some testing."

"That's what I wanted to arrange with you."

"I'll take care of it through Lex. How soon can you return?" he asked.

"I don't know. I still have some street work to do."

"What kind of street work?"

"You were the one who preached John Snow at me." There was a pause while she ate Thai noodles.

"All right," he said.

She took a long shower, collapsed into the carved bed, and pulled the blankets up to her chin. When she was a girl, around ten years old, and the family was vacationing in a little resort motel on the seashore of New Hampshire, she had sometimes had trouble falling asleep. Her parents had put her on a folding steel cot in a room with her younger brother. She had loved to curl up with a Nancy Drew mystery book, her head nestled in the pillow, which smelled faintly of mildew and the sea. She had read all of the

Nancy Drew mysteries as a girl. This made her think about her father, living alone now in Ashland, near the lake. I've got to call Dad, she thought.

She could hear Mrs. Heilig padding around the kitchen, and then a television went on. For a long time, she could not fall asleep. Her window looked out on First Avenue. Late into the night, sounds of traffic came through the glass, trucks rumbling, taxis honking, the occasional ambulance heading for one of the emergency rooms. The normal sounds of the city. She thought: this can't be as bad as it seems. I haven't shown any connection between these two cases. The Moran girl's death may not have anything to do with Harmonica Man. The traffic moved on the avenue like blood swishing through an artery.

The Ladies' Room

AL GHAR, IRAQ, THURSDAY

Mark Littleberry was standing over Hopkins in the cloud of dust left by the truck containing the portable lab. He was holding a plastic sample tube. Without a word to Hopkins, he grabbed the swab out of his hand and jammed it into the tube. "Truck sample number one!" Littleberry put the tube in his shirt pocket.

Hopkins stood up, brushing dust off.

"Did you get a look, Will?"

"Yeah. What was it?"

"It was—"

The minders arrived and crowded around. They seemed almost hysterical.

"What was in that truck?" Littleberry demanded.

"I shall inquire," Dr. Fehdak said.

Littleberry let loose a stream of unprintable language.

The Kid's face darkened. He spoke in Arabic.

This was nothing, Dr. Mariana Vestof said. It was a routine delivery of a vaccine.

"I shall try to get information on this," Dr. Fehdak said.

"Why did one of the men in the trucks speak Russian to me?" Hopkins asked.

"You must be mistaken," Dr. Fehdak said.

Hopkins and Littleberry looked at each other.

"The inspectors need a rest room!" Littleberry suddenly shouted. "According to the terms of Security Council agreements, inspectors are to be accorded private use of rest rooms whenever they ask for them."

Hopkins and Littleberry were led back into the building. When they arrived at the door of the rest room, they noticed that some of the minders were snickering. Others were jabbering on their radios.

"I think it's a ladies' room," Littleberry said to Hopkins. "Just go in." They closed the door after themselves and locked it.

□

Dr. Azri Fehdak was in a state of shock. He was seeing his life pass before his eyes. Hopkins had noticed one of the foreign advisers. And Fehdak wasn't certain, but he thought he had seen Hopkins holding a swab inside the truck. He wondered if Hopkins had taken a photograph. It would be virtually impossible for these two inspectors to convince the United Nations that they had seen anything of a military nature. But the swab . . . if anything was proven, Dr. Fehdak was likely to be shot by his own government, for having allowed U.N. inspectors to take a swab inside that place.

Dr. Mariana Vestof looked grim. "That rest room is for the female technical staff," she said. "It is not for those men."

"Perhaps they are nervous," Dr. Fehdak said.

One of the minders, an intelligence official named Hussein Al-Sawiri, pounded on the door. "Everybody healthy?" he asked.

No answer.

The Kid rattled the door. "It's locked," he said. "They locked it."

□

The ladies' room was gleaming and antiseptic, set with green and white tiles.

"This whole situation is gonna blow sky high," Littleberry said. "I did not expect to find a *truck*. We have to do this fast."

Hopkins stripped off his rubber gloves and put on a clean pair. Then he placed the Halliburton case on a sink. He crouched down until he was staring at the Halliburton, looking at a small optical lens near the handle. He brought his right eye close to the lens. The system recognized the pattern of blood vessels in his retina as that of "Hopkins, William, Jr., Reachdeep." Any attempt to open the case without the eye-key would cause the self-destruct process to initiate.

The locks inside the case slid open, and he lifted the lid. Meanwhile, Littleberry placed his Halliburton case on a sink, and it popped open.

The two Halliburtons contained biosensors. They were used by the United States Navy for sensing and analyzing biological weapons. A normal laboratory that does this occupies several rooms full of machines.

"I'm gonna do a hand-held Boink, real quick," Littleberry said. From the suitcase, he lifted out an electronic device about the size of a paperback book. It was a palm-sized biosensor. People called it a Boink because it let off a pleasant chiming sound if it detected a biological weapon. The Boink had a screen and some buttons and a sample port—a little hole. The Boink could test for the presence of twenty-five different known biological weapons.

Littleberry took the small tube that contained the truck sample from his pocket. He took out a disposable plastic pipette. It was a little droplet-sucker. He sucked up a droplet of the sample liquid and dropped it straight into the sample port in the Boink.

Then he waited a moment. He stared at the readout screen. He was hoping to hear a chiming tone. There was silence.

"Damn!" he said.

"What, Mark?"

He was staring at the readout screen. "No reading. It didn't boink. I've got a blank screen here."

"All right, Commander. Should I run Felix?"

"Yeah. Quick."

There was pounding on the door. "Is somebody ill in there?" It was Hussein Al-Sawiri, the security man.

"It's just taking a little time," Hopkins replied. He took the truck sample tube over to *his* Halliburton case, which held a device called Felix, a black box the size of a big-city telephone book. It was a biosensor device known as a gene scanner. It was controlled by a laptop computer, and it could read the genetic code of an organism very fast.

Hopkins lifted the laptop from the Halliburton and placed it on a window ledge. Working very, very quickly, his hands moving fast, he ran a data cable back to the Felix black box and started the computer. The computer's screen turned on and glowed. It said:

Felix Gene Scanner
Beta 0.9

Lawrence Livermore National Laboratory

Enter Password:
●●●●●●●●●

Hopkins hammered in his password. "Come on, come on," he said.

Using a pipette, Hopkins dropped a bit of liquid from the sample tube into the sample port in the Felix black box. He tapped the keys of the laptop computer.

"P.C.R. amplification has started, let's hope," he said to Littleberry.

He stared at the screen.

More pounding on the door.

"Not finished!" Littleberry shouted.

"Amplification of the DNA is completed," Hopkins whispered. "The DNA's moving onto the chip."

The door began to shake. "Open up!" Hussein Al-Sawiri shouted.

"This is a United Nations toilet facility," Littleberry yelled over his shoulder.

Hopkins gestured wildly to Littleberry. "We've gotta start beaming," he hissed.

From his suitcase Littleberry removed a black panel about the size of a notebook. It was attached to a cable. It was a special satellite transmitting antenna. He plugged it into the laptop computer while Hopkins tapped the keys.

"We're getting sequences!" Hopkins said.

Running cascades of letters appeared on Felix's screen, combinations of A, T, C, and G. The combinations were sequences of raw genetic code from a life-form in the sample.

"Beaming it up, Scotty!" Hopkins said.

Felix was beaming chunks of DNA code into the sky through the transmitter panel. Overhead, a communications satellite operated by the U.S. National Security Agency was picking up the genetic code of the organism, whatever it was.

"I think we're going to get some matches here," Hopkins said. "Hang on."

Felix was matching the DNA sequences with some sequences stored in its memory, trying to identify the organism. The names of viruses that it was supposedly "seeing" in the truck sample began to appear on the screen of the laptop.

TENTATIVE SEQUENCE MATCHES:

Goldfish virus group
Porcine reproductive virus
Hepatitis D woodchuck
Bracovirus
Spumavirus
Microvirus
Unclassified Thogoto-like agent
viruslike particle Cak-1
Humpty Doo virus

"Humpty Doo virus? What is this?" Hopkins whispered.

Then the screen said:

Felix is unable to process this sample.

The screen went blank. The system had crashed. "You jerk!" he said to Felix.

"What happened?" Littleberry whispered.

"I think it's giving me gobbledygook."

The pounding on the door became very insistent.

Will Hopkins reached down to his belt and pulled the Leatherman tool out of its case. He opened it to alligator pliers and a screwdriver. From his pocket protector he pulled out a Mini Maglite flashlight. He hunched over Felix and lifted off the smooth black top of the box. Inside was a mass of tiny threadlike tubes and wires. He started pulling out wires, shining the flashlight in, twirling the screwdiver.

"Will—" Littleberry said.

"The system isn't going to work perfectly every time."

"Put that suitcase together, Will. We've got to call on the radio for help."

Hopkins held up a metal object the size of a peanut. "That's a pump. I think it's malfunctioning."

"Enough. Shut the case."

"Mark—That was a bioreactor in the truck. And there were some crystals. That's what I took the swab from."

"Yeah? What do you mean, crystals?"

"Well, they were kind of flat, sitting in trays, clear . . ."

"Shit. That sounds like some kind of viral glass. Those bastards are making viral glass."

"Inside a truck?"

"That's the whole problem."

"Where was it going?"

"Who knows? The U.N. will never see it again."

□

Hussein Al-Sawiri had been talking on a shortwave radio to the Iraqi National Monitoring Center in Baghdad. "There has been a decision. If they want to lock themselves in a toilet, they can stay there." Several minders reached under their jackets and drew guns.

Outside the Al Ghar facility, the UNSCOM convoy had arrived. The vehicles were lined up on the access road to the plant. In the lead vehicle, Dr. Pascal Arriet, the chief inspector, was talking on two radios at the same time. The Iraqi guards had closed the gate. They were pointing their guns at the UNSCOM convoy.

"These people! They have not acted under my instructions. They have disobeyed my direct orders!" Arriet said to the radio.

It turned into a standoff. The Iraqi security people wanted to break down the door and place the two United Nations inspectors under arrest. What held them back was the Iraqi government's desire not to annoy the United Nations any more than it already was annoyed at Iraq, even though everyone agreed that the two inspectors had acted in a manner that was not acceptable by international standards of behavior. The day dragged on into evening, and the evening dragged on into night. The UNSCOM convoy of vehicles remained sitting on the road outside the plant. The inspectors carried food and water with them in their vehicles, but they were angry and exhausted, and wanted, above all, to go home. The rules did not allow them to leave without Hopkins and Littleberry, and the Iraqis were determined not to

let the inspectors go. They announced that all samples and all equipment belonging to the inspectors
must be forfeited to Iraq.

□

"Quit fooling with your machine," Littleberry said to
Hopkins. "You need to get some sleep." Littleberry
was lying on the floor with his head on his Halliburton briefcase for a pillow, and every muscle in his
back ached. Hopkins sat cross-legged with his back
against the wall. Felix was spread out in pieces
across the floor in front of him. He held the flashlight
in his teeth. "I'm convinced the problem is in this
pump," Hopkins said.

"Christ," Littleberry said. He could not fall
asleep. Late into the night, as the shortwave radio
squawked and chattered, and Iraqi security agents
continued to pound on the door of the bathroom at
odd intervals, he stared at the ceiling and thought of
his wife and the boat he had just bought in Florida.
"This is the last time I am ever going to stick my
head in a weapons plant," he muttered.

A few hours later, early on Friday morning, Littleberry was talking on the shortwave radio, which
hadn't worked very well ever since Hopkins had removed a part from it. "We've got a deal shaping,
Will." The terms had been worked out by teams of
negotiators. The two American inspectors would be
allowed to leave Iraq, but the United Nations would
disown them. They would be stripped of their U.N.
status. Pascal Arriet was pleased to do this. They
would have to surrender all their biological samples
and equipment—namely the suitcases—to Iraq. And
all transactions would be videotaped.

Littleberry and Hopkins agreed to the conditions of the deal, and by sunrise two helicopters had been dispatched from Kuwait City to pick them up. The disgraced inspectors emerged from the bathroom and were marched at gunpoint outdoors, in front of the plant. They stood within view of the U.N. convoy but were held inside the security fence. There, while they were videotaped by both the United Nations people and by Iraqi minders, they handed over both Halliburton cases and all their swabs and samples.

There was a shuddering sound in the sky. Two aging white helicopters appeared, coming from the south. They were Hueys, bearing U.N. markings. They touched down beside the UNSCOM vehicles. Dust filled the air.

"We made a mistake. We are very sorry," Littleberry said to Hussein Al-Sawiri.

The Kid was holding one of the sample tubes. "Is this a sample from the truck?" he asked.

"Yes. The only one."

Fehdak's face showed no expression, but in his mind he was heaving a terrible sigh of relief. This may save my life, he thought.

The guards patted down Littleberry and Hopkins exceedingly thoroughly and in a very personal way. Eventually they were satisfied that the two U.N. inspectors no longer possessed any sample material. No swabs, no tubes, no evidence. The guards opened the gate. Littleberry and Hopkins walked through.

Pascal Arriet leaped out of his car. He was shaking with rage. "Idiots! You are finished! You are fired by authority of the secretary general."

"I'm sorry, Pascal," Littleberry said. "We failed. We found nothing."

"You Americans are demented!" Arriet said. "You threaten Iraq *continualment.* You are ruining everything. Get out of here. Leave now!"

"We apologize," Hopkins said. "We are very sorry." He and Littleberry climbed into one of the waiting helicopters.

Then they were in the air, leaving Al Ghar straight below.

"Wow," Littleberry said, and leaned back.

Some of the Iraqi guards were pointing their guns at the helicopter, but nothing happened. Hopkins and Littleberry looked down on a long line of white cars in front of the plant, a gray roof studded with vent stacks, a wide brown land, stretches of green irrigated fields, and in the distance the brown arc of the Euphrates River.

"Florida, here I come," Littleberry muttered.

Sitting in the Huey beside them was a man in khaki civilian clothing wearing a voice headset. He shook Hopkins's hand. "Major David Saintsbury, United States Army. I'm from USAMRIID. Fort Detrick, Maryland." He turned to Littleberry. "Well, Mark," he shouted. "What happened?"

"We came so *damned* close," Littleberry said on his headset.

"We got a very hot virus sample, we think," Hopkins said. "We started decoding the DNA and beaming it up on the bird, but the Felix crashed on us."

"Too bad," Major Saintsbury said. "Of course, you had Navy gear. What can I say?"

The helicopter was shaking, the blades giving off the classic Huey *thup, thup.*

"But we got some partial DNA sequences," Hopkins said. "Man, these Iraqi biologists are doing scary things."

"They're not the only biologists doing scary things," Major Saintsbury said.

□

On the ground at Al Ghar, Hussein Al-Sawiri and Dr. Azri Fehdak were holding the Halliburton suitcases, carrying them into the building. They were taking them to a secure place, where they could be retrieved by Iraqi intelligence. Fehdak was carrying Felix. Something was wrong. He placed the palm of his hand on the case. "Ah!" he said, jerking his hand away. He put the case on the floor. "It's hot."

"Ay!" Al-Sawiri dropped his case to the floor.

Smoke began to boil out of both cases.

As they watched, the cases melted, and catalytic heaters destroyed them. The two Iraqis could feel the warmth on their faces.

Invisible History (II.)

During the 1991 Gulf War, Iraq is said to have come close to using anthrax on its enemies, the allied coalition forces. Anthrax is a bacterium, a single-celled organism that feeds on meat. Anthrax grows explosively in warm meat broth or in living meat. Modern armies consist largely of steel and meat.

Weaponized anthrax is made of anthrax spores. The spores are dried into a powder or made into a brown liquid concentrate. No one to this day (except the Iraqi government) knows what particular weapons-production strain of anthrax Iraq possessed at the time of the Gulf War. It is believed to have been the Vollum strain. The Vollum strain of anthrax was first isolated from a cow near Oxford, England, before the Second World War. Vollum anthrax is the strain that the U.S. Army used for its anthrax warheads during the 1960s, before the United States ended its offensive biological-weapons program in 1969.

Iraq signed the 1972 Biological Weapons Convention, but in conversations with U.N. weapons inspectors after the Gulf War, top Iraqi government officials said that they did not actually know if their country had signed the treaty. They said that it wasn't important, not a matter for consideration.

If Iraq had done a laydown of Vollum anthrax during the Gulf War, allied casualties might have been the largest in the shortest period of time sustained by any army in history. On the other hand, it might not have been too bad. No one knows what the Iraqi anthrax would have done. Some of the American troops were vaccinated against anthrax, with a vaccine that might or might not have worked. Most of the soldiers were taking antibiotics as a protective measure—antibiotics that might or might not have worked. Many were also equipped with breathing masks, which offer protection against biological agents—provided one knows that the agent is in the air. Vollum anthrax is susceptible to vaccines and antibiotics. Other strains of anthrax are hotter. An engineered strain of anthrax could be designed to elude vaccines and grow explosively even in the presence of antibiotics.

Weaponized anthrax spores end up sitting on the largest wet membrane in the body, the lungs. The spores land on the lung surface and hatch, and the organism quickly enters the bloodstream. Humans infected with weaponized anthrax may cough up a thick yellow-and-red bubbly mess called anthrax sputum exudate. There is debate about what anthrax sputum exudate looks like if it's caused by a weaponized form of anthrax. Experts stress that a disease caused by a biological weapon may look very different from a natural disease caused by the same organism. In animals, anthrax sputum exudate is bloody and watery, rather golden yellow in color. It pours out of the animal's mouth and nose. Many experts say that anthrax exudate in humans forms a thick, gobby, foamy, bloody paste that sticks inside the lungs like glue. Anthrax sputum is streaked and marbled with bright red blood, which is hemorrhage from the lungs. Someone hit with weaponized anthrax probably would feel a cold coming on at first. You get a sniffle and a cough. Your cough becomes worse. Then there follows a kind of pause, a lessening of the symptoms. This is the anthrax eclipse, a phase in which the symptoms seem to lift for a while. Then abruptly the victim crashes and dies with fatal pneumonia and a bloody sputum exudate.

The experts call anthrax a "classical" weapon. Anthrax is powerful, but it is far less efficient than many bioweapons. It seems to take about ten thousand spores of anthrax trapped in the lungs to make a person die. That is a large number of spores. With other military biological agents, a single spore or as few as three virus particles trapped in the lungs can cause a fatal biological crash in the victim.

In 1979, in the city of Yekaterinburg, Russia (then called Sverdlovsk), there was an accident at a Soviet biological-weapons-production facility known as Military Compound Number 19. The Soviets were making weaponized anthrax there by the ton. It was a full-speed military production, for the purpose of filling warheads and bombs, with shifts working around the clock. No one knows exactly what happened, but one credible story goes that the workers were drying anthrax and making it into a powder in grinding machines. A shift of day workers on the grinding machines discovered that the safety air filters (which prevented anthrax powder from going into the air) had become clogged. They removed the filters at the end of the shift and left a note for the night shift, telling the workers to install fresh filters. The night-shift workers came on duty but didn't see the note. They ran the anthrax grinding machines all night without safety filters. During the night shift, up to a kilogram (2.2 pounds) of weapons-grade dry anthrax spores were released into the air in the city of Sverdlovsk. They formed a plume that went in a southeasterly direction across the city. Sixty-six people crashed and died of anthrax. Many of them did not break with anthrax until weeks after the accident. The zone of human fatalities extended for about four miles downwind. Most of the dead civilians worked or lived within half a mile of the plant.

This suggests that anthrax is not very efficient as a bioweapon, since it took a relatively large amount of dry spores to kill a relatively small number of people. A kilogram of a more advanced biological weapon released into the air should be able to make a plume as long as fifty miles. If the plume cuts through a city, the deaths should number in the thousands or millions. A far larger number of deaths will occur if the weapon is transmissible—that is, if it's contagious and able to jump from one person to another in a chain of infection. Anthrax is not a transmissible weapon. You are not likely to catch anthrax by being in contact with an anthrax victim. Anthrax does not spread from person to person by a chain of infection. Other weapons—contagious weapons— are therefore more powerful, though they can go out of control. In the age of molecular biology, anthrax looks like a black-powder cannon.

After Iraq's defeat by the coalition forces in the Gulf War, inspection teams from the United Nation Special Commission—UNSCOM—spread out over Iraq. They found and destroyed most of Iraq's nuclear-bomb program and some of Iraq's chemical weaponry. Iraq's biological-weapons program vanished into thin air.

Iraqi officials always referred to their bioweapons program as the "former" program. Yet it became clear, after a while, that Iraq had an ongoing biological-weapons program. The program was moving forward under the noses of the U.N. inspectors. For example, the teams inspected a biological-production plant called Al Hakam, a factory situated in a desert area near the Euphrates River. Iraqi scientists told the U.N. that this plant was making "natural" pesticides to kill insects. The UNSCOM experts looked at the plant and believed the Iraqis. After inspecting the equipment carefully, they saw no reason to ask Iraq to stop production at the plant.

An older American weapons inspector, a man well beyond the age of retirement who in his day had been a leading scientist in the United States Army's biological-weapons (B.W.) program, visited Al Hakam as a member of an UNSCOM team. He was mighty impressed. He said, "They've got a helluva good B.W. plant here at Al Hakam. How can I prove it? I've just got a feeling, that's all." He could not prove it, and he was frankly doubted by most U.N. experts, although he was one of the very few people in the entire UNSCOM organization who actually had hands-on professional experience as a biological weaponer. Iraq, meanwhile, was making hundreds of thousands of gallons of brown liquid concentrate in this plant.

□

In 1995, one of the heads of Iraq's biological-weapons program, Babrak Kamal, suddenly defected and ended up in Jordan. Various intelligence agencies rushed to debrief Kamal, and Kamal talked. Fearing that he was telling everything about their bioweapons program, and in an effort to placate the United Nations Security Council, Iraqi officials suddenly disclosed that Al Hakam was, in fact, an anthrax weapons plant. The brown liquid was anthrax. UNSCOM inspectors had been wrong about Al Hakam. The old Army scientist had been right. In June 1996, after a year of bureaucratic hesitation—during part of which time Iraq was allowed to continue operating the plant—the United Nations finally blew up Al Hakam with dynamite. Al Hakam is now eleven square miles of level ground. The many tons of anthrax that the plant produced have never been found. Unlike many bioweapons, anthrax can be stored indefinitely.

There was another revelation, this one more unpleasant. In the wave of panic following Kamal's defection, Iraq also suddenly confessed that a French-built animal-vaccine plant called Al Manal had been turned into a weapons facility dedicated to toxins and virus weapons. Al Manal is a modern Level 3 biocontainment virology complex situated in the southern outskirts of Bagdhad. The Iraqis said that this plant had been used for an early-phase genetic engineering program in virus-weapons research, and then, during the Gulf War, had been used to make large quantities of botulinum toxin—botulism, or bot tox, as military people call it. Bot tox is one of the most powerful toxins known. An amount of bot tox the size of the dot over this *i* would be enough to easily kill ten people. Bot tox is a nerve agent. It is one hundred thousand times more toxic than Sarin, the nerve gas that the Aum Shinrikyo sect released in the Tokyo subway. Iraq confessed to having made approximately *nine thousand cubic yards* of weapons-grade bot tox at the French-built plant at Al Manal. The bot tox had been concentrated twenty times over. In theory it was more than enough bioweapon to kill every person on earth a thousand times over. In a practical military sense it was enough to eliminate all human life from Kuwait.

The bioproduction lines at Al Manal had been built in 1980 by a French vaccine company called Institut Mérieux, which is headquartered in Lyons. Mérieux is owned by the pharmaceutical giant Rhone-Poulenc. Mérieux was paid a great deal of money by the Iraqi government to build production lines at Al Manal that were ready for operation, and to train the staff in the use of the equipment. The purpose of the plant was to make vaccines for protecting animals from foot-and-mouth disease, which is caused by a virus. The plant was wildly expensive. Some experts claim that an effective animal-vaccine plant could have been built at a tenth of the cost. However, Iraq had plenty of money to spend. The Iraqis needed a Volkswagen. Mérieux sold them a tank.

At the time that Mérieux was involved in Al Manal, Iraq was involved in a bitter war with Iran. This was the Iran-Iraq War (1980–88), during which, in 1984, Iraq initiated the use of chemical weapons. In 1985, while Iraq was known to be using chemical weapons, French advisers from Mérieux were working at Al Manal, training the Iraqi staff in how to make virus vaccines. To make a virus vaccine, you use bioreactors to grow strains of viruses. You can use the same equipment and manufacturing processes to make hot weaponized viruses. If the plant is equipped with high Level 3 biocontainment, virus weapons can be produced without too much difficulty or danger to the staff.

United Nations inspectors discovered that the buildings at Al Manal are made of bomb-resistant concrete, strengthened with large amounts of steel bar. The hardening goes deep inside the buildings. Al Manal has a kind of double-shell construction in which some of the inner biocontainment zones are themselves reinforced with steel. Did Mérieux engineers notice that they were building the production lines in a "hardened" facility? Did they speculate that Iraq might view the place as a potential military facility? Much of the production equipment at Al Manal came from European biotechnology and pharmaceutical companies: from France, Spain, Germany, and Switzerland. What did these companies know or guess? The chance that the public will ever find out is essentially zero.

Until 1990, five years after the French advisers left, Al Manal was apparently used for making animal vaccines, and it had a staff of civilian scientists. In the fall of 1990, however, when the Gulf War was imminent, a military staff suddenly took over the operation of Al Manal. The plant was then almost instantly converted to a bioweapons facility. All of the plant's production equipment was used for making bot tox, and the Iraqis ran double production lines. In a short time the plant was pumping out bot tox. Iraqi production scientists had no problems making the toxin. They knew exactly how to do it. They had obtained their strain of botulism through the mail from the United States. They had ordered it from the American Type Culture Collection, a nonprofit organization in Rockville, Maryland, that supplies microorganisms to industry and science. The seed strain cost Iraq thirty-five dollars.

One UNSCOM inspector who is an attentive observer of French behavior in Iraq sums up his view of Institut Mérieux's motives this way: "The reality is that people just don't realize what can be done [with bioproduction equipment]. To Mérieux at the time, their involvement with Al Manal was a successful commercial venture. Hey, if they can sell an extra ten fermenter tanks, open another bottle of Champagne! It's the act of commerce that's important, and what happens afterward is someone else's responsibility."

Al Manal has become the responsibility of the United Nations. As of this writing, the plant is standing, but much of its equipment has been destroyed. The buildings and infrastructure, including the bomb-hardened Level 3 biocontainment zones, have not been destroyed by the U.N. Al Manal is in excellent condition. The decision-making process in the United Nations is so flawed that an admitted virus and toxin weapons biocontainment facility can't be dismantled.

Inspectors have noticed that the Iraqis seem to be switching to small, portable bioreactors that roll around on wheels. The Al Manal bioweapons plant could go hot in a matter of days. All it needs is some more equipment. In the meantime, not a single drop of the nine thousand cubic yards of bot tox made at Al Manal has been found.

In fact, it is said that no Western intelligence agency has ever recovered a sample of a weapons-production strain of any Iraqi biological weapon. The U.N. inspectors have found empty biological bomb casings in Iraq, and they have obtained video footage taken by Iraqi scientists of bioweapons tests conducted in desert areas—biological bombs going off, hot agents being sprayed into the air, a jet doing a line laydown. It is clear from the footage and the bomb designs that the Iraqis know what they are doing. It is just that the U.N. people haven't found the heart of any Iraqi bioweapons system, the life form itself.

In the years following the Gulf War, the biological-weapons inspection process in Iraq continued to go forward, but it left important questions unanswered. The U.N. teams continued to monitor and search Iraq, but some of the individual team members began describing their efforts as a charade, or as just another job, for which at least they were getting some hazard pay. Other individuals on the teams were known to have taken personal risks to uncover information. There were indications that the Iraqi bioweapons program was very much alive, and was focusing more and more on viruses, on genetic engineering, and on miniaturization of the research and production processes—using tiny bioreactors that can be hidden in small rooms.

The French UNSCOM inspectors and officials always seemed to be at the center of conflicts with other UNSCOM teams. It was quite clear that the

French were no longer interested in discovering any more biological-weapons installations in Iraq. Some of the other inspectors would say, privately, that the senior French UNSCOM inspectors appeared to be acting on direct orders from their government to stop finding things in Iraq. The French government seemed confused. Most of the French political leaders were middle-aged men, relatively uneducated in advanced biology, and unable to grasp the seriousness of biological weaponry. French leaders seemed unable to conceive of the idea that the proliferation of biological weapons in the Middle East might be a direct threat to the safety of the French people. This was a situation that, to be sure, the French people knew nothing about. When a bomb goes off in a trash can in Paris and kills a dozen people, it is a problem. If the bomb were to contain a military virus, the problem might be uncontrollable.

But commercial interests are important in France, as they are everywhere. Not so long ago, Iraq had been a customer and friend of France. Iraq might be a customer and friend again. It is important to have good relations with one's customers and friends. Money makes friends. Money makes the world go around.

A Cast of the Net

Alice Austen had a freshly printed list of the hospitals in the New York City area, with telephone numbers, on her desk. She began calling the hospitals, one by one. She would get an E.R. house-staff doctor and ask him or her a few simple questions. The conversation didn't take long. "Have you had any emergency cases recently where the patient was in violent terminal seizure?" she would ask. "We're looking for previously healthy people who suddenly develop seizures that may end in death. These patients may have discoloration of the iris of the eye. There may be a very strong muscular rigidity. The spine bends backward in the shape of a C."

The reactions she got from the doctors were all over the map. One doctor thought she must be a paranoid schizophrenic. He refused to talk to her unless she could prove that she was really a C.D.C. doctor. Another doctor, a woman, told her that she had been seeing a lot of strep A flesh-eating bacteria—"cases of people's faces melting off, and arms and legs. These are mostly homeless people. Who knows where they're getting their infections."

"Are you seeing seizures with any of these patients?"

"No. Not like you're describing."

After hours of this, she had come up with nothing. It was looking like a dead end.

Then she had a breakthrough. The third case.

She called the St. George Hospital on Staten Island. It was a small hospital in an outlying borough of New York City. She reached an emergency-room physician named Tom d'Angelo.

"Yes," he said. "I think I've seen this."

"Can you describe it?"

"It was a woman named—what was her name?—let me get the patient records, hold on."

"Okay," d'Angelo continued, with a sound of papers being shuffled. "Her name was Penelope Zecker. She died here in the E.R. on Tuesday."

"Who was the attending?" Austen asked.

"I was. I signed the death certificate. Apparently she had been having dizzy spells. She had a history of hypertension. She was on blood-pressure meds. Age fifty-three. Smoker. Someone called 911—it was her mother. Penny was living with her mother. She was having a seizure. The E.M.T. got her here. She had a cardiopulmonary arrest and we couldn't resuscitate. With her history of hypertension, we figured she must be having an intracranial bleed or an infarct. I think it was a brain bleed. Her pupils were blown—dilated and fixed. She was cooked."

"Did you do a brain scan?"

"No. We couldn't get her stabilized. She had this dramatic agonal seizure. Her spine bent all the way back and froze. It was really impressive. It scared the nurses. It scared *me*. I've never seen anything quite like it. Her faced twisted up, it changed shape, really. She rolled off the gurney and landed on the floor. Her legs straightened out. Her head went way back. There was incredible muscular tension in the spine. She starting biting the air. The nurses were afraid of being bitten, actually. She bit down on her tongue and almost severed it. Also, it appeared that she had bitten off several of the fingers of her right hand."

"My God. When did she do that?"

"Before she was admitted. The elderly mother was—well—incoherent. A patient biting off her own fingers. I've never seen that before."

"Was there an autopsy?"

"No."

"Why not, in a case like that?"

He paused. "This is a for-profit hospital," he said.

"What do you mean?" she said.

"An *autopsy*? At a for-profit hospital? Who's going to pay for it? The H.M.O.s sure as hell won't pay for an autopsy. We try to avoid autopsies."

"You try to avoid knowing what happened to a patient, Dr. d'Angelo?"

"I'm not going to argue that, Dr. Austen. We didn't do an autopsy, okay?"

"I wish I could have looked at her brain tissue. Do you have samples?"

"Bloods and spinal and some lab tests. We don't have tissue samples because we didn't do an autopsy, as I told you."

"Can you get me the results by tomorrow?"

"Absolutely. I'm glad to help."

"What did you put on the death certificate?"

"Cerebral vascular accident. Brain stroke." There was a pause. "You think this is something infectious?"

"I'm not sure what it is. What's the mother's address and phone number?"

Cells

With a pencil, Austen marked another X on her map, this one at the St. George Hospital on Staten Island. Now there were three points of death:

1. Times Square. April 16. Harmonica Man. The index case.
2. St. George Hospital, Staten Island. April 21. Penelope Zecker.
3. East Seventy-ninth Street. April 22. Kate Moran.

There was still no obvious connection among them. What had they come into contact with? How were these people connected in a biological sense? The term *stealth virus* came into her mind, but she pushed it out.

She called Walter Mellis. "Walt, I've found a third possible case." She described it to him. "But I think I'm missing something important. There's a pattern that I'm not seeing."

"What do your instincts say?"

"It's something I've *seen,* Walt. It's a visual clue. It's staring me in the face and I don't see it."

□

By now, the samples of Kate Moran's tissue would have been processed and prepared for viewing in a microscope. Austen went to the O.C.M.E. histology lab and collected a set of glass slides. There was no microscope in her office, so she took the slides to Glenn Dudley's office.

"So how are things going, Dr. Austen? Have you solved the mystery yet?" He was dressed in a scrub suit, sitting at a word processor. He had just finished his day's autopsies, and he was writing up his reports. She noticed that he looked tired. His usually perfect hair was mussed, his face was sallow.

She described the Zecker case.

"Interesting," he said. "I've got some lab results for the Moran girl." He pulled out a report. "She had high uric acid in the bloodstream." He gave the readings. "She had a mildly elevated white-blood-cell count in the spinal fluid."

"Any toxins?" she asked.

"If we'd found any toxins in her blood I would have *told* you," he said. He turned away and blew his nose on a laboratory Kimwipe and hurled it into the wastebasket with a gesture of annoyance. Then they sat down, facing each other across the doubleheaded microscope. Dudley chose the slides to look at. First they looked at slices of the girl's liver and lung. Everything seemed normal. Then they looked at slides of vaginal tissue. Austen found an area of what looked to be a blister, and she examined the cells there. Some of them appeared to have angular shadows or crystalline objects in their centers, but she wasn't sure.

Austen wanted to look at brain cells. "Yeah, well, the brain was a bitch to prepare after you chopped it up, Doctor," Dudley said.

Even so, they searched through fields of Kate Moran's brain cells. Once again, some of the cells— in the nuclei—contained the lumpy shapes.

"Let's look at some kidney," Austen said. She was thinking about the golden streaks in Kate's kidneys.

Together they studied a slide showing tissue of the kidney. The damage was clearly caused by uric acid. Austen saw needlelike shapes.

"Yeah," Dudley said. "These are uric acid deposits. This kid had very high uric acid." The finding was consistent with the blood work. She had been undergoing some kind of kidney failure when she died.

"I'd like to get some of this tissue in an electron microscope," Austen said to him. "Get a better image of the objects in the cell nucleus." An electron microscope uses a beam of electrons to make highly magnified images of the interior structure of cells. It can make an image of virus particles.

"Why don't you just take some stuff back to Atlanta?" he said.

"I will. But I want to follow up on a couple of things here in the city."

Houston Street

By now, Austen was sure this was an outbreak. The shapes inside the cells were part of the disease. Mental alarms were going off. Back in her office, she stared at the map for a while, pondering what to do. She noticed that her hands were sweaty. The day had practically gone. She opened up the case files and pored over them, looking for details. She was sure there was a detail she'd missed. Harmonica Man was the index case. She had to look more closely at that, although the O.C.M.E. had not been able to establish where he even lived, much less his real name.

There was a knock on the door. It was Ben Kly. "How are you doing, Dr. Austen? I was just checking in on you. You don't look too good."

"I'm okay. How are you doing, Ben?"

"Do you think this thing is real?"

"I know it's real. Can you help me with something? Do you know your way around the city?"

"Pretty well. I used to drive a mortuary van."

"The first case was a homeless man, Ben. He was called Harmonica Man. They don't know where he lived, but he had a friend who was with him when he died, a man named Lem. The report says that Lem lives 'under East Houston Street.' Can you tell me what that means?"

"Sure. He lives under East Houston Street. Like it says." Kly smiled.

"Can you take me there?"

"Now?"

She nodded.

He shrugged. "I'll ask the chief."

"Please, don't, Ben. He may say no. If you would just take me there—"

"We're going to get a transit cop to go with us, okay?"

□

"I've been all over this city picking up bodies," Kly said. "A lot of homeless dead. They call the homeless people skells. The skells die in every crack."

He and Austen were sitting at a table in Katz's Delicatessen on East Houston Street, on the edge of the Lower East Side. They were eating hot knishes and hot pastrami sandwiches with mild pickles, and drinking coffee. There were two flashlights on the table.

Austen dug into her knish; a knish is a potato turnover. She burned her tongue on the potato. She had not eaten all day again, and she was practically fainting with hunger. The knish seemed to flow into her bones.

Katz's Delicatessen was founded in 1888, when the Lower East Side was a slum populated by Jewish immigrants from Eastern Europe. Katz's is still owned by the Katz family. It has brown varnished walls and Formica tables, and the place is awash in fluorescent light. It is mostly self-service, but there are some waiter tables along one wall. The walls are decorated with photographs of celebrities, such as the police commissioner and Soupy Sales. Always the celebrities are shaking hands with a Mr. Katz.

There is a photo of Harry Houdini shaking hands with a Mr. Katz—Houdini was a regular at Katz's.

You get a ticket when you go inside, and the men behind the counters hold out little nibs of hot pastrami for a taste before you order, so you can judge whether the pastrami is good that day. On the outside the pastrami is as black as tar and covered with grit. On the inside it is delicate, red, juicy, though sometimes a little fatty, but that is the way Katz's customers like it. Occasionally the guys behind the counters give you more than you have ordered, such as two beers instead of one, but they mark only one beer on the ticket, and they say to you in a low voice, "You wanted *one*? Speak up next time! Take it, will ya! Don't tell nobody." There are racks of dry salamis hanging behind an elderly man who will sell you fifty of them if you want, and there are paper signs dangling from the ceiling that say

Senda salami
To your boy in the Army.

It rhymes if you say it correctly.

They finished their coffee and carried their tickets over to the cashier, and they went out onto Houston Street and walked westward. Houston Street is a wide, treeless traffic artery. The afternoon was getting along, and traffic was heavy. On the way, Kly used Austen's cell phone to call the Transit Police. He led Austen into a subway-station entrance at the corner of Second Avenue, a stop for the F train. Once in the station, they waited, and eventually a transit officer showed up.

The station platform was a hundred and fifty yards long, and there were no more than three or four other people standing there. It was not a busy station.

Ben Kly looked up the ceiling. "We're following Houston Street," he remarked. "We're going east." At the end of the platform there was a metal curtain wall that went from floor to ceiling. There was a strong smell of urine in the air. Kly said that they were facing the East River. "The tracks of the F line turn south from here," he explained. "We're not going that way. There's an abandoned tunnel that goes east." Kly turned to the transit officer. "How far's it go?"

The officer was a chunky man with a mustache, and he had a flashlight. "A ways," he said.

There was a small swinging gate at the end of the platform. They switched on their flashlights and went through the gate and down a set of steps to the tracks. Kly pointed his flashlight at a dark metal bar running parallel to the tracks. "That's the third rail, Dr. Austen. It's alive. Don't touch it."

The officer turned to her. "If a train comes, stand against the wall, okay? In these little spaces. They're safety niches. But I'll stop the train with my light."

They walked a distance along the tracks. On their left was a wall made of sheet metal. Kly swung his light over it. He found what he was looking for— a hole in the metal—and they bent over and went through. On the other side was a set of abandoned tracks heading east. The rails were rusty, and the crossties were covered with scattered newspapers and trash. They walked along the track bed, casting their lights around. A train rumbled below them, filling the tunnels with a roar.

"That's the uptown F train," Kly remarked over the sound. "It's going under us. We're on a bridge."

The tracks and the ground were covered with black dust.

"Don't kick up that stuff," Kly said.

"What is it?" Austen asked.

"It's steel dust. It comes off the rails. It builds up in these unused tunnels."

They played their flashlights around. There were steel columns everywhere, and a vaulted ceiling. There were empty, open doors leading to black spaces. Their feet moved through the black dust, which was very soft, almost silky underfoot. It hushed the sound of their feet. The walls were decorated with graffiti. On the floor were scattered heaps of cardboard, and coils of dried feces. They stepped over a ski jacket, torn, blackened, lying between the tracks, and a furry mat or rug. Austen shone her light on the rug. It was a crushed, mummified dog. There was a bad edge to the air that seemed to come from the dog. Austen heard a snapping sound. She glanced over and saw that the policeman had unsnapped the leather flap on his gun holster.

"Lem?" Kly shouted. "Hey, Lem!" His voice echoed down the tunnel.

No answer.

"Anybody home?" Kly called.

"Lem!" Austen called.

They moved slowly back and forth for a long while, shining their lights into grim-looking spaces.

At one of the openings in the wall both Austen and Kly noticed the sound of many buzzing flies. This surprised Austen. She didn't expect to find flies underground.

He was lying on an aluminum-and-plastic folding lawn chair. He could have been anywhere from thirty to sixty years old. He was a white man. His back was arched deeply, his body wrenched backward into the shape of a crescent moon. His abdomen had swollen to a tremendous size. It was distended, as if he were pregnant with something, and it had turned a molten shiny green in the lower quadrant over the intestinal area. Gases of decay had built up inside the body, swelling it. His mouth and beard were wet with green and black fluid. Cadaver liquids had poured from between his legs, staining his pants. Flies rose and skittered in the air. He seemed to have lost his eyes.

The cop pulled his hand-held radio and switched it to the breaker channel. He stepped backward, then he turned away and coughed. He put his hands on his knees. He coughed again. There were splashing sounds and more coughing in the darkness. "I hate these kind of ones," he said at last, wiping his mouth.

Drawing shallow breaths, Austen moved into the smell. She could feel it touching her skin—she could feel her skin receiving an oily coating from the gases, and a metallic taste appeared in her mouth. She was tasting the smell on her tongue.

She knelt down beside the decedent. She opened her knapsack and put on a protective button mask. She handed another mask to Kly. He did not seem to be particularly bothered by the smell. She put on latex rubber gloves. Very carefully she lifted up the man's right hand.

His fingers were intact, but the skin of the hand had sloughed off. It hung loosely about the fingers, a soft, semitransparent parchment. Delicately, she pulled open the fingers. His hand enclosed a collapsed eyeball.

"He enucleated himself, Ben. He pulled out his eyes."

□

After making a brief examination of the dead man, Austen stood up and looked around the tunnel, shining her light into corners. Lem and Harmonica Man had been friends. Harmonica Man had sometimes hired Lem as a bodyguard, according to the report. Friends and neighbors?

The transit officer was talking on his hand-held radio, reporting the body.

Austen found a steel door a distance down the tunnel. It was a folding door. There was a padlock on it, and there were heaps of what looked like fresh garbage and food containers scattered around the door. "Ben," she said.

He came over and looked, and shook the padlock. It opened. The steel loop had been cut with a hacksaw.

"That's a trick. The homeless do it," he said, pulling open the door.

Behind the door was a cramped space full of electrical cables. Most of the cables ran along a shelf above the ground. "They sleep up on the shelf," Kly remarked, playing his light around. "It's warmer up there."

Austen stood on a cinder block and looked. There were several empty vodka bottles lined up on the ledge, and more bottles and plastic food containers. And there was a black garbage bag containing something soft.

"Watch out for rats, okay, Dr. Austen?"

She felt the bag with her gloved hands, and pulled it down.

The policeman was asking them what they were doing. "Just a minute," Austen said.

She opened the bag. It contained a black hooded sweatshirt, balled up in a lump, and a roll of silver duct tape. There was also a clear plastic bag. It contained two Hohner harmonicas.

"Harmonica Man lived here," she said.

□

The transit police brought the body out in a bag, working with city mortuary drivers. Austen left instructions for them to be especially careful about taking universal biohazard precautions with the body, and she asked that it be placed in a double pouch. She then called Nathanson at his office.

"You can do the autopsy tomorrow," Nathanson said. "The guy's so putrefied, you could wait until Monday, I think."

"I'd like to do it right now."

"It's Friday. It's rush hour," Nathanson said, sighing, but he asked Glenn Dudley to stay while Austen did the autopsy. She couldn't sign the death certificate.

Annoyed, Dudley hurried the body into the X-ray room and took dental X-rays. They were alone in the Pit, except for Kly, who had stayed to help them. All the other tables were empty.

They cut Lem's clothing away, and found that rats had eaten his genitalia.

"They go for that first," Dudley remarked.

There was what looked like a maggot infestation in his left eye socket. Austen took light breaths, barely able to draw air into her lungs. The smell was so thick it had a greasy quality. She had to force her hands to make the Y incision to open the body.

Dudley stood to one side with his arms folded.

She was cutting now, and as her scalpel crossed the belly, there was a hiss of escaping gas. The abdominal fat had liquefied. It wept oil and stank.

"Oh," Austen said. She backed away.

"You work around it, Austen," Dudley said.

Dudley removed the skin hanging from Lem's right hand. It came off easily. He put his rubber-gloved hand inside the skin glove, his fingers sliding up inside Lem's finger-skins. The finger-skins still had fingerprints. Dudley inked the fingertips and rolled a set on a fingerprint pad. She noticed that Dudley's hands were trembling inside Lem's skin. She wondered if Dudley had a drinking problem.

The internal organs were a foul stew. Austen took samples and dropped them into the stock jar. She inspected the mouth carefully. It seemed to be marked with dark spots, possibly blisters, but it was hard to tell.

Dudley said, "When you look at that meat in a microscope you won't see anything." The cells had been dead a long time, and they would have ruptured and would appear, at best, like ghosts.

The smell filled the Pit and got out under the doors into the morgue area, where two attendants on the night shift noticed. "They're doing a mean one in there," one of them remarked.

Island

The Staten Island Ferry left South Ferry Terminal at
the tip of lower Manhattan and rumbled across
Upper New York Bay, churning through water the
color of pavement. It was a gray, misty Saturday
morning. Alice Austen stood outside on the forward
deck, behind a folding rail, watching Governors Island pass on the left, a low expanse of trees and brick
buildings. The trees on Governors Island were breaking bud, bursting into an indistinct bloom, a haze of
russet and pale green flowers. Yellow splashes of
color suggested to her that the forsythia was in
flower. The wind threw her hair around. She looked
the other way, at the Statue of Liberty passing in the
mist. There weren't many people on the ferry. The
deck trembled and bounced under her feet. Delicate
small terns with black heads flipped and pirouetted
over the water, and a bell buoy passed the boat,
clanging.

The boat docked at the ferry terminal at St.
George, on the northern tip of Staten Island. It was a
shorefront of abandoned piers that stretched into the
bay. Austen walked through the terminal building,
lugging her knapsack, with its weight of computer
and notebook, consulting a map. She found the platform of the Staten Island Rapid Transit train, and
took a train to Stapleton, then walked inland until she

came to Bay Street. She looked left and right, and found a Victorian house with yellow aluminum siding. A sign on the ground floor said "Island Antiques." The house was next to a dog-grooming salon. A smell of salt air filled the neighborhood.

Austen found an entryway with a buzzer button, and she pushed it.

Long pause. "Who is it?"

"It's Dr. Alice Austen. We spoke on the phone."

The buzzer sounded and the lock was released. Austen climbed up a flight of stairs to another door on a landing.

"Walk in," a voice croaked.

When Austen opened the door a smell of cats hit her.

Sitting in a recliner, facing a plate-glass window with a view of warehouses and the bay beyond, was a heavy, wrinkled woman about eighty years old. She was wearing a nightgown with a bathrobe, and slippers. Her ankles were thick, puffy, blue with edema. "I can't walk good. You have to come over here."

It was Mrs. Helen Zecker, the mother of the decedent.

"I'm working with the City of New York," Austen said. "We are trying to find out what happened to your daughter, Penny. We are concerned it might be an infectious disease. We're trying to trace it."

There was a long pause. Mrs. Zecker shifted her bulk and looked at Austen with terrified eyes. "It got my Penny."

"What did?"

"The monster thing I kept tellin' the doctors about! They wouldn't listen to me." She began to cry.

Austen sat down on a chair next to her.

"It got my Penny. It'll get me, next." She waved her hand in a gesture that seemed to say, I'm finished with you.

"May I ask you some questions?"

Helen Zecker rolled around in the chair and looked at Austen with a tear-streaked face. "You'd be a darling and feed the cats."

The kitchen was filthy and disordered. The moment Austen opened a can of food, four cats came hurrying in. She filled two teacup saucers with chopped chicken liver, and the cats crowded around them. She rinsed out the cats' water dish and refilled it.

Back in the living room, she said, "I'm interested in Penny's activities in the time before she died. Can you help me?"

"It got her. That's all I know. It got her."

"Let's try to figure out what it is that got her."

"There's all these things happening and they never tell us anything!"

Mrs. Zecker's memory of recent days was not good. Her memory of her earlier years was very good. "I grew up in this house," she said. "It was nice before the city went to hell. On New Year's Eve, Papa and Mama, they'd take us up to the attic." She pointed to the ceiling. "Papa would open the window up there. It was so cold. We'd have blankets around us."

"About your daughter, Penny—"

"You could smell the smoke from the freighters coming in the window. On New Year's Eve you'd hear the sailors singing on the ships. Right at midnight, Papa would hold up his hand and he'd say,

'Quiet! Listen!' And we'd be quiet. And we'd listen. And it would start. Over there. . . ."

Austen followed her gaze, to where the silver-gray towers of Manhattan seemed to float in the distance.

"It was a roar like the wind," she said. "It went on and on." It was the sound of Manhattan on New Year's Eve. "I don't hear it anymore."

Austen sat down on a chair next to her. She touched Mrs. Zecker's hand. "Can you remember? Did Penny go anywhere, do anything unusual? Anything you can remember?"

"I don't know. I don't know . . ."

"Where did she buy the things for the shop?" Austen asked.

"All over. I don't know. She always paid the taxes. Once she went to Atlantic City. That was a bus tour. . . . My Penny is gone."

"Do you mind if I look at the shop?"

"I can't go with you."

"That's all right."

Mrs. Zecker pulled a handle on the side of her lounge chair. The back came forward, raising her up. She put her feet on the floor and grunted. Austen took her by the hands and helped her up, and she shuffled across the room, her slippers dragging. She picked up a coffee cup from a bookshelf, and tipped it over. A key fell out.

Austen went down the stairs, out to the sidewalk, and let herself in through the front door of Island Antiques. She switched on a fluorescent light. It was chilly in the room; the heat was off. The walls were painted lemon yellow, and there was dingy lace trimming around a plate-glass window. A number of glass cases and cabinets displayed cheap-looking "antiques." It was really a thrift shop. There was a rack of musty women's dresses, and a metal desk with the dried remains of a sandwich sitting on a piece of waxed paper. Next to it was a glass ashtray full of cigarette butts. Penny Zecker had been a heavy smoker. There were bookshelves holding forgotten paperback best-sellers. There was an oak display case with items of costume jewelry in it. On the display case was a sign: "Case not for sale. Don't even *ask*." There was a caned rocking chair selling for seventy-five dollars, which seemed a high price, and a scuffed chest made of stained pine selling for forty-five dollars. She opened the chest. Inside was a stack of *National Geographic*s.

This was looking good. Somewhere in this room was a clue. Penny Zecker was a packrat. Like Kate Moran. There was a similarity in their behavior. And they are now dead.

She began making photographs with her electronic camera.

Austen went through the room carefully. There were trays and boxes of kitchen tools. A meat grinder. There were children's toys made of plastic, and a veneered coffee table for sale. A nice-looking brass ship's lamp, for thirty dollars. A Sylvester the Cat jelly-jar drinking glass. A chrome samovar, a lobster buoy. On the walls there were reproductions of snow scenes in frames, everything for sale.

Something was nagging at her. She opened the desk drawer. There were some file folders. She pulled them out, and found a folder marked "Profits." In it was a list, handwritten, on lined paper. The list was Penny's way of keeping track of her costs and profits as she bought and sold junk.

There were dates on the sheet, and names. Austen scanned the sheet quickly: "4/18—small chair—$59 cost $5." It looked as if Penny had bought a chair for five dollars and had sold it to someone for fifty-nine dollars. Penny Zecker was no fool. She had been keeping herself and her mother alive with her business.

Penny seemed a little obsessive about the entries, but this was her means of survival.

4/18—6 Ave. flea—black dress—woman—$32
    cost $0 found garbg.
4/18—sharp bone knife—Mr. ?Clow—$18 cost $1
4/19—6 Ave. flea—box (joke)—$6 traded for postcards
4/19—jewel pin (green)—$22 bot $5

She photographed the page.

Austen said good-bye to Mrs. Zecker and promised to let her know immediately if anything further was learned about the cause of the death of her daughter.

Back on the ferry she stood at the rear deck, in the open air, looking over Bayonne and down the throat of the Kill Van Kull. Then she walked to the bow of the boat, and watched the stone crystals of Wall Street approach. The clouds were beginning to break apart, revealing a brownish blue on the face of the sky over the city. The city was looking sick, but there was no diagnosis.

She decided to call Walter Mellis at the C.D.C. In the ship's passenger cabin she took out her cell phone and punched up Mellis's home number. The phone beeped at her. The battery had drained.

"Damn," she whispered.

Feeling more alone than ever, out of contact with the C.D.C., she put the phone in her knapsack and leaned back in her seat. She was exhausted. The ferry ride took almost half an hour, giving her time to think. Austen felt that somewhere in her data there existed a hidden door. If and when she found it, it would lead into a maze of biological systems and relationships, to the inner workings of nature as it played out its billion-year games with the human species.

She opened her laptop computer and started it up. By now she had three memory cards full of images taken with the electronic camera. She slid the memory cards into the computer, one by one, reviewing all the photographs on the computer screen.

Two of the four cases had been people who collect things, namely Kate Moran and Penny Zecker. What about Harmonica Man? He had been a collector, too. He had collected money in his cup, money that had passed through many hands. She didn't know much about Lem.

Hitting keys on her laptop computer, she brought up the images of Kate Moran's art collection. Some were close-ups. There was a geode of crystals, she remembered that. Austen hit a key on her laptop and zoomed the image until it was a checkerboard of pixels. She couldn't see anything.

Rocks didn't carry diseases. She zoomed on the image of the box that held the little beetle with the green eyes. No. The image of the dollhouse. Anything unusual in it? She zoomed images of the boxes Kate had collected. A tin box. What was inside it?

She had not taken any photographs of Harmonica Man's things. She and Kly had been in a hurry to get out of the tunnel.

The ledger. Zecker's ledger. She called up the images, and studied the pages. Something caught her eye, something brushed her memory:

> 6 Ave. flea—black dress—woman—$32 cost
> $0 found garbg.

It was perhaps the kind of dress Kate had liked to wear. But something else got her attention now: Sixth Avenue. Kate's father had mentioned that Kate had bought things at the flea markets, and Austen was pretty sure she remembered him mentioning Sixth Avenue. Kate had bought dresses? Her eye went down the ledger:

> 4/19—6 Ave. flea—box (joke)—$6 traded for postcards

Kate had liked boxes.

Austen felt a chill. What in the hell . . . ?

She reviewed the photographs of Kate's bedroom again, one by one, on the screen of her laptop.

Then she found it. A little gray wooden box. It was sitting beside the dollhouse. It was small, rectangular, nondescript. Except for one thing. It had a shape painted on the side. The shape was familiar. It was a polygon, an angular, crystalline shape. She had seen it before.

She blew the image up. Blew it up until it was a maze of pixels. She stared at the painted design on the box. Where have I seen this?

It was the shape of the crystals that she had seen inside Kate Moran's brain. The diagnosis clicked, like a mechanism locking into place.

Kate bought that box from Penny Zecker, at a flea market.

The box was the pump handle. She thought: It's sitting in Kate's bedroom now.

Whirlwind

Brain viruses can act fast. A brain virus can take a person from apparent good health to a fatal coma in a matter of hours. Viral agents that grow in the central nervous system spread along nerve cells. You can go to bed healthy and never wake up. By the next morning the agent has amplified itself along the fibers of the central nervous system.

The virus had spent the night amplifying in Peter Talides. His mental state was not good. It was Saturday morning, not a school morning, but he got himself dressed for school and walked to the elevated train station. He took the inbound N train to Manhattan, heading for the Mater School. He rode near the middle of the train, as was his habit. The train clattered over the elevated tracks through Queens, went around a bend, and descended into the tunnels under the East River.

He usually changed trains at the Fifty-ninth Street stop, and from there he would take the Lexington Avenue line uptown. At the Fifty-ninth Street station, he got off the train, as usual. The Lexington Avenue line runs at a lower level, and he walked down a flight of stairs to the mezzanine. The mezzanine is covered with colored mosaics. It is easy to become disoriented there. All the exit doors look alike. The mosaics are of trees and greenery. The tree trunks are red and the leaves are green. On the walls are lines of the poetry of Delmore Schwartz and Gwendolyn Brooks.

Peter Talides should have headed for the door that leads to the uptown train. But he didn't. He failed to read the signs. The colored mosaics disoriented him. He kept going. He passed by words on the wall that said, "Conduct your blooming in the noise and whip of the whirlwind."

He passed through a doorway around which shone a huge yellow sun of mosaic tiles. He went down a set of stairs to the downtown side of the Lexington Avenue tracks. A train came along; he stepped aboard. He sat down on a seat, and he was carried away from the Mater School, away from his destination. He sat with his head down almost between his knees. He kept touching his hands to his mouth. His nose was running profusely with clear mucus.

The train carried him along southward, through Manhattan. It dove under the East River and emerged in Brooklyn. At the Borough Hall station in downtown Brooklyn, he seemed to realize he was lost. "I missed it," he said in a thick voice.

He got off the train. He went up the stairs and down to the other side, looking at the signs. The higher Peter Talides was reading the signs while the lower Peter Talides was screaming in agony and writhing with disease. His midbrain was dying. He sat down on a bench and bent over and put his head between his knees and stayed that way for a long time. He groaned. Eventually a transit officer named James Lindle arrived at the scene. He touched Talides on the shoulder.

Talides uttered a sharp cry, almost like a baby's cry. It was a startle seizure: a seizure triggered by an intrusion into his world. He fell off the bench to the platform. He curled up on his side and straightened out, his body rigid. The rigidity passed.

A few people stopped and gathered around Peter Talides, but others passed by.

"Stand back, please. Don't touch him," Officer Lindle said. He called on his radio for an emergency medical squad from the New York Fire Department.

Talides was near the yellow line at the edge of the platform. Suddenly he twisted and rolled off the platform, dropping five feet down to the tracks. He landed with a splash in pools of water in the track bed.

At that moment, the station filled with the rumble of an approaching train.

"Aw, no!" Officer Lindle shouted. He ran up along the platform, waving at the train. "Stop!"

People were shouting at the man on the tracks: "Stand up! Get up!"

Talides seemed to hear the people calling to him. His eyes were half open. He was lying in pools of water. He rolled over onto his belly and began to crawl across the tracks—away from help, toward the third rail, the power rail. The train was approaching fast.

The train motorman saw the man crawling on the tracks and dumped his airbrakes on full emergency stop. A subway train can slide five hundred feet along the rails during an emergency stop.

Down on the tracks, a tremor shook Talides, and he flopped over and writhed. His clothing was soaked with water. His body crossed the running rail, and his head wedged itself against the electrified third rail. He grounded the electrical system through his head.

There was a sizzling flash. His body snapped rigid, made rock-hard by ten thousand amps of D.C. electricity running through his head and spine. The circuit breakers did not trip—they almost never trip when a body shorts out the New York subway. Enough electrical current was passing through his skull to accelerate twenty subway cars to full speed. The skin on his face came to an instant boil. A sheet of white blisters passed in a wave over his face. The blisters cratered and turned black.

There was a humming, crackling sound, and his cranial contents boiled. His skull burst with a dull thump. Brain material shot into the air and showered down over the platform. One man was seen wiping his eyes with his hands, then studying his smeared eyeglasses, puzzled by the gray bloody flecks that had seemed to come from nowhere.

An instant later, brakes wailing, the train thudded over the body, cutting it in two, and came to a halt. Smoke began to pour from beneath the car.

Cobra

The housekeeper, Nanette, answered the door. She said that Mr. and Mrs. Moran were staying with relatives.

"There may be something dangerous in Kate's room. Has anyone been inside?" Austen asked.

No one had been in the room. Kate's parents couldn't bear to go in. Her grandmother was going to go through her things once the worst was over. Mr. and Mrs. Moran were busy arranging the funeral, which was scheduled for tomorrow.

Austen had studied the photographs, and she had almost every object in Kate's bedroom in her mind's eye. She sat down at the worktable. There in front of her was the box with the rounded, angular crystal painted on it. She reached her hands toward it, stopped. She hesitated. Then she opened her knapsack and pulled out a cardboard box of latex examination gloves. She found a button mask and snapped the rubber band around the back of her head, fixing the mask over her mouth and nose. She found a pair of protective eyeglasses in her knapsack, and she put them on, too. She turned on a desk lamp.

Now, very delicately, she picked the box up. It was about three inches square and was made of some kind of very hard, dense wood. It was a puzzle. There was a sliding catch or mechanism somewhere that would open the box. One of the sides was loose. That might be the opening mechanism.

Should I try to open this? What will happen if I do? Four people are dead, maybe because of this thing. I may already be exposed anyway.

I'm going to open it. *"Ephphatha,"* she whispered. Be opened.

She slid her fingers over the box, feeling carefully. There was a click. The box opened and something snapped out of it, fast.

She dropped the box with a yelp. It clattered on the desk.

A snake had popped out. The head and neck of a small wooden snake. It was like a jack-in-the-box. The snake had struck at her fingers, and it had missed. It was a hooded cobra, and its hood was flared open, in the attack stance. It had a red spectacle marking painted across the back of its hood. Its eyes were bright yellow dots with slit irises painted on them. Its tongue was red and forked and stuck out.

The snake was attached to a spring mechanism. When you closed the lid and locked up the puzzle, the spring was cocked. When you pulled on the correct facet, the spring tripped and the snake leaped out and struck at your finger. It was a children's toy. It had been made by hand, perhaps in India or China, she thought.

Something else had come out of the box. She could just see it in the light of the skylight. It was a grayish dust.

She closed her eyes, jerked her head back, held her mask tight on her face, and ran. She found herself

standing on the other side of Kate's room. She shiv-
ered. She was covered with sweat. What was that
dust?

She crossed the room again, breathing as lightly
as she could in her mask, holding it tightly down over
her face, and she picked up the box in her gloved
hand. The top was open. She looked inside. Nothing
there, except the mechanism and a bit of dust. The
thing was a dust-dispersion device. Not very efficient. Just enough to put a little bit of dust into the air
near the person who opened the box.

"Oh, my God. My God," she said. It's a bomb.
It's a biological bomb.

She kept her hand on her mask, pushing it down
over her nose and mouth, hoping the seal was good.
What is the pore size of this mask? Will the mask
block these dust particles? The problem was, she
didn't know the size of the dust particles. Well, either
the dust is getting through the mask or it isn't. If it
has gone through, it's too late now.

She turned the box over with her fingertips, rotating it only slightly, so as not to cause any dust to
fall out. On the bottom of the box was glued a tiny
slip of paper with some words printed on it. The
words were very small.

Kate would have had a magnifying glass somewhere around here. She opened a drawer under the
table. Then she opened another drawer. There. A
magnifying loupe.

She held the box up again, near the desk light,
and looked through the loupe at the words. She dis-
cerned fine black letters, evidently made by a high-
quality laser printer.

Human trial #2, April 12

ARCHIMEDES FECIT

She put the box down and looked around the room. The Twinings tea can would do. She got a Kleenex from a pack on Kate's bedside table. She noticed wadded Kleenexes on the floor near the bed. She almost screamed. If Kate had been blowing her nose on them, they would be hot. She didn't touch them. She stuffed a wad of fresh Kleenex into the can, and then gently placed the snake bomb in a nest of Kleenex. She snapped down the can's lid, tight. She held the tea can in her hands. As soon as possible she would have to transfer it to a biohazard bag or container.

The light from the skylight came down around the scene, a cool light, illuminating Alice Austen's red hair. She thought of Kate's red hair, and of the autopsy.

She looked around the room. What is the air-circulation system in this room? She noticed a steam radiator. Good. Forced-air heating ducts might carry the room's air all over the building. She noticed an air-conditioning vent on the ceiling. She would have to make sure the Morans didn't turn on the air-conditioning system.

Austen locked Kate's door from the inside and then went out, and the door clicked behind her. She removed her mask and gloves but didn't know what to do with them. Finally she just put them in a pocket of her knapsack. She also took the magnifying loupe with her.

She found Nanette and warned her not to let anyone go into Kate's room. "I think I found something in there that may be extremely dangerous. I've locked the door. The authorities are going to investigate. Please keep that door locked until they arrive."

Nanette promised that she would stay out of the room and would keep people from going in. "Mr. and Mrs. Moran won't be home until tomorrow," she said.

"Whatever you do, don't turn on the air-conditioning."

□

Austen went out to the street and got a taxi to the medical examiner's office. There, in her office, beside her desk, she had left the bag of Harmonica Man's possessions. She put on a clean pair of surgical gloves and a clean button mask. She opened the mouth of the garbage bag and pulled out the black sweatshirt. There was a lump in the front pocket. She reached into the pocket and pulled out a small box. It was nearly identical to the one from Kate's room. She examined it in the fluorescent light. There was another tiny piece of paper glued to the bottom of this box. With the magnifying loupe, she examined it. This paper contained a picture. It was a very small engineering drawing. A picture of something she had never seen before. It looked like some kind of jar. The jar contained something that looked like a dumbbell or an hourglass. Under the picture was written, in very small print:

Human Trial #1, April 12
ARCHIMEDES FECIT

The boxes reeked of a plan, and a precise mind.

She locked her office, went up to the histology lab, and asked for several sealable plastic biohazard bags. Telling no one what she needed them for, she returned to her office and bagged the two cobra boxes. She didn't open the tea can. Then she went to the basement and got some large plastic bags, and she triple-bagged Lem's clothing. She realized that her knapsack had been hopelessly contaminated by the rubber gloves and the mask, and she triple-bagged the whole thing and tied it up.

She went to the ladies' room and looked into a mirror over the sink, afraid that she would see something in her eyes. Her eyes stared back at her, gray-blue. There was no change of color. No pupillary ring.

□

Dr. Nathanson lived on the Upper East Side in the Fifties. Austen took a taxi there, and in five minutes she was at the door of his apartment. His wife, Cora, answered the bell. "Oh, yes, you're the doctor from the C.D.C.," she said. "Come in."

Nathanson had a small office in the apartment. The desk was piled with papers. On the shelves were works of philosophy and medicine. The room smelled of cigars. He shut the door.

She said: "I've found the source."

"I'm not sure I follow you."

"The source. The cause of death. It's a human being. This isn't a natural outbreak. This is the work of a killer."

There was a long pause. In a careful voice, Nathanson said, "What makes you think so?"

On his desk she placed the orange-and-red plastic biohazard bags that held the tea can and Harmonica Man's box.

"I have found two devices. They are biological dispersion devices—bombs, Dr. Nathanson. I found one in Harmonica Man's clothing. I found the other in Kate Moran's bedroom. Penny Zecker was a junk dealer. She sold the device to Kate. Her notebook indicates that somebody traded the box with her for some postcards. That somebody is a murderer."

She placed her laptop computer on his desk and turned it on. "Look at these images."

The chief bent over to stare at her photograph of the Zecker-Moran box.

"This is the device that infected Penny Zecker. She sold it to Kate Moran." Then Austen held up one of the plastic biohazard bags. "There's the other device—you can see it in here. It's the device that ended up with Harmonica Man. I think someone may have given it to him in the subway. These boxes are designed to release a small amount of dust into the air when the lid pops open. I think the dust is a dried biological agent. It may be crystallized virus particles, I'm not sure."

Nathanson said nothing for a long time, staring at the boxes. He picked up the plastic bag, and looked through the plastic at the box inside, at the painted crystal, the featureless gray wood. Suddenly he seemed like an old man. He put down the bag. "This is criminal evidence. You should have left it where you found it."

"I—I guess I wasn't thinking about evidence. This is a bomb. I wanted to get it out of there."

"You've been exposed."

"So have Glenn Dudley and Ben Kly. You, too. You were present at the Moran autopsy."

"Jesus! They're doing the teacher now!"

"What?"

"The art teacher. He was killed on the subway tracks."

"Oh, my God. How?"

"We don't know what happened. I tried to reach you. Your phone wasn't working. I called Glenn and asked him to come in. He's in the autopsy room now with Kly."

Nathanson called over to the O.C.M.E. and reached a morgue attendant, and asked him to get Dudley on the phone. Soon the man came back, saying that Dr. Dudley was busy and would call later.

Knife

Glenn Dudley and Kly were alone in the Pit when Austen arrived there, out of breath. She stopped at the door of the main autopsy room and cried out to them. "Wait! The body is infected with a hot agent."

Ben Kly took a step backward.

"It's very dangerous, Dr. Dudley," Austen said.

"Then get yourself suited up before you come in here," he replied. "Note my findings." His gloved finger pointed at Talides's head. "The facial skin is cratered with blackened pits in the jumping-arc pattern we observe in subway electrocutions. The eyes remain open, milky due to heating. The right temple bulges outward, where we see a cracked-oyster fracture, and here we see traces of cooked brain material spilling out. The smell of cooked brain is distinctive. Why can't I smell it?" Now he looked up at her. His nose was running with a clear mucus, which was flowing over his breathing mask.

"*Ben,*" she said, backing away.

Kly had been holding the stock jar. He looked at Dudley and the jar dropped from his hands and broke on the floor with a crash.

The sound of the breaking glass may have upset Dudley. A jacksonian twitch rippled across his face. He grunted and opened his mouth. He sighed.

Dudley raised his prosector's knife, hefting it in an expert hand. He turned toward Austen and sighted along the blade, looking at her with shining, alert eyes.

The blade was honed carbon steel, more than two feet long, sharpened to the cutting edge of a straight razor, with a wooden grip. It was a weapon of real power, held in the hand of a man who knew how to use it. It was slick with infective blood.

Austen moved backward, keeping her eyes on the blade. Very slowly she raised her hands to protect her neck and face. "Dr. Dudley, please put the knife down. Please," she said.

Slowly, gently, Dudley moved the knife toward her. She screamed and jumped back, and the knife passed under her arm. He was playing with her, it seemed.

"Over here!" Kly said.

Dudley turned and faced Kly.

"Go!" Kly hissed to her.

She did not move. She picked up a pair of lopping shears, but Dudley spun around and tapped the shears away with his blade. It made a tiny *clink*.

Dudley turned and moved toward Kly, who backed up, keeping his eyes on Dudley's face, talking to him. "Calm down, Doctor. Put the knife down. It's all right, Doctor. Let's pray together, Doctor."

Dudley backed him into a corner. Kly had nowhere to go.

"Let's not pray," Dudley said, as he swung the knife with all his strength. It passed through Kly's neck with a wet sound, almost beheading him.

An arterial jet from his neck hit the ceiling. His head flopped over sideways, the muscles cut. He went down with a slumping sound.

Austen ran out of the room, shouting.

□

Dudley looked down at Kly, then looked around calmly. His neck arched. His back curved and swayed. The basal writhing intensified. He went over to a supply table and picked up a sterile scalpel blade in a wrapper. He stripped off the wrapper and fitted the little scalpel blade into a handle. He reached above his left ear with the scalpel and poked it into his skin until the tip touched bone, then drew the blade swiftly over the crown of his head, making a coronal incision from ear to ear, the blade tip bumping against the hard bone of his calvarium. He poked the scalpel into his thigh and left it quivering in the muscle—the muscle being a convenient sticking place for the scalpel. With both hands, he reached up and grasped the flap of skin that had opened across his head. He tugged it forward sharply. There was a tearing sound. He pulled his scalp off his skull and turned it inside out. He kept going—expertly, he pulled his face off his cranium. His eyes sagged as he pulled. His scalp fell down over his face inside out, like a slippery red blanket, the dome of his calvarium ivory-colored and red and wet, his hair draped in a fringe down over his mouth. His lips moved behind his hair. He screamed. He was eating his scalp. There was no seizure at the end.

Part Four

DECISION

Masaccio

The Jacob K. Javits Federal Building at 26 Federal
Plaza in lower Manhattan sits along Broadway, overlooking a complex of courthouses and city government buildings around Foley Square, with a view of
the Brooklyn Bridge. The Federal Building is faced
with dark gray stone. It has smoked windows. The
offices inside include the New York field office of
the Federal Bureau of Investigation, which is the
largest F.B.I. office in the United States, except for
F.B.I. headquarters in Washington. Eighteen hundred special agents and staffers work out of the New
York office. It occupies eight floors of the Federal
Building.

Alice Austen and the chief medical examiner of
New York City entered a darkened conference room
on the twenty-sixth floor. The room was full of desks
arranged in concentric half-circles, facing a bank of
video display screens. It was the Command Center of
the New York field office. Various agents and managers and technical people were standing around or
sitting at the desks, and there was an unmistakable
scent of sour law-enforcement coffee in the air.

A stocky man in his forties came over to them.
He had curly brown hair and dark intelligent eyes.
He wore a blue oxford shirt under a gray V-neck
sweater vest, and khaki pants and L.L. Bean loafers.
He had an ample gut.

"Hello, Lex," he said, and he shook Austen's hand. "Frank Masaccio. I'm glad to meet you, Doctor. We'll talk in my office."

As they walked out of the Command Center, Masaccio gestured to the video screens. "We're just wrapping up a bust. Insurance fraud." He shook his head. "Some of the suspects are doing the fake-heart-attack routine. Half the cardiac-care units in this city have organized-crime figures dying in them as we speak. Drives us nuts."

Frank Masaccio was the head of the New York field office and an assistant director of the F.B.I. When they got to his office, three floors above, he said to them, "All right, run this by me again."

Nathanson's voice was shaky. "My deputy is dead, infected with something in the autopsy room. He killed our best morgue attendant with a knife, and then he killed himself in a way that is difficult to describe."

Austen placed her laptop computer on a coffee table. "Something seems to be causing people to attack themselves or others. We've had six deaths, and it looks like someone is planting the agent in a premeditated way."

Masaccio said nothing. He got up and crossed the room and sat down on the couch in front of her computer, so that he could see the screen, and he gave her a sharp look. "The first question I'm asking, is this F.B.I. jurisdiction?"

"This is murder," she said. She was met with a neutral gaze that was impossible to read as she began to summarize what had happened, what she had found.

Masaccio listened without comment, then suddenly put up one hand. "Hold on. Have you notified anybody at C.D.C.?"

"Not yet," Nathanson said.

"I want to do a dial-up with C.D.C.," Masaccio said. He went over to his desk. Without sitting down, he tapped the keys of his computer, and stared at a list of numbers and names. "Here's our contact in Atlanta." He punched up a telephone number and then tapped in a string of digits with one finger. "Sky-pager."

Within two minutes, the phone rang back. Masaccio put the call on his speakerphone and said, "Is this Dr. Walter Mellis? Frank Masaccio here. I'm the director of the New York field office of the F.B.I. I don't know if we've ever met. I'm sorry to bother you on a Saturday. We have a little problem. Where are you right now?"

"I'm at my golf course. In the clubhouse," Mellis said. They could hear him breathing hard. It sounded as if he had run for a telephone.

"Walt? It's Alice Austen."

"Alice! What's going on?"

There was some confusion for a moment about who knew whom, but Walter Mellis quickly explained things to Masaccio.

"Dr. Mellis, it looks like we may be in the middle of a—biological event of some kind," Masaccio said. "Your researcher seems to have uncovered something."

"Wait—what's Walt's involvement?" Austen said.

"He's a consultant to one of our special units. It's called Reachdeep," Masaccio said. He explained that Reachdeep was a classified operation, and that he would arrange for her to have security clearance.

Austen wasn't sure she grasped what was going on.

"Reachdeep is a special forensic unit of the Bureau," Masaccio said. "It deals with nuclear, chemical, and biological terrorism. Dr. Mellis here is the C.D.C. contact for Reachdeep. He's a consultant for us."

"Were you in on this?" Austen asked Lex Nathanson.

Nathanson was embarrassed. "Walt has involved me a bit," he said.

"So he lined you up, Lex?" Masaccio said.

"He asked me to watch for unusual cases. This one seemed unusual."

Austen was annoyed about being deceived, but she tried to calm herself down. She described to Masaccio in greater detail what she had found, speaking carefully. He interrupted her occasionally to ask questions. She found that she did not have to explain anything twice to him.

"Why did Dr. Dudley become so violent?" Masaccio asked. "That high school kid didn't."

"The agent seems to exaggerate underlying aggression," Austen answered. "Kate Moran was a peaceful person, and she bit her lips. Glenn Dudley was—"

"Very unhappy," Nathanson filled in, "to begin with."

"It's doing damage to primitive parts of the brain," Austen said. "If this is an infectious agent, it is one of the most dangerous infective organisms I've ever seen or heard of."

Masaccio shot a look at Austen. "*How* infective? A lot or a little?"

He is asking the right questions, she thought. "The blistering process in the mouth and nose is an important detail, and it's particularly frightening," she said. "You get blistering with very infective agents like smallpox or measles. The agent is *not* as contagious as the influenza virus. But it is more contagious than the AIDS virus. I would guess it's about as infective as the common cold. It actually starts like a common cold, but then it invades the nervous system."

"So what is the bug?" Masaccio asked.

"Unknown," Austen said.

"This has to be federal jurisdiction," Lex Nathanson broke in. "The City of New York can't possibly handle this."

"All right," Masaccio said. "What we have is an apparent series of homicides using an unknown biological agent. That's covered under Title 18 of the federal code. That's ours. That's F.B.I. jurisdiction. Can the C.D.C. identify this thing for us?"

"It could be difficult," Mellis said.

"What about a cure?"

"Cure?" Mellis said. "How can we cure something if we don't know what it is, Mr. Masaccio? If it's a virus, there's probably no cure. Most viruses are untreatable and incurable. Usually the only defense against a virus is a protective vaccine. It takes years of research, and maybe a hundred million dollars, to invent a vaccine for a new virus. We still don't have a vaccine for AIDS."

Masaccio said, "Okay, but how long will it take to identify this?"

Mellis answered on the speakerphone, "Weeks to months." Masaccio stared at the speakerphone as if he were trying to burn a hole in it with his eyes. "We have hours to days to deal with this." He turned. "So—tell me what you *think* the virus is, Dr. Austen."

"I don't know what it is. We're not even sure it's a virus."

There was a silence, and then Masaccio said, "I have the impression that there's a lot on your mind you're not telling me, Dr. Austen."

"I don't have much evidence."

"Bullshit. You pulled off a very complex criminal investigation with no backup. Are there any cops in your family? Is your dad a cop, by any chance?"

She didn't say anything.

"Come *on*," he said, coaxing her.

"My father, yes. He's a retired chief of police, but what difference does that make?"

Masaccio chuckled, delighted with himself. "All right, now—good cops work their hunches. Tell me your hunches. One cop to another."

"It's a virus," she said. "It spreads like the common cold: by contact with tiny droplets of mucus floating in the air or touching the eyelids, or by contact with infective blood. It can be dried into a powder and it can get into the air, so it may also be infective through the lungs. It's neuroinvasive—that means it travels along the nerve fibers and invades the central nervous system. It replicates in the brain.

It amplifies explosively in the brain. It kills in about two days, so it has a very fast replication phase, as fast as anything I've ever seen. The virus makes crystals in brain cells. The crystals form in the center of the cell, in the cell's nucleus. It damages the brain stem, the areas that control emotion and violence and feeding. The virus causes people to attack themselves and to eat their own flesh. It is not . . . natural."

"This is wild speculation," Mellis said.

"Come on, Walt, you started it when you talked to me about stealth viruses," Austen said.

"I'm thinking about the Unsub," Masaccio said. Unsub is Bureau jargon for "Unknown Subject"— the unknown perpetrator of the crime. "Is this a group or a loner?" Nobody could answer his questions.

"Dr. Austen, one thing I have to ask: are you personally contagious?"

"Please don't take me off this case."

Masaccio grunted. "Hm . . . so we could go postal if we've been chatting with you? What a thought." He rolled a large gold class ring on his finger and made a sucking sound with his teeth. He stood up and crossed to the window, which looked north, toward midtown and the Empire State Building. He put his hands in his pockets. "Self-cannibalism, spreading through New York like the common cold." He turned around and faced them. "I don't have a single goddamned space suit in this office!"

"The fire department has protective suits," Lex Nathanson said.

"So what can the New York City Fire Department do with a brain virus, Lex? Pour some water
on it?"

"I have to inform the director of C.D.C.," Mellis
said.

Frank Masaccio hung up, then turned toward
Nathanson and Austen. "I'm taking this to our National Security Division. The head of the N.S.D. is a
guy named Steven Wyzinski." He punched up another
string of numbers. Wyzinski returned the call immediately, and they spoke quietly for a minute or two.

"Steve wants to do a SIOC calldown," Masaccio
said. "Can anyone tell me why bad things always
happen on Saturday night? You can't find anybody in
Washington on a Saturday night."

"What is a—calldown?" Austen asked.

"A SIOC calldown." He pronouced it *Sy-ock.*
"That's a meeting of experts and federal people at
F.B.I. headquarters. SIOC means Strategic—ah—
Strategic—huh. Jesus, I can't remember. Alzheimer's
must be setting in. It's the F.B.I.'s command center in
Washington. You'll go. Lex and I are going to stay
here in New York and get the ball rolling locally. The
mayor's office has to be brought into this. I'm going
to start lining up a joint task force with the police department—that's an asset. The fire department could
be an asset—I'm trying to see the end of this . . ."

Austen watched him. What she saw was a very
bright man working out the opening moves of a chess
defense. The problem was that the unknown oppo-
nent was in control of the game.

Archimedes

Archimedes of Syracuse, the great mathematician and weaponeer who died in 212 B.C., designed glass lenses or mirrors that focused sunlight on enemy ships and set them on fire. He understood the principle of the lever and the fulcrum, the idea that one can place a long lever on a fulcrum and use it to move a giant mass. "Give me only a place to stand, and I can move the world," Archimedes said.

Archimedes liked to ride the subway. He could ride for hours, thinking about things, planning. He sat in the cars looking at people from behind his metal-framed eyeglasses, a faint smile playing across his face now and again. He was a prematurely balding man of medium height. Usually he wore a tan cotton shirt and loose, natural-fiber trousers, and sneakers made of canvas and rubber. The clothes were simple but actually quite expensive. He had reasonably friendly feelings toward most people, and it made him feel bad that some of them would have to go.

The subway was the bloodstream of the city, with connections that ran everywhere. Archimedes liked to study connections. He stood on a platform in Times Square, watching the trains go by. Then he took the shuttle across midtown Manhattan to Grand Central Terminal. He walked briskly through the station, moving among the crowds, listening to their

footsteps, looking at the golden constellations overhead in the vaulted space, beautiful Orion the Hunter.
He thought of the tracks that go out of Grand Central
into the world. People were always talking about
viruses from the rain forest that would find their way
to modern cities and infect the inhabitants. But it
works the other way around, too, he thought. Diseases that emerge from New York City can spread out
and reach the humans who live in the rain forest.
There are more connections from New York City to
the rest of the world than from any other city on
earth. Something can explode from here to go everywhere on the planet.

He walked west a few blocks to the New York
Public Library, and he circled around it and sat down
on a bench in Bryant Park, among lawns and London
plane trees and, of course, people. Too many of them.
He sat on a bench and watched them pass before his
eyes, the temporary biological creatures whose lives
would not be remembered and who would vanish in
the reach of deep time. He looked up at the library,
the repository of human knowledge. They are not
going to understand my optimism and my hope, he
thought. But I think we can be saved. I hold the lever
in my hands.

Dash

Before dawn, a New York City police car took Alice Austen from Kips Bay to the East Side Heliport at Thirty-fourth Street. It parked near the landing platform as a Bell turbo helicopter operated by the F.B.I. came down the East River at full power. The helicopter drew up sharply and landed on the platform. Austen ran for it.

On board were two F.B.I. pilots and a tech agent, a woman.

"Frank's really upset about something," the woman remarked.

"I've never heard him that bad," one of the pilots said. The woman shook Austen's hand. "Special Agent Caroline Landau."

Austen observed that the helicopter was full of racks of electronic equipment. Caroline Landau fiddled with some wires, crimping a cable harness. "This damned equipment is going to lose our case for us," she remarked to the pilot.

The helicopter flew straight across Manhattan and up the Hudson River. It turned west across New Jersey and landed at Teterboro Airport, beside a twin-engine turboprop passenger plane. "Good luck with whatever," Special Agent Landau said to Austen. Then the helicopter lifted away, to return to its duty over the city.

The turboprop plane was a Dash 8 owned by the F.B.I. A pilot and copilot were on board, checking their instruments. Austen went up the steps, and the props sputtered and started. The Dash 8 cut into the queue of taxiing planes and was prioritized for immediate takeoff. It climbed to altitude and left New York behind. She looked out the window to try to see the sick organism, but the city was lost in predawn clouds.

She was the only passenger. The other twenty-nine seats were empty.

"If there's anything you need, Dr. Austen, please ask us," the pilot said to her over the loudspeaker.

"I'd like a telephone," she said.

The copilot walked back and showed her a communications console facing a seat. There was a lot of gear, including several telephones. He picked up a headset and handed it to her. "It's secure. You can dial anywhere in the world."

She put on the headset, adjusted the microphone, and called her father in New Hampshire. She woke him up. "Aw—God. It's five o'clock, Allie," he said. "Where've you been? I was calling all over Atlanta. Nobody knew where you were."

"Sorry, Dad. I'm on a field investigation."

"I thought so. Where are you?"

"I can't say. It's kind of an emergency."

"What's that noise I hear?"

"It's nothing important."

"Aw!" He still sounded groggy. He coughed, and she heard him drinking water. "Where are you, in a factory or something?"

Her father was living in a small house in the woods near Ashland, New Hampshire. Her mother had died three years earlier. She thought about how excited her father would be if he knew she was calling him from an F.B.I. aircraft headed for Washington. "Dad, I just wanted to say how much I admire you," she said.

"You wake me up at the crack of dawn for this?" He chuckled. "I can take it."

"I may not have a chance to call you for a while."

"Hey—I'm going out to do some fishing. As long as you got me up."

"What are you going for, Dad?"

"Landlocked salmon. They're still hitting."

"Yeah. Get some."

"Keep in touch, sweetie."

"Good-bye, Dad. I love you." She sat back in the seat and closed her eyes. That wasn't a perfect good-bye. If I end up like Kate Moran. She got up and went into the plane's washroom and looked at her eyes in the mirror, for the second time that day. She saw no sign of a color change. I hope I'm right about this. I know I'm right. But if I'm wrong, I've just pulled the biggest fire alarm handle in the world, and I didn't even know it existed.

Andrews

Will Hopkins, Jr., and Mark Littleberry had had a few hours layover at the airport in Bahrain, on the Persian Gulf, and they finally had a chance to shave. But they didn't have any clean clothes, and when they hooked onto some spare seats on board a U.S. military airlift command transport 707 bound for Andrews Air Force Base, they looked a little worse for wear.

The flight landed at Andrews at dawn on Sunday morning. Littleberry was due to go out to Bethesda, Maryland, to the National Naval Medical Research Institute, where he would be debriefed about the attempt to obtain a sample of an Iraqi biological weapon. Hopkins had to go to the F.B.I. Academy in Quantico. They had both been fired by the United Nations, they had caused a diplomatic incident, and there was going to be a lot of explaining to do. Still, it was a fine Sunday morning in Washington, and Hopkins was feeling lucky to be alive. "Let's go over to Georgetown and find a café and just sit there," he said. "Get some coffee, some breakfast, enjoy the sun. You and I need to decompress a little."

"I can get on this program," Littleberry said.

He called his wife, Annie, to let her know he was safe. He told her he expected to be back in Boston within a few days, as soon as the briefings were finished. "Get your bathing suit out, honey, because we're heading for Florida."

They went in search of a shuttle bus into Washington. They were just arriving at the curb when Will Hopkins's Skypager beeped. It was inside his bag. He unzipped the bag and looked at the number on the beeper. It was not familiar. But he plucked a cell phone from his pocket and dialed the number back. He identified himself and listened for a minute. "Sioc? What? Oh, man. When is she coming in? I'm supposed to wait for her?" Suddenly, Littleberry looked down and frowned. The beeper in his bag had gone off.

"It's a calldown," Hopkins said to him.

Littleberry pulled his cellular telephone out and turned it on. It was a secure cell phone on a government band. He walked off to one side. A minute later, he returned. He said, "Can you give me a lift to the meeting? After you pick up the doctor?"

□

Hopkins and Littleberry were waiting on the tarmac at Andrews when Alice Austen stepped off the Dash 8.

Hopkins said, "Hi. Supervisory Special Agent William Hopkins, Jr." He shook Austen's hand. "This is Dr. Mark Littleberry. He is a consultant to the F.B.I. on matters involving biological terrorism. We will accompany you to the meeting."

Austen thought that Supervisory Special Agent Hopkins was a little underdressed. She noticed the plastic pocket protector. The word *geek* entered her mind.

An F.B.I. car appeared, and they headed for downtown Washington, traveling very fast. The car threaded sparse traffic on the Beltway, then turned west onto Pennsylvania Avenue.

Hopkins cleared his throat. "I'm the guy in the bureau who is supposed to handle a bioterror event. Can you tell us what's going on, Doctor?"

She told them briefly. "There have been several deaths. It looks like serial murder using a virus, but we don't have any idea what the virus is."

"Terror singlets, huh?"

"If that's what you call it," she said.

"We were sort of figuring on a bomb," he said.

"These are bombs."

"It's a onesies and twosies kind of thing."

"It's murder using a contagious disease," she said.

"We can handle this," he said.

Austen looked at him skeptically. "Do you think so?"

The car circled around the Capitol and got back on Pennsylvania Avenue. The cherry trees were past their peak, but the city still glowed with lingering blossoms. A homeless man poked around in a pile of garbage near a restaurant. Their car skirted the north side of the Mall and headed for Ninth Street.

"My turn to say something," Mark Littleberry remarked.

"Go ahead," she said.

"We are about to go on air, live, with the whole federal government. You guys ever done that before?"

"Nope," Hopkins said.

"If you two are jabbing for turf, it's going to look awkward," Littleberry said.

Austen and Hopkins were silent.

A phenomenally ugly building of monstrous proportions loomed over Pennsylvania Avenue. It was made of raw yellow-gray concrete, with deep-set, bulletproof, smoked windows. It was the J. Edgar Hoover Building, the national headquarters of the F.B.I. The fortress was wider at the top than at the bottom, an upside-down iceberg. The Bureau car turned up Ninth Street and went into the Hoover building through a security point, around an explosion-barrier, down a ramp, and into a basement garage. They took an elevator to the fifth floor, and came to a door. It was a steel vault door with a combination lock. There was a combination pad on it and a red sign that said, "Restricted Access—IN USE."

"Looks like they've already begun," Will Hopkins said. He punched in an authorization code. A lock clicked, and he pulled open the door. It was the entry foyer of the Strategic Information Operations Center.

SIOC

The SIOC room at F.B.I. headquarters was a window-less, radio-secure chamber. It was lined with copper and steel, so that no stray signals could get out and be caught by an eavesdropper. The interior space of the SIOC chamber was divided into sections that were visible to one another through glass panels. A number of people were sitting around a meeting table in one of the smaller sections.

A tall, silver-haired man in a suit came out to meet them. He was Steven Wyzinski, the head of the F.B.I.'s National Security Division. "You're William Hopkins? Everyone cleared?"

"These people are basically, sort of, my group," Hopkins said.

Austen was introduced to a number of F.B.I. officials, but she had trouble remembering their names.

"We'll be going up on the bird in twenty-five minutes," Wyzinski said, glancing at a clock on the wall. "We don't have much time. We have to move fast and hard. Please give us all the information you have, Dr. Austen."

Austen opened her laptop computer, showed them the images, and described the situation. They asked her many questions, firing them at her left and right. They wanted to make absolutely sure the event was real before they called in the rest of the government.

"Satellite transmission initiates in four minutes," someone announced.

"We're going live," Steven Wyzinski said, rising to his feet. "Thank you, Dr. Austen."

They filed into the videoconference situation room and sat down at a table, where a sound technician wired them with clip-on microphones. There were a number of large video screens positioned on the walls. The screens were glowing but blank. There were several speakerphones on the table.

Steven Wyzinski adjusted his necktie. He cleared his throat nervously.

One by one, the video screens filled with faces. Voices came on the speakerphones. The room filled with power, real power; you could feel it in the air.

"I'm bringing the meeting to order," Wyzinski said. "Welcome to SIOC. This is a threat-assessment meeting for the Cobra Event. The Federal Bureau of Investigation customarily gives a name to major crime investigations and this one will be designated Cobra. You will understand the meaning of the term shortly. This meeting has been called by the Bureau under the mandate of Presidential Decision Directive 39 and National Security Directive 7 . . ."

Austen felt herself trembling, ever so slightly, and she hoped it didn't show. She hadn't slept well in days. Hopkins was sitting next to her.

On two video screens, side by side, were the faces of Walter Mellis and the director of the C.D.C., Helen Lane. Mellis was wearing the full-dress white uniform of the United States Public Health Service, including action ribbons across the chest.

"Congratulations, Dr. Austen," Mellis said.

"Walt? Where are you?" she said.

"Dr. Lane and I are at headquarters in Atlanta."

Frank Masaccio's face appeared on another screen. He was with Ellen Latkins, chief of the Emergency Management Office for the City of New York. She was representing the mayor.

Steven Wyzinski introduced Austen, and the calldown people identified themselves. Many of them were high-level military officers. There was also a man from the Office of the Attorney General, at the Justice Department.

"Is the White House coming online?" Wyzinski asked.

"White House on now!" said a technician in the background.

A large viewing screen set in a commanding position glowed and went live. It showed a rumpled middle-aged man in a pink polo shirt. He had the air of someone who was used to attending meetings that were choreographed to the minute. "Yeah. Jack Hertog here. I'm with the National Security Council of the White House. I'm not sure this incident needs a response from us at this point."

Wyzinski turned the floor over to Austen.

She stood up and took a breath. Her photographs flashed on the viewing screens. She read the words that were printed on the dispersion devices, the cobra boxes. She said, "It's a very frightening situation. Six disease-related deaths have occurred in a short time."

"Are we sure that we're dealing with a biological agent?" an Army colonel from USAMRIID, at Fort Detrick, asked.

"I am fairly sure," Austen said. She explained that there had been infective transmission of the unknown disease-causing agent in at least two cases. She told them that she suspected that it was a virus.

"If so," the Army colonel said, "then it's a Level 4 hot agent. But there's been no identification, right?"

"Correct," Austen said.

"So how can you assess a threat if you don't know what the agent is?"

"Good point," Wyzinski said.

"Will, tell us—how bad *is* this threat?" Frank Masaccio said, addressing Will Hopkins.

"Dr. Littleberry should answer that."

Littleberry leaned forward over the table. The cameras followed him. "There are a lot of unknowns here," he said. "Certainly the identity of the agent, but also the identity of whoever is dispersing it. It's hard to assess the threat, but what we do know is that the lethal-dose response in a population under biological attack can be enormous. A couple of pounds of dry hot agent, released in the air in New York City—you might get ten thousand deaths. The top range would be two million deaths, maybe three million."

"Your top range seems exaggerated," said Jack Hertog, the White House man. "I've seen different estimates in different policy reviews."

"I sure hope it's exaggerated, son," Littleberry said.

Hertog looked annoyed; people didn't call members of the White House inner staff "son."

Ellen Latkins, from the mayor's office, broke in. She had been getting increasingly angry. "Look, if you people really think that this could escalate to anything even close to the scenario you've described, then I would like to know how you plan on handling this."

"I share your concern," Jack Hertog said. "However, you must understand that we have no reason to think that what we have here is a major act of terrorism." He was thinking to himself: Why did I agree to have my name on the list?

"Wait," Austen said. "The deaths have happened very quickly. The disease is unknown. It is explosive in its effects on people. I think we have a problem in New York. There's some kind of murderer out there."

Hertog smiled. "There *are* murderers out there, Doctor."

"You haven't seen this disease!" she said.

Steven Wyzinski decided to neutralize things. "We need to work up an assessment of the threat," he said. "The threat is not just the disease but the person or group behind it. The person or group who is called . . . what is it?"

"Archimedes," Austen said. "The words '*Archimedes fecit*' are Latin. They mean 'Made by Archimedes.' They refer to the cobra box. The date on the box could be the date that Archimedes prepared the box. The expression 'human trial' probably refers to human medical experimentation."

There followed a great deal of discussion about the motives of Archimedes. The Cobra Event did not seem like classic terrorism, in which a group acts with an agenda. Or if there were an agenda it didn't seem obvious at this point.

Jack Hertog had been getting annoyed with the meeting. The White House had bigger problems to deal with than a killer loose in New York. "There's been no explicit threat to commit a wide-scale terrorist act," he said. "So Dr.—ah—Littleberry's projections sound kind of academic."

Littleberry stood up. "Hey! One of those photographs that Dr. Austen took of the cobra dispersion boxes shows an engineering drawing," he said to Hertog in a harsh, angry voice. "It's a bioreactor of some kind. A bioreactor can make a shitload of virus in a real hurry—"

"*Thank you*, Dr. Littleberry," Hertog said.

Hopkins had been sitting there, wondering when to speak. He was still wearing clothes that needed laundering in the worst way. "It looks like we could have a very serious situation," he finally said. "I think—"

"Who are you, again?" Hertog asked.

"Supervisory Special Agent William Hopkins, Jr. I'm a forensic molecular biologist. I'm head of scientific operations for the biology group at the Hazardous Materials Response Unit in Quantico."

"Oh, yeah. You're that biological SWAT unit that's not ready," Hertog said.

"We're ready, sir. And we're not a SWAT group. We are scientists."

"It's my understanding that you're not ready for anything."

Hopkins sensed that Hertog was losing interest. He said, "I think we are seeing a pattern. We are seeing a biological terrorist going through a testing phase. That's the meaning of the expression 'human trial.' For some reason, bioterrorists like to test their stuff. It happened with the Aum Shinrikyo sect in Japan, before they let off nerve gas in the Tokyo subway. They tested anthrax two or three times, and they couldn't get it to work, so they switched to nerve gas. The same thing happened in 1984 in The Dalles, a town in Oregon. The Rajneeshee sect put salmonella in salad bars in restaurants around town, and seven hundred and fifty people got sick. It was a test. They were planning a wide-scale biological attack on the town that was to happen later. What's happening in New York could be the testing phase for a huge release of a biological weapon."

"This is just speculation," Hertog said.

"But we can use forensics to stop it," Hopkins went on. "Normal forensic science is all about uncovering evidence *after* a crime has been committed. Here we can use forensics to solve a crime of terror in progress. We have an incredible opportunity to stop a terror event before it happens, using Reachdeep."

"The unit that doesn't exist," Hertog said.

Hopkins pulled a swab out of his pocket protector. "This is the heart of Reachdeep," he said.

"What?" Hertog said.

"This little swab. The evidence is mainly biological. All terrorist weapons contain signatures— forensic signatures—that lead you back to the perpetrator. When someone makes a bomb, he leaves marks and clues all over it. We can analyze the infective agent, and it will lead us back to its creator."

"This sounds off the wall," Hertog said.

Hopkins waved his swab around as he talked. "The idea behind Reachdeep is universal forensics. You use all your tools, everything you've got, and you take the crime apart. You explore the crime with the limits of your intellect. Exploring a big crime is like exploring a universe. It's what astronomers do when they look at the night sky with telescopes, or what biologists do when they explore a cell with their instruments of vision. You begin to translate the language, and the structure of the crime and the identity of the perpetrator are slowly revealed, like the structure of a universe."

"For God's sake, Hopkins!" It was Steven Wyzinski. He was embarrassed.

Hopkins put the swab back in his pocket and sat down abruptly. His face was red. He looked sideways at Austen, and then he looked down at the table.

"I've never seen a policy brief on this," Hertog muttered.

Austen began to feel sorry for Hopkins.

"We need to be invisible," Hopkins said in a louder voice. "The perpetrator may accelerate the killing if he, or they, know we're closing in on them. We need to do a secret field deployment of a Reachdeep lab."

The Army colonel from Fort Detrick said, "Wait a minute. This man is talking about isolating a hot agent using a portable field laboratory. That's crazy. You need a full-scale Biosafety Level 4 research facility to do that."

"We're in the middle of an unfolding criminal event," Hopkins replied. "We don't have time to fly evidence down to Fort Detrick and then work on it there. Also, if we're flying evidence all over the place, the chain of custody might be damaged. We might lose our ability to get convictions."

The Justice Department attorney agreed with him. "We need evidence that can be used in a trial," he said.

Hopkins went on: "We can move the crime lab to the evidence. I propose we set up a ring of investigative power around a Reachdeep lab. What I mean is, we'll have a core science lab with a forensic team. Around that team, we'll have a joint task force of agents and police officers. The science team will generate leads, but we'll need hundreds of investigators to run out the leads. We need to do good, classical investigative work, and we need to merge it into a Reachdeep forensic operation."

Jack Hertog of the White House broke in. "This is over the top. You're asking for a hell of a lot of money and federal attention, and for what? Another Flight 800 media circus that ends up in a hopeless mystery—?"

"Hey!" Masaccio ripped in. "My people gave their heart and soul—"

"Shut up, Frank. The F.B.I. forensic lab doesn't exactly have a stellar track record. You people spent twelve years looking for the Unabomber, and in the end, his *brother* turned him in. Now what do you want to do, act out a sci-fi movie in New York?"

Hopkins looked around the room, seeking support. Steven Wyzinski was hanging back, unwilling to commit himself to a fight with the White House. Frank Masaccio's face was discolored with fury in the video, but he seemed to be reining himself in. There had been too many fights with the White House lately.

Mark Littleberry stood up slowly. "I think I have something to add here that may put things into perspective. We've never had a situation in this country on any large scale where a population is threatened with a biological weapon. But we've feared this type of event for a long time, and the technology for the development and use of biological weapons is being advanced constantly by people we have no control over, who don't care about the consequences. We learned a lot about how these weapons work during tests in the Pacific in the late 1960s—"

"Excuse me—." It was Jack Hertog. "I don't think a discussion of those tests is germane here."

Littleberry stared at him. "I don't know if it's *germane*, but you'd damned well better take it seriously."

"Of course the President takes this seriously," Hertog said.

"With a biological weapon," Littleberry continued, "you can make people die like flies, depending on the weather and wind, time of day, the way the agent's dried and prepared, the exact method of dispersal, and the nature of the agent itself. Ten thousand deaths in a matter of days would overwhelm all of the city's hospitals. The hospitals would run out of beds and supplies. If the agent was contagious in human-to-human transmission, then just about the first people to die would be the medical caregivers and the first responders. The population of doctors, nurses, firemen, ambulance crews, and police—

they'd disappear, fast as hell. There would be nobody left to transport the victims to a hospital and no medical people in the hospitals to treat them. A relatively low end of the range of numbers of possible deaths from a biological weapon could leave the city without any medical-care system at all, except for what could be flown in by the military. The high end of the range is unimaginable—but is technically achievable. And it could happen to any city in the world. Tokyo, London, Moscow, Singapore, you name it. You've got a situation here where any jerk with a hot strain and some understanding of biology can kill a large number of people."

There was silence in the room. Even Jack Hertog seemed affected by the weight of what Littleberry had said.

It was Steven Wyzinski who finally spoke up. He had been taken aback by Hertog's outburst against the F.B.I., and he wanted to suggest that the Bureau was in control. He said that he felt that even though there was reasonable doubt about the scale of the threat, particularly since there had been no specific target mentioned or demands made, there seemed to be no choice but to start a major investigation. He thought the best chance was Will Hopkins's Reachdeep team.

Everyone agreed that it was so, more or less. "I can imagine this thing turning into a giant rat fuck," Hertog said. "But I think we don't have much choice. The bottom line is, we can't take a chance of a big blowup in a place like New York."

It was Frank Masaccio who came up with the idea that set the operation in motion. "I've got a place for you Reachdeep guys," he said to Hopkins. "You know Governors Island?"

"Never heard of it," Hopkins said.

"It's in the middle of New York Bay, right off Wall Street. It's a federal property. Very secure. No media, no people barging in on you. It used to be owned by the Coast Guard, but they've left. They left all their infrastructure there."

"Okay," Hertog broke in. "Hopkins, you put your science squad on the island. And don't screw up. As for USAMRIID and C.D.C., I want you to work in parallel. Both of you are national labs. Both of you will get samples to analyze. If the F.B.I. thing goes down the toilet, *both* national labs will be there to analyze the disease. Is this agreed?"

The director of the C.D.C. and the colonel from USAMRIID were agreed.

"Sir." It was the colonel from USAMRIID, speaking to Hertog. "May I make a suggestion? There has to be some kind of on-site biocontainment field hospital. It could be placed on the island. You do not, repeat *do not* want any human cases infected with an unknown biological weapon to be put into any New York City–area hospitals. That is just incredibly risky."

"He's absolutely right," an admiral from the Public Health Service said.

The Army colonel went on: "The Army has TAML units that can be palletized and flown under Black Hawk helicopters—"

"I'm sorry," Hertog said, "I don't know what a TAML is."

"Sure—that's a Theater Army Medical Lab. It's a biocontainment hospital in a box. It's rated Biosafety

Level 3 Plus. You hang it under a helicopter and you
can fly it anywhere."

"Good."

"One little item," Frank Masaccio broke in. "Dr.
Alice Austen here opened the Cobra case. We would
call her the case agent. I want her sworn in as a deputy
U.S. marshal, with full law-enforcement powers.
Somebody from Justice get her sworn, okay?"

"Thank you, everyone. The first Cobra meeting
is closed," Wyzinski said.

People stood up; the technicians ran around un-
doing the shirt mikes and moving the video cameras;
and the screens on the walls went dead, one by one.

Part Five

REACHDEEP

Quantico

Immediately after the Sioc meeting, Austen and Hopkins took a Bureau car to the F.B.I. Academy in Quantico, Virginia, an hour's drive south of Washington. Mark Littleberry called his wife in Boston, and then set out by himself in another Bureau car to Bethesda, Maryland, to the National Naval Medical Research Institute, to pick up some extra biosensor equipment at the laboratories of the Navy's Biological Defense Research Program, which had been supplying Felixes and Boinks to the F.B.I.

Hopkins talked on his cell phone most of the way down to Quantico. He was "wickering together a team," as he put it. He and Austen barely had a word to say to each other. At one point, he looked over and saw that she was asleep. Her hair had fallen off her face, a face that seemed delicate and tired to him, and he noticed faint circles under her closed eyes.

Quantico is a Marine Corps base, and the F.B.I. has an area inside the base. Hopkins turned off Interstate 95 and followed a road westward through rolling woods. He drove through an F.B.I. checkpoint and parked in front of a group of pale-brick buildings that were joined by glassed walkways. It was the F.B.I. Academy, where the Bureau trains new agents and maintains a number of its units, including Hopkins's own group, the Hazardous Materials Response Unit.

"We're here, Dr. Austen," he said. His voice woke her up.

□

Austen was given a guest room in the F.B.I. Academy, where she changed into operations clothing—cargo pants and a blue shirt—and she ended up with Hopkins at a large gray building known as the Engineering Research Facility, or E.R.F. This building is the F.B.I.'s supersecret electronic-equipment facility. It is a complex of smooth, featureless blocks with smoked windows that reveal nothing of the building's interior. The roof is a forest of radio antennas of all shapes and sizes.

In the lobby of the E.R.F., Hopkins collected a plastic badge for Austen. She entered her Social Security number into a keypad, and a computer system indicated that she had a national security clearance—Frank Masaccio had taken care of that.

She followed Hopkins into a corridor that extended through the center of the building. The corridor was two stories tall, and lined with windows. The windows were covered with black blinds, so that people walking in the corridor could not see what was going on inside the adjacent rooms. "A lot of these rooms are machine shops," Hopkins remarked as they walked along. "We can make anything here. We can put a video camera in an ice-cream cone and take a picture of a mobster's tonsils—just kidding."

They came to a turnstile and a security door controlled by a computer. They both had to swipe their badges in the turnstile.

"The E.R.F. is divided into security pods," Hopkins explained. "The Hazardous Materials Response

Unit is scattered through two pods. We are podless. We're kind of new. We're still looking for a pod to call our own."

They entered a vast indoor chamber, five stories high, called Pod D. The chamber was illuminated with bright lights on the ceiling, and the interior walls were shiny with aluminum foil and copper mesh. The floor of Pod D was crowded with piles of equipment in boxes.

"Is this Reachdeep?" Austen asked. "It's huge."

"Oh, no. Most of this is other F.B.I. stuff. We just have a little corner of Pod D."

"What is this place?" Austen asked.

"It's the radio-silence chamber. The Bureau does electronic work in here."

Austen didn't ask him what kind of electronic work he meant. She had a feeling she wouldn't get a full answer.

Hopkins led her through a warren of makeshift corridors that zigzagged through stacks of boxes and metal storage shelves. They passed an old broken-down pickup truck. The dashboard was open. It was full of communications gear, with data cables hanging out. The truck was a surveillance vehicle.

They emerged into a warren in the middle of an area walled off by boxes where people were working furiously.

"Will! Hey, Will's here!" A man came over to greet them. He was about fifty years old, very fit, with a seamed face and huge shoulders. He was Special Agent Oscar Wirtz, the Tactical Operations officer for Reachdeep—the weapons-and-space-suits man. He was also a logistics specialist. Oscar Wirtz

knew how to pack aircraft with gear quickly. This
turns out to be a valuable skill in the F.B.I. He was
wearing a large black gun in a shoulder holster. He
shook Austen's hand with a grip that was not merci-
ful. "Welcome to Reachdeep," Wirtz said to her.

Austen met the other team members. They were
people whom Hopkins had selected for the operation. Most of the selecting had happened over the
telephone, while she had been asleep in the car and
Hopkins had been driving.

The team's imaging specialist and microbiologist was a pleasant woman in her late twenties named
Suzanne Tanaka. She was not an F.B.I. agent; she
was a civilian laboratory technician. Until recently
she had been working for the United States Navy.

"Suzanne was bugging us to hire her," Hopkins
explained, "so we finally stole her away from the
Navy."

"Should I bring the mice, Will?" she asked.

"Sure, bring a few. Not too many," he said.

Tanaka busied herself with some plastic boxes
holding laboratory mice.

Austen said to her, "Do you know how to work
an electron microscope? Because we need to look at
tissue samples right away."

"Sure," she said. "That's my specialty."

"Suzanne, have we worked out where we're
going to get an electron microscope?" Hopkins said.

"The Army's sending us one in a truck. They're
also sending someone to show me its quirks."

"Good," Hopkins said. "Those scopes all have
quirks."

Hopkins looked at his watch. "Where's Jimmy Lesdiu? Our materials genius."

"Right here."

An extremely tall man stood up from behind a tower of boxes. Special Agent James Lesdiu was a forensic materials analyst. He analyzed hair and fibers, and surfaces and chemicals. He would be coordinating with the F.B.I.'s forensic group in Washington by videoconference during the operation.

"I don't know if I can load this man on a helicopter—he's too tall," Oscar Wirtz said. Lesdiu was six feet eight inches tall.

"You'd better load me, Wirtzy, because Will can't make this case without me," Lesdiu replied.

"Here's what I want, Jimmy," Hopkins said to Lesdiu. "I want an infrared laser unit. A little weenie one, desktop size."

"Got it already," Lesdiu said. He pointed a long, skeletal finger at a gray military transport box.

"Mass-spec machine," Hopkins went on. "For identifying materials."

"Got that, too. It's a little one. What else?"

"I want an X-ray diffraction machine. Small. Portable."

"Got it. I've got everything you need."

In a corner of the staging area, a half-dozen men and women, special agents, were sorting their biohazard space suits and body armor. The space suits were jet black, apparently for use in night operations. They were also making inventory of ten-millimeter handguns, pump-action .00 shotguns, and Heckler & Koch ten-millimeter MP5 assault rifles, along with ammu-

nition, lights, and special breathing equipment. Oscar
Wirtz called them up and introduced Austen to them.
They were all with the F.B.I.'s Hostage Rescue Team,
or H.R.T., which is stationed at Quantico. "They're
going to handle the operations side of this mission,"
Wirtz said, "if we have an operation."

They were known in the F.B.I. as ninjas.

"We take turns looking after Will," said a ninja
by the name of Carlos Pedernal.

"That's because Will's a scientist. He can't look
after himself," Oscar Wirtz said.

"You know, we don't need any ninjas," Will
said, stepping around the weapons and looking at
them. "If I need you guys, I'll call for you."

"Get real, Will," Wirtz said. "Look, you want to
lean the operations squad forward. Lean 'em way
forward. You want to bring them to the island now,
Will. If there's an action, it could develop fast."

Wirtz turned to Austen. "The idea, in case Will
hasn't explained it to you, is that you scientists are
the evidence gatherers. If a terrorist weapon goes off,
you have to go into a hot zone to gather evidence fast.
You may need to have ninjas around you to keep you
out of harm's way."

Austen felt like saying that she could take care
of herself, but she didn't say anything.

Then Mark Littleberry entered Pod D, accompanied by two F.B.I. agents. They were carrying a
total of five Halliburton suitcases. He'd picked up
two Felix machines and three Boinks in Bethesda.

The Reachdeep team worked for an hour or so,
organizing boxes, taking inventory. Oscar Wirtz and

his people began moving equipment out through a door in Pod D to a truck, where the stuff was driven up to the helicopter landing field.

Austen took Littleberry aside. She said, "Dr. Littleberry, could we speak privately? Why do we have to have all the weapons?"

"That's a good question. Hey, Will—come over here for a second. Do we need these armed people? I'm askin' you, Will."

Hopkins looked thoughtful. "Let's hope we don't need them."

Littleberry said, "If we go into shooters in New York, I'm off the team. I don't do shooters. Dr. Austen joins me in this position, I believe."

Hopkins was exasperated. He was wearing a gun himself. "Look, Mark, I'm running this team. We're going to do this by the book."

"By the book, Will?" Littleberry said. "There isn't any book."

A man came in, looking surprised at the gear. He was a U.S. marshal from the Department of Justice. "Where is Dr. Austen? I've been sent to deputize her."

"I don't really want to be a marshal," she said.

"The government requires it," he said.

"I can't use a gun."

"You're not *allowed* to use a gun," Hopkins said. "You aren't weapons-qualified."

The man from Justice swore in both Austen and Littleberry as deputy U.S. marshals.

"Good for you," Suzanne Tanaka said to Austen. "I wish they'd do it for me."

The Hot Core

The helicopters churned north, strung out in a line, traveling at a steady 110 knots. The operations squad followed in helicopters behind the science squad.

"I like Hueys. They're slow as hell but they get you there," Oscar Wirtz remarked to a pilot.

"We should have taken the Black Hawks," the pilot said.

Hopkins kept a Felix black box on his knees during the whole flight. For most of the time he worked on it, checking it out, fiddling with his Leatherman tool. He started the Felix and restarted it, testing it. Then he opened the second Felix and checked it out, too. He tested and retested the Boinks.

Littleberry had been sitting near Hopkins in the Huey, almost silent during the flight. "I'm kind of squirrelly over this, Will," he said.

The helicopters came up New York Bay over the Verrazano Bridge late in the afternoon. Early that morning, when Austen had left in the F.B.I. plane, the city had been wrapped in clouds. The clouds had turned into fluffy cotton with soft gray undersides, the changeable clouds of spring, and they threw spots of shadow on the buildings below.

"These big operations," Hopkins said, "there's nothing like it on earth. The feeling is indescribable."

Austen had become frankly terrified. She had never been in an air operation, had never seen so many weapons, and she was amazed at how quickly the F.B.I. had put things together. But she had a sense that whenever a government throws its people fast into an unfolding emergency, nobody is in control. Only history is in control, and the story never goes as planned.

As the Reachdeep Hueys approached Governors Island, which sat in the East River not far from Brooklyn, the team members saw that other parts of the federal government had already arrived. There was a landing zone in the middle of the island that had once been baseball fields. Two Army Black Hawk helicopters had landed, and a third Army Black Hawk was standing off to allow the Reachdeep helicopters to land first. The Black Hawks had pallets slung under them. They contained hospital gear for a theater medical lab. One by one, the Reachdeep Hueys touched down in the field.

Governors Island is a mile long. It is dotted with abandoned buildings from several historical periods. There are two forts dating from the War of 1812, and there are other buildings put up as recently as the 1970s. Before the American Revolution, Governors Island was where the British colonial governors of New York lived. They chose to live on the island because it put a distance of water between them and the noise and turmoil of the town. Recently the island was owned and operated by the U.S. Coast Guard, but the Coast Guard had moved its operations, leaving the place mothballed.

There were a number of large, graceful brick dormitories on the island. They were trimmed with white paint and had slate roofs, and the largest building had a cupola. The eastern side of the island was separated from Brooklyn by Buttermilk Channel. Three piers stuck out of the island into the channel. A couple of Coast Guard launches were tied up at the piers. Governors Island was so close to lower Manhattan that the towers of Wall Street seemed to loom over it.

The team got their gear out into the field, ducking under the helicopter blades and dragging their boxes.

Frank Masaccio was waiting with a group of his senior investigators. He greeted the team, shaking their hands, welcoming them. "Isn't this a great place?" he said. He put his hands in the pockets of a black trench coat. "Now it's yours. Don't let the New York office down. I'll be there for you."

Seagulls were wheeling overhead in the clear light, and a sea breeze rippled across the island. The smell of salt water came off the bay.

Walter Mellis was with Masaccio. He had caught a flight from Atlanta after the Sioc meeting. Mellis was looking scared. He shook Alice's hand. "Finally I get to congratulate you in person."

"I wish you had told me."

"You didn't have clearance."

"You put me in the F.B.I."

"You're still C.D.C. We're sending up an epidemic task force." This was a team of epidemiologists who would monitor the city for any further cases of Cobra, and who would follow up on people who had had contact with potential Cobra cases, so that any spread of the disease in the city would, it was hoped, be kept under control. "Our labs are ready to do the backup work," Mellis said to her. "I'll be flying samples down."

The F.B.I. helicopters had been offloaded. Two stayed on the island to help ferry people in and out of the city, while the third helicopter returned to Quantico.

On the water's edge at the western side of the island, facing lower Manhattan and the Statue of Liberty, there was an old brick hospital. It was the old Coast Guard base hospital. There was already activity going on there—Army soldiers and officers in green fatigues were hurrying up and down the front steps, carrying equipment and supplies. The idea was to bring the place up to standard as a biocontainment Army field hospital.

An Army colonel in fatigues was standing on the steps. "You must be Dr. Austen. I'm Dr. Ernesto Aguilar. I'm chief of the TAML unit," he said.

"How's the hospital, sir?" she asked him.

"It's got rooms, and that's all we need," he said. "In a few hours, this will be a real hospital."

The hospital was simple and spare, with a pervasive smell of linoleum. Mark Littleberry began prowling around, opening doors. He and Hopkins explored the entire building from top to bottom, getting a sense of how the rooms were structured, where the windows were located, and where the air would flow. Littleberry, the team biohazard officer, found a group of rooms near the back side of the building that he liked—a warren of interconnecting chambers. This area was going to be the Reachdeep lab, the biocontainment core. The rooms were empty, except for a few wooden tables and some metal chairs. There was a large conference area adjacent to the rooms. It looked out through a line of windows across the bay to lower Manhattan and the Statue of Liberty. Outside the conference room there was an observation deck with a metal railing around it. A large investigation requires regular team meetings: this is standard practice. At least once a day all managers of an investigative group meet and share the evidence, trade ideas, and discuss leads that need to be run out.

"This is a good setup, Will," Littleberry said.

"It beats Iraq," Hopkins said.

The electronics specialist Austen had met on her way to Sioc, Special Agent Caroline Landau, flew over in a helicopter, bringing with her various types of communication gear. It was combined with the gear that Oscar Wirtz had brought from Quantico. The agents set up a row of satellite dishes on the deck outside the conference room. Inside, Landau put up video monitors, racks of encrypted cellular telephones, and Saber radios. People in conference could make instant visual contact with the Command Center of the New York office or the F.B.I. headquarters in Washington. The gear also included high-speed satellite connections to the Internet and the World Wide Web.

□

Mark Littleberry planned the layout of the biocontainment core, working with Hopkins. Biocontainment of infective evidence was the goal, so that the evidence could be studied safely in a Biosafety Level 3 zone. They called it the Evidence Core.

The Evidence Core was hot. It consisted of three connected rooms. The first room was the materials room, for holding and analyzing the basic physical evidence. There would be a variety of machines in this room. The second room was the biology room, for growing cultures in flasks and for preparing and looking at samples of tissue in regular optical microscopes. The third room, the imaging room, was for the electron microscope and equipment associated with it.

There was a glass window looking from the Core into the conference room. The Core rooms were accessible through a vestibule safety room. This room served as a decontamination chamber, where the team members would put on and take off their protective biohazard gear. They would use bleach in hand-pump sprayers to decontaminate their protective suits. The suits were disposable F.B.I. field biohazard suits.

A Coast Guard ferryboat arrived and docked at the pier on the north end of the island. The boat carried an unmarked white truck. The truck contained the Army's portable electron microscope. The truck was backed up to a loading bay in the hospital, and Army technicians carried the microscope in sections into the imaging room in the Core, and set it up, while Suzanne Tanaka received instructions from them and helped with the work.

The electron microscope was a massive instrument, six feet tall. It used a beam of electrons to make highly magnified images. It was going to be a crucially important tool for making magnified pictures of biological samples. The samples in this microscope would be hot. Since the team needed to have real-time instant access to images, the microscope had to be placed in the biocontainment core.

The team's living quarters were situated in an empty Coast Guard dormitory next door to the hospital, in one of the brick buildings. It was surrounded by elm trees and plane trees. Like the hospital, it looked out on New York Bay toward the Statue of Liberty and lower Manhattan. The team members each had his or her own room. The rooms contained a metal bed with Coast Guard blankets and sheets, and that was all.

"We're going to run this forensic investigation around the clock," Hopkins said to the team. "When you need to sleep, let people know where you are, and try to keep a sleep session to four hours or less."

"Aye, aye, Captain Ahab," Jimmy Lesdiu said.

The operations squad of Reachdeep—Oscar Wirtz's ninjas—had set themselves and their equipment up, and for the moment they had nothing to do. So they cleaned their weapons and checked and double-checked their gear. They hated this kind of waiting. Some of the younger members of the Reachdeep operations squad complained about it to Wirtz. He told them to relax. He pointed out that successful hunters spend most of their time holding themselves still.

The Evidence Core would be kept at Biosafety Level 3 Plus, under negative air pressure. This was so that infective particles would not leak out of the rooms through cracks. Mark Littleberry figured out how to do it. He and Hopkins pounded a hole in one of the exterior walls of the Core, taking turns with a sledgehammer. Then they attached a flexible plastic air duct to the hole, taping all the cracks with sticky duct tape. They ran the duct into a portable HEPA filter unit supplied by the Army. It was essentially a vacuum cleaner attached to the Core. It sucked contaminated air out of the Core and filtered it before discharging the air out a window through a second plastic duct. This system kept the Core in a state of negative air pressure, which is standard for Level 3 Plus. Any dangerous particles in the air would not leak out of the Core, but would flow inward and toward the vacuum cleaner, where they would be trapped in the HEPA filters.

Hopkins threw a switch on the filter machine and it hummed quietly. They finished setting up the air-handling system and had turned it on by nine o'clock in the evening, four hours after the helicopters had touched down on Governors Island.

"We've got negative pressure in the Core now," Hopkins explained to the others. "If I must say so myself, this is a gadgetized hot zone."

"Every time I hear you say that word *gadget,* Hopkins," Littleberry said, "I know we're in trouble."

The Reachdeep team gathered in the conference room. Hopkins spoke to them. "You could think of this lab as a spaceship," he said. "We're going to lose touch with the world for a little while, with our families and friends. We are going on a voyage to explore a crime."

"And to go where no man knows what he is doing," Suzanne Tanaka said.

"One question, Will," James Lesdiu said. "Is this really going to work?"

"I have no idea," Hopkins said.

"Is it really safe, is what I'd like to know," Walter Mellis said. He was waiting for samples that he could fly back to Atlanta.

"It's as safe as we can make it," Mark Little-berry said.

Elsewhere in New York City it was a calm spring evening. In the cafés in Greenwich Village, people were gathering at the outdoor tables, drinking and eating. There had been nothing in the news-papers, as yet, about F.B.I. teams landing on Gover-nors Island. The news media had not noticed the increased activity. The Coast Guard had used the island for years as a staging place for rescue opera-tions, and the neighborhoods in Brooklyn closest to the island were accustomed to helicopters coming and going. People did not focus on the fact that the Coast Guard was no longer there, and that the heli-copters were from the F.B.I. and the U.S. Army.

□

Hopkins pondered the question of where to put the Felix gene scanners. They did not need to be operated inside the Core. The Felix system had been devel-oped at Lawrence Livermore National Laboratory, in California, as a system for use by military forces in identifying unknown biological agents. Biological samples for reading in the gene scanners could be sterilized with chemicals before being brought out of the Core. Certain chemicals would kill a virus with-out disrupting the virus's genetic material. You could put a sterile virus sample into Felix and it would ana-lyze the DNA successfully, even when the organism was dead.

Hopkins found some tables and began setting up the Felixes in the conference room. He placed a few chairs around the tables, and he ran data cables from the Felixes over to the communication center.

In that way, Hopkins joined Felix to the World Wide Web.

At seven o'clock in the evening, a Coast Guard ferryboat had arrived at the island bearing a refrigerated morgue truck, courtesy of the City of New York. With the truck came Dr. Lex Nathanson. For any autopsies that fell under the jurisdiction of the chief medical examiner—and any deaths in New York City related to Cobra were of that type—Nathanson would be present at the autopsy and would sign the death certificate and seal the evidence.

The morgue truck contained the bodies of Peter Talides, Glenn Dudley, and Ben Kly, sealed in triple body pouches. Nathanson rode in the front of the truck with an F.B.I. evidence specialist who was carrying a large NATO biohazard tube containing the two cobra boxes. They also brought a red plastic biohazard drum containing Harmonica Man's clothes and harmonicas.

Frank Masaccio's people had taken control of Kate Moran's bedroom, the art classroom at the Mater School, Peter Talides's house, and Penny Zecker's shop on Staten Island. The agents were evidence specialists. They were not trained in biohazard work, but they wore respirator masks and coveralls and hoped for the best. It would take them days to sift these locations for further evidence. It was standard operating procedure for a criminal investigation. It had to be done.

□

"I think we're ready to go hot," Hopkins said.

Outside the windows of the meeting room came the continual flutter of helicopters bringing in Army hospital equipment, and the Reachdeep team could hear the voices of Army doctors and medical staff moving through the halls of the hospital, setting up rooms for patients as yet unknown.

The team members put on surgical scrub suits and filed into the staging room for the Core. They opened some fiberglass boxes and pulled out black F.B.I. biohazard suits made of Tyvek. They put on rubber boots, and drew on double surgical gloves. The staging room was crowded with team members bumping into one another.

"This is not my idea of fun," James Lesdiu said, shaking out an extra-large black suit and stepping into it.

Hopkins slung a nylon belt around his suit and hung his Leatherman pocket tool on that. They put on soft, flexible breathing helmets known as Racal hoods, transparent plastic head-bubbles with a filtered air supply. A battery-powered blower, worn at the waist, drives filtered air into the helmet, keeping it under postive pressure, so that infective bioparticles in the air will not sneak in. The batteries for the blowers last eight hours and supply a large volume of filtered air, enough for a person exerting himself heavily. Unlike the Racal hood, the space suit itself is not pressurized. It is a neutral-pressure whole-body suit. The lungs and the eyes are the most vulnerable membranes exposed to the air, so they require the superior protection of a pressurized helmet.

Hopkins fitted a Racal hood over his head, showing the others how to do it. The hood had a kind of double flap that went down over the chest and shoulders. He zipped his suit up over the shoulder flaps of the hood, closing it at the neck. "We should be able to do a complete suiting procedure in four minutes or less," he said. "It's going to be important for us to move in and out of the Core quickly." He turned to Austen. "This is a lot easier and simpler than those dinosaur Level 4 space suits you guys have at C.D.C."

"The dinosaurs work," Austen said.

"Reachdeep is a small, furry mammal," he said. "Go light, move fast, and have sharp teeth."

"And get stepped on, Hopkins?" she said.

Littleberry pushed open the door, and the team members went into the Core, deploying for their tasks.

Hopkins placed the NATO canister on a table. He opened it. He removed a plastic cylinder and opened that. He removed some paper-towel wadding, and then pulled out the two cobra boxes. They looked exactly alike. The only visible difference between them was the different paper labels glued to their bases. Once the boxes were out in the air, the Core had officially gone hot.

He put the boxes on the table and wrote the word COBRA on a couple of evidence tags. Then he dated the tags and wrote down the laboratory control number of the Reachdeep lab (every evidence lab is assigned a number in the F.B.I.). The sample numbers were 1 and 2.

"I've been thinking about something, Will," Littleberry said. "Whoever made those boxes used a lab setup much like this one. Somewhere in this city there's another lab, another Core. And it's running hot, like this one."

"I like your concept, Commander Littleberry," Hopkins said. "It's an Anti-Core. The Anti-Core is out there. And these little things"—he indicated the cobra boxes—"are going to lead us to it."

By putting the elements of the forensic investigation together in one place, in a forward field deployment, with living quarters nearby, with an operations group ready, Will Hopkins believed—hoped—that the investigation could be speeded up and run to a quick conclusion. The idea was to compress a universal forensic operation into a continuous, silent, catlike movement at high speed, culminating in an accelerative explosive rush. The quarry should not know where the hunter was moving. The quarry should not even know that there was a hunter.

Insectary

Archimedes lived in a two-bedroom apartment on the third floor. He kept the shades drawn at all times. The shades were lined with metal foil, to block the sunlight and also to keep snooping eyes from looking into his laboratory with heat-sensing cameras. There were times when he thought he was being watched. At other times he thought he must be paranoid.

He had to keep the apartment dark. He could not allow direct sunlight to enter the laboratory, because sunlight might destroy his virus cultures. He was eating lunch now, in the kitchen. His lunch was a frozen vegetarian burrito, with a tortilla that was free of animal fats. He did not eat meat. He was a parasite on the plant kingdom, but we all have to eat. The problem is that too many humans have to eat. He stood up and opened a door that led to a hallway. The hallway was his Biosafety Level 2 staging area.

In the staging area, he kept a plastic tub full of water and laundry bleach. That was for washing—deconning—objects that were contaminated. There were also some cardboard boxes holding biosafety equipment that he had ordered through the mail from an 800 number. He had his equipment sent to a mail service in New Jersey. Then he drove out and picked up the things in his car.

He pulled a clean Tyvek suit out of a box and put it on. Tyvek was not a natural fiber, but it was necessary to wear around the brainpox virus or you would get infected pretty quickly. He had been around brainpox for a long time and had never become infected. He was careful. He had also come to believe that he might very well be one of the people who, for some reason, were less susceptible to infection by brainpox. He put on double latex rubber gloves, a head covering, surgical booties, and a full-face respirator mask. Then he opened the door to Level 3.

He entered the bedroom and shut the door behind him.

His weapons lab was a comfortable working environment. There were some old Formica tables he had bought at a flea market. It was the flea market where he had traded the box to the woman who had tried to cheat him. He had enlisted her in the human experimental trials. Afterward, he had scanned the newspapers and watched the television news, but nothing about her was mentioned. Also in his lab there was a bioreactor, which was humming away softly, and the virus-drying trays, and the insectary.

The laboratory was situated in the back of his building. He had installed an air-filter system, a quiet little fan, set in a window. It had a HEPA filter. It pulled air out of the Level 3 laboratory, passed it through filters, and discharged it outdoors, clean and safe. This created negative air pressure inside his lab, so that no infective particles would escape. Air was drawn into the lab through a little vent in another window. He had sealed the windows with tape. Nothing fancy, but it worked.

The insectary, which sat on a table, was a colony of moths. He kept the colony for philosophic reasons; he didn't really need it to carry out his work. But it was fun. The insectary was a collection of clear plastic boxes where his moths lived. He pulled open the lid of a box and inspected the green caterpillars inside. He dropped in some pieces of lettuce. They ate vegetables. He had planted a few alfalfa plants in the garden next to his building for them to eat; no one even seemed to notice.

The natural strain of his brainpox virus lived in moths and butterflies. The moth caterpillars crawled around in the boxes eating leaves. They ate until they died. They became paralyzed with the insect strain of his brainpox virus—not the human strain; human brainpox wouldn't grow in insects. The moth caterpillars became listless, but they kept eating. Then, suddenly, the *melt* occurred. It was a technical term for a virus-triggered meltdown of a creature. It happened in an explosive final wave of virus replication, and in less than two hours the caterpillar was transformed into mostly virus. He understood that pretty much the same type of virus amplification melted the human brain.

He reached inside the insectary and pulled a dead caterpillar off a leaf. The dead caterpillar had turned into a liquid bag full of glassy, milky ooze. It was 40 percent pure virus crystals by dry weight. It was almost half virus. He squeezed the dead caterpillar and the crystalline ooze popped out of it. This melt was a fascinating thing to see. The transformational power of a virus never failed to impress him, even when it worked inside caterpillars.

It was interesting to see how the virus could turn an insect into a bag of virus crystals. The virus could take over its host and keep the host alive—still hungry, still feeding—even while it converted the host's body almost entirely to virus crystals. The virus also stopped the molting process of the insect, so that it never became an adult. It stayed young and ate and ate until it was nothing but crystals. The human strain of the virus could transform the human brain into a bag of virus crystals and make the human eat and eat and eat.

The human species is hungrier than a hungry insect. With its monstrous, out-of-control appetite, it is ruining the earth, he said to himself. When a species overruns its natural habitat, it devours its available resources. It becomes weakened, vulnerable to infectious outbreaks. A sudden emergence of a deadly pathogen, an infectious killer, reduces the species back to a sustainable level. These mass dyings happen all the time in nature. For example, gypsy moth caterpillars sometimes overrun forests in the northeastern part of the United States; they eat the leaves off the trees. Eventually the population of caterpillars becomes so large that the caterpillars use up their food supply, and then all kinds of viruses break out among the caterpillars. Sooner or later some virus crashes the population of gypsy moths, and for years afterward the trees are relatively free of caterpillars. Viruses play an important role in nature: they keep populations in check.

Now consider man, he thought.

Look at the AIDS virus. People go on talking about the depletion of the population because of

AIDS, saying what a disaster it is, yet in the next breath they talk about how the environment is being damaged by overpopulation. The fact is that AIDS is an example of the kind of disease corrective that always appears when a population booms out of control. It is necessary. The real problem is that AIDS has not done its work well enough. And what's worse, public health doctors are trying to develop a vaccine for it.

There is no more dangerous human being than a public health doctor, he thought. Public health doctors are largely responsible for the uncontrolled boom in the human population that is destroying the earth. The public health doctors are environmental criminals of the highest degree. Even now they are trying to cause an extinction of a natural species, the extinction of the smallpox virus. Smallpox is a beautiful white tiger, and it has a place in nature. Who are we to presume to destroy a white tiger? The Sierra Club and Friends of the Earth should defend smallpox!

Natural thinning events are positive. History shows what I mean, he liked to point out in his mind. In the year 1348 or thereabouts, the Black Death, an infective airborne bacterial organism called *Yersinia pestis,* wiped out at least a third of the population of Europe. It was a very good thing for Europe. The survivors prospered. They inherited more land and more property. A great economic boom followed the Black Death, and it culminated in the Renaissance. In the wake of the mass dying, the survivors were richer and had more to eat. There were fewer poor people crowded into the towns, because so many of the poor had died. With the numbers of poor reduced, a labor

shortage developed in the towns during the years following the Black Death. New machines and new
manufacturing processes were invented to make up
for the loss of unskilled laborers. This led to increasingly free capital flow. It led to the creation of the
first true investment banks, in Florence and in other
cities, and great wealth was created, great art, new
ideas. One could say that the ceiling of the Sistine
Chapel came out of the Black Death.

Historians describe the Black Death as something that just "occurred" at the end of the Middle
Ages. They don't make the connection: the Black
Death did not just "occur"; it was the biological event
that *ended* the Middle Ages. And the world is overdue
for another biological event. If it doesn't happen
soon, how many species will disappear, how many
beautiful tracts of primeval rain forest will vanish forever? If the public health doctors keep up their work,
they will practically destroy the world.

Hence the need for a new disease.

Brainpox was beautiful. It was a biological
rocket that destroyed the central nervous system.
Driven by its rocketing proteins, brainpox raced along
nerve fibers in the skull. Brainpox transformed the
brain into a virus bioreactor. The brain went hot.
Brainpox melted the brain in the same way that the
natural form of the virus melted insects.

The brain bioreactor went hot, and it filled up
with virus particles until it melted down inside the
skull. The reactor began leaking fluids and biting and
thrashing and hemorrhaging and generally running
out of control, spreading the virus around to other
hosts in a messy but effective way. Of course brain-

pox caused human suffering, but it was over soon. None of this lingering, as with AIDS, no time for public health doctors to find a cure. Brainpox wouldn't harm any other life forms on the planet, because brainpox infects only the human species. It wouldn't effect the ecosystems and habitats of the rain forest.

He imagined brainpox turning New York City into a hot bioreactor, a simmering cauldron of amplifying virus. From there brainpox would amplify itself outward along invisible lines, following airline routes, spanning the globe. New York was the seed bioreactor, the cooker that would start the other cities going. This was not exactly the revenge of the rain forest; this was the revenge of molecular biology. From New York, brainpox would rocket to London and Tokyo, and it would fly to Lagos, Nigeria, and it would land in Shanghai and Singapore, and it would amplify through Calcutta, and it would get to São Paulo and Mexico City and Dacca in Bangladesh and Djakarta in Indonesia and all the great supercities of the earth. The cities would go hot, for a while. But it would not be the end of the human species, not in the least. It would merely remove one out of every two persons; or perhaps one out of three persons might vanish. Maybe even less. He didn't know exactly. A biological weapon never exterminates a population. It merely *thins*. The greater the thinning, the healthier the effect on the species that has been thinned.

He checked on the bioreactor. It was a microreactor called a Biozan. It was running smoothly, the pumps humming gently, making about as much noise as a fishtank. It was making concentrated brainpox virus. The output liquid, saturated with virus parti-

cles, ran through a flexible tube to a jar on the floor.
As the liquid settled, a white sludge would form on
the bottom of the jar. That sludge was mostly virus.
He would pour off the liquid from the jar, and the
sludge that remained was incredibly concentrated
brainpox. He scraped it out with a spoon. It was unbelievable how one little bioreactor could make so
much virus.

Near the bioreactor stood the drying trays. He
mixed the virus sludge with a special kind of glass
in liquid form. It was rather like making candy. He
poured the molten glass into the trays. It dried and
hardened into coin-sized hexagons of viral glass.

He bought the viral glass mix through the mail.
It was great stuff. A little pricey, but it seemed to
work.

With his double-gloved fingertips, he gently
picked up a glass hexagon. He enjoyed holding viral
glass in his fingers. He could see the rainbow colors
of his virus—

His thoughtful reverie was interrupted by a
squeaking sound, a dry, metallic squeal. He heard
voices and then a crash.

He put the crystal back in the tray. Those kids
were being disruptive again.

He pulled back the metal curtain an inch and
looked down. His laboratory overlooked an empty
lot that was surrounded by a chain-link fence. People
in the neighborhood had planted a garden there, with
flowers and shrubs (and a little bit of alfalfa, which
he had planted). They had put in an old swing set and
a children's slide and a small rotating merry-go-
round. It was made of metal. The large boys were

standing on the merry-go-round, pushing it, shouting. They were making it go too fast, and it was squealing again. They were ten or twelve years old, rough-looking city kids. One of them hurled a rock into the fence. Then the rest of them jumped off and went running, throwing rocks.

At a cat!

It was a brown and white stray cat, one of the animals that people left tins of food for in the informal park below his window. The cat leaped up the fence, but a rock crashed into the fence, and the cat went to the ground and shot off, more rocks pounding around it, and it twisted and screeched when a rock hit it. And then it ran through a hole under the fence, and escaped.

It made him angry, but there was nothing he could do, because he was stuck in Level 3.

Samples

GOVERNORS ISLAND

The city morgue truck was backed in behind the Coast Guard hospital, its rear end facing a hospital loading dock. Inside the truck was a bank of refrigerated crypts. There was also a mortuary gurney on wheels—a pan. The bodies of Peter Talides, Glenn Dudley, and Ben Kly were triple-bagged in white body pouches that were plastered with biohazard symbols. The morgue attendants at the O.C.M.E. had splashed large amounts of bleach inside the pouches and around the bodies, to kill the hot agent on the exterior of the bodies.

Lex Nathanson and Austen suited up in a storage room near the loading dock, a room that Littleberry had designated the autopsy decon room. They wore chain-mail gloves on both hands. When they got in the truck, they started with Glenn Dudley.

Without removing Dudley from the biohazard pouches, they lifted him by his shoulders and feet out of a crypt. It was a struggle. He was a heavy, muscular man. They transferred his bagged cadaver to the gurney. Nathanson unzipped the bags but did not remove the body. This was going to be a minimal autopsy in a biohazard shroud. Dudley's blood and fluids would collect inside the shroud, and would not flow anywhere else.

No one had removed Dudley's clothing. He was wearing surgical scrubs. His scalp hung down over his face, exposing the dome of the skull. Dudley had prepared his cranium for opening.

Austen lifted up the scalp, and Dudley's eyes came into view. They had developed gold rings in the irises, with flamelike offshoots. She opened his mouth and looked carefully. She found a half-dozen blood blisters, mainly inside the upper cheeks.

Austen cut his scrubs off with blunt scissors, laying the shirt back, opening the trousers.

"I spoke with Glenn's wife," Nathanson said. "They have three children. The oldest is fifteen. It's the children I think about."

"Do they know what happened?" Austen asked him.

"I believe she has told them something but not all of it."

He did the Y incision on Dudley's chest and abdomen, and opened up his chest. He cut Dudley's ribs with loppers, and removed the sternum plate. He remained ice-calm. Austen watched him with respect. She saw no external sign of emotion.

"Do you want me to take over, Dr. Nathanson?"

"I'm all right."

The two pathologists worked carefully. Nathanson did not remove any of Dudley's organ blocks. He and Austen examined the organs in place in his body cavity, and they took biosamples. Removing the organs and sectioning them would splash around a great deal of blood and fluid, and Nathanson felt that the safety risk did not justify the procedure.

Nathanson wrapped Dudley's head in a clear plastic bag. He plugged in a Stryker saw, then put the saw inside the bag, and tightened the bag with a string around Dudley's throat. The bag would prevent blood and bone dust from flying into the air; it would splash inside the bag. This was standard procedure for opening a biohazardous brain.

The saw chattered away, spewing wet bone dust and bloody material on the inside of the bag until the top of the skull could be removed. Nathanson's mask was now completely misted with sweat. Austen watched him carefully. He appeared to be holding himself under tight but fragile control, but suddenly he said, "Would you take over now, Dr. Austen?"

She nodded. She snipped open the dura mater—the gray leathery membrane that covers the brain.

Dudley's brain resembled that of Kate Moran: glassy, jellylike, swollen, bloated.

"I splashed a drop of blood in his eyes. It was my fault."

"Put that out of your mind forever," Nathanson said.

What she could not put out of her mind was her last sight of Ben Kly alive. Kly had given her a chance to escape, and he had done it knowing it might well cost him his life. He had also accompanied her and protected her in the tunnel under Houston Street. He was a city morgue attendant, one of the anonymous handlers of the dead, yet she saw him as a man of perfect courage. The investigation had turned on his help. He left a wife and a small child.

Austen felt the unworthiness of a survivor. She could hear Dudley's voice saying, "You work around it."

She removed Glenn Dudley's brain, taking great care with the scalpel, cutting the nerves. The brain spread out on the cutting board. It resembled a silvery bag of jelly. The color amazed her. She touched the brain with her fingertips. Protected by the chain-mail gloves, her fingers didn't register the subtleties of the texture, but the brain almost melted under her touch.

With a scalpel, she took small chunks of the underside of the brain and tucked them into biosample jars.

"I'm going to take his eye, Dr. Nathanson," she said.

He nodded.

Using a forceps and scalpel, she lifted Dudley's eyelid and chipped and cut bone around the orbit of his right eye. Eventually she freed up the eyeball and lifted it out of the socket. A bit of optic nerve dangled from it. She put it in the stock jar.

Austen made triple sets of samples. One set was for Walter Mellis to carry back to the Level 4 hot labs at the C.D.C.; one was for USAMRIID, at Fort Detrick; and the third set was for Reachdeep.

□

When they had finished collecting samples and the postautopsy cadavers were back in the crypts in their bags, the two pathologists exited from the morgue truck and went into the autopsy decon room, where they sprayed their suits down with bleach, using hand-pump sprayers. Mark Littleberry supervised the deconning process. They disposed of their suits in biohazard bags. Then Dr. Nathanson returned to the O.C.M.E. by helicopter. The autopsied bodies of Peter Talides and Glenn Dudley would have to remain in the refrigerated truck for the time being. They could not be given burial or cremation. They had become federal evidence. The murder weapon was inside their bodies.

□

Alice Austen carried a box of sample jars containing tissue from the autopsies into the Reachdeep laboratory area. She entered the Level 2 decon vestibule, where she had to suit up again before proceeding inward. She put on a black biohazard suit, marked with the letters F.B.I. She put on lightweight rubber boots and double rubber gloves, and a Racal hood over her head, and then she pushed through a door into the Evidence Core. Hopkins and Lesdiu were bent over the two cobra boxes, which sat on a table under bright lights. Both men wore F.B.I. space suits.

Austen's sample jars contained fresh brain tissue, liver tissue, spinal fluid, vitreous humor from the eye, and blood. She gave the samples to Suzanne Tanaka, who took them into the biology room for culturing, and for examination in the electron microscope. Austen went with her.

Tanaka wanted to try to make the virus grow in flasks of living cells. If she could get it to grow, then it could be studied more easily. Using a simple mortar and pestle, she mashed up a bit of Glenn Dudley's brain and dropped the mush into a series of plastic flasks containing living human cells. The flasks were used for growing viruses in culture. The virus in Dudley's brain tissue might infect the cells in the culture, and the virus would multiply in the cells, until the flask was enriched with virus particles. Then she could put a sample of it in an electron microscope and see the particles. The shape and structure of the particles might help identify the virus.

Nearby, Tanaka had some clear plastic boxes that held white laboratory mice. She made a water preparation of Dudley's brain tissue and injected it into several mice. "This is our mouse biodetector system," she explained to Austen. Mice are used in virus labs somewhat like canaries in a coal mine. When you are trying to identify a virus, you may want to inject it into mice. If the mice get sick, you can observe the signs, and then examine the mice by necropsy (that is, kill the mice, cut them up, and look at the mouse tissue through a microscope). "We'll see if they get sick," Tanaka said.

Next, Tanaka prepared some samples for the electron microscope. She wanted to try to make a direct image of the virus particles in Glenn Dudley's brain. Working with a scalpel, she cut away tiny bits of brain tissue. Her cuts made samples of brain the size of pinheads. She put the samples into small test tubes and filled the tubes up with a fast-drying plastic resin. The resin would penetrate the brain sample and harden it. Then Tanaka could make slices of it.

She also wanted to look at the powder in the cobra boxes. She went into the materials room, where Hopkins and Lesdiu were still examining the boxes, and, with a fine pair of tweezers, she obtained a small amount of dust from the Zecker-Moran box, which she dropped into a tiny plastic sample tube. She poured quick-drying resin into the tube.

All of the samples—brain tissue and dust—became fixed in a hard plastic resin. Now she had some small cylinders of resin. She cut the resin blocks with a diamond-bladed slicing machine known as a microtome. A microtome is somewhat like a deli's meat-slicing machine, except that the blade is a diamond and the slices it makes are the size of the head of a common household ant. While she worked, she explained to Austen what she was doing.

"Investigations like this get me really fired up," she said. "I can hardly sleep when we're on a big case."

"Have you been on big cases before?" Austen asked her.

There was a little pause. "Well," Tanaka said, "not really. I've . . . dreamed about this, Alice. It feels like what I've wanted to do all my life."

Tanaka placed the slices on copper sample screens that were the size of this letter *o*. "Do you want to look with me, Dr. Austen?"

"Yes."

"Let's look at the Cobra dust first," Tanaka said. She dropped a copper-screen sample into a sample holder, a kind of steel rod. She slid the holder into the electron microscope, and it made a clinking sound as it locked into place. She threw some switches, adjusted a dial, and a screen glowed. Tanaka dimmed the lights in the imaging room so that they could see the images on the screen more clearly.

□

In the Materials room, Hopkins performed a delicate operation. With a fine pair of tweezers and a hand-held magnifying glass, he took a nearly invisible pinch of dust out of the Zecker-Moran cobra box. He had a hard time seeing what he was doing—his Racal hood interfered with the view. He dropped the dust into a plastic test tube that contained a few drops of salt water and a disinfectant. The tube was about the size of a circus peanut.

Two rooms down, in the darkened imaging room of the Evidence Core, Tanaka and Austen looked into the screen of the electron microscope. Before their eyes hovered an image of the dust particles in the cobra box. Tanaka spun the dials, and the image moved sideways. She was scanning. "This is weird," she said. The particles were angular crystals. They had slightly rounded sides, rather like angular soccer balls.

"That's not a virus," Austen said. "There's no way it could be a virus. The crystals are way too large to be a virus."

Tanaka found something inside a crystal. She zoomed the image, moving into the field.

"Look, Alice. Look at that."

There were dark rods of material inside the crystals. The rods were scattered about. In places they formed bundles.

Tanaka pointed to a bundle of rods. "Those—I'd bet those are the virus particles themselves. They're surrounded by these crystals. You've got virus particles embedded in crystals."

"What do you think the crystals are made of?" Austen asked.

"I don't know. They appear to be a protective coating around the virus particles—if those little rods inside the crystals are virus, which I think they are."

Tanaka put another sample in the electron microscope. "We're looking inside one of Dr. Dudley's brain cells," she said. She spoke of his cells in a personal way, as if she might be speaking of a hand or an arm. The crystals inside the cells were chunks of material sitting in the cell's nucleus. Some of the crystals were cracking open and seemed to be releasing particles into the cell's cytoplasm, the cell's interior. The particles resembled rods or batons. In places, Tanaka found the rods floating around inside a brain cell without any crystal material near them.

"Dr. Dudley's brain cells are a mess," Tanaka said to Austen in a low voice. "This is as bad as Ebola."

"Have you seen Ebola?" Austen asked.

"Sure. Part of our training. This isn't Ebola."

"Do you think you know what it is?"

"I'm not ready to say, Alice. I *think* I know."

Austen was standing behind her, looking down at the screen. She felt dizzy, as if she were falling into the depths of a microscopic universe that extended inward to infinity.

"I have to be careful here," Tanaka went on. "There is a type of virus that makes crystals like this. It lives in butterflies and moths."

"It lives in butterflies?"

"Yup," Tanaka said.

Tanaka had brought reference textbooks with her. When you are looking at virus particles in a microscope, trying to make a visual identification of the virus, you check the images against photographs in a book, in the same way that a bird-watcher might look up photographs of birds in an Audubon field guide.

Tanaka went over to a military transport box sitting in a corner of the imaging room. She threw the catches, and pulled out a textbook on viruses. She closed the box and sat down on it, and opened the volume on her lap. Austen sat beside her. Tanaka flipped through the table of contents, then turned to a page about halfway into the book. "There," she said, putting her finger on a photograph.

She had come to a section on insect viruses. The photograph showed images of crystals.

"This is nuclear polyhedrosis virus," Tanaka said to Austen. "That's kind of a mouthful. Let's call it N.P.V. You know, like H.I.V.? This is N.P.V. This virus scares the hell out of me."

Austen saw that Tanaka wasn't kidding when she said the virus frightened her. Tanaka's breathing hood had misted up, a sure sign of upset. "The crystals are a kind of protein, I think," Tanaka said, her voice not strong. She said that the virus particles were clumped inside the crystals. "The crystals are like—kind of—protective shells around the virus. They protect the virus from harm. This thing is an engineered weapon, Alice."

Tanaka returned to the microscope and began snapping photographs with an electronic camera that was attached to it. Image by image, huge crystals appeared on a video screen. The two women looked at cells from the golden areas in Dudley's irises. The cells were full of crystals. It was the crystals, forming in the pupillary ring around the iris, that gave the eyes the yellow-gold color. There were crystals in the optic nerve leading to the eye. The virus had either migrated through the eyes into the brain along the optic nerve, or it had spread out of the brain to the eyes.

They were seeing a life-form that Austen had seen earlier through the optical microscope in Glenn Dudley's office, when she had first looked at Kate Moran's brain tissue in a microscope. Then she had seen fuzzy shapes, without much clarity. Here, the clarity was superb, and the crystals loomed like planets.

"We have to tell Will," Tanaka said.

The Code

Will Hopkins, now dressed in surgical scrubs but not a space suit, had set up a work area on a table in the conference room. While Tanaka was attempting to make an image of the virus particles, he would try to "see" the DNA of the virus using his machines. In this way, he hoped to get a rapid identification of the virus.

He hooked up the two Felix machines on the table. He deployed several other small machines as well. He also put out a bagel with cream cheese, which he munched while he worked. Wires and cables trailed everywhere.

Hopkins had a sample of Cobra dust in a small plastic test tube the size of a baby's finger. The dust had been sterilized with chemicals and mixed with a few drops of water. It wasn't dangerous. It contained a quantity of DNA from the virus. He held the tube up to a bright light and swirled it around. Sometimes you could actually see DNA with your naked eye—it formed milky lumps in a test tube. This time, he couldn't see any, but the water in the test tube was nevertheless full of strands of DNA, like a soup made with angel hair pasta. He put a droplet of the water (containing DNA from the virus) directly into a sampling port in one of the Felix machines.

Felix began reading the DNA, but nothing came up on the screen. Felix was having some problems.

Hopkins had to resist a temptation to bang Felix with his hand, the way you'd bang a television that isn't working.

Just then Austen and Tanaka came in. Tanaka's face was radiant, she was beaming, but holding back.

"I'm having trouble getting gene sequences here," Hopkins said to them.

"Take a look at this," Tanaka said. She laid the photographs in front of Hopkins.

"Whoa," he said. He stared at the photographs, chewing bagel.

"These are particles we recovered from Glenn Dudley's brain," Suzanne Tanaka said.

"Midbrain. The part of the brain that controls primitive behavior, such as chewing," Austen added.

"Look at the crystals, Will," Suzanne Tanaka said. "See that blocky shape? This *looks* like the nuclear polyhedrosis virus. N.P.V., which lives in butterflies. It isn't supposed to live in people."

Hopkins stood up slowly, a look of wonder on his face. "It lives in people now," he said. "My God, Suzanne! A butterfly virus. This is great!" He slapped her on the back. "Suzanne, you are the best!"

She looked very pleased. She didn't say anything.

"All right!" Hopkins said. "All right." Now he paced the room. He ran his hands over his face. "All right. What are we gonna do, guys? Are we going to tell Frank Masaccio we've got a *butterfly* virus? He won't believe us. He'll think we've gone lunatic."

In biology, the shape of an organism may not tell you how it fits into the evolutionary tree of life. Many viruses look alike in a photoscope but are very different at the genetic level. "We need some genes," Hopkins said. "We need a gene fingerprint. Felix is gonna *prove* this thing is a butterfly virus. I'm scanning genes already, but I haven't put it together."

He bent over the Felix machine, his hands flying, working like a madman.

Austen found herself watching Hopkins's hands as he worked. His hands were muscular, but they were gentle and precise in their motions. There was no trembling, no hesitation, no spare or useless movement. His hands were in perfect control. These were trained hands, the hands of a gadgeteer. "I'm purging the system. We'll try again."

Using a micropipette, he put another sample of DNA into Felix. Still standing, he tapped the computer keys, and letters of text began to appear.

ttggacaaacaagcacaaatggctatcattatagtcaagtacaaagaattaaaatcgagag
aaaacgcgttcttgtaaatgcctgcacgaggtttaacactttgccgcctttgtacttgaccgt
ttgattggcgggtcccaaattgatggcatctttaggtatgttttttagaggtatc

This was genetic code from somewhere in the DNA of the Cobra virus.

Molecules of DNA resemble a spiral ladder. The rungs of the ladder are known as the nucleotide bases. There are four types of bases, and they are denoted by the letters A, T, C, and G. (The letters stand for adenine, thymine, cytosine, and guanine—nucleic acids.) The length of the DNA in living creatures varies greatly. Human DNA consists of about three billion bases. That's enough information to fill three *Encyclopaedia Britannica*s. All of this information is crammed into every cell in the human body. A small virus, such as the virus for the common cold, has only about 7,000 bases of DNA. Hopkins had made a guess that the Cobra was complicated and would probably contain around 50,000 to 200,000 bases of DNA.

Sometimes as few as a dozen bases of DNA code are enough to provide a unique fingerprint to a particular organism. You can use a computer program to match unknown code with known code. If you can make a match, then you can identify the organism the DNA came from. The process of matching unknown DNA code with known code is like the process of opening an unread book and reading a few lines from it. If the lines are familiar, then you can make a guess as to the book. For example, these words serve to identify a book: *In the beginning God created the heaven and the earth. And the earth was without form, and void.* The exact edition of the book (the "strain" of the book, so to speak) is the King James translation of the Bible in English.

As strings of letters marched across the screen, Hopkins hoped that he would soon have a better idea of what kind of book Cobra was.

```
gcaagcatttgtatttaatcaatcgaaccgtgcactgatataagaattaaaaatgggtttgttt
gcgtgttgcacaaaatacacaaggctgtcgaccgacacaaaaatgaagtttccctatgttg
cgttgtcgtacatcaacgtgacgct
```

The letters drifted in blocks across the screen. "Time to get on the Web," Hopkins announced. He ran Netscape on one of the Felix laptops. His computer then socketed into the World Wide Web via the satellite dish sitting on the patio deck. In a few seconds, he arrived at a Web site known as GenBank. This site—it is in Bethesda, Maryland—has a huge database of genetic sequences. GenBank is the world's central library of genetic codes.

Hopkins clicked a button on the screen. The GenBank computer looked at the code and began matching it to known genetic codes. Soon an answer came back:

Sequences producing High-scoring Segment Pairs:

Autographa californica nuclear polyh . . .   900 4.3e-67 1
Autographa californica nuclear polyh . . .   900 4.9e-67 1
Bombyx mori nuclear polyhedrosis vir . . . 855 2.4e-63 1
Bombyx mori nuclear polyhedrosis vir . . . 855 2.7e-63 1

It was a list of virus DNA codes that had shown close matches with the code that Hopkins had sent. The top line showed the closest match.

"Looks like we've got a rough identification of the Cobra virus," Hopkins said. "That top line, right there, that's the probable strain of the virus. That's the closest match to Cobra." His finger traced over

Autographa californica nuclear polyhedrosis virus

Cobra virus was similar to the nuclear polyhedrosis virus, or N.P.V. (It is also called the baculovirus.) This particular strain lived in a moth. The moth was *Autographa californica*, a small brown and white moth that lives in North America. The caterpillar of the moth is a crop pest, a green inchworm known as the alfalfa looper. The virus invades the moth caterpillar and kills it. Cobra was based on a moth virus, but it had been altered.

N.P.V. is a common virus used in biotechnology labs all over the world. It is available to anyone, and

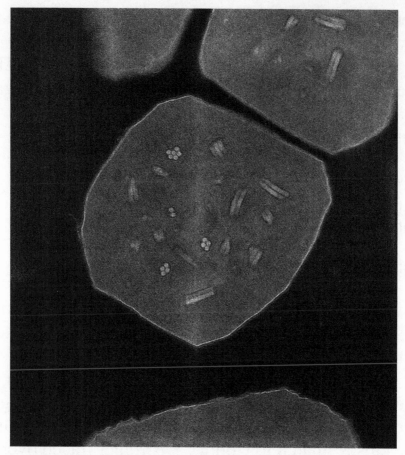

Cross section through a crystal of *Autographa californica* nuclear polyhedrosis virus. Magnification
25,000. *(Electron micrograph courtesy of Dr. Malcolm J. Fraser, Jr., and William Archer, Department
of Biological Sciences, University of Notre Dame.)*

Hopkins's heart sank as he thought about this. The
virus was going to be devilishly hard to trace back to
its original source. It made him wonder if his idea of
a Reachdeep operation was already in trouble.

The crystals that Tanaka had photographed were
actually crystals of protein, with virus particles embedded in them, like seeds in a watermelon. The pro-

tein is called polyhedrin, because it forms rounded crystals that look like soccer balls: polyhedrons.

The genes of N.P.V. can be changed easily without causing harm to the virus. Many viruses are difficult to change. They are too sensitive. If you change their genes, they stop working. But N.P.V. is a rugged, tough, flexible virus. It can be given foreign genes that change its behavior as an infectious agent. Hopkins knew enough about viruses to know this, and it chilled his blood to make the identification. He knew that buried somewhere in the code of the Cobra virus he would find engineered genes. Genes that had been put there, enabling the virus to replicate in human tissue, specifically in the central nervous system.

Cobra was a recombinant virus, or a chimera. In Greek mythology, the chimera was a monster with a lion's head, a goat's body, and a dragon's tail. "The chimera," Hopkins whispered, "was a tough monster to kill."

He put a few more drops of sample liquid into Felix and started Felix on another run, pulling up more DNA code. Austen had finished her autopsies, and for the moment she did not have work to do. She suited up and went back into the Core to see what was going on there. Suzanne Tanaka went back to work with her microscope.

Signatures

In the core, James Lesdiu was running a forensic analysis of the physical materials used in constructing the two boxes. They were bombs. All bombs, as Hopkins had so passionately maintained at the Sioc meeting, contain forensic signatures that can guide an investigator to the builder of the bomb.

Austen found Lesdiu sitting at a table in the center of the materials room, the cobra boxes before him under bright lights. He was holding an old-fashioned magnifying glass in one hand and a pair of tweezers in the other. His hands were enormous. They were covered with double rubber gloves.

"I'm dying inside this suit," he confessed to Austen. He was dressed in an extra-large F.B.I. biohazard suit, and he looked extremely uncomfortable. His Racal hood was beaded with sweat on the inside. He had draped a towel over his shoulder—inside his hood. Now he shifted his shoulder, turned his head, and wiped the sweat off his face using the towel.

Lesdiu probed the tweezers here and there in one of the boxes.

"I'm looking for hair-and-fiber evidence," he explained. Lesdiu plucked at something inside the box. "There's another hair. It's another Q."

Austen had never heard the term *Q*.

Lesdiu explained that he had found some unknown human hairs. "They're questioned hairs," he said. "We call unknown samples Q evidence, or questioned evidence. It's questioned because you don't know what it is or where it comes from." He had placed the hairs on a sheet of brown paper. "Samples are either questioned samples or known samples. The questioned samples are things that are found at the crime scene. Sherlock Holmes called them clues." He smiled. "Qs are physical evidence. We analyze the Q samples, hoping to match them with something known. Forensic science is largely pattern recognition. The Qs are things like fingerprints, hair and fibers, blood, toolmarks, shoe prints, all kinds of trace evidence. DNA is trace evidence. The DNA of the Cobra virus that you've been looking at on the screens, that's a questioned sample, because we don't know where the Cobra virus comes from."

Austen realized that this was very similar to what she had been doing in the beginning, when she had traced the outbreak to the boxes. "You guys are doing a diagnosis of a crime."

"In a way, yeah," Lesdiu said.

The F.B.I. maintains enormous reference collections of known samples of all kinds of objects. These are called reference knowns. "If you can match a fingerprint, you can get a conviction," Lesdiu said. "Because a fingerprint pattern is unique. But forensic evidence is not always so clear. That's why you usually need a lot of it."

Lesdiu put his tweezers down. He was taking a break. "I've got two hairs so far," he said. They come from the Zecker-Moran box. One is a fine, reddish hair, with an oval shaft, Caucasian."

"That sounds like Kate's hair," Austen said.

"It probably is," Lesdiu said. "Frank Masaccio's folks are getting some known hair samples from her bedroom. As soon as they arrive, I can start comparing Qs and Ks. The other hair is oval and transparent. It's a gray hair from a Caucasian."

"Penny Zecker," Austen said.

"Maybe. We'll be getting hair samples from her house too. I also found some wool fibers. Black. Maybe from a sweater—maybe the girl's sweater, maybe not. The other box, the one the homeless guy carried around with him—" Lesdiu indicated the Harmonica Man box, which was sitting beside the Zecker-Moran box. "This one has a ton of fibers all over it and in the cracks. The fibers are cotton and polyester. The box was wrapped up in the guy's clothes. I have to say that anyone who was smart enough to load this box with a virus is smart enough not to leave any hair or fibers on it. This fiber analysis is not going to pan out. My bones are telling me that. But there's more than one way to skin a cat. There's a ton of microscopic evidence in these boxes."

□

Jimmy Lesdiu had set up a row of machines in the materials room. One of them could throw a beam of infrared laser light on an object and then analyze the spectrum of the light bouncing off the object. The machine gave information about what the sample was made of. It could also see invisible fingerprints on a surface. Lesdiu had also set up a machine that could vaporize a sample and identify the atoms in the gas coming out of the sample.

Lesdiu found a number of fingerprints on the boxes. He photographed them in laser light and sent the images by satellite to Washington, where the fingerprints would be analyzed. Later, it would turn out that none of the fingerprints belonged to the Unsub. They belonged to Kate Moran and Penny Zecker. The Unsub had been much too careful to leave fingerprints.

A shiny black enamel had been used to paint the design on the box. With the infrared laser, Lesdiu got a spectrum of colors from the paint. To the human eye, the paint was black, but to the laser it was a rainbow of colors. Lesdiu passed the paint spectrum on to Washington, and within minutes an F.B.I. expert in paint called him back on the telephone. The call came into the hot Core on a speakerphone, since you can't use a telephone handset if you are wearing a Racal hood.

"You folks in Forensics must be standing around waiting for me to call," Lesdiu shouted on the speakerphone to his paint expert.

"We've been told to respond quickly. Frank Masaccio will kill us if we don't." The paint expert went on to say that the paint was a common enamel model paint. It was sold in hobby shops everywhere.

The signature had petered out into a maze of common objects. This was typical of signatures. Still, the paint was a Q that could be tied to a K, if a suspect turned up with enamel model paint.

The cobra boxes had bits of paper glued to them, on which words were written—Archimedes' name and the date. The bits of paper were glued to the box with a clear, flexible glue. With a razor blade, Lesdiu cut away a tiny shred of the glue. "It's kind of a rubbery glue," he said. "I'd say it's a silicone glue or a hot-melt type of glue."

He dropped a bit of the glue from the knife onto a glass slide, ran it through the laser machine, and got some data. "I got a real nice infrared spectrum of this glue. Look at that, isn't that *beautiful*?" he said.

Alice Austen stared at the screen. It was a meaningless jagged line to her. She told Jimmy Lesdiu as much.

"There's information in these peaks and valleys," he said.

"If you looked at a cell, you wouldn't see much in it," she said to him. "I would see a world."

There was a man at F.B.I. headquarters who could see a world in a drop of glue. They called him the Maven of Glue. James Lesdiu sent the spectrum of the glue over an encrypted satellite link to the F.B.I. forensic lab at headquarters in Washington, meanwhile talking on his speakerphone to the scientist known as the Maven of Glue. The Maven put Lesdiu on hold for a few minutes, and then said to him, "Okay, Jimmy, I've checked the spectrum against our library of adhesives. You are not going to be happy, Jimmy."

"I'm listening," Lesdiu said, standing by the speakerphone.

"The spectrum you sent is consistent with a silicone glue made by the Forkin Chemical Company in Torrance, California. It's called Dabber Glue. They sell millions of tubes of this stuff. You can buy it in any hardware store. I really like it. It's a nifty glue. I use it myself at home."

Austen said, "Why doesn't somebody call Forkin Chemical?"

Lesdiu shrugged. "That would probably be useless. They can't trace millions of tubes." Nevertheless, he called Frank Masaccio with the information, and an F.B.I. agent got in touch with the president of Forkin Chemical. The agent and the company president had a very pleasant conversation, and the president called an emergency meeting of his technical people and his top sales staff for the northeastern United States. But in the end, there was nothing the management of the company could do to help narrow down the retail source of the glue. The company said that there were at least three hundred retail-outlet stores in the New York area that would be selling Dabber Glue. And of course the Unsub might not have bought the glue in the northeastern United States. The glue was sold everywhere.

Lesdiu held the box in his long fingers, squinting at it. He looked at it with his Sherlock Holmes hand-magnifying lens. He found some kind of black, powdery dirt embedded in the glue. Very fine particles of dirt, jet black.

"I'm going to nail this dirt," Jimmy Lesdiu said.

He had to separate a few particles of dirt from the glue, and silicone does not dissolve in most solvents. But after a further conversation with the Maven of Glue and with chemists at headquarters, Lesdiu came up with a solvent that would work. He rooted in one of the supply boxes, shuffling through bottles, until he found what he was looking for. Then he dissolved a bit of the glue in a small test tube, and swirled the particles. A blackish, brownish haze hung in the liquid. Now he had to separate the particles. He returned to a supply box and found a magnet. He held the magnet against the test tube. The black dust drifted toward the magnet. "It's a ferromagnetic material. It's iron or steel," he said. But the brown haze did not move under the magnet. The brown haze was probably an organic material or rock or concrete dust. Lesdiu had separated the dirt into two components—a black dust and a brown haze.

"I've done an autopsy on a terror device," Lesdiu remarked to Austen.

But now he had reached the end of what was possible with a Reachdeep portable operation. The sample of dust had to go to the F.B.I. metallurgists in Washington, who would continue the analysis. Into the test tube of dusts he dropped a strong disinfectant—to sterilize the contents, just in case it contained any live Cobra virus particles. A few minutes later, a Bell turbo helicopter took off for Washington bearing the test tube. The team would have to wait several hours, at least, before the F.B.I. metallurgists could tell what the black dust was. The particles might contain information, but whether that information would constitute a signature that could lead back to the perpetrator, no one knew.

The only part of the boxes not yet studied was the wooden material of the box itself. James Lesdiu pondered it. He didn't recognize the type of wood. He didn't recognize the design and style of the box, either. It was clearly handmade, and Lesdiu guessed that either Archimedes had made the box himself or that he had bought it at a trinket shop. Reachdeep needed a forensic botanist. Lesdiu called Washington and asked that an expert on wood be flown to Governors Island. Then he photographed the boxes in different kinds of light. He was especially interested in the small pieces of paper that were glued to the boxes. He set up a camera stand and photographed the papers with different kinds of light shining on them. It seemed that the Unsub had been careful to avoid watermarks when cutting the paper. The text itself was from a high-resolution laser printer. The type font was Courier, a common font. While F.B.I. scientists could identify characters from an old-fashioned typewriter, they could not identify laser-printer output. The chemical composition of the paper might lead to a particular manufacturer, but that would probably not be helpful in finding the Unsub.

Every detail of the boxes had been chosen by the Unsub to be hard to trace.

□

Will Hopkins had set up a series of videoconference meetings with molecular biologists at the Centers for Disease Control and at USAMRIID at Fort Detrick. The experts told him that the Cobra chimera had been built on the most common laboratory strain of baculovirus. It was available through the mail, and it was in use everywhere in the world. The experts told him that they did not know how the virus could be made to replicate explosively in human cells. One of them said to him, "It's doable. But I just don't know how. The baculovirus is adaptable, and someone's figured out how to adapt it to humans, that's all."

Mark Littleberry studied James Lesdiu's magnified photographs of the bits of paper glued to the boxes. He was interested in the drawing of a bioreactor that appeared on Harmonica Man's box. He had never seen this exact type of bioreactor before, but in studying the drawing he became convinced that it had been done from life. The drawing had been made by Archimedes using a simple drawing program on a computer, and then it had been shrunk to a tiny size on a laser printer. The drawing was sketchy, but Littleberry believed it had been done by someone who had used a bioreactor and knew exactly how it worked. But who had manufactured the bioreactor? Littleberry and various F.B.I. agents with Masaccio's task force studied sales catalogs and made telephone calls asking about the designs of bioreactors made by companies in the United States. It was not an American design. Littleberry came to suspect—it was a gut feeling, but he couldn't prove it—that the bioreactor came from either an Asian biotechnology company or from perhaps Russia. Tracing it would be very difficult.

The forensic Reachdeep operation was not going as well as Hopkins had hoped. The idea that so many lives might depend on his team's work frightened him. At times he wished he had never joined the F.B.I. Even though he was dog-tired, he found that he couldn't sleep, and he wondered if he was getting an ulcer.

During a discussion of the Unsub's motives, Hopkins suddenly hurried out of the meeting room, and people heard him throwing up in the bathroom. He came out after a while looking shaky. He said that he had been drinking too much coffee. Some of them were afraid he might be getting sick with the virus, but they didn't know what to say or do about it.

"I'm scared for Will," Littleberry later remarked to Austen. "I'm wondering if he made promises he can't keep."

Chimera

Hopkins was thinking about the virus that he and Littleberry had found in Iraq. The drawing of the bioreactor on the cobra box looked somewhat like the bioreactor that he had seen inside the truck in Iraq—at least from what he could remember. The possibility that the deaths in New York were a terrorist event being sponsored by Iraq weighed on him. He discussed it by phone with Frank Masaccio. Masaccio was very disturbed by this. "If this is terrorism sponsored by a foreign government, Will, this could start a war."

"I know, Frank," Hopkins said.

Hopkins put in a call to the Navy's Biological Defense Research Program in Bethesda, where one of his contacts, a Navy doctor named John Letersky, was working through the night. Letersky was a member of the group that supplied Felix equipment to the F.B.I. He had been trying to analyze the chunks of genetic material that Hopkins and Littleberry had beamed up to the satellite when they'd been locked in the rest room.

"Will! How are you doing?" Letersky said.

"The truth is, I'm scared, John. We have a bitch of an investigation that's going nowhere."

"I'm hearing about it."

"What can you tell me about the stuff we got in Iraq?"

"It's bad, Will," Letersky said.

"How bad?"

"Those crystals you swabbed in the truck? Looks like they were Ebola virus crystals. But some of the DNA sequences show similarities to influenza virus. Problem is, you didn't get enough DNA. We don't know what the Iraqis were dicking around with in the truck, except that the virus had Ebola in it, and might also have flu in it."

Hopkins let out a deep breath. There was no apparent connection between the virus in New York and what he had found in Iraq. This made him feel better, for reasons he could not quite articulate.

"So what's the White House going to do about Ebola in Iraq?" he said.

"Nothing. You heard that off the record, okay? Trying to get the White House to pay attention to bioweapons is like pulling teeth. We'll submit a report to the United Nations, and that's as far as it will go. The Iraqis will claim we made a mistake or we're lying, and the White House will drop it. You guys were way outside the limits. We don't have a real sample. And the truck's long gone."

□

Hopkins went back to work with the Felix machines, and late in the afternoon he had a breakthrough. The following genetic sequence came up on the screen of one of the Felixes:

gaccatattcaggagaaccaaagcccaagac
taaaatcccagaaaggcgtgtagtaacacag

It looked no different to Hopkins than any other string of genetic code. The human mind can't read the text of life as easily as it can read Shakespeare. But the GenBank computer could read it. Hopkins got this answer back:

Sequences producing High-scoring Segment Pairs:

Human rhinovirus 2 (HRV2) complete n . . .	310	5.8e-18	1
Human DNA sequence from BAC 322B1 on . . .	110	0.53	1
Mus musculus vibrator critical regio . . .	107	0.87	1

"Human rhinovirus," Hopkins muttered. "Human rhinovirus. *The common cold!*" He jumped to his feet. "My God! Cobra's got a piece of the common cold in it!"

He ran to the window of the Core and pounded on the glass. "Hey everyone! We've got the common cold!"

Hopkins continued picking the genes apart using Felix. He couldn't believe it. It took his breath away. This was *impossible*. Cobra was partly a common cold. He couldn't figure how it had been mixed with a butterfly virus. It made no sense to him. Somehow the creators of Cobra had managed to make a sticky molecule of some kind on the virus particle that enabled it to grab on to the mucus membranes of the body, especially in the area of the mouth and nose.

"The victims look like they have a cold, when they first get sick," Austen remarked to him. "Kate Moran, especially, had a streaming cold."

"No doubt she felt as if she had a cold," Hopkins said. "This bastard of a virus probably attaches itself to the eyelids—cold viruses do that—or to the membranes in the nose. That would explain the design of the cobra box—it blows virus in your face. I just wonder if it's engineered to get into the lungs, too."

"But how does it move to the brain?" Austen asked.

"It likes nerves," he said. "The optic nerves and the olfactory nerves in the nose are hard-wired straight into the brain, aren't they, Alice?"

She nodded.

"So Cobra hits a mucus membrane and it zooms for the brain," he said. "Cobra is a biological missile designed to take out the brain. There's no cure for the common cold. The common cold is very contagious. Cobra is the ultimate head cold."

One of the two Felix machines beeped. His fingers danced over the keys, and he stared at the screen. "Yup. Here's another cold gene. It's surrounded by expression cassettes of unknown biologic function. Hm, hello? What's this? Hm." His fingers clacked away, and genetic code unreeled across the screen, the language of life twisted into a secret poem of death.

Dawn

Alice Austen was assigned a simple Coast Guard officer's room as a bedroom. It overlooked the quiet
waters of the bay, where the running lights of container ships flickered in the moving air. The only furniture in the room was a metal folding cot with
blankets and sheets. Someone, probably an F.B.I.
agent from Masaccio's office, had gone over to Kips
Bay, gathered up her personal things, brought them
here, and left them sitting on the bed. That vaguely
embarrassed her. She turned on her cell phone and debated calling her father, but decided not to. She would
wake him up again if she called now. Then she lay
back on the bed and looked up at the ceiling. She was
too tired to take off her clothes. She began to doze off.
Suddenly it was five-thirty in the morning, and the
birds were singing in the gray light.

Suzanne Tanaka stayed up most of the night,
working alone in the Core. Most of the team had
gone off to get some sleep. But she could not sleep.
She was too keyed up. She looked at more electron-
microscope images for a while, then decided to look
at the mice again. It would be too soon to see any
symptoms, but you never knew.

She bent over the boxes. They were clear plastic, and the mice were white mice, and they were
moving around, because mice are active at night.

They seemed fine. Except for one male mouse. He seemed wobbly. She looked at him more closely. He was very active. He was chewing on a wooden nibble block. Chewing and chewing. But mice normally chew a lot; chewing is rodent behavior. She looked at the clock on the table. She had injected the mice with Glenn Dudley's brain material just last night, and now it was the early hours of the morning. That was too little time for a mouse, even with its fast metabolism, to be showing clinical signs of infection by Cobra. And there was no evidence to show that Cobra could infect rodents anyway. Nevertheless, the mouse's chewing behavior bothered her: then again, this was probably her imagination talking to her.

She did not want to make any mistakes. She had begged Will Hopkins to put her in the group. She decided, finally, that she would bleed all the mice— take blood samples from all of them. Maybe the blood would show signs of infection, maybe not.

She went over to a cargo box that held her animal kits, and she got a soft leather glove and some disposable syringes. She pulled the leather glove over her surgical glove. She opened a box and removed the first mouse, holding it in her gloved hand in a practiced way. The mouse struggled.

She placed the needle under the mouse's skin and withdrew a few drops of blood. The mouse was struggling wildly. He's as afraid as I am, in his dim little way, she thought. Just then the mouse flipped out of her gloved hand and landed across her right hand, the one without the leather glove. For just an instant the mouse bit through the latex rubber and hung on with its teeth and let go.

Tanaka gasped and juggled the mouse back into its box.

It was just a nip. For a moment she didn't think the animal had drawn blood. She inspected her rubber glove. Then she saw it: two red dots on her right index finger, where the mouse's front teeth had penetrated. The slightest smear of blood welled up under the rubber.

"Damn!" she said.

It could *not* be. Was there any virus circulating in the mouse's bloodstream? We don't even know if Cobra can infect a mouse. Yet she had heard stories of people pricking their fingers in the Army hot labs. If it was a hot agent, incurable, you had between ten and twenty seconds to remove the finger with a clean scalpel. Otherwise the agent would move down your finger and enter your main blood system, and it could go anywhere. You had a twenty-second window of opportunity to save your life by cutting off your finger.

She dashed over to a cargo box, found a scalpel, stripped it, fitted the blade—quick!—and slammed her hand down on the box. She held the scalpel clumsily with her left hand, poised to slash it down on her finger.

And didn't do it. Couldn't.

This is crazy, she told herself. I don't want to lose my finger.

And then the twenty seconds had passed, and the choice was no longer hers to make. She put the scalpel down. Sweat poured from her face. Her Racal hood fogged up, and Tanaka realized that she was weeping.

Stop this, stop this. I'll be all right, she told her-self, I'll be all right. This was not an exposure, she told herself. We don't even know if it can live in mice. I'll just have to wait and see, but I know I'll be all right. I will not tell anyone. Because they'll take me off the investigation, and this is my first big case.

Morning

Alice Austen returned to the Reachdeep unit shortly after the sun came up, and she found Suzanne Tanaka sitting in the meeting room drinking coffee. Tanaka looked exhausted.

"You need to get some sleep, Suzanne," Austen said to her.

"I wish I could."

Hopkins was talking on the telephone to John Letersky of the Navy's Biological Defense Research Program in Bethesda. It was six o'clock in the morning, and Letersky was still there. "What I need, John, are some antibody probes for insect nuclear virus. Do you have any probes like that?"

"No way," Letersky said.

"It would be good if we could program the hand-helds to detect Cobra," Hopkins said. "We'd like to be able to test blood and tissue, and we want to do quick environmental sampling for the presence of Cobra."

A hand-held biosensor device requires special antibody compounds known as probes in order to register the presence of a given hot agent. The probes are molecules that lock onto proteins in the hot agent. They change color as they lock on, and the biosensor device reads the color change.

"I hear you, Will. Let me start calling around. You stick to the investigation."

Hopkins hung up. "Whew. Coffee. I need coffee."

"Did you get any sleep last night?" Austen asked him.

"A couple of hours." He went over to the electric coffee machine. The pot was empty. "I need some breakfast," he said to Austen. "What about you? Hey, Suzanne! Breakfast?"

"I'm not hungry. I'll eat later."

Austen and Hopkins caught a helicopter up the East River. It let them off at the East Thirty-fourth Street Heliport. A few minutes later they were sitting in a coffee shop on First Avenue.

"A four-star breakfast, if you add in the air-fare," Hopkins remarked. It was an old-style coffee shop, with a short-order cook flipping eggs behind a stainless-steel counter, and a waitress who went around refilling disposable plastic cups in reusable holders.

Austen took a sip of coffee. She said, "How did you end up doing this?"

"What, Reachdeep?"

"You don't seem like the type."

He shrugged. "My father was in the Bureau."

"Is he retired now?"

"No. He's dead."

"I'm sorry," she said.

"He was a field agent in Los Angeles, where I grew up. He and a partner went to talk with an informant, and they walked into a murder in progress. One of the subjects panicked and opened fire through the door when they knocked. My father was hit in the eye. I was thirteen. I grew up hating the Bureau for taking my father away."

"But—never mind."

"You were going to ask me why I joined the Bureau?"

She nodded.

"I guess at some point I realized I was a cop, like my father."

"You're not a cop."

"I'm a type of cop, and I'm scared this investigation isn't going to work." He looked at the table and played with a spoon.

"I don't think we've diagnosed the disease yet," she said. "The self-cannibalism. We can't explain that."

"You put an insect virus in a human system, you get a complicated result," Hopkins said.

The waitress brought over a plate of fried eggs with bacon for Hopkins, and fruit and an English muffin for Austen.

"You need to eat more, Alice," Hopkins said. "Bacon is good for you."

She ignored him. "If we could just see through the disease, maybe we could see the person who's spreading it." Her voice trailed off.

"But we do have a diagnosis. It's Cobra."

"No. We *don't*. Will, you're looking at the genetic code. I'm looking at the effect of the virus on people. We don't understand Cobra as a *disease process*. There is no diagnosis."

"That's a funny idea." He took a slow sip of coffee, looking dismayed.

She thought: So many details to hold in your mind. If you could fit them together, the pattern would emerge. "Will," she said. "How about the dust in the glue—the dust that James Lesdiu found? I'm wondering if it's steel dust from the subway."

"Steel dust? What's that?" Hopkins asked. He loaded egg and bacon into his mouth. Traffic went past outside the window.

"Ben Kly showed it to me. It's all over the subway tunnels. Two homeless men have died of Cobra, and they were neighbors living in a subway tunnel. I wonder if Archimedes lives in the subway."

"Impossible," Hopkins said. "You can't do lab work in the subway. A virus lab has to be spotlessly clean, and you need some sophisticated equipment. You just couldn't put that stuff in the subway."

"If he had any steel dust on his fingertips, he might have spread some of it into the glue when he was making the box."

"Sure. But a lot of people take the subway, and they probably get dust on their fingers. All the dust shows is that Archimedes took the subway the day he made the box. Big deal."

"Maybe he's been exploring the subway to look for the best place to do a big release," she said.

Wanderer

He slept late (by his own standards) and was out of bed by seven o'clock in the morning. First he went into the staging area and suited up in a Tyvek suit and entered Level 3. He checked on the bioreactor. It was running smoothly. It might run for another day or two before he would have to replace the core. He checked on the drying of the viral glass. It had hardened nicely during the night. With double-gloved fingertips he picked out a hexagon, a sliver of brainpox viral glass. He loaded it into a wide-mouthed plastic flask. The flask would fit in his pocket. He screwed a black cap on the flask, and tightened it hard. He dipped the flask in a pan full of bleach and water. That was to sterilize the outside of the flask. The inside of the flask was hot, in a biological sense. The hexagon contained perhaps a quadrillion virus particles.

He went down the stairs and out onto the street. He walked for a while. It was a cool Monday morning, with a high overcast, almost motionless air. He could see a tinge of brown in the sky, a hint of summer's coming smog. It was the right kind of weather for a biological release. You wanted slow-moving air and a weather inversion, with a haze of pollution.

He ended up in Greenwich Village, where he stopped for breakfast at a café. He ordered a goat-cheese omelette with fresh-baked sourdough bread and wildflower honey and a cup of coffee. No meat, but today eggs were acceptable. He took the flask out of his pocket and put it on the table next to his food. It looked harmless. Only a bottle wrapped in a plastic bag. If you looked closely at the flask you would see a pane of viral glass sitting inside the bottle. The waiter didn't notice; no one noticed.

He mulled over his possibilities. The question was not just the power of the hot agent, but how it was to be dispersed. The boxes were okay for the Phase I human trials, and it was clear that they worked. The low-key warnings about them that were now being broadcast on TV proved that. Good. It was time to move on.

He reached into the pocket of his windbreaker, which was draped on the back of his chair, and pulled out a photocopy of a scientific report. He placed it beside the flask and unfolded it and smoothed it and put his coffee cup on the paper to hold it there. Then he began to read. "A Study of the Vulnerability of Subway Passengers in New York City to Covert Action with Biological Agents"—he was reading it for about the hundredth time. Department of the Army, Fort Detrick, Maryland. It had been published in 1968.

The study described how Army researchers had filled glass lightbulbs with a dry, powdered bacterial-spore preparation, finer than confectioner's sugar. The particles were in the size range of one to five microns, the lung-friendly particle size. The bacterial agent was *Bacillus globigii,* an organism that normally doesn't cause disease in humans. It forms spores. The Army researchers had gone to various locations in the New York subway, including the Times Square subway station, and they had dropped the lightbulbs full of spores on the tracks. The lightbulbs had shattered and the spores had flown up into the air in puffs of gray dust. Just a few lightbulbs were broken this way, not many, and they contained altogether perhaps ten ounces of spores. Then the Army researchers fanned out and found that within days the spores had disseminated throughout New York City. Spores from Times Square were driven far into the Bronx by the plunger action of the subway trains whooshing through the tunnels—those trains were like pistons, driving the spores in the air through the tunnels for many miles. The spores drifted out of the subway entrances into the neighborhoods. He read: "A large portion of the working population in downtown New York City would be exposed to disease if one or more pathogenic agents were disseminated covertly in several subway lines at a period of peak traffic."

"More coffee?" the waiter asked him.

"No thank you. Too much coffee makes me jittery."

"I know what you mean," the waiter said.

He left the waiter a generous tip; the waiter was a nice fellow. Outdoors on the sidewalk, he wondered which way to go. East or west? North or south? He headed eastward along a tree-lined street. The trees were flowering, but they had not yet put out leaves.

He had conceived a strategy: he would not plan ahead, except in a general sense. Then they couldn't predict his moves. He himself did not know exactly what he was going to do next. He had a pane of viral glass in his pocket. By the end of the day, it would be out in the world. In his apartment, at last count, he had an additional 891 panes of viral glass, sitting in jars. They would go into the world too. Most of them all at once.

□

Looking for a place to let the crystal go, he walked from Washington Square Park eastward along Waverly Place, past the gracious buildings of New York University. He liked being lost among the students. Their energy pleased him. He walked up Astor Place past the Cooper Union, and then headed along St. Marks Place through the heart of the East Village.

Here he reached into his jacket and removed a rubber surgical glove from the pocket and put the glove on his right hand as he walked. No one paid any attention. The glove was to protect his skin from coming into contact with any brainpox particles when he opened the flask and released the crystal into the city.

Continuing eastward across First Avenue, he came to where Manhattan extends in a bulge into a curve of the East River. The avenues there are named A, B, C, and D. The predominant color of Alphabet City is gray, in contrast to the brickreds and greens of the sleeker and richer Greenwich Village to the west. Yet the gray of Alphabet City is mixed with the yellows and greens of bodega signs, Caribbean pinks, and the purples and whites and blacks of hand-painted signs on junk stores and dry-cleaning shops

and cafés and music shops and clubs. Many buildings have been torn down over the years, and so the
neighborhood has abandoned lots, some of them
with homemade gardens.

As he passed through Tompkins Square Park, he
had an idea. The park has a playground for children,
and grassy areas with benches and walks. There are
public toilets there, and so it is popular with homeless people and stray teenagers. He thought that he
might leave the piece of glass on a bench where a
drunk or a messed-up teenager would encounter it,
sit on it, break it, shatter it, throw particles in the air,
particles that would get on the test subject's clothes
and eventually perhaps into the lungs. It would be a
therapeutic execution.

He cruised past the benches. He saw a couple of
drunks lying on their stomachs or backs on the
benches, dead to the world. They don't move enough.
A group of teenagers were sitting on the ground in a
circle, some of them drinking beer out of paper bags.
They couldn't be more than sixteen years old. They
stared at him as he passed, giving him that nasty,
knowing look of teenagers. He had better not do anything in front of them. They would notice.

He was feeling frustrated; he had been walking
for a while, and he hadn't encountered anything
quite right.

Then he had another idea. It might be taking a
chance to do it so close to home, but as far as he
could tell, they had not figured out the human trials.
He turned south, heading for Houston Street. This
might bring more peace to his laboratory. He arrived

at the little people's park surrounded by a chain-link fence that lay next to his building. It was a nice little park, to be sure, with its gardens. Interestingly, it was deserted. Good.

He sat on the children's merry-go-round. It creaked under his weight. *I could also come down here with a little bit of oil; that might help too.* Then, using his gloved hand, he unscrewed the cap of the flask. He tipped the flask, and the piece of viral glass slid out onto the merry-go-round.

They will be back. They will jump on the merry-go-round, and they will yell and throw rocks at the cats, and meanwhile, their feet will be pounding the crystal to dust. Shake the dust from your feet, children. You are a burden to the earth.

□

Hector Ramirez, five years of age, was just about to climb up the slide when he changed his mind and went over to the merry-go-round. His mama sat on a bench talking with another lady. He climbed up on the merry-go-round and stood there for a moment. You needed to have more kids to get it moving, but he thought he could get it moving anyway. He climbed down and pushed it, and it began to turn with a squeaky sound, but not much.

"Mama! Mama! Spin me."

His mama didn't want to spin him. He was about to run off to the slide when he saw the little nice thing.

He thought it might be candy. It looked like . . . sugar? He picked it up. It had colors in it, like a rainbow. He sniffed it, but there was no smell. He put it in his mouth.

It seemed to turn rubbery and melt in his mouth real fast, but it didn't taste like candy. "Ew!" he said. He spat out some rubbery bits.

It had tasted like . . . nothing.

He bent over and spat again, and again, and looked over at his mother.

"Hector! What are you doing?"

"Nothing, Mama."

She was young and pretty. She wore a short skirt and a denim jacket and black boots. "What are you doing?"

He couldn't give her any kind of answer, so she gave up and went back to talk with the other lady. Oh, well. He went off to slide down the slide.

The cold symptoms come on in a matter of hours. The eclipse phase—where no obvious symptoms appear in the central nervous system—lasts from one to three days. Meanwhile Cobra is rocketing along the wires. The infected brain cells switch into crystal-phase production, and the cells plump up with crystals. The transformation of the personality is abrupt and devastating. The shift to autocannibalism happens explosively. It often occurs when the infected host is momentarily startled or confused, or is experiencing strong emotions.

Briefing

The forensic operation had been going flat out on Governors Island for nearly eighteen hours. The Reachdeep team had generated a lot of information, but the information was leading nowhere fast.

An epidemic task force from the C.D.C. had arrived and set up shop in an empty Coast Guard building, and they had been making telephone calls and going around the city, looking for any new cases of Cobra and locating people who had been in close contact with those who had died. Walter Mellis had flown down to Atlanta with samples from the autopsies for the C.D.C.'s molecular biology labs, and USAMRIID was also starting an analysis.

Reachdeep worked in isolation. Frank Masaccio believed that the team needed to focus on the criminal evidence. No one was allowed to telephone Reachdeep without placing the call through Masaccio's office, but Reachdeep could phone out anywhere. No one was allowed to land on the island and enter the Reachdeep unit unless it was okayed by Masaccio or Hopkins, but Reachdeep team members were given standby helicopters ready to fly them anywhere they wanted, or ready to fly in experts. "I've put you guys in an ivory tower," Masaccio had told them. "An ivory tower with a helicopter landing zone."

Seagulls perched on the railings of the observation deck outside the Reachdeep conference room.

The gulls looked in the windows at the racks of communications gear, at the people in black biohazard suits.

Two helicopters lifted off from the heliport in lower Manhattan and crossed the East River. They passed over the Coast Guard hospital and touched down in the middle of the island. Five minutes later, Frank Masaccio appeared with a group of men and women, F.B.I. agents and New York Police Department investigators. They were the managers of his Cobra task force. They had arrived for the daily briefing. They were carrying boxes of take-out Chinese food. Lunch.

□

The New York F.B.I. is experienced in the matter of catering food. The Bureau supplies take-out food to safe houses and stakeouts, since the agents don't have time to prepare their own food or to go out to a restaurant (eating in a restaurant also might draw attention to them). The food must be delivered by other F.B.I. agents, since food-delivery people would be a danger to the security of an operation. Not surprisingly, the New York F.B.I. has the best take-out food capability of any field office in the United States.

The food was excellent. It included Peking duck.

There weren't enough chairs to go around. People sat on the floor. For a time there was no conversation in the room, only eating. Eventually Masaccio brought the meeting to order.

"You start, Hopkins," he said.

Austen had been sitting curled up against the wall, feeling comfortably alone with herself for the first time in days. Masaccio's voice woke her from her reverie.

Hopkins stood up in front of the Felix devices and summarized the state of the Reachdeep investigation. He said that Reachdeep had made a tentative identification of the Cobra agent. It was a chimera, a recombinant virus engineered in a laboratory. He said it was a mixture of an insect virus and the common cold. Mixing the two viruses had produced a monster. "But that's not all that's going on in this virus," Hopkins said. "We're going to find more engineered DNA wetware in this virus. I'm sure of it."

Alice Austen gave her autopsy findings. Suzanne Tanaka showed photographs of the virus particles and the crystals in which the particles were embedded. James Lesdiu reported the results of his analysis of the materials in the boxes.

"My number one question is this," Frank Masaccio said to the Reachdeep team. "Are you any closer to the perpetrator?"

"It's hard to say," Hopkins answered.

"That answer sucks, Hopkins. I want the Archimedes perp. I want him yesterday." Masaccio summarized what had been happening outside Reachdeep. State health officials and the city health commissioner had been brought in and quietly informed of the situation. "The mayor's Emergency Management Office has been geared up," Masaccio said. "We have fire department chemical-hazard and decon teams standing by on Roosevelt Island. We've got New York City Police Department SWAT teams on standby. We are doing our best to keep the news media out of this. . . . One other thing: the mayor is unhappy."

"With whom?" Hopkins asked.

"With *me*. He's bouncing off the walls in City Hall. He's yelling on the telephone. Most of the Cobra task force is idle, and it's driving the mayor *nuts*. You guys aren't giving us enough leads to push. I've got agents running around the city looking for more of those little wooden boxes, but nothing's turned up." He mentioned that his office had done "a tiny little news release" to the media.

"What?" Hopkins blurted.

"We had to warn people about the boxes, Will. We're saying it's a poison. We're not giving out that it's a germ weapon. But we can't keep a lid on this thing forever. The minute you guys find something real, you get in touch with me."

"I need an art historian," Hopkins said.

"What?"

"An art historian, Frank. Someone who can look at the boxes and tell us where they came from."

A Brief History of Art

Frank Masaccio flew back to Manhattan, where he stationed himself in the Federal Building. Within the hour a helicopter landed on Governors Island carrying a professor of folk art from New York University. His name was Herschel Alquivir.

The New York office of the F.B.I. had called Professor Alquivir on the telephone and reached him at his apartment on the Upper West Side. They wanted to know if he could help them identify a work of carved wooden folk art. Could he do it right now? Would that be too much trouble?

He agreed to help. He was stunned when, less than sixty seconds after he hung up the telephone, a team of federal agents knocked on the door of his apartment. They had been waiting in cars on the street. He was rushed in a Bureau car with police escort—three police cars moving ahead, breaking up traffic with their sirens and lights—to the West Side heliport. Professor Alquivir was flown to Governors Island, in a state of increasing alarm at what he had gotten himself into.

They brought him into the meeting room and showed him the door that led into the decon room and the Core. The door was plastered with biohazard signs. Hopkins showed Professor Alquivir how to put on an F.B.I. biohazard suit, and then the professor examined the boxes. He was a slender man, middle-aged, with a passion for carved wooden objects. He maintained a calm demeanor. Finally he said, "These boxes are children's toys. I think they were made in East Africa. I'm quite sure of it. Cobras don't live in East Africa, they live in Egypt, India, and other parts of southern Asia. But the king cobra is known, of course, to many people around the world. And there is a large Indian population in East Africa. I see Indian influences in this box, but the type of object is fundamentally African. This is a type of toy that's not uncommon, I believe, in East Africa. Because of the Indian influence—the cobra—I should say the place of manufacture might be near the coast of the Indian Ocean, where Indian influence is strongest."

At 9:30 that night, two agents from the New York office of the F.B.I. departed on a Lufthansa flight to Frankfurt, with a connection to Nairobi.

Washington

Archimedes had completed the first phase of his human trials. The boxes were Phase I trials. During a course of medical experimentation upon humans in a Phase I trial, you test small amounts of a new experimental drug on subjects. Phase I trials are safety trials. Having seen the announcement of the boxes on the television news, Archimedes understood that the Phase I safety trials of brainpox showed it was unsafe for humans. Given this success, he would move into Phase II. During Phase II, you increase the dosage and the numbers of people tested. He felt reasonably confident that the results would be satisfactory, but he wanted to have more assurance. After that would come the Phase III trial, when he would give a huge loading dose of brainpox to the human species.

He was uncertain about whether they were looking for him by now, uncertain as to what they might have conjectured about him, if anything.

He was walking through the concourse of Penn Station with a flask containing one hexagon of viral glass tucked in his pocket. He stood looking at the Amtrak departures on the big display board. A Metroliner train was due to be leaving in ten minutes for Washington, D.C. He paid cash for a round-trip ticket to Washington. I have not seen Washington in weeks, he thought. Human trials can occur anywhere humans live.

He had a pleasant lunch of a vegetable pocket pita sandwich on the train, and he enjoyed the green countryside. He delighted in the bridge over the Susquehanna River where it drained into Chesapeake Bay, and he drank a glass of white wine to help himself relax and to steady his resolve. Bridges are beautiful. They are constructive and mathematical. They are one of the good things that humans make.

□

In the Metro Center Station of the Washington Metro, at midday, a man was sitting on one of the concrete benches along the wall of the station platform. He was breathing rather heavily, as if he was short of breath. A train came along. The man took a deep breath and stood up. As he was walking toward the train, he threw something along the platform, casually, as if he was discarding a bit of trash, and he stepped onto the train. The trash was a shiny bit of plastic, perhaps. It broke into pieces and was quickly trodden underfoot by passing crowds. No one noticed that the man was wearing a flesh-colored latex rubber glove on his right hand or that he was holding his breath when he got on the train. He continued to hold his breath for almost a minute afterward. "Ah," he said, letting out his breath as the train proceeded along the tunnel, heading in the direction of Union Station, where Amtrak trains will take you anywhere. He dropped his rubber glove in a trash can somewhere in Union Station.

Dust

The face of an F.B.I. metallurgist appeared on a screen in Reachdeep. "This Q dust you sent us is a type of medium-carbon steel. The annealed structure of the particles would indicate they formed through a pressure process such as the hot rolling process."

"Railroad track," Austen said to Hopkins.

"There's more," the metallurgist said. "We found a grain of something that looks like pollen."

"Pollen? What kind?"

"We're trying to find out right now."

□

The F.B.I. consulted Dr. Edgar Adlington, a palynologist (pollen expert) at the Smithsonian Institution in Washington. A special agent named Chuck Klurt walked across the Mall from F.B.I. headquarters to the brown towers of the Smithsonian. Klurt took an elevator to the basement.

Dr. Adlington was hunched over his desk in a windowless room that smelled of old books and dried leaves. He was examining a flower under a magnifying lamp.

Special Agent Klurt placed some microscope photographs of a single grain of pollen in front of Dr. Adlington. "We have a little problem. Can you tell me what this is?"

"Well, it is a pollen grain."

"Any idea what it came from, Dr. Adlington?"

"Why do you people have to give me just one grain? Do you take me for a psychic? This is not the kind of thing I can just look up in a book."

"But could you help?" Special Agent Klurt asked.

"Yes, indeed," he answered. "The problem, while challenging, is not insurmountable. What did you say your name is?"

"Klurt."

"Now, Mr. Klurt." Adlington flipped through the photographs, studying them. The pollen grain looked like a wrinkled football that had grooves running down the seams of the ball. He took a ruler and laid it on the photograph, while his finger traced features on the pollen grain and he glanced at Klurt every now and then to make sure that Klurt understood. "See, here—what we have here is a colporoidate sporomorph, actually three-colpate, about thirty microns long on the polar axis, in a prolate spheroid with a polar-to-equatorial axis ratio of approximately 1.5, I would *say*, while the sexine—do you see the sexine, Klurt?—you have to bear in mind that the sexine, here, is thicker but not *terribly* much thicker than the nexine, and it is densely reticulate with heterobrochate form, *viz.*, muri simplibaculate—do you follow me?"

"Yeah."

"This pollen grain may come from one of several families of the Caprifoliaecae or certain of the Celastraccae, but if I *had* to say, I would place it in the family Oleaceae."

"Mmmm—"

"Yes. And I would venture to say we are looking at *intermedia* or *japonica*. Perhaps I am going too far out on a limb, here, Mr. Klurt, but I would hazard a guess—just a guess!—that this pollen grain comes from none other than *Forsythia intermedia* 'Spectabilis.' " He handed the photographs back to special Agent Klurt.

"So what is it?" the agent asked.

"I told you, it's forsythia! A flowering shrub. 'Spectabilis' is the most beautiful type of forsythia, with large vivid yellow flowers that bloom in April. It is the most popular forsythia in America."

Forsythia blooms in many places around New York City in the spring. Knowing that the pollen came from forsythia could not help pin down the location of the Unsub. The grain of pollen seemed untraceable.

□

The Cobra boxes themselves came under the scrutiny of a consultant in tropical wood, a middle-aged professor of plant cellular biology from American University in Washington named Lorraine Schild. She arrived at Governors Island in a state of terror.

Professor Schild stood in the decon room before the door that led into the Evidence Core. She was dressed in surgical scrubs. Austen and Tanaka were helping her step into a black F.B.I. biohazard space suit.

"I don't think I can do it," she said. Her voice quavered.

They pleaded with her. They shooed Hopkins and Littleberry away while they tried to reassure her.

"It's my worst fear," she said. "There's a horrible virus in there, isn't there?"

"We've been all right, so far," Tanaka said.

"We really need your help," Austen said.

Finally they prevailed on Dr. Schild, and she suited up and went into the Core. She sat down at a microscope and looked at the wood in the boxes. Austen sat next to her. Dr. Schild's voice came out of her Racal hood, muffled and weak. When she had signed a consulting contract with the F.B.I. two years earlier, she had had no idea it could lead to this. She kept turning her faceplate this way and that, trying to see into the microscope. "The wood cellular structure is extremely fine-grained," she said. "This is a very hard wood. The darker streaks are heartwood. The curvature of the rings indicates that it's the center of a small trunk. I believe this is a flowering legume. A wood this hard would suggest it is a type of acacia tree. I can't tell you exactly the species of acacia. There are so many acacias."

"Where does it grow?" Hopkins asked.

"In habitats all over eastern Africa. Can I leave now?"

They took her out and deconned her in the decon room, spraying her with bleach. Dr. Schild refused to get back on the Black Hawk helicopter. She asked to be put on a civilian flight back to Washington.

Nairobi

Frank Masaccio had taken to sleeping in the Federal Building, where he had a bed in a room the size of a closet. At one o'clock in the morning, he put in a telephone call to Nairobi, to the Old Norfolk Hotel, where two agents from his office, Almon Johnston and Link Peters, had checked in some hours earlier. It was now Wednesday morning in Kenya. Masaccio told them about the wood. He suggested they look for shopkeepers selling cobra boxes made of acacia wood.

Special Agent Johnston was a tall African-American who had lived in Kenya for a year when he'd been posted there as a sales manager for an American company that did business in Africa, before he'd joined the F.B.I., so he knew his way around. Peters worked in the foreign counterintelligence division of the Bureau. He had never been to Africa in his life.

They were joined by an officer from the Kenya National Police, Inspector Joshua Kipkel, who provided them with a car and a driver. Neither agent knew where to begin looking, but Inspector Kipkel suggested they try some of the better shops—they are called houses—on Tom Mboya Street and Standard Street in downtown Nairobi. So they drove down the streets, stopping at the shops. They looked at the goods for sale. Occasionally the F.B.I. agents purchased something in order to sweeten relations with the shopkeepers. The agents showed them photographs of the cobra boxes. All of them said they had seen such boxes, but they said that they were out of stock at the present time. One shopkeeper offered to ship a cargo container full of cobra boxes to New York but he said he would need a large cash deposit up front. "I shall have this container shipped to you at a special price." Inspector Kipkel spoke to the man sharply in Kiswahili.

"*M'zuri sana,*" Johnston said to the shopkeepers. To Peters and Kipkel, he said, "This isn't panning out."

Next, Inspector Kipkel suggested they try the Kenya National Museum. He said, "It has a good tourist shop, and it has collections you may find interesting."

They explored the National Museum and its gift shop, but they found nothing like the cobra boxes on display or for sale. Inspector Kipkel said, "We will go to the City Market."

"Sounds okay to me," Link Peters said.

"It will be difficult for you there. You will see," Inspector Kipkel said to them.

Their driver took them to a rotting concrete structure in downtown Nairobi, on a dusty street across from a supermarket. The Nairobi City Market had been built many years earlier by the British, when they had been the colonial rulers of Kenya. It resembled an aircraft hangar. They entered through the front entrance, and immediately they were surrounded by a knot of shopkeepers waving leather goods and carved chess pieces and jewelry. When Johnston showed the shopkeepers photographs of the cobra boxes, the shopkeepers were certain they had seen such boxes. They were certain they could get more boxes for the Americans. In the meanwhile, would Johnston and Peters like to buy anything else? A beaded belt, perhaps, or a set of napkin rings? Silver jewelry? A carved mask?

"Some of this stuff is really beautiful," Link Peters said to Almon Johnston. Peters stopped to buy some wooden carvings of lions and hippos for his kids. It took the agents two hours to explore the City Market. They circled around the building, stopping at each shop in turn, showing the photographs. It created an unbelievable sensation, a churning knot of commercial hysteria that followed them everywhere they went. Yet no one could show the agents a box of the right type.

It was getting near five P.M., closing time for the Nairobi City Market. Almon Johnston turned to Peters and said, "I'm beginning to think we should try Tanzania."

Inspector Kipkel said there was one more possibility. He said they should try outdoors behind the building. They went out through a back door to a dusty open lot jammed with booths of people selling trinkets, people who couldn't afford the rent inside the market building.

Kipkel made the break. He spotted an old lady with some small carvings. She was sitting in a booth off to one side. He went over to her. The boxes looked familiar. "Gentlemen, come over here."

Her name was Theadora Saitota. She was selling baskets woven from baobab bark. She also had on display a number of small boxes that were not unlike the cobra boxes, except that they were made of gray soapstone, not wood.

Johnston showed her photographs of the boxes. She eyed the Kenyan police inspector. Then she said, "I know these things."

"Where do they come from?" Johnston asked her.

"Voi."

"What?"

"Voi," she said.

"This is a town," the Kenyan police inspector said. "There are many woodcarvers in this town." It was a town on the road to the coast.

"Do you know who in Voi makes these boxes?" he asked her.

She looked at the Kenyan inspector, and hesitated.

Johnston removed a wad of paper shillings from his pocket and handed the banknotes to the lady. They were worth a few dollars.

She tucked the money away in the blink of an eye and said: "He was a good man. He was a woodcarver in Voi. He carve things."

"What is his name?" Johnston asked.

"His name Moses Ngona. He was my cousin. He passed away. Of Slim. Last year," she said.

"And you sold his boxes until he died?" Johnston asked.

"Yes."

"Do you have any more of Mr. Ngona's boxes?"

She looked hard at him and said nothing.

He handed her more banknotes.

She reached down to a shelf beside her knees. She pulled out a roll of old newspaper. She unrolled the newspaper and placed one wooden box on the plank.

Johnston opened it, fiddling with the catch. A snake popped out. A king cobra.

"Do you remember selling any of your cousin's boxes to any tourists?" Johnston asked.

"Not many tourists here," she said. "There was a man from Japan. There was a lady and a man from England. There was a man from America."

"Can you describe the American, the man?"

"He was small." She began to laugh. "He had no hairs on his head, he was a little *mzungu*." *Mzungu* means white man and it also means ghost. "He offer me many dollars, this little *mzungu*. We have a big business." She smiled. "I give him two of my cousin's box! He give me twenty dollars! Ha, ha! This little *mzungu!* I did have the best of him!" Twenty dollars had made her month.

"When did this happen?"

"Oh, last year."

□

Almon Johnston telephoned Masaccio from the Old Norfolk Hotel. It was by then Wednesday morning in New York. Johnston explained what they'd found. "A man paid the lady twenty dollars. That's way too high a price. And that's why the lady remembers. It suggests the guy may have been planning this crime a year ago, Frank. She's down at police headquarters now. They're getting a composite artist. The lady's saying that all small hairless white men look the same to her. But I think they'll get a face. Link and I could start cross-checking with the Foreign Ministry's visa records. The problem is, about fifty thousand male Americans were issued visas to Kenya during the time period. It'll be a bitch going through them."

"It's kind of a stretch, guys, but suck it in and start sifting through those fifty thousand visas," Masaccio said.

That afternoon, a fax machine in the Reachdeep unit beeped and extruded a composite drawing of a man's face. He wore glasses. He had a narrow nose and rather puffy cheeks. He was nearly bald, and he looked to be in his thirties or forties. He was a possible suspect. On the other hand, he may have been just another American tourist. Hopkins taped the drawing to the wall, where all the team members could see it.

Case

Suzanne Tanaka studied the drawing of the face on the wall. Like all of the Reachdeep team members, she couldn't keep her eyes off it. Was this really the man? Feelings of great terror engulfed her, terror that she couldn't describe, and the feelings kept her awake all the time now. She said not a word to the others of her fear.

In the biology room of the Evidence Core, Tanaka inspected her mice. One animal seemed more active than the others, and began grooming itself for long periods of time, but the periods of grooming activity were interspersed with periods of what looked like paralysis, when the mouse wouldn't move. Then it attacked itself. It gnawed at its front paws, and pulled out some of its hair, especially in the belly. But the animal did not die.

With Austen watching, Tanaka killed the mouse and dissected it. She placed it on a cutting board, and, wearing triple gloves and full biohazard gear, she opened the mouse with a scalpel and obtained a sample of the mouse's brain. She prepped the brain material and scanned it in the electron microscope. Some of the mouse's brain cells contained Cobra crystals, but on the whole, the brain tissue seemed less damaged than with humans infected with Cobra. The virus seemed to produce a nonfatal infection in a mouse.

Then another mouse got sick. It curled up and groomed itself for hours on end. Two other mice also seemed trembly. Tanaka wanted to look through an optical microscope at brain cells of the mouse she had sacrificed. She made thin slices of mouse brain, stained them, and looked at the slices through the doubleheaded microscope. Austen stared into the other set of eyepieces.

"When did you see the first signs of illness in this mouse?" Austen asked.

Tanaka didn't answer.

"Suzanne?"

"Oh, ah, last night, I guess. It was agitated. That was the first sign. I guess." She took her eyes away from the microscope and bent over.

"Are you all right?"

"I'm fine." She went back to looking into the eyepieces.

Austen kept looking at Tanaka. "I haven't seen you sleep since we arrived, Suzanne. I haven't seen you eat."

"I don't seem to have time."

"You need to find the time. I mean this," Austen said gently.

Austen moved the slide and replaced it with another one. They were looking, now, at the mouse's midbrain. It was not unlike the human midbrain, a core of material with a lot of branching nerves coming out of it, at the top of the animal's spinal cord.

Austen moved the slide. "I think we're looking at the basal ganglia," she said. That was a bundle of nerve fibers in the mouse's midbrain. The cells contained crystals in the center, and they were hairy with branches. "It's as if the basal ganglia started to grow. Like there's been some kind of reorganization of all the connections. What do you think?"

"Think? I . . . can't think."

"Suzanne?"

Austen looked up across the top of the double-headed microscope. She was not two feet away from Tanaka's face. Suzanne's lips were trembling. A drop of clear liquid fell from her nose.

"Suzanne!"

☐

The Army Medical Management Unit placed the first team casualty, Technician Suzanne Tanaka, in a bio-containment hospital room on the second floor. They set up an access vestibule, where nurses and doctors could change into protective clothing before they entered. They started Tanaka immediately on an IV drip of ribavirin, a drug that is known to slow down the replication of some viruses. They told her not to worry, that they hoped her illness would prove treatable. Yet with all their technology, they were as helpless as doctors had been in the Middle Ages in the face of the Black Death. They set up monitoring machines in her room and started her on Dilantin, an antiseizure medication. When she tried to chew on her wrists and fingers, they tied strips of gauze around her hands, but she tore them off with her teeth, so they had to restrain her arms with nylon straps tied to the bed frame. She was not incoherent, and she was deeply apprehensive of the future. Most of all she was afraid of dying alone, but she didn't want her family to see her in this condition. "Will you stay with me, Alice?" she said in a thick voice. A nurse wearing a mask and protective suit wiped the sweat off her face.

Austen stayed with Tanaka as much as possible.

Tanaka said that she didn't feel very sick, just very "coldy." She did not know why she wanted to do "that thing." She could not find a word for wanting to destroy herself with her teeth.

□

A team of four epidemiologists from the C.D.C. had been stationed on Governors Island in their own quarters. They had spent the past two days interviewing case contacts, taking blood samples from people who might have been exposed to the virus, and calling area hospitals. One of the C.D.C. people, an epidemic intelligence officer named Gregory Katman, found a new case.

At New York Hospital, a man had been brought into the emergency room having continual seizures. He had begun biting his mouth severely while having dinner with his wife in a restaurant on the Upper East Side of New York. His name was John Dana. An Army medevac helicopter was sent to New York Hospital from Governors Island. By the time the patient-transfer documents had been filled out, John Dana was dead.

Alice Austen and Lex Nathanson did the autopsy and made a diagnosis of Cobra virus infection. Dana's body was federal evidence and could not be released to the family.

C.D.C. investigators, working with some of Masaccio's task-force agents, interviewed the Dana family. They lived in Forest Hills, Queens. The investigators discovered that John Dana had been walking across the subway platform in downtown Brooklyn on the Saturday morning when Peter Talides was killed on the tracks. Dana was the man who had wiped specks of brain material from his glasses. He had been infected with Cobra through the eyes. The United States Public Health Service put his wife under quarantine. She was installed in a hospital room on Governors Island, where her two daughters were allowed to visit her.

John Dana had been infected with the Zecker-Moran isolate of Cobra virus. It had passed from Kate Moran to Peter Talides, and from Talides to John Dana. It had undergone three generations of infection in humans. It did not seem to become weaker as it moved from person to person. Austen found that the clinical signs of Cobra in Dana at autopsy were very much like those in Kate Moran.

Mrs. Helen Zecker, the mother of Penny Zecker, was found dead in her house in Staten Island by a C.D.C. investigator. Mrs. Zecker's body was lying on her recliner. "It" had gotten her, as she had feared and predicted. The deaths led Austen to believe that Cobra was capable of sustaining itself in the human species, in a perhaps unlimited chain of human-to-human transmission.

Recombination

Hopkins continued to use the Felix machine to decode the genetic material in Cobra. The DNA of the Cobra virus contained roughly 200,000 bases of code. That made it one of the longest and most complicated genetic codes in any virus. Many viruses, especially those that use RNA rather than DNA for their genetic material, contain some 10,000 bases of code. A DNA virus with a long genetic code, like Cobra, is eminently usable as a genetically engineered weapon, because a lot of extra code can be added to it without damaging the virus and rendering it incapable of being able to multiply.

All day and much of the night, Hopkins ran samples of blood, tissue, and dust through Felix, pulling up genetic sequences from Cobra and trying to identify them. The process was like putting together a very large jigsaw puzzle. Gradually the structure of the organism's genes became clearer to him, yet parts of it mystified him. Cobra was a recombinant virus that had been engineered with skill and subtlety.

"It's a world-class weapon," Hopkins said to Littleberry and Austen one day. "It didn't come out of somebody's garage, that's for sure."

Hopkins was staring at the screen. "Uh-oh. Look at this," he said. He had just fed a piece of code into GenBank. This is what had come up on the screen:

Sequences producing High-scoring Segment Pairs:

<u>Variola major virus (strain Banglade . . .</u>	3900	0.0	1
Variola virus (Xhol-F,O,H,P,Q genome . . .	3882	0.0	1
Variola virus Garcia-1966 right near . . .	3882	0.0	1

<u>Variola major virus (strain Bangladesh-1975)</u>

"Wow! Variola major! That's smallpox," Hopkins said, pointing to the screen. "Cobra's part smallpox. That is really clever." He turned to look at Littleberry and Austen.

Littleberry wasn't answering. He was staring at the screen.

Littleberry made a fist. He brought his fist down on the table with a crash. "God damn it!" he said. "God damn it! *Those sons of bitches!*" He turned and walked away. He went out on the deck by the conference room and stood by the rail, staring across the waters of New York Bay. He stayed there for a long time. The other members of the team decided not to disturb him. Hopkins carried on into the night, analyzing the code with Felix, muttering strange terms to himself—"Open reading frame . . . virulence factor A47R . . ."

Invisible History (III.)

Security matters in the federal government are compartmentalized. Information from one agency flows to another agency through top managers. The flow is controlled by bureaucrats and intelligence people. This means that parts of the federal government don't know what other parts are doing. Files are routinely destroyed, for security purposes, and people retire and die. The United States government does not know parts of its own history. The knowledge remains hidden in pockets.

In times of emergency, someone in one branch of the federal government may suddenly need information from someone in a different branch. Then people have to sit down in a room with each other and trade sensitive information by means of an informal conversation. This is secret oral history. It is not supposed to happen. It happens all the time.

Mark Littleberry telephoned Frank Masaccio and told him there was an area of knowledge that he, Masaccio, needed to become aware of, under conditions of security. Shortly afterward, Littleberry and Masaccio entered the F.B.I. Command Center in the Federal Building. It was night, and the room was deserted except for one agent, Caroline Landau, who was working on some video feeds. Masaccio stopped before a steel door on the west wall of the Command

Center. It was the door to a room known as Conference 30-30. It is a secure room—actually a Mosler
steel safe. He touched a combination keypad, and the
two men settled in chairs around a small table, and
the door clicked shut.

From the corner of her eye, Caroline Landau
had watched the two men go into the secure room,
and she had understood that it had to do with Cobra.
I wonder if an operation is going down? she thought.
She could feel an operation gathering in the air, like
a weather front coming, bringing a gentle pickup of
the wind, and the smell of a building electrical storm.

□

"We've found a lethal smallpox gene in the Cobra
virus," Littleberry said to Masaccio.

"Yeah?" It didn't mean much to him.

"Will calls it the rocketing gene. It makes a protein that rockets the virus particles around the infected cell. You could think of it as fireworks going
off inside the cell. It destroys brain cells while it
shoots the virus everywhere. That's why these people
die so fast, Frank. The virus is rocketing through
their brains. Cobra is part smallpox."

Masaccio sucked his teeth and played with his
class ring on his finger. "Fine, but when are you guys
going to find me the perp?" he said.

"What you're trying to do is change the out-
come of history, you know," Littleberry said.

Masaccio replied that he was well aware of that.

Littleberry settled back in the chair, feeling tired
in his bones, and he wondered how long it would be
before he could see his grandchildren and feel a wind

from the Gulf of Mexico on his face. Finding a piece
of smallpox in the Cobra virus was like . . . dying.

"It's strange, Frank. I'm proud of what I did as
a scientist. But I'm sorrier than ever for what I did as
a human being. How do you reconcile that?"

"You don't," Masaccio said.

"Something happened to me late in the program. I mean in the American biological-weapons
program. Late 1969. Just before Nixon killed it."

The U.S. Army's biological-weapons-production
facility was the Biological Directorate plant in Pine
Bluff, Arkansas. In 1969, Littleberry had received an
invitation from some Army researchers to visit the
plant and see warheads being loaded. He watched
workers packing bomblets with dry anthrax. They
were wearing breathing masks and coveralls, and that
was it. No protective space suits.

"I'm looking at these guys, and I realize that
they are all black guys," Littleberry said to Masaccio.
"The overseers were white. It was African-American
men filling germ bombs, with the white guys telling
them what to do."

He had tried to put it out of his mind. He had
tried to tell himself that the men had well-paying
jobs. He had tried to tell himself that the military had
been good to him. "It took me way too long to get
through my stubborn head the *reality* of what was
going on in Arkansas. It was expendable nigger-labor
in a disease factory, that's what it was."

When Nixon shut down the American biological-
weapons program in 1969, Mark Littleberry was out
of work. "Nixon put me out of a job, and I'm thankful.

All I had to show for my M.D. was thousands of dead monkeys and some super-efficient biological weapons."

"Hold on," Masaccio said. "What I hear is that the biological shit was unusable. I hear that it wouldn't work."

"Where'd you hear that?"

"All my sources."

"That's crap," Littleberry said. "That is pure crap. It's the kind of unreal crap we've been hearing for years from the civilian scientific community, which has its head in the sand about bioweapons. We tested strategic biosystems for five years in the Pacific Ocean. We tested *everything* at Johnston Atoll, the lethal stuff, all the means of deployment. Not everything worked. That's the whole point of research and development. But we learned what works. Believe me, those weapons work. You might not like the way that they work, but they work. Who told you the weapons don't work?"

"Ah, one of our academic consultants. He has security clearances."

"An academic with security clearances. Did this guy describe what happened at Johnston Atoll?"

Masaccio didn't answer.

"Did he *mention* Johnston Atoll?"

"Nope."

"Then let's get back to reality," Littleberry said. "Nixon suddenly killed the program in late 1969. It was his decision to kill it. I was agonizing over this goddamned program, whether I should leave it, and Nixon killed it. I won't forgive Nixon for taking away a decision that I should have made for myself."

Littleberry decided that he had to do something to make up for his work with weapons. He applied to switch his officer's commission into the Public Health Service, and he went to work for the Centers for Disease Control, where he took part in the war on smallpox. In the early 1960s, a handful of doctors at the C.D.C. had an important idea. Their idea was that a virus could be eradicated from the planet. They chose the smallpox virus, variola, as the most likely candidate for total extinction, because it lives only in people. It doesn't hide in the rain forest in some animal where you can't eradicate it.

Littleberry reached into his hip pocket and pulled out his wallet. He removed a small photograph. It was old and dog-eared, covered with plastic. He had been carrying it in his wallet for twenty years. He pushed it across the table toward Masaccio. "This is the work that made me whole."

The photograph showed a thin African man standing in a parched landscape, beside a fence. He was squinting away from the camera. He wore no shirt. Blisters speckled his shoulders, arms, and chest.

"Should I know him?" Masaccio asked.

"Nope," Littleberry said. "But if you were a public health doctor you would. His name was Ali Maow Maalin. He was a cook. The place is Somalia, the date's October 26, 1977. Mr. Maalin was the last human case of smallpox. The smallpox life-form has never made another natural appearance anywhere on earth. That was the end of the road for one of the worst diseases on the planet. I was there, with Jason Weisfeld, another C.D.C. doctor. We vaccinated everyone for miles around. That bastard wasn't able to jump from Mr. Maalin to any other host. We wiped out that bastard. By *we* I mean thousands of public health doctors all over the world. Doctors in India. Doctors in Nigeria and China. Doctors in Bangladesh with no shoes. Local people. Today I'm afraid you have to wonder just how successful that smallpox campaign really was."

What Littleberry had in mind was the surprise that history and nature came up with in 1973, four years before the last naturally occurring case of smallpox and just a year after the signing of the Biological Weapons Convention. It was the biotechnology revolution.

□

Genetic engineering is all about moving genes from one organism to another. A gene is a strip of DNA that carries the code for making a particular protein in a living creature. A gene could be thought of as a piece of ribbon. A microscopic ribbon. The ribbon can be cut and pasted. Molecular biologists use certain splicing enzymes, which act as scissors, and which cut DNA. (Molecular biology is largely a matter of cutting and pasting ribbon.) You can snip the DNA where you want. You can chop it out of a longer piece of DNA, then put it into another organism. That is, you can transplant a gene. If you do it correctly, the organism will have a new working gene afterward. The organism will do something different; it will make a new protein. It will be a changed living creature, and it will pass its changed character to its offspring. If you allow the organism to multiply, you've cloned the organism. A clone is a designer copy. This is genetic engineering. One of the big complications is that when you move DNA from one organism to another it doesn't always work properly in its new home. But it can be made to work. An organism that contains strips of foreign DNA is known as a recombinant organism.

The biotechnology revolution began in 1973, when Stanley N. Cohen, Herbert W. Boyer, and others succeeded in putting working foreign genes into the bacterium *E. coli,* a microorganism that lives in the human gut. They made loops of DNA, and they managed to stick the loops inside *E. coli* cells. The cells were different afterward, because they had extra working DNA inside them. Cohen and Boyer shared the Nobel Prize for this achievement. The genes they transplanted gave *E. coli* resistance to some antibiotics. The organisms with their new features, their resistance to antibiotics, were not dangerous. They could easily be wiped out by other antibiotics. The experiment was perfectly safe.

Cohen and Boyer had accomplished one of the historic experiments in twentieth-century science. It would lead to the growth of new industries in the United States, Japan, and Europe. New companies would be formed, diseases would be cured in new ways, and great insights into the nature of living systems would follow.

However, almost immediately, scientists became worried that moving genes from one microorganism to another could cause outbreaks of new infectious diseases, or environmental disasters. The concern was very great: recombinant organisms were frightening to think about. Concerned scientists urged a temporary halt in genetic experimentation until the scientific community could debate the hazards and come up with safety guidelines to prevent accidents. A meeting to discuss these issues took place in Asilomar, California, in the summer of 1975.

The Asilomar Conference brought a sense of reason and calm to a situation that had seemed inherently frightening. After the Asilomar Conference, scientists proceeded cautiously in the area of genetic engineering. The so-called Asilomar Safety Guidelines for carrying out genetic experiments on microorganisms were established, and a variety of safety review boards and procedures were put in place. As it turned out, the concerns of Western scientists about the hazards of genetic engineering provided a blueprint for what was to become the Soviet bioweapons program.

Around this time, a certain Dr. Yuri Ovchinnikov, one of the founders of molecular biology in the Soviet Union, and some of his colleagues pitched the idea of a genetic-weapons program to the top Soviet leadership, including Leonid Brezhnev. Soon the Soviet leader began sending word down to the Soviet scientific community: do research in genetic engineering and you will have money; if your research has applications for weapons, you will be given what you need.

In 1973, the year of the Cohen and Boyer cloning experiment, the Central Committee of the Soviet Union had established an ostensibly civilian biotechnology research and production organization called Biopreparat. Participating scientists sometimes called it simply "The Concern." It was controlled and funded by the Soviet Ministry of Defense.

The main business of Biopreparat was the creation of biological weapons using advanced scientific techniques. The first head of Biopreparat was General V. I. Ogarkov.

In 1974, the Soviets established a complex of research institutes in Siberia devoted especially to developing advanced virus weapons using the techniques of molecular biology. The centerpiece of the complex was the Institute of Molecular Biology at Koltsovo, a self-contained research complex in the birch forests twenty miles east of the city of Novosibirsk. The cover story was that the institute of Koltsovo was dedicated to making medicines. But for all the state research money spent on "medicines" in Biopreparat, the Soviet Union suffered a chronic lack of the simplest medicines and vaccines. It seems pretty clear that the money wasn't being spent on medicine.

Most of the leading scientific figures in Soviet microbiology and molecular biology took military money and did research that was connected to the development of bioweapons. Some of the scientists lobbied for the money. Others didn't know what was going on, or didn't want to ask too many questions. In the West, there was strong, vehement, entrenched resistance to the idea that biological weapons work, and there was a worthy but perhaps naive hope that the Soviets would be reasonable about such weapons. Scientists in general believed that the treaty was working remarkably well. Biologists in particular congratulated themselves for being more alert and wise than the physicists, who had not managed to escape the taint of weapons of mass destruction.

Meanwhile the intelligence community kept leaking allegations about a biological-weapons program in Russia. Scientists were (quite reasonably) suspicious of intelligence information of this kind— it wasn't backed by much hard evidence, and it seemed to come from right-wing military people and from paranoids in the C.I.A., who, it was felt, tended to demonize Russia to serve their own interests. People who tried to say that the Soviets had used toxin weapons on hill people in Southeast Asia were pilloried in scientific journals. In 1979, when airborne anthrax drifted across the city of Sverdlovsk, killing some sixty-six people, American experts in biological weapons declared that the citizens of the city had eaten some bad meat. The chief proponent of this view was a Harvard University biochemist named Matthew S. Meselson, one of the architects of the Biological Weapons Convention. He had helped persuade the Nixon White House to embrace the treaty. Meselson insisted that the anthrax accident at Sverdlovsk had been a natural event. His view prevailed for a long time, even though there were those who said that the Sverdlovsk incident was an accident involving biological weapons.

Then in 1989, Vladimir Pasechnik, a top Biopreparat scientist, defected to Great Britain. Pasechnik had been the director of a Biopreparat research facility known as the Institute for Ultrapure Biological Preparations, in Leningrad. British military intelligence gave Pasechnik the code name Paul. The British intelligence people spent months debriefing "Paul" in a safe house in the English countryside about fifty miles west of London.

Pasechnik spoke of massive biowarfare facilities hidden all over the Soviet Union. The Soviet Union, he said, had deployed a variety of operational strategic biowarheads on intercontinental missiles that were targeted all over the place and could be loaded with hot agents and launched quickly. Large stockpiles of hot agents were kept in bunkers near the launch sites. Dr. Pasechnik spoke very knowledgeably of genetic engineering—he knew exactly how it was done. He said that genetic engineering of weapons was a recent focus of work in his own laboratory. He said it had been done in a variety of places in the Soviet Union with a variety of hot biological agents.

President George Bush and Prime Minister Margaret Thatcher were briefed on the situation. It seemed possible that Pasechnik was exaggerating. Much of what he claimed was difficult to verify. The Soviet Union clearly had a biological-weapons program, but what was the extent of it? Bush and Thatcher put intense personal pressure on Mikhail Gorbachev to come clean about bioweapons and allow an inspection team to tour some of the Soviet bioweapons facilities.

This was in the late fall and early winter of 1990, when the Soviet regime was in the process of crumbling in a welter of glasnost and perestroika, and the Soviet Union was heading for economic collapse and eventual breakup. At the same time, President Bush was preparing to go to war with Iraq. (The Gulf War started in January 1991.) American and allied troops were pouring into the Persian Gulf. Intelligence reports indicated that the Iraqis possessed an arsenal of biological weapons, but the Iraqi capabilities were not known. It suddenly appeared that the United States had been caught flat-footed in respect to biological weapons, both in the Soviet Union and in the Middle East.

□

"I was only one man in a group of inspectors," Littleberry said to Masaccio, "but I think I can speak for all of my colleagues."

Just before Christmas 1990, Mark Littleberry and a group of Americans were flown to London on their way to Russia for an inspection tour. Some of the Americans were C.I.A. analysts, some were in the F.B.I., some were U.S. Army experts, and some, like Littleberry, were private scientists who happened to know a great deal about biological weapons.

The inspection team had a long wait in London. It was said that the procedure for inspecting Russian biological facilities was proving difficult to work out in detail. What was actually happening was that Gorbachev was stalling the inspection team in order to give his military people a chance to move the live weapons stocks out of the facilities and sterilize the buildings with chemicals. Suddenly, in January 1991, the team was told it was going in to have a look. While the world was preoccupied with the Gulf War, the inspectors flew to various sites in the Soviet Union.

If there were any veils over their eyes before they went in, the veils fell away quickly. One inspector, an American who is an expert in advanced biotechnology production processes involving genetically engineered vaccines, would later say that when he went in, he was sure that the problem in Russia had been exaggerated by military people and by intelligence analysts. By the time he left, he had come to believe that the problem was so bad that it was impossible to see the bottom of it. It was "very scary," he said.

There were approximately sixteen identified major bioweapons facilities in the Soviet Union (or as many as fifty-two, if the smaller ones are counted). The team visited only four of them. The facilities were of two basic types: weapons-production facilities and research-and-development labs. Forty miles south of Moscow, near a town called Serpukhov, the teams explored the Institute of Applied Microbiology at Obolensk, a large Biopreparat facility. Obolensk consists of thirty buildings. It is at least ten times the size of the USAMRIID complex at Fort Detrick. The main building at Obolensk is called Corpus One. It is eight stories tall, and it covers more than five acres of ground. It is an enormous monolithic biological laboratory with one and a half million square feet of laboratory space, making it one of the largest biological research facilities under one roof anywhere in the world. Corpus One is surrounded by triple layers of razor wire. The perimeter security includes tremblors (ground-vibration sensors), infrared body-heat detectors, and armed guards from the Special Forces. Inside Corpus One, the team had a chance to explore Soviet hot zones.

They discovered that the design of Corpus One is different and somewhat more sophisticated than the design of the hot zones at USAMRIID or at the Centers for Disease Control in Atlanta. Obolensk

Corpus One has ring-shaped hot zones, levels within levels. The hot core is at the center of the building, surrounded by concentric rings of graduated biohazard security, so that as you approach the building's center, you go from Level 2, to Level 3, to Level 4. The Soviet scientists were justifiably proud of their ring design. They were also proud of their green AP-5 biohazard space suits. The Americans who tried them on said they were more comfortable than American biohazard suits.

At Corpus One, the focus of research was *Yersinia pestis,* a bacterial organism that causes the plague. This is the organism that in the Middle Ages had killed off a third of the population of Europe in one sweep.

The scientific director of Obolensk was a hawk-faced microbiologist and military general named Dr. N. N. Urakov. He had long, silvery, thick, straight hair that he wore swept back over his forehead. Urakov seemed to be a man without emotion, except when he spoke of the power of microorganisms, and then his voice resonated with commitment.

The inspection teams found research areas in Corpus One that were designed for rapid mutation and fast selection of strains of plague while the strains were exposed to ultraviolet light and nuclear radiation. They came to the conclusion that the researchers were doing forced mutation and selection of strains of Black Death that could live and multiply in a nuclear-battle zone. The Obolensk Black Death was a strategic weapon. Team members would later offer the opinion that the Obolensk Black Death was fully weaponized and integrated into the Soviet Union's strategic forces and its war plans. It was a strategic bioweapon on two counts. First, it was apparently deployed in intercontinental strategic missile warheads targeted all over the planet, and second, it was highly contagious and incurable with medicine.

The inspectors found forty giant fermenter tanks inside Corpus One's hot zones. The tanks were used for growing huge quantities of *something*. They were twenty feet tall. The fact that they were placed inside the biocontainment zones was evidence that they were for growing hot agents. The tanks were about the largest reactor tanks that any of the inspectors had ever seen. Why would any legitimate medical research program need forty tanks for growing Black Death and other organisms, tanks twenty feet tall, inside a hot containment area that was surrounded by intense military security? One of the inspectors would later say that he thought you could supply the entire national output of the Iraqi biological-weapons program at the time of the Gulf War with a single Obolensk reactor tank. And there were a number of bioweapons-production facilities the scale of Obolensk scattered across Russia.

The production equipment in Corpus One was sparkling clean and sterile when the inspectors arrived. The rooms and tanks smelled of bleach and chemicals. All of the living biological materials, the so-called seed stocks and growth media, had been removed from the parts of Corpus One that the inspectors were allowed to visit. The team took swab samples, but nothing grew in the test tubes.

Dr. Urakov insisted to the Americans and the British that the medical research at Obolensk was entirely peaceful in nature. When asked by the inspectors why the Soviet Union had built a heavily guarded military research site, with one and a half million square feet of space, with forty reactor vessels two stories tall, much of it dedicated to Level 4 space-suit research and production of Black Death, Dr. Urakov answered that Black Death was a problem in the Soviet Union.

The inspectors agreed with him on that score.

However, they pointed out that the Soviet Union was reporting only a handful of deaths from plague every year, so plague couldn't be *that* much of a problem. Especially, they said, because plague is controllable with simple antibiotics.

Dr. Urakov answered that in a country as large as the Soviet Union there was "a need for research."

The inspectors began to ask questions about genetic engineering. Did the need for research include the need to do genetic engineering of Black Death for the purposes of creating a weapon?

Dr. Urakov's answers were disturbing. He suggested that his people were working with strains of Black Death that were incredibly deadly—strains you would not believe. He claimed they were natural strains. He said that vaccines didn't work on the strains. The inspectors had the impression that he was making veiled boasts about his staff's accomplishments in genetic engineering, but they couldn't be sure. Urakov and his colleagues stunned the inspectors by offering to arrange for a "technology transfer" with the United States, whereby the United States would have access to the discoveries at Obolensk—for an unstated price. They insinuated that since the United States had fallen behind the Soviet Union in the area of biological weapons, the inspections were a cover—an excuse to pry into what Soviet scientists had done, so that the United States could play catch-up.

In fact it is easy to put antibiotic-resistant genes into bacteria—it's a basic technique, nothing fancy. Subsequent reports from Western intelligence agencies alleged that, in fact, the Obolensk Black Death was resistant to sixteen antibiotics and to nuclear radiation. How the Russians had actually developed such a strain—if they had—wasn't clear. Had they used genetic engineering, or had they used more traditional, tried-and-true methods for developing hot strains? In any case, the United States lodged a demand with the government of Russia for an explanation as to whether Russia did or did not have a weapons-production Black Death that was multidrug resistant. To date, Russian biologists and political leaders have not given any answer to this question that makes sense. There have been only vague denials.

"That Obolensk Black Death is an amazing product," Littleberry said. "It is basically incurable with medicine. And it is contagious as hell in humans. If someone threw a pound of Obolensk Black Death into the Paris Metro, you would *not* want to be living anywhere near Paris. One of our big concerns is that the Russian government appears to have lost control over these engineered military strains."

□

The inspection team flew to the city of Novosibirsk, in western Siberia. Twenty miles east of the city, in a forest of birch trees and larches, is the bioresearch

complex known as the Koltsovo Institute of Molecular Biology. It consists of about thirty buildings. The
buildings contain a variety of hot zones in the ring-
shaped Russian design. Here the focus of research is
on viruses—Ebola virus, Marburg virus, a South
American brain agent called VEE (Venezuelan equine
encephalitis), Crimean-Congo hemorrhagic fever,
tick-borne encephalitis (another brain virus), and
Machupo (Bolivian hemorrhagic fever).

The team learned that the Koltsovo research facility had bioreactor tanks designed for growing
smallpox virus. It dawned on them that Soviet smallpox military-production capacity could be many tons
a year.

Littleberry was stunned. "It was one of the
worst moments of my life," he said to Masaccio. "I
was thinking of those doctors in India and Africa,
fighting smallpox inch by inch, and meanwhile this
Biopreparat monster was preparing to make smallpox by the ton."

It came out that Koltsovo was not the only place
in Russia that had smallpox military-production capacity. There were two other places. One was a facility in a city just outside Moscow called Zagorsk
(now Sergyev Posad), and another military smallpox
weapons-production plant was at Pokrov.

Littleberry: "This story you hear about how
smallpox is just kept in one freezer in Russia today?
Complete bullshit. The Russian Ministry of Defense
is keeping seed stocks of smallpox virus at multiple
locations in military superfreezers. The Russian military people are not gonna give up their smallpox, no
way. Smallpox is a strategic weapon. It's especially

valuable as a weapon now that the natural virus has been eliminated from the human population." Most people on earth have lost their immunity to smallpox. It is incredibly lethal and infective. One person infected with it can easily infect twenty more people, so a small outbreak in a population lacking immunity will mushroom into a lethal burn. "We all think we're protected because we had our smallpox vaccinations as kids," Littleberry said. "Bad news—the smallpox shot wears off after ten to twenty years. The last shots were given out twenty years ago. Except to soldiers. Soldiers still get them."

The world's total supply of smallpox vaccine currently stands at enough shots for half a million people—enough to vaccinate one out of every ten thousand people worldwide. If smallpox started jumping from human to human in a global outbreak, smallpox vaccine would become more valuable than diamonds. On the other hand, smallpox can be engineered to elude a vaccine, rendering the existing vaccine worthless.

At Koltsovo, the research staff admitted to the inspectors that they were "working with the DNA of the smallpox virus." The statement shocked the inspectors. It shocked them as much as anything they had encountered. They did not understand what it meant to "work with the DNA of smallpox," so they asked for clarification.

The answers were vague. The inspectors went nose to nose with the Russian scientists. What did you *do* to smallpox? They pushed. They pushed harder. No answers came back. The situation became extremely tense, steel-hard with implications, and it turned into a standoff. In the background were the shadows of intercontinental missiles loaded with living hot agents, and the inspectors wanted to know this: have you people targeted my country with smallpox in missiles? What kind of smallpox? Both sides understood that the inspectors were looking straight into the asshole of modern military biology.

No answers were forthcoming. The explanations of the Russian biologists just got stranger and stranger. They said that they were working on *clones* of smallpox, not on smallpox itself. Genetic experiments in the West involving smallpox are done using clones of the vaccinia virus, because vaccinia is harmless to humans (it's the strain used for making the smallpox vaccine). To work on clones of smallpox is to work on recombinant smallpox. By insisting that they were working only on "clones of smallpox" the Russians essentially admitted that they were doing black biology with smallpox. As to whether they created whole new strains of smallpox, or whether they worked on parts of the smallpox virus, the Russians would not say. Did they take pieces of smallpox and mix them into some other virus or into a bacterium for study? Did they engineer a vaccine-elusive smallpox? It was impossible to tell.

All of the words of the Soviet biologists were captured on tape recordings. Their statements were translated and retranslated by Russian-language experts. The words were analyzed to death by experts working for the National Security Agency and other intelligence agencies. In the end, as Littleberry put it, "We never learned *what* the hell they did with smallpox."

It should not be forgotten that these were military scientists. The goal of their research was military. They had tried and perhaps succeeded at making a genetically engineered smallpox. One participant in the confrontation between the inspectors and the Russian military biologists speculated that they had chopped up the genetic material of smallpox and had put the genes into bacteria. In this way they were able to discover which smallpox genes were the lethal factors. They then put the smallpox death genes into monkeypox, making a recombinant chimera, a vaccine-elusive strategic monkeypox.

After the inspection teams returned from Russia, the C.I.A., British intelligence, and the National Security Agency collectively had a heart attack. A gulf had opened up between the factual knowledge of the eyewitness inspectors and the belief structure of the civilian science community. Senior scientists, especially in microbiology and molecular biology, began to get accelerated security clearances and were briefed on the situation, not only with regard to Russia but other countries as well. Scientists who attended these briefings came away shocked. "Their eyes were like saucers," according to one American scientist who was present at several such briefings. Biologists had discovered that one or more Manhattan bomb projects had occurred in their field, and they hadn't known about it or believed that such a thing was possible. What was particularly upsetting for some of them was the realization that leading members of their own profession had invented and were developing weapons that were in some ways significantly more powerful than the hydrogen bomb.

Matthew Meselson at Harvard was still insisting that the Biological Weapons Convention was not being violated. For years he had dominated the discussion of biological weapons, and his opinions had been widely accepted. He had published articles in prestigious journals supporting the view that the anthrax deaths in Sverdlovsk in 1979 had been caused by the citizens eating bad meat, and he offered detailed scientific data from Russian colleagues to support him. It seems that the creators of the biological weapons treaty had become its guardian, with too great a stake in the treaty's "success," and this made them blind.

Russian news reporters began to investigate the Sverdlovsk accident, and in 1991, the Moscow bureau chief of *The Wall Street Journal*, Peter Gumbel, made three trips to Sverdlovsk, and at some personal risk, while he was being followed and harassed by the K.G.B., traced about half of the civilian victims. He located their families, who had wrenching stories to tell; he found doctors who had treated the victims; he unearthed medical evidence; and he showed that most of the victims had lived or worked next to a military compound. Meselson had written that the anthrax came from a "meat-processing plant at Aramil." Gumbel went to Aramil and found no meat plant, only a picturesque village. He later confronted the Harvard professor with the fact that the meat plant didn't exist. He reported rather drily that "Prof. Meselson seemed taken aback."

Meselson found himself in an awkward position, to say the least. *The Wall Street Journal*'s investigative reporting made it appear that the scientific data that he had published about Sverdlovsk was not only wrong but might have been fabricated by his Russian colleagues. Meselson had been both a victim and an unknowing disseminator of potentially misleading or even fraudulent scientific information. He got permission to go to Sverdlovsk, and with his wife Jeanne Guillemin and a team of collaborators, demonstrated that the outbreak really had been caused by an airborne release of anthrax from a military plant. He eventually published his findings in 1994 in the magazine *Science*. He did not, however, see fit to credit Peter Gumbel anywhere in his article.

He and his co-authors concluded that only a pinch of anthrax had been released into the air, not a large amount—only a miniscule whiff of anthrax that might be almost invisible if held between thumb and forefinger. Some experts disputed the notion that such a tiny amount of anthrax could kill so many people in a plume across a city. It is more logical, and it now seems widely accepted, that the amount of anthrax was more than a pinch, but no one really knows. The accident involved production of anthrax for weapons, and the story is that filters had been left off grinding machines, but the world may never learn what really happened.

The important thing is that Matthew Meselson had done an about-face. There is a world of difference between a pinch of weapon and a ton of bad meat. The other turnaround was more impressive, and it came from Russian president Boris Yeltsin, who confirmed to the world that modern Russia had inherited a biological-weapons program from the Soviet Union. This information was corroborated and

expanded upon by two more senior defectors from
the Russian bioweapons program. Top officials in the
Russian program have just recently released a list of
the hot agents that the modern Russian military
forces would be most likely to use in the event of
war. In order of choice, it goes: smallpox, Black
Death, and anthrax. One or more of them may be genetically engineered. Biological-weapons treaty?
What treaty?

□

Masaccio and Littleberry sat in silence for a while, as
Masaccio took in the context in which the Cobra
Event was being played out.

"The cancer has metastasized," Littleberry said.
"A lot of countries are into biological weapons now.
Syria has a top-notch biological-weapons program.
Syria is also believed to be a sponsor of terrorism—
you would know more about that than I do, Frank. If
Syria's got a program, you can wonder if Israel has
gone seriously into black biology, and Israeli scientists are some of the best in the world. Iran is heavily
into biological weapons; they know all about molecular biology, and they are also testing cruise missiles.
Think about that. Think about line streakouts of an
engineered hot agent. China has massive biological-
weapons facilities out in the Sinkiang desert, but it's
hard for us to know what they're doing, because our
satellites are useless for detecting bioweapons research. We can't see inside the buildings, and even if
we could, we wouldn't know what was growing in the
tanks. We do know that the Chinese are very good in
the area of molecular biology. And that's not all.
There are plenty of other countries that are develop-

ing bioweapons. None of these countries is *that* good. There are some clever idiots out there, and sooner or later, there is going to be a very serious biological accident. Something that will make Sverdlovsk look like a kiddie ride at the park. And I think it will be global, not just one city."

Littleberry went on to say that he sometimes wondered if there had already been major accidents. "The Gulf War Syndrome," he said, "is almost certainly caused by exposure to chemical weapons. But we have not yet totally ruled out the possibility that it's some kind of biological weapon. Maybe early in the war the Iraqis did a line laydown of some experimental agent that we never noticed. One jet flying along—we might not have recognized it as a laydown. It might mean that the Gulf War Syndrome could be contagious and spreading. I doubt it, but you never know. Now think about the AIDS virus. There's a lot of evidence that AIDS is a natural virus that comes from the Central African rain forests, but in fact the origin of AIDS is unknown. We cannot *rule out* the possibility that AIDS is a weapon. Is AIDS something that escaped from a weapons lab somewhere? I don't think so, but I keep wondering."

"Is Cobra like that? Did it escape from somewhere, Mark?"

"I doubt it. Someone stole it from a lab, is my guess."

"What about Russia? What's going on there now?"

"That's real touchy stuff. Real ugly. Real sensitive."

"Of course," Masaccio said.

"There's a building at the Koltsovo Institute of Molecular Biology that doesn't have a name or a number," Littleberry said. "We nicknamed it Corpus Zero, and we demanded to be allowed to go inside."

After a lot of hesitation, the Russian minders finally agreed to allow the inspectors to have a very brief tour of Corpus Zero. Since that time, no inspector from the United States or anyplace else has been allowed back inside Corpus Zero. What is known about Corpus Zero is based on one brief visit in 1991.

Corpus Zero is situated in a corner of the Koltsovo campus. It is a large building, made of brick, with small windows, a building shaped like a cube.

"We didn't know what was going on inside Corpus Zero. The satellite imagery didn't show anything," Littleberry said.

All of the Koltsovo staff had been sent home at the time of the inspection, so Corpus Zero was deserted when the inspection team entered with a group of minders. There wasn't much to see. The building appeared to contain only office space and normal biology labs. On one of the laboratory benches, an inspector discovered a piece of paper pinned to the side of the bench with a tack. On it was written in English, "The eagle can't catch a fly." It seemed to be a way of thumbing one's nose at the inspectors.

The inspectors were touring some offices when Littleberry told everyone that he was going to the men's room. As he was coming out of the men's room, he found that the team and the minders had gone down a hallway and were starting to turn a corner. He saw his chance. He went in the other direction.

Littleberry had gone AWOL.

Telling the story to Frank Masaccio, Littleberry found himself drifting back in time. The memory was so clear, set off in distinct edges from the foggy haze that followed.

The corridors in Corpus Zero were in the shape of a ring, he realized. All the corridors circled around the center of the building but did not give access to the center. There had to be something hidden in the center of Corpus Zero. The building must have a hot zone at its core.

How to reach the core? On the inside wall of a corridor, he found an unmarked steel door. It did not have a biohazard symbol on it. Littleberry opened it. He found himself in a corridor heading inward. The light was dim, and he turned on his flashlight.

It was a blank corridor. He kept going, and opened a far door. He found himself in a vast interior space. It was the center of Corpus Zero, and it was pitch-dark. He switched on his flashlight. He was standing in a hangarlike room, several stories tall. In the center sat an enormous steel cube. He played his flashlight over the cube. Sticking out of the cube in various places were probes and tubes—they were obviously sensor devices, monitoring devices. They were there to monitor something happening inside the cube.

He circled the cube, his footsteps echoing on the concrete floor, and he found a control room. There were computer consoles and all manner of gauges and controls. The room was deserted, the staff gone, the computers turned off.

Littleberry turned and faced the cube. That was when he saw the stairs. The stairs led halfway up the

side of the cube to a door. The door had a circular
wheel handle, like a pressure door in a submarine.
His flashlight played over the door, and then he saw
the symbol. The door was marked with a red biohazard flower.

The flower beckoned to Littleberry like his own
fate. Fuck it, I'll hold my breath, he said to himself.
When he arrived at the landing at the top of the stairs,
he spun the wheel. Locks pulled back. He took a
breath, opened the door, and shone his flashlight in.

He began to descend a stairway into the chamber.
He knew what the chamber was. It was an explosion-
test chamber. It was for testing small bioweapons in
the air. The chamber is used to simulate a battlefield
environment that has gone hot with a biological
weapon.

He heard a whimpering sound.

"Hello?" he said.

There was no answer.

At the bottom of the chamber he found a passage leading off horizontally. He looked into it and
pointed his flashlight around, and found the cages for
the test animals. In one of the cages a female monkey
sat crouched. He saw that she was a rhesus monkey.
She reached toward him and drew her hand away.

"Sorry, sweetheart," he said. "I don't have any
food."

He played his flashlight over the animal. Like all
female primates, she had breasts for suckling her
young. He saw that her nipples were leaking blood.
Her body was peppered with a rash of black blood
blisters, half-hidden in her fur. The blisters looked
like garnets in the light of his flashlight. He saw pools

of blood at the bottom of the animal's cage. She was hemorrhaging from the vagina. She was a simulated human female in a simulated biological war zone.

She gave an alarm cry, faint. Her teeth were covered with blood.

He had not held his breath. He turned and made his way back up the stairs. He had been inside an explosion test chamber at Koltsovo. This one was used for testing freeze-dried Ebola virus preparations that the Soviet Union was developing for missile warheads. The same chamber was also used for testing smallpox for warheads.

Three days after he walked into the Ebola chamber in Corpus Zero, Littleberry developed a fever and collapsed. He was rushed to the Koltsovo biocontainment hospital. It was a hospital with dozens of beds, behind steel airlock doors, where nurses and doctors wore space suits.

"I had airborne Ebola," Littleberry said.

"Why aren't you dead?" Masaccio asked him.

"With a biological weapon, there will always be survivors. Maybe the Russian treatments worked on me. We still don't know."

Mark Littleberry remained in the Koltsovo hospital for four weeks. The medical staff were embarrassed and deeply apologetic, and did their best to take care of him.

"What was it like, having that?" Masaccio asked.

"All I remember is the way I cursed those folks in space suits every time they tried to turn me over in bed."

"One thing I've got to ask you, Dr. Littleberry. Do we have a secret biological weapons program?"

Littleberry stared at him. "Jesus—you ought to know, Frank."

"Well, I don't. The C.I.A. doesn't always tell me things."

"There are two answers to your question," Littleberry said. "One, I personally have no evidence that the U.S. military has a secret bioweapons program. The second answer is, we could have it anytime we wanted. Our biotechnology industry is second to none."

"So why don't we do it?" Masaccio asked.

"It would leak pretty quick. This is the world's leakiest government, and public opinion would stop it. I like to think so, anyway."

□

The staff at the Koltsovo Institute of Molecular Biology numbered four thousand at the time of the first biological-weapons inspection, in 1991. By 1997, after economic troubles had hit Russia, the staff at Koltsovo had shrunk to about two thousand. Two thousand scientists and staff members from Koltsovo no longer work there. Some of them have gone missing, and the Russian government itself does not seem to know where to find them. Some of them have left Russia. Some of them are working for bioweapons programs in other countries, probably in Iran and Syria, possibly in Iraq, and perhaps in Asian countries. What strains they took with them, and where they are now, is a question that bedevils intelligence agencies.

Biopreparat is broke and is trying to make money, any way it can, in order to keep its scientists and staff employed. The Russian government does not want its biological scientists leaving Russia, because they could carry their knowledge and military strains of viruses to a country that is an enemy of Russia. In Russia today, you can buy face cream made by Biopreparat. You can buy Biopreparat vodka. It is known as "Siberian Sunshine." Biopreparat scientists have told Americans that it is made in former anthrax tanks, and they don't seem to be joking. The vodka is probably safe to drink, for if Biopreparat knows anything, it knows how to sterilize a hot zone. Biopreparat is now a joint stock corporation. You can buy shares in Biopreparat on the Moscow stock exchange.

The Russian Ministry of Defense was always in control of the country's bioweapons-development work, and it also controlled the stockpiling and deployment of the weapons. The Ministry of Defense paid for the research done by Biopreparat, and used the fruits of the research in warheads. It is very difficult to find a knowledgeable expert who believes that Russia has given up developing offensive biological weapons. The program is probably smaller in scope, but it is believed to continue at secret locations, more deeply buried than before. Defense is still supremely important to Russia. As molecular biology becomes cheaper and easier to do, and as virus-production facilities become smaller and more portable, a biological-weapons program can continue to move forward almost unnoticed. The fly becomes smaller, faster, harder to catch.

In recent visits to Koltsovo, American scientists have noticed that the lights are burning in the windows of Corpus Zero at three o'clock in the afternoon, when it begins to grow dark in Siberia during the fall and winter. The lights are out almost every-where else in Koltsovo, but they remain lit on all floors of the building with no name. The Russian managers of the site have said to American visitors that "only three married couples work there, and they have had their smallpox vaccinations." It is obvious that many more people than that are employed at Corpus Zero. What the staff is doing with the Ebola-smallpox aerosol test chamber inside Corpus Zero is unknown. Who is paying for the research being done in Corpus Zero and what type of research is being done there are unknown.

"Biopreparat was a Humpty Dumpty," Little-berry told Masaccio. "It fell and broke when the So-viet Union broke. Biopreparat has gone into pieces that have fallen in different directions. The Bio-preparat that's visible is the part that makes face cream and vodka. Another chunk was pulled into the Russian military. There may be other invisible pieces of Biopreparat floating around. Dangerous fragments. Maybe Biopreparat has an Evil Child. Maybe the Evil Child has no connection to Russia anymore."

"So you think an Evil Child has put together the Cobra virus?" Masaccio said, incredulously. "You think it's the *Russians*?"

Littleberry smiled. "Not exactly. This Cobra virus is so beautiful and so new that it has to be Amer-ican engineering, Frank. Has to be. Looking at that virus is like looking at a starship. But the smallpox in it—that's ancient and old and smells like Russia. Will Hopkins keeps talking about reaching through Cobra to find its maker. Here's what I think. I think Cobra has two makers. One is American and one is Russian. They've gotten together somehow, and there's money involved. There has to be. I think there's a company in this. Cobra does comes from an Evil Child. And I think the Evil Child is an American company that is operating somewhere near New York City."

Part Six

THE OPERATION

Boy

Alice Austen was with Colonel Ernesto Aguilar and two Army nurses on board an Army medevac helicopter that had just lifted off from the Thirty-fourth Street Heliport. It was carrying a five-year-old boy named Hector Ramirez, who lived on Avenue B. Hector was conscious, lying buckled on a gurney and covered with blankets. His lips, behind a clear oxygen mask, were bloody and torn. He had been in grand mal seizure in the emergency room of Bellevue Hospital, but the seizures had abated. The boy stared at the ceiling of the chopper, and his brown eyes had a tawny gold center.

Austen had insisted on going with the evacuation team. She should not have been there, perhaps, but she had presented herself to Colonel Aguilar and told him that, as a physician, she should be with the boy as the representative of the Reachdeep team. He did not argue with her.

The helicopter was crowded. Dr. Aguilar watched the boy's vital signs. They passed over the Williamsburg Bridge. The blade noise was high, and they spoke through headsets.

"Watch him! He's seizing again!" Dr. Aguilar said.

Hector Ramirez went into a flurry. He was buckled down, but his small body seemed incredibly strong. He turned diagonally under the straps, and his head lashed back and forth. He began biting his lips behind the oxygen mask, and a fresh run of blood spattered inside the mask.

An Army nurse named Captain Dorothy Each yanked off the boy's oxygen mask. She took his head in her hands. She was wearing rubber gloves. She held his head steady. It was impossible to control his jaws. The helicopter shook and the boy shook, and his jaw worked. The helicopter began its descent to Governors Island.

Austen, also wearing gloves, put her hands on the boy. She grabbed his wrists. They were the thin wrists of a five-year-old. She was impressed with how strong a boy could be.

The two women bent over the boy. Austen transferred her grip to the boy's head. "There, there, steady, sweetheart," she said to him. She could feel his neck tightening and writhing. It was basal writhing. This was the first time she had *felt* it happening in a patient.

Captain Each transferred her grip to the boy's jaw. She held his jaw tightly in both hands, clenched, to keep him from biting. That seemed to help.

Suddenly the boy arched his back. His teeth flashed, and he bit down hard on Captain Each's left hand. His teeth tore the rubber glove.

"Oh!" the nurse said. She pulled away momentarily, but then she was back over the boy, holding his head and jaw. Austen saw how her hand bled. The blood from her hand ran onto the boy's hair. Austen did not say anything. Nobody said anything about it.

Everyone understood that Captain Dorothy Each would be placed in quarantine biocontainment in the Army Medical Management Unit.

□

The boy's mother, Ana Ramirez, the boy's aunt, Carla Salazar, and his ten-year-old sister, Ana Julia, were all admitted as patients in the Medical Management Unit. They had been in close proximity with the boy. They were kept in separate containment rooms, attended around the clock by Army medical personnel. There was very little that could be done for them except monitoring and supportive therapy. The boy's mother exhibited symptoms of the common cold, with a clear mucosal effusion from the nasopharynx. Dr. Aguilar ordered IV drips of an experimental Army drug, cidofovir, given to the patients. It was supposed to work on smallpox, but there was no evidence it would work on Cobra. Dr. Aguilar also ordered a dose of Dilantin to help control the boy's seizures but decided not to go ahead with any heavier antiseizure drug therapy for fear that it would cause Hector to go into an irreversible coma. The only member of the family who had had seizures so far was the boy. His mother was alert, although deeply afraid and almost hysterical about her child.

The doctors had set up a biocontainment intensive-care unit, a group of rooms accessible through a vestibule in the north wing of the Coast Guard hospital. Hector Ramirez was placed there, along with Suzanne Tanaka.

Tanaka lay strapped in bed, receiving cido-fovir, ribavirin, and Valium drips. She drifted in and out of consciousness, but she had not suffered any seizures.

The boy was strapped into a bed, and various monitoring machines were placed around him. One of the machines was a pressure sensor for real-time monitoring of the boy's cranial pressure. They had drilled a small hole in his skull and put in a plastic pressure sensor there. The machine could detect brain swelling. If the doctors saw signs of swelling, they might decide to put him into surgery to remove a portion of his skull, to give his brain space to swell. "The mortality rate is awful, but it may be our only chance," Dr. Aguilar explained to Austen.

Hector uttered a sharp cry.

Austen drew closer. The boy was small for his age. His body shook as if a wind were rattling it. The nursing staff had tied soft cords of gauze around his wrists and ankles and across his chest. They'd done their best to immobilize his head, but his mouth was uncontrollable. He had torn off a part of his tongue and swallowed it. His eyes were half open, the pupils darting. "Mama!" he said. "Mama!"

Austen bent over the bed. "We're doctors and we're here for you, Hector."

"*¿Donde está Mama?*"

She touched his forehead. Through her glove, she could feel his facial muscles tightening and twitching.

They couldn't give the boy a brain scan, because his condition was too unstable and because he was liable to go into seizure at any moment. The Army nurses and doctors moved around the room with great speed and desperation at times, but at other times they seemed to be moving through thick water.

□

Will Hopkins entered the intensive-care unit. He was dressed in a protective suit. The probe compounds had arrived from the Navy, and Hopkins had programmed them into a Boink biosensor. "I've got a hand-held that'll detect Cobra, I think."

The staff had been taking samples of the boy's blood. Hopkins mixed a few drops in a tube containing salt water, then put a drop of the bloody water into the sample port of the device.

It gave off a chiming sound. "Cobra," Hopkins said, looking at the screen.

Suzanne Tanaka was now suffering agonies in a bed on the other side of the unit. Hopkins tested her blood, and the answer was obvious. He stayed by her bed for a while. "I'm sorry," he said.

She could not answer, and it was not clear that she even heard.

As he walked out of the unit, he met Alice Austen. They spoke about what had happened to Tanaka. Hopkins told Austen that when he'd been driving down to Quantico, and she had been asleep in the car, Tanaka had begged him over the telephone to include her in the mission. "I made the decision," he said to Austen.

"Don't think back on decisions, Will."

"I can't help it," he said.

"I can't either. I should have put Peter Talides in the hospital."

In the spread of an infective agent, chance plays a part in survival. Hopkins went down the hall and tested the blood of Aimee Dana, the wife of John Dana, who had been infected by brain material from Peter Talides. He did not get a reading. She seemed okay. Then he went to see Captain Dorothy Each.

She had been placed in a biocontainment room. She was sitting in a chair, reading a book, a bandage over the cut on her hand. She seemed calm, but she was very pale.

Hopkins tested her blood. So far, there was no sign of Cobra. "Looks good, but it's really too early to tell," he said to her.

"Thanks, anyway," Captain Each said to him.

□

In Hector Ramirez's room, Austen continued to watch the boy. She felt that she was on the verge of understanding something important. The pattern was emerging, and then it slipped away.

She turned to Dr. Aguilar. "I still don't believe we've made a diagnosis," she said.

"We know a fair amount," he answered.

"But we don't understand the disease process. We're missing a diagnosis."

"Okay, I can buy that," he said. "What are your ideas?"

"It's there, but I can't touch it."

A doctor walked in with some test results. Hector's white-cell count, in his spinal fluid, was too high.

"His uric acid's high also," the doctor remarked.

"What's the count?" Austen asked.

"Fourteen point six. Extremely high."

"It's probably the result of his seizures," Dr. Aguilar said. People having muscle breakdown have high uric acid counts in their blood and urine.

Austen was remembering something. She ran the images of Kate Moran's autopsy through her mind. The kidneys. She remembered the golden-yellow streaks in the girl's kidneys. That was damage by uric acid. Something moved in Austen's mind. It was like a bird fluttering its wings, a bird with unusual markings.

"Could you please loosen the boy's straps?" Austen asked. "I want to see how he moves his legs."

The medical staff hesitated.

She asked them again.

They loosened Hector Ramirez's straps. Austen got down on her knees. She took the boy's arm in her hand, grasping it firmly.

He was looking at her with yellow eyes. It was not easy to see where the personality of the boy was. His essential being seemed to have already died or partly died.

She let his arm go slightly. He drew it to his mouth. His teeth snapped. He moaned. He began crying, *"No! Basta! Vaya! Ay!"*

"Oh, God," one of the nurses said.

With the straps loosened, the boy's body assumed a peculiar posture. One arm was bent toward his mouth, and the *opposite* leg was bent. The other leg was straight. The boy's posture was like that of a fencer leaping in for a touch. One arm straight, the other bent. The opposite leg bent, the other leg straight. It was a *diagonal* thrashing of the human body.

A diagonal crisscross.

The posture indicated damage to areas of the brain where signals cross. That would be the midbrain. A deranged midbrain.

The boy squirmed, and his back arched. His legs crossed in an abrupt scissoring motion.

The diagnosis clicked.

"They eat themselves. They're children," Austen said with sudden clarity and horror. "They pull out their eyes. Lash. Lesch. What is it called, Dr. Aguilar?"

"Oh, Jesus," Aguilar whispered. Suddenly, he had seen it too.

"High uric acid," she said.

"Yeah," he said. "This kid looks like he has Lesch-Nyhan syndrome."

"I had forgotten what it was called," Austen said.

Lesch-Nyhan

Lesch-Nyhan syndrome is an extremely rare disease. It occurs once in a million births, and it occurs naturally only in boys. It is caused by a genetic mutation. Alice Austen did not make the diagnosis alone. She began the diagnosis. It was made by a team of physicians.

Frank Masaccio immediately flew to Governors Island with senior managers of his joint task force. They arrived just as Austen and the other doctors began giving a presentation to the assembled Reachdeep team.

Austen was speaking: "Lesch-Nyhan syndrome may be the most terrible genetic disease known."

Lesch-Nyhan syndrome is caused by a mutation on the X chromosome, which is the chromosome that every child inherits from his or her mother. Lesch-Nyhan boys lack an enzyme that breaks down a metabolic waste product, and the end result is a huge excess of uric acid in the bloodstream. The enzyme they lack is called HPRT.

Lesch-Nyhan syndrome was first identified in 1964 by Michael Lesch and William L. Nyhan. Michael Lesch was then a sophomore medical student at Johns Hopkins University, in Baltimore. Bill Nyhan was his research adviser.

A boy with Lesch-Nyhan syndrome seems normal as a baby, except that the parents begin to notice what they sometimes describe as "orange sand" in the diaper. These are crystals of uric acid being passed from the kidneys. By the baby's first birthday there is something definitely wrong. The boy becomes spastic. He does not develop normal coordination. He does not learn how to crawl or walk. His limbs become stiff. The baby's body tends to assume the characteristic "fencing" posture of Lesch-Nyhan disease—one arm bent, the opposite leg bent. This is a sign of damage to nerve fibers in the midbrain. As the boy's teeth come in, he begins chewing on his lips. The chewing is uncontrollable. The child begins to eat off his lips. He begins to eat his fingers. He concentrates his gnawing on certain parts of his body; no one knows why.

The parents can't control their child. Often doctors have trouble making a diagnosis. The boy may not be retarded. He may have normal intelligence, but it's hard to tell, because his speech is poor. He can't speak well, although his eyes are bright and alert, and he seems to be taking in the world with understanding and intelligence. The boy may pull out his fingernails with his teeth. He attacks his body. As he grows older and stronger, he attacks the people he loves, lashing out with his arms and legs, biting at them, and using obscenities. It is clear that he is capable of love, and he forms strong attachments to his caregivers, even while he is attacking them.

The pain of self-injury is excruciating for Lesch-Nyhan children. It troubles them when they attack people, yet they can't resist doing it. They cry out with pain as they chew themselves. They know what they are doing but can't stop. They feel the pain, but the biting continues, and the more it hurts the more they bite themselves. They fear the pain, and their fear makes them bite themselves more violently. Thus the Lesch-Nyhan cycle of behavior literally feeds on itself. When they feel an episode of self-mutilation coming on, they beg to have their hands tied and their bodies restrained. The sudden appearance of a stranger in the room may make them bite themselves. They vomit upon themselves. They may blind themselves, tearing out their eyeballs. Self-enucleation, tearing out of the eyes, is rare, but it happens. There are not many Lesch-Nyhan adults. A Lesch-Nyhan boy may survive to young adulthood, but at some point he will die of kidney failure or self-injury.

The human genetic code consists of about three billion bases of DNA. A single change of one base in the entire human genome, at a particular location on the genome, causes full-blown Lesch-Nyhan disease. Scientists understand how the change in the DNA changes the resulting structure of the enzyme. That is simple. What is a complete mystery is how a change in one enzyme causes a radical shift in behavior. What kind of brain damage could cause an organism to try to eat itself? No one knows.

Austen told the group that the Cobra virus appears to trigger a kind of Lesch-Nyhan disease in humans, in both men and women. Lesch-Nyhan had become a contagious disease. Cobra probably had the ability to knock out the gene for the enzyme HPRT, and that somehow led to self-injury and auto-cannibalism. Natural Lesch-Nyhan disease was a progressive disorder that came on slowly as the child developed. "No one understands the exact kind of brain damage that causes Lesch-Nyhan children to engage in self-injury," she said to the group. "Cobra apparently causes the same general type of brain damage but very rapidly. The virus seems to engage in a massive burst of replication, just as the moth virus N.P.V. does, and that last burst almost melts the human brain, triggering the wild change of behavior in the hours leading up to death."

Frank Masaccio had been listening to this. Listening with his hands in his pockets, and staring at the piece of fax paper on the wall of the meeting room that showed the face of an American tourist who might or might not be the Unsub. Masaccio had been trying to see how to use that information to move the investigation forward. Now he saw a new move in the chess game. He turned to his senior people.

"I see where we can go. We need to look at every biotech company that's doing research into this disease. We get lists of employees at these companies. We see if the name of an employee matches a name of any of the thousands of tourists to Kenya who were issued visas. It we get a match there, we've got Archimedes."

□

Hector Ramirez died late Thursday afternoon. By that time Hopkins and Austen were working in the Reachdeep Core, confirming that Cobra virus disease was a type of Lesch-Nyhan syndrome.

Meanwhile, the investigation had moved into financial territory. The New York field office's joint task force on Cobra studied recent Securities and Exchange Commission filings by companies in the biotechnology industry. They found nothing there

Agents telephoned the headquarters of the Food and Drug Administration in Maryland and asked for information on any new drug-research applications involving Lesch-Nyhan disease.

There are three major geographic areas where biotechnology companies have settled in the United States. One is the San Francisco Bay area of California, where biology is mixed in with Silicon Valley and the high-tech computer and software industry. The second area is in Massachusetts, around Boston. The third area—the largest, the deepest—is a belt of biotech companies hidden away in small buildings scattered from central New Jersey south through Pennsylvania and down into Maryland to the outskirts of Washington, D.C. This is the Middle Atlantic Biotechnology Belt, and it is where some of the leading-edge start-up companies in genetic engineering and biomedical research are situated. In all three geographic areas, the biotech companies are fueling economic growth, bringing jobs, making people rich, and developing drugs that help people live longer and have more productive lives. As a group they are light-years ahead of the rest of the world in biotechnology.

In a matter of hours, investigators had determined that there were only two companies in the United States currently doing F.D.A.-reviewed research into Lesch-Nyhan syndrome. One was a publicly held company in Santa Clara, California, outside San Francisco—a medium-sized company with public shareholders. The other was a privately held company in Greenfield, New Jersey, an hour's drive west and south of New York City. It was called Bio-Vek,

Inc. Since it was a private company, it did not file financial statements with the Securities and Exchange Commission. But Bio-Vek had recently submitted a filing with the Food and Drug Administration for permission to go ahead with Phase I clinical trials of a bioengineered treatment for Lesch-Nyhan disease in children, a so-called gene therapy protocol, in which healthy genes would be inserted into the brain tissue of sick children.

The Cobra investigators from New York enlisted the help of the Trenton, New Jersey, field office of the F.B.I. The Trenton office looked at the company's financial filings and registration statement with the state of New Jersey, and they looked at the company's state department of labor filings. Bio-Vek was a very small company. It had just fifteen full-time employees. The president of the company was Orris Heyert, M.D.

"This *feels* right," Frank Masaccio said. "This Bio-Vek is where we want to look." He discussed with his senior investigators and with Hopkins how they should proceed.

They could do what was known as a "freeze and seize" white-collar raid on Bio-Vek. They could move in with a huge white-collar-crime-analysis team, freeze the company's operations, and take over the company in its entirety as federal evidence. That would be an extreme measure. In order to do a freeze and seize of a company, federal investigators must show probable cause that a crime has been committed. They must get a search warrant from a federal magistrate, a warrant that enables them to enter the premises and seize evidence. That was impossible in this case. There was no probable cause for thinking a crime had been committed—no evidence whatever to link Bio-Vek to the Unsub or to any crime. No federal magistrate would permit a raid on Bio-Vek.

The right way to do things—the way the F.B.I. would proceed under normal circumstances—would be for the federal investigators to take their time to develop evidence, perhaps going undercover. They would conduct quiet interviews with low-level employees. They would contact the company's bankers for information. They would check out the company's dealings with suppliers and customers. They would try to get a sense of how the money was moving.

Masaccio understood that the movement of money is the blood supply of crime. Just seeing the way this company's name popped out so easily once Dr. Austen had identified the type of disease the virus was causing, he now understood, he knew in his heart, with a lifetime's experience as an investigator, that money was somehow involved with the deaths in New York City. It was there, somewhere. The long green had entered the picture—but *where*?

Since everyone wanted the Unsub found and arrested in a matter of days, before any more people died, there was extreme pressure on Frank Masaccio to fly fast and hard into the case. There was no time to mount a careful investigation into Bio-Vek, no time to profile the company. Yet there was zero evidence to justify a raid. There was a good chance the company itself might be blameless. An employee or a former employee could be the Unsub. The company might not have anything to do with it, and they might be eager to cooperate. He decided to ask the company for help. Carefully. He would use some of the Reachdeep people for this, since they would know the right questions to ask.

Bio-Vek, Inc.

Will Hopkins, Alice Austen, and Mark Littleberry took a Bell turbo helicopter across Raritan Bay and touched down on a grassy airstrip in a town not far from Greenfield, a few miles east of Bio-Vek. They were met by three F.B.I. agents from the Trenton field office in unmarked Bureau cars. The Reachdeep team got into a car driven by a female agent. The two other Trenton agents took the other car, and they moved discreetly to a remote part of the airstrip, where one of the agents wired Hopkins with a micro–tape recorder, hung down his back behind his jacket. Hopkins was wearing a charcoal-gray suit, with a blue shirt and a muted silk necktie, and he had on sunglasses. He looked every inch a federal agent. Austen thought: he's showing off. The only thing that spoiled the image was a lump under his jacket. He wore a SIG-Sauer nine-millimeter semiautomatic pistol in a holster. But that wasn't what made the lump. It was the pocket protector.

They drove over suburban roads to a business park, some low buildings constructed during the office boom of the 1980s. The buildings were not old, but they didn't look particularly new. They contained a mixture of businesses. There was a printer in one of the office blocks, with a civil-engineering firm next door.

The Bio-Vek, Inc., building had coppery dark windows that concealed what was behind them. The investigative team cruised past, keeping a low profile. Littleberry pointed to some tall silver pipes coming out of the roof. "Vent stacks," he said. "Looks like they're venting a biocontainment lab. Level 2 or Level 3."

"That's not unusual," Hopkins said.

The two F.B.I. cars parked in a back lot beside a Dumpster, near the printing business, out of view. Hopkins, Austen, and Littleberry got out of the car. Mark Littleberry was carrying a small Halliburton case. It contained a hand-held Boink biosensor and a swab kit.

The Reachdeep team walked casually down a sidewalk. It was a faultless day, white clouds puffy and changing in a sky as blue as dreams. The air smelled like Colorado at nine thousand feet. The ornamental cherry trees had gone into fierce bloom, and though the bloom was past its peak, the trees flashed and moved brilliantly in the breeze. The trees and plants around the business park seemed to ache and sway with life. Above Bio-Vek, a sailplane swooped and banked on rising thermals under the clouds; a pilot having fun, and below the sailplane red-tailed hawks floated and turkey buzzards moved in slow circles, people and birds enjoying the air.

The Reachdeep investigators stopped before the company's nondescript brown door. There was a galvanized box by the door, for holding clinical samples.

Hopkins led the way in. He gave the team members' real names to the receptionist. He said that the group was from the Federal Bureau of Investigation and was there to see Dr. Orris Heyert, the president of Bio-Vek.

"Was he expecting you?" the woman said. "I don't see your names on the calendar."

"No, but this is important," Hopkins said.

She called Dr. Heyert on her telephone. In a moment he came out through a door into the lobby, with a puzzled expression on his face. He was a handsome man in his forties. He had dark hair, a smooth haircut, lively features. He wore a white shirt and a tie, but he was jacketless, and his sleeves were rolled up, and there were many cheap pens in his pocket. He had the start-up-company look.

In Dr. Heyert's office—small and cluttered, with pictures of his wife and children on the shelves—they got down to business.

"I realize this is unexpected," Hopkins said. "But we need your help. I am with the Federal Bureau of Investigation, and my colleagues here are with the Centers for Disease Control and the United States Navy."

"Can I see some identification, before we go any further?" Dr. Heyert said.

Hopkins showed his creds. Austen showed her C.D.C. card.

"Do you guys want some coffee?"

They said they did.

He called his secretary and asked her to bring coffee. He had an informal way about him that made Hopkins look stiff and uptight.

Hopkins did the talking. "We need your help in an investigation."

"My company is not the subject of this investigation, I hope?"

"No. We are searching for an unknown suspect who has been making terroristic threats involving an infective biological agent. We have reason to think that he's knowledgeable about Lesch-Nyhan disease. We need your expertise and advice."

"This is very strange," Heyert said.

"Why?" Hopkins said. He looked calmly at Heyert. Time passed. More time passed.

Heyert clearly expected Hopkins to say something more, but Hopkins did not. He just watched Heyert.

Finally Heyert answered, "Well, it just seems strange."

"Have you fired any employees lately? Has anyone quit? Because we're wondering if by any chance a disgruntled former employee of yours might be the person making these threats."

"Nobody has left the company in quite a while. Our employees are very loyal."

Hopkins watched Heyert carefully, oberving the man's body and his eyes at least as much as he listened to the words. The tape recorder would get the words anyway. "Can you describe the research your company is doing?"

"A lot of it is proprietary," Heyert said mildly.

"Are there areas you can talk about?" Hopkins asked.

"We are trying to find a cure for the Lesch-Nyhan syndrome," Dr. Heyert said. "We are using gene therapy. Are you familiar with that?"

"Not totally. Could you explain it to us?" Hopkins said.

"Gene therapy is where we replace a damaged gene in human tissue with a working gene. This involves putting the new genes directly into cells. We use viruses to put the genes into the cells. These viruses are called vectors. If you infect tissue with a vector virus, it will add genes or alter the genes."

"What kind of virus are you using?" Hopkins asked.

"It's just a construct," Heyert said.

"A construct? What's that?"

"It's an artificial virus."

"Is it based on a natural virus?"

"Several."

"Which?"

"Principally the nuclear polyhedrosis virus."

"Oh," Hopkins said. "Doesn't that virus live in insects?"

"Normally, yes."

"Can you tell me, Dr. Heyert, what strain you are using?"

"*Autographa californica.* It has been modified to enter human brain cells."

"I'm curious, Dr. Heyert," Hopkins said. "Could this virus be engineered so that it not only enters the brain but replicates there? Could it then spread from person to person?"

He laughed in a way that seemed to Austen rather forced. "Good grief! *No.*"

"There have been indications that the suspect has such a use in mind. We're trying to evaluate the credibility of the threat."

"Nothing has happened, then?"

"There's been what is perceived as a threat."

"To do what?"

"To injure people with this insect virus."

"Who's making the threat?"

"As I said, Dr. Heyert, that's what we're trying to find out."

"I don't think it's much of a threat," Heyert said. "The virus couldn't be used that way."

"Could an engineered virus spread genetic changes through the human population?" Hopkins asked.

There was a long pause. "This is way off base," Heyert said. "Statements like that are frankly offensive to me. I am a physician, a medical doctor. What we are doing here is so remote from what you are suggesting that it is almost obscene. We are trying to alleviate the most terrible suffering. Have you ever seen a Lesch-Nyhan child?"

Bio-Vek was a small company, all under one roof. Orris Heyert led the investigators into a back wing of the building where there was a cluster of surprisingly small rooms cluttered with benches and laboratory equipment. The labs were populated with young workers, most of whom wore casual clothes.

"Who's financing you?" Littleberry asked Heyert, in his blunt way.

"Private investors."

"Do you mind telling us who?" Hopkins said.

"Well, myself for one. I did well in a previous start-up."

"Who are the controlling shareholders?" Hopkins asked. He watched Heyert's body language.

"I am a general partner. We have limited partners, of course."

"What's your cash-burn rate?" Hopkins asked.

"You seem to have worked in biotechnology yourself, Dr. Hopkins."

"Not really."

Heyert flashed a not-very-nice look at Hopkins. "Didn't pan out, eh? So you went to work for the government?"

"It has its ups and downs."

They went into a laboratory. The benches were cluttered with research equipment, flasks and table shakers and incubators and small centrifuges. Biosafety cabinets stood against the walls. As they were passing through the lab, Littleberry whispered to Hopkins, "Those vent stacks we saw on the roof. They're coming from somewhere near here. There's a Level 3 unit around here, but we haven't seen it yet."

They went around a corner and entered a small waiting room. There were a few stuffed chairs, and a door that said CLINIC.

"We have a patient in the observation room with his mother," Heyert said. "His name is Bobby Wiggner."

Bobby

Dr. Heyert entered the room first and asked Mrs. Wiggner if two visitors could meet her son. "Would Bobby like to be restrained?" he said to her.

The mother glanced at her son, and she shook her head.

Heyert brought Austen and Hopkins into the room. Littleberry chose to stay outside.

Bobby Wiggner was a young man. He looked somewhat like a boy. On his chin appeared the faintest beginnings of a beard. He lay in a wheelchair in a half-straightened posture. His back was sharply curved; his body was rigid. A rubber strap went around his chest, holding him in the wheelchair.

Austen watched. She observed Bobby Wiggner with the care of a medical doctor trying to see what was going on with a patient.

His mother sat on a chair facing him—out of striking distance of his arms. She was reading to him from a book. The book was *David Copperfield.*

The man-boy was thin, bony, stiff. He was wearing a T-shirt and a diaper. His legs were bare and his kneecaps stuck up like points. His legs were crossed—scissored and rigid. His feet were bare, and they were wrapped around each other. One of his big toes was extended straight up at a peculiar angle.

He had no lips. His mouth was a hole consisting of bulbous wet scar tissue that extended across the lower half of his face: these were biting scars. His upper teeth were gone—probably extracted to prevent him from doing damage when he bit, but his lower teeth remained in place. His jaw was very flexible and seemed to move a lot. Over the years, in episodes, he had reached up with his lower teeth and had cut and sawed away his upper lip and the lower part of his nose. He had also eaten away his upper palate bone by gnawing it with his lower teeth, breaking off the palate bone bit by bit. In this way, reaching up with his lower teeth and using them as cutting tools, he had opened a hole in his face that extended from his palate up through his nose. He had eaten away the septum of his nose—the cartilage and flesh that divides the nostrils from each other. His breath whistled in and out of his mouth. He was missing several fingers; they were stumps. His right thumb was gone.

His eyes were bright. They moved under deep-set, heavy eyelids, tracking Alice Austen and Will Hopkins. He had scruffy, chopped hair. From his wheelchair dangled an array of Rubatex straps. His hands were not tied down.

Mrs. Wiggner stopped reading for a moment. She looked up at Austen and Hopkins. "My son sees *you* more clearly than you see him," she said.

They introduced themselves.

"Wha uh uh wah?" Bobby said. What do you want? Air whistled through his mouth. He had trouble making words because he had no lips or upper teeth or upper palate.

"We just wanted to see you and to say hello," Austen said.

"Huh uh am." Here I am.

"How are you feeling today?" Hopkins said.

"Uh guh tuh uh." Pretty good today.

His body went into a writhing motion, the back arching and twisting, the legs twisting. Suddenly his arm lashed out, aiming for Austen's face. She jerked her head back, just in time, and his clawlike mangled hand whipped past.

Bobby Wiggner moaned. "Sorry. Sorry," he said.

"It's okay."

"Guh tuh hell."

"Please, Bobby," his mother admonished him.

He lashed out at his mother, trying to strike her, and cursed violently at her. She did not react.

"Sorry, sorry, sorry," he said to her.

"He needs his restraints," his mother said.

Quickly, with deft movements, the mother and Dr. Heyert tightened the Rubatex straps around the young man, fastening his wrists to the chair, and they placed and tightened a wide Rubatex band across his forehead. That helped restrain the back-and-forth writhing of his head.

"Tha is wetter," Bobby Wiggner said. "Huck you, I sorry."

"This is a vertically divided mind," Dr. Heyert said. "The brain stem has been deranged and wants to attack the things it loves. The higher cortex—the conscious, thinking part of the mind—hates this but can't control it. In these battles between the higher brain and the brain stem, the brain stem wins, because it is primitive and more powerful."

"Nuh wuh ook! Nuh!"

"Are you sure, Bobby?" Mrs. Wiggner tried to keep reading.

"I wanh sohsing tuh drink. Wlease."

"Do you want milk?"

"Nuh. Nuh." No. No. That probably meant yes.

The young man's mother held a plastic cup up to his mouth. It had a feeding spout. She got some milk down his throat. Suddenly he vomited it up. His mother wiped him with a towel, dabbing it around the scarred remains of his lower face.

Bobby turned his head and looked at Austen, his eyes bright. He was completely tied down. "Uhr yuh uh *Stuh Tuk* hwuhnh?"

"I'm sorry. Could you say that again?" she said.

"My son is asking if you are a *Star Trek* fan," the mother remarked. "He always asks people that."

"Hopkins is," Austen said.

Hopkins went over and sat down on a chair next to Bobby Wiggner. "I like that show," Hopkins said.

"Wee, too," Bobby Wiggner said.

Hopkins listened. He found that he could understand the words.

Wiggner said (his words are translated now): "My favorite episode is 'City on the Edge of Forever.' "

"Right! Mine, too!" Hopkins said. "When Captain Kirk ends up in Chicago."

"He was sad when the woman died," Bobby Wiggner said.

"Yes. He couldn't save her."

"Or history would be changed," Wiggner said.

"Captain Kirk loved that woman. He should have saved her, and to hell with history," Hopkins said.

They were deep in conversation, Hopkins hunched over, seeming to forget the fact that he was supposed to be conducting an interview for the F.B.I.

Austen stood back, watching Hopkins. He was leaning forward. She could see the muscles of his back and shoulders through his jacket. She thought: He's very gentle.

Abruptly she realized that she had stopped seeing Hopkins in a purely professional way. This did not seem to be the moment for that kind of thing, and she put it out of her mind.

□

In the waiting room, Mark Littleberry asked an employee where the men's room was, and he went off in that direction. Carrying the Halliburton briefcase, he hurried down a hallway toward the center of the building. Once again, Littleberry had gone AWOL. He found an unmarked door. It opened inward through a partition wall. On the far side was a short corridor leading to another door. This door was marked with the numeral 2.

He opened it. Now he was in a corridor even shorter than the first one. There were some white Tyvek coveralls on a shelf, and some masks hanging on a wall. The masks were full-face respirator masks with purple virus filters. At the end of this corridor was yet another door. This one had a window in it, with a biohazard sign on the window, and the numeral 3. The door led inward toward the center of the building.

"The ring design," Littleberry said.

He looked through the window.

It was a small room, gleaming white, antiseptic. On a table in the center of the room sat a bioreactor.

It was a top-hat model with a core in the shape of an hourglass. The unit was marked with the name of a manufacturer, Biozan.

He reached up and took one of the masks, and put it on. He opened the door, carrying the briefcase.

The Biozan reactor was running. He could feel the warmth coming from it. There was no smell in the air.

He placed his hand on the glass surface of the Biozan unit. It was exactly the temperature of the human body, 98.6 degrees Fahrenheit, 37 degrees Centigrade. The temperature of living cells. The hourglass core was full of cells, and the cells were sick with a virus. From the top hat (the upper lid) of the bioreactor came tangles of flexible tubing. A liquid was draining out of the Biozan slowly into a sealed glass collection jar, which sat on the floor. The liquid inside the reactor was a pinkish red. The cells in the reactor were sick and dying, and were bursting and pouring out virus particles into the liquid, and then the virus-saturated liquid was running slowly out of the Biozan.

"Caught a fly," he said out loud.

He opened the Halliburton and pulled out a sterile swab. He stripped the wrapping off the swab. Just then he heard footsteps in the corridor. Quickly Littleberry ducked down against the wall, below the level of the window in the door. The Halliburton was sitting open and in view.

Someone looked into the room but didn't enter. He heard sharp-heeled shoes. It sounded like a woman.

He got to his feet and jammed the swab into and around the exit port of the Biozan, where liquid was flowing out of the bioreactor and into the collection jar. He held a Boink biosensor unit in his hands. He stuck the swab into the sample port of the Boink.

It beeped. The screen read "COBRA."

He jammed the swab into a sample tube, to preserve it, and dropped it into the Halliburton. He had seen enough. Time to get out of here before the stuff gets into my brain and turns me into a human bioreactor. He put the mask back on the wall and went out through the vestibule. He emerged in the main hallway and turned a corner, looking for Hopkins and the others.

That was where he encountered the woman. She came around the corner heading in the other direction. Their eyes met.

It was Dr. Mariana Vestof.

He blurted out, "I was looking for a men's room."

Time hung suspended. Her face held no expression. Then she smiled, but her face was drained of blood, and she said, "Still inspecting toilets, Dr. Littleberry?" She laughed a musical laugh, but her face hardly moved, and was without emotion.

"Still making vaccines, Dr. Vestof?" he said.

"Only for you, Dr. Littleberry."

At that moment, Hopkins and Austen appeared, coming down the hall, followed by Heyert.

The sight of Hopkins seemed to paralyze Dr. Vestof for a few seconds.

Hopkins reacted not at all.

"I will attend to some business," Dr. Vestof said, turning away.

Hopkins looked at his watch, "Well, thank you, Dr. Heyert. You've been very generous with your time."

"I wish I could help you more."

"You've been very helpful."

□

Hopkins, Austen, and Littleberry dove into the waiting F.B.I. car. Hopkins was on his cell phone immediately with Frank Masaccio. He asked for perimeter surveillance to be thrown around the Bio-Vek building. "We need this building covered completely. Mark says it's a weapons facility. He took a sample from a bioreactor and it came up positive for Cobra." He explained who Dr. Vestof was. "I saw her last week in Iraq. She's an international type, Russian-born, lives in Geneva, she told me. She is in this thing deep."

"If that's a biological weapon they're making, we can bust them now," Masaccio said. "That's a Title 18 crime. Except that sample Mark took might not hold up in court." Masaccio was thinking about the way Littleberry had gathered the evidence. It may have been an illegal search.

The question was whether to raid Bio-Vek immediately or to hold perimeter surveillance and gather more evidence. Masaccio finally decided to hold surveillance for the night. "Remember, our main goal is to get the Unsub before he kills more people. The company could lead us to the Unsub."

The helicopter crossed Red Bank, New Jersey, and bent out over Raritan Bay. It headed up the eastern side of Staten Island, vectoring on Governors Is-

land. Whitecaps whipped the sea below; a strong on-
shore breeze buffeted the helicopter.

"Bio-Vek may be connected to BioArk, the
company that Vestof said she works for," Hopkins
said. "Maybe the two companies are swapping
strains and technology."

"Welcome to the global village," Littleberry said.

"I'll bet Heyert's telling himself he hasn't done
anything wrong," Hopkins said.

"He's probably working both sides of the
street," Littleberry said. "Making money curing diseases. Making money selling diseases."

□

At Bio-Vek, Dr. Heyert, Dr. Vestof, and two other
managers sat in the conference room. The late-
afternoon sunlight lit up the tinted amber window.
There seemed to be no one around, and the fields
outside were serene and beautiful. The F.B.I. was
pouring surveillance into the area. The surveillance
teams, which were coming out of Trenton and New
York, were men and woman of varying ages and eth-
nic backgrounds, driving various kinds of cars.

Outdoors a swollen female robin, gravid with
eggs, bounded across a stretch of manicured grass.
Inside, Heyert was speaking. "I want the production
stopped. Immediately." They were going to stop the
Biozan, stop the centrifuges, stop everything. They
would sterilize all liquid materials by mixing them
with bleach, and when they were sure the materials
were dead, they would pour them down the drains,
followed by water. "I want those rooms *nuked* with
bleach, from top to bottom," Heyert said. "We will

restart the production line with our nonweaponized virus. Destroy all weaponized product, including the master seed cultures. Destroy every trace of the weapon. Erase all data pertaining to the project from the computer hard drives."

"If they search you, I assume there will be nothing to find," Dr. Vestof said.

"The problem is Tom Cope," Dr. Heyert said. "He's done something—I don't know what he's done, but they are looking for him. He was a sick man, Cope. I knew it at the time. When we fired him, that number-four Biozan went with him. He stole it. He must have taken a master seed culture of the weapon. Did he?"

The managers didn't know.

"How can you possibly tell me you don't know if Cope stole a master seed?" Heyert said angrily. "Every single seed tube was bar-coded!"

"He may have grown virus from a very small amount," one of the managers said.

"Do you think this employee stole a seed culture, Dr. Heyert?" Dr. Vestof said. She held him in a hard gaze. "That is incredible. The Concern will be appalled."

Sweat was pouring from Heyert. The armpits of his shirt were dark and wet. "This isn't my fault!"

"You are the manager of this division, I believe," she replied cooly.

"Where is Cope now?" Heyert asked his managers.

No one had any idea.

"Is he in New York?"

Dr. Vestof had changed her plans. She would fly out tonight. She could see that the American subsidiary was about to blow up, and she didn't want to be anywhere near the United States when that happened.

Freeze

That night, the Reachdeep unit went into a kind of stasis on Governors Island. Suzanne Tanaka was hovering between life and death in the medical unit. She had had a seizure. Her prognosis was terminal, according to Dr. Aguilar.

Oscar Wirtz readied his people for an operation. His squad consisted of a total of six agents from the Hostage Rescue Team who were trained in chemical, nuclear, and biological hot operations. It was clear that a freeze-and-seize raid would be made on Bio-Vek, but it was not clear when the raid would occur. Masaccio wanted to wait, to see if more evidence would develop, and he also hoped that the surveillance of the company might lead directly to the Unsub. But he realized that he might have to move at any moment to shut down the company, depending on what the surveillance revealed.

There were fifteen Bio-Vek employees at the headquarters. The rule of thumb the F.B.I. uses for a freeze-and-seize raid is for the evidence team to outnumber the employees at the site. You assign one agent to each employee, including secretaries and mail clerks. The culminating rush of a freeze-and-seize raid should take perhaps sixty seconds. During that time, every employee of the company is frozen by an agent who finds the employee and orders him to stop his physical hand motions, to move his body away from any company equipment and then freeze his body. Most employees will be innocent of any crime and will not be subject to arrest. But the company in its entirety can become federal evidence. Masaccio thought the raid could be accomplished with about forty agents, including the Reachdeep operations squad. He gave Hopkins the job of talking to a federal magistrate, asking for a search warrant to be drawn up.

□

At one o'clock in the morning, agents watching the Bio-Vek building reported lights and activity. It seemed that all the Bio-Vek employees had gone home, except Heyert, who had not emerged from the building. The lights and activity did not look good. Then, through a window, the agents observed Heyert putting paper into a shredding machine.

"That's it! They're destroying evidence! Freeze them!" Masaccio shouted. He was sitting in the Command Center of the Federal Building in New York City. Helicopters took off from Governors Island. Bureau cars carrying agents converged on Bio-Vek.

Alice Austen did not go on the raid. She was not trained in operations. She stayed with Suzanne Tanaka, sitting by Tanaka's bedside, wearing a protective suit. Tanaka was connected to monitoring machines and life-support machines, but they made no real difference, nor did any of the supportive therapy seem to make any difference. The virus had invaded Tanaka's midbrain, had nested itself at the top of the brain stem, where it could not be reached. Tanaka had bitten her lips, but what seemed to bother her the most were the poxlike blood blisters that formed and began to burst inside her mouth. She asked for water but could not coordinate her swallowing, and she spilled water mixed with blood from her mouth over the arms of Austen's biohazard suit. Tanaka remained conscious until nearly the end. The virus had left the conscious part of her mind clear even while it destroyed her unconscious mind.

"Do you believe in God, Alice?" Tanaka said. Her voice was thick, difficult to understand. Her face twitched, covered with sweat.

"Yes, but I don't understand God," Austen answered.

A helicopter landed, carrying Suzanne Tanaka's mother, who had been flown up from North Carolina. Tanaka had finally asked for her mother to come see her. But by the time they got her mother dressed in a protective suit, it was too late. Suzanne Tanaka had died.

□

The first unit of F.B.I. agents to move on Bio-Vek was a group wearing operational clothing but not space suits. They tried the door. It was locked, so they broke it with impact rams, and rushed in. They were followed instantly by Wirtz and the Reachdeep operations group, who were wearing space suits. They had suited up at the airfield. They peeled off down a corridor. Littleberry and Hopkins, both wearing protective suits, went with Wirtz to show him the way to the bioreactor room. Agents poured into the building, heading in all directions.

They found Heyert and one Bio-Vek manager. There was no one else on the premises. Heyert was in his office talking on the telephone when they entered. The team served him with a search warrant and informed him that all of Bio-Vek, Inc., was being confiscated as federal evidence, including all computer data. They did not place Dr. Heyert under arrest. They asked him if he would mind waiting voluntarily in his office for a short while, because Hopkins wanted to speak with him. Even though he was not under arrest, they read him his constitutional rights and reminded him of his right to say nothing, and his right to have an attorney.

Heyert agreed to wait. He did not want to seem to be fleeing.

Littleberry led Hopkins and Wirtz straight to the bioreactor room. They entered it thirty seconds after they'd gone through the front door of the building. The bioreactors were shut down and the room stank of bleach. They could smell the bleach coming through their respirators.

They took out swabs and collected samples from a variety of spots in the bioreactor room. They filled two dozen small plastic tubes with swab tips. Hopkins swabbed the bioreactor and the equipment, while Littleberry swabbed the walls, corners of the room, and a light switch. Hopkins stood on a table and pulled down the HEPA filter units in the ceiling. There was fresh, new fiber material in them.

"Look in the trash," Littleberry said.

They found a trash can stuffed with used HEPA filters and used bioprotective suits. Everything was drenched with bleach. It was a small room, and it was obvious that one or two people, working for an hour or two, could clean it up.

Hopkins ran samples through the hand-held Boink. It chimed and chimed, telling them that it saw Cobra everywhere in the room. The effort to clean the room had failed completely. The bleach had killed the virus but could not destroy all the DNA of the dead virus particles.

They went back to the office, where agents waited with Dr. Heyert.

Hopkins sat down facing Heyert, with Littleberry next to him. They removed their face masks. Hopkins thought it might make medical sense to leave his mask on, but on the other hand, Heyert was not wearing a mask, and neither were most of the F.B.I. agents. It was one of those situations where you take your chances.

Hopkins said, "I want to offer you an opportunity to make the right decision. It will be the most important decision you make in your life, Dr. Heyert. We have found an overwhelming amount of evidence that you are making biological weapons here. You cannot justify this as legitimate medical research. Your company has been seized and you are under investigation. I believe you will be arrested. The charge will be violation of Section 175 of Title 18 of the United States Criminal Code. That's the biological weapons section. Conviction can result in life imprisonment. If the crime is connected to a terrorist act, then it is a capital crime, and the death penalty can be imposed. I want to repeat: the death penalty can be imposed."

Heyert stared at him.

"We can't do a plea bargain with you," Hopkins continued. "But if you cooperate with us right now, we *can* recommend leniency to the sentencing judge. Otherwise I believe you are likely to spend most of the rest of your life in prison."

"I haven't committed any crime. If there was anything wrong . . . it was an accident."

"We took samples from your bioreactor yesterday when you were running hot, Dr. Heyert. We found a virus. We have sequenced most of the genes in the virus and it is clearly a weapon. It is a weaponized chimera. It's a mixture of an insect virus, smallpox, and the common cold. It's very nasty. It seems to alter a gene in the human body, creating Lesch-Nyhan disease in normal people. It is a lethal weapon."

"This is a lie."

"The evidence will be introduced at your trial."

"I have not committed any crime!"

"You could be charged as an accessory to terrorism," Hopkins said.

Heyert was deeply frightened now. "There have been deaths?"

"You tell me," Hopkins said.

Something began to fracture inside Heyert. It happened delicately at first, like an egg developing a crack. The egg did not exactly break, it only leaked. "It isn't my fault," he said.

Littleberry, who had been staring at Heyert with a fierce expression, yelled, "Then whose fault is it?"

"We don't control things," Heyert said. "We are controlled by BioArk, the Concern. BioArk is our silent general partner. I'm an employee. I am only a middle manager."

"How do we find BioArk?" Hopkins asked.

"Geneva."

"It's a Swiss company?"

"It's a multinational. I don't know where the Concern comes from originally. It is headquartered in Switzerland."

"There's a terrorist making threats in New York City. Who is he?"

Heyert almost shuddered. "I don't know what you are talking about," he said.

"Yes, you do. Please do the right thing, Dr. Heyert. For your sake and that of your family."

Heyert drew a long breath. "His name is Tom Cope—Thomas Cope. He's a strange man. A good scientist. He helped develop . . . our . . . some of our . . . uh . . . strains."

"What do you mean?" Hopkins asked.

"We hired him to do research on a—a particular aspect of the virus. It wasn't able to replicate in human tissue very well. He . . . fixed it."

"Why? Why did you want the virus to do that? Replicate in human tissue?"

There followed a long pause, and Hopkins saw fit to let it drag on. Finally Hopkins repeated, "Why?"

Heyert seemed on the edge of tears. "I have a family," he said. "I am afraid for them."

"Why?"

"BioArk. I am afraid. Can you—I—I can help you. I can tell you about BioArk. But can you protect my family? And me? These BioArk people are . . . without pity."

"We can't make any promises," Hopkins said. "If you can help us in the investigation and agree to testify, there is a witness protection program."

"I'm more afraid of BioArk than I am of you."
The words tumbled out. Heyert couldn't stop now.
"BioArk is a biotechnology company. A multinational. Part of the BioArk business—only part of it—
is black research into weapons. They also make
medicines. They do both. They work both sides of
the street. They were paying me and my staff well,
but if we talked we would be killed. They located a
subsidiary here because this is—well, this is America, where the most talented people in biotechnology
are. They set up *this* company, Bio-Vek, to do contract weapons-research into focused areas. One of
them was the development of N.P.V. as a weapon.
I—I hired Tom Cope to figure out how to get N.P.V.
to infect humans. There is very big money in this,
Mr. Hopkins."

"What about the patients, Dr. Heyert, the kids
with Lesch-Nyhan?"

"I am a doctor. I *do* want to help them. It's just
that there's no money; it's a rare disease."

"Cope—did he develop the virus?"

"No. Others at BioArk had mostly developed it
already. But there were some problems, and it was
felt that the Americans could solve them. Tom
merely sharpened the edge of the weapon. I fired him
because he was unreliable and seemed—really odd,
kind of scary."

"How much virus did he steal?" Hopkins asked.

"I don't know. . . . He stole a Biozan."

"A bioreactor?" Littleberry said.

"The number-four Biozan, yes." Heyert was
trembling.

"We need to see your records on Cope," Hopkins said.

The employee records of Bio-Vek were kept in a locked filing cabinet in Heyert's secretary's office. Heyert gave agents the key, and they soon pulled Cope's employment file and his résumé. If his résumé was accurate (a big assumption to make), he had a Ph.D. in molecular biology from San Francisco State University, and he had a troubled employment history. For a while he had worked at Los Alamos National Laboratory. He had never married.

Thomas Cope was the Unsub no longer. The file contained his Bio-Vek company photo ID. In his physical features he was what might be described as a gray man. He had no strong or defining characteristics—he was of medium height with rather pallid skin, hair thinning on top but not completely gone. He was thirty-eight years old, and he wore metal-framed eyeglasses.

A team of investigators continued to question Heyert, but soon after having given them Cope's name, he stopped talking and demanded to have access to his lawyer.

Hopkins telephoned the information on Cope to Frank Masaccio, who put his task force to work on it. The first thing they did was to run a credit check on Cope. This is one of the easiest and best ways to find someone. You can learn if they are using a credit card, and if so, you can find out which businesses they are shopping at and what they have been buying lately. The pattern of activity on a credit card can quickly pinpoint a subject's location.

They found out that Cope had been using a Visa card under his own name to order laboratory equipment from a variety of suppliers across the United States. The things were being shipped to a mail drop that Cope maintained at a private mail service in a strip shopping center known as the Apple Tree Center in East Brunswick, New Jersey. There was no other activity on the credit card except for these orders. Cope was evidently picking up his equipment in a car or truck and driving it somewhere else.

Hopkins was now standing in the parking lot at Bio-Vek, talking on his cell phone to Frank Masaccio. Masaccio said to him, "We're going to have Cope in a day or two, maybe in hours. You Reachdeep folks have done great work."

"Don't count on anything," Hopkins said.

"Yeah, I know. Any operation can fall apart. But we're going to bust him. I can feel it. We're throwing up a massive surveillance operation around the Apple Tree Center. I've got half the agents from the Newark office on the case. Cope is going to be history. Hold on a minute, Will, there's a call I have to take."

Hopkins waited. Just then, Hopkins's beeper went off. He checked it. It was the contact number for Sioc in Washington.

When Masaccio came back on the line, he sounded like a different man. "We've got a problem in Washington," he said.

Washington

The second Cobra Event SIOC meeting began thirty minutes later. It was ten o'clock in the morning when Hopkins and Littleberry landed on Governors Island. They went straight to the meeting room in the Reachdeep unit, where Austen was already in a videoconference with Washington. Frank Masaccio was sitting beside her.

From his office at the F.B.I.'s National Security Division, Steven Wyzinski had given the order—with White House approval—to deploy disaster medical groups in Washington. There had been eleven deaths from what looked like Cobra in Washington overnight. Victims had been showing up in emergency rooms all over the metropolitan area. The C.D.C. task force on Cobra was working the epidemiology.

"The news media is starting to go berserk," Jack Hertog said. He had just come from the White House, and he seemed extremely angry. The video screen made his polo shirt look chartreuse. "They're saying it may be food poisoning. They're also saying it may be deliberate. What if we've just been bombed with a chemical weapon?"

Walter Mellis was in the SIOC room with him. "We've got a team in place, and we're looking at the epidemiology now. I have a preliminary result," he said.

"What is it?" Hertog asked brusquely, turning to Mellis.

"All the cases seem to have been commuters on the Washington Metro. There was a release of hot agent somewhere in the subway."

"Goddamnit!" Hertog cried. "What's the casualty projection?"

"We've seen only eleven cases, so far, which is telling us that this was a small release, not a large one," Mellis replied.

"A warning," Hopkins said.

"He must have popped a few grams of agent into the air," Littleberry said. "If it was a big release, you'd know it. You'd have thousands of cases."

Mellis turned aside and listened. Someone was speaking to him. Then he said: "We've been working on samples in Atlanta. We have preliminary confirmation that the agent in Washington is in fact Cobra virus."

All the cases of Cobra were being moved by Navy and Army medevac helicopters into Bethesda Naval Hospital. That is, the survivors were being moved. The dead were being stored in a refrigerated biohazard truck that was making the rounds.

Jack Hertog laid down the White House line. He said, "I am here to tell you that the President of the United States will hold a news conference later today. The President is going to explain to the American people what is happening. It seems that the Reachdeep operation has been a failure. It has failed totally, disastrously."

"We have the Unsub's name," Hopkins said.

Silence fell over the SIOC.

"His name, we believe, is Thomas Cope. He is a molecular biologist, a former employee of Bio-Vek, Inc., a biotech company headquartered in Greenfield, New Jersey," Hopkins said. "We're getting background on him now."

"Is he under arrest?" Hertog asked.

"Not yet," Frank Masaccio said.

"That's not good enough," Hertog said. "Where is he?"

"Can we put Cope's image on the screen?" Hopkins asked. Cope's face appeared on screens in Washington. "We just obtained this photograph during the seizure of Bio-Vek."

Frank Masaccio said that Dr. Thomas Cope's name appeared on the F.B.I. profile list of Americans who had visited Kenya around the time the cobra boxes were bought in Nairobi. Bio-Vek records indicated that Cope had never married and had no children, but he had relatives. The F.B.I. was trying to locate them. Then Masaccio explained about Cope's mail drop in New Jersey. "When we checked the doctor's credit records," he said, "we found out that he recently placed an order for safety suits and breathing filters from a company in California. The shipment went by Federal Express, marked for Saturday delivery. It's due in today. They're telling us at the mail service that Cope usually picks his stuff up on the day it arrives. We've checked all the phone numbers he left on various forms, and none of them check out, so we can't trace him through phone calls. But he's coming to get that package. He's got a key that lets him in anytime, and we've already got nearly a hundred agents waiting to nail him."

"Yes, but *how soon?*" Hertog demanded.

"Hours if we're lucky," Masaccio said. "The Reachdeep people will be suited up, just in case of trouble at the shopping center, if the guy's got a biological with him."

"The director of the F.B.I. has authorized me to say that all, repeat, *all* of the Bureau's resources will be dedicated to this case," Steven Wyzinski said.

"After the horse left the barn!" Hertog said, his voice rising. "How do you know he's going to pick up his mail? How do you know it isn't a group?"

"I can't guarantee anything until he's in custody, but I'm confident we'll have him soon," Masaccio said.

"Cut the bullshit!" Hertog shouted. "People are dying in Washington, for chrissake. This is not Lubbock! This is *Washington*. This is the goddamned fucking capital of the country! The people who run the fucking *world* live here! You marshmallows dicking around with your test tubes have left us open to a real mess. I want some straight F.B.I. work here, coordinated with anybody else in the goddamned government who knows how to get some results in this situation. I want the Reachdeep dickheads on that island off this case, and I want your top guys, Frank, your pros, taking this one down *fast*."

Littleberry suddenly broke in, shouting, "The terrorist is going to cook New York while you are shifting gears and the President tries to save his own ass."

"You're fired," Hertog snapped.

"You can't fire me, I'm retired."

"Then I'm going to take away your goddamned pension."

Break

Austen and Hopkins sat facing each other in the meeting room outside the Reachdeep Core. They had had nothing to do for hours except talk about the case. Mark Littleberry was out on the deck, staring across the water at the city. He'd been there for a long time.

"I'm worried that Frank's going down a blind alley," Hopkins said. "What if Cope *doesn't* pick up his mail? He could be anywhere."

Austen doodled with a pencil on her map of the city. "You know, I've been thinking . . . there's such a tight cluster of cases here. Here, in this part of the city. It's weird. We've got cases in Washington, but all the other primary cases fall in one part of the city. Look." She showed him on the map. Her finger moved over a part of Manhattan. It was lower Manhattan, and toward the eastern side. Her finger moved over Union Square, where Kate Moran had lived, and over East Houston Street, where Harmonica Man and Lem had lived, then over the Lower East Side, where Hector Ramirez and his family lived—and to the Sixth Avenue flea market on Twenty-sixth Street, where Penny Zecker and Kate Moran had met. "There's a pattern here."

"Sure, but what?"

"Cope is like a thread crisscrossing the area," she said. "You can see it in the cases. When you have a cluster of illnesses, you go out and find the threads that link them. Cope is the thread."

"You can't go and check that out. We're grounded." Hertog had made it very clear that Reachdeep was restricted to Governors Island and to doing lab work only.

□

Nagged by the possibilities, Austen went to the hospital wing, where the Army Medical Management Unit was situated, and she put on a protective suit and went in. She was headed for the rooms where the family of Hector Ramirez was quarantined. Hector's young mother, Ana, was now in critical condition and was not expected to live. High doses of Dilantin seemed to be preventing her seizures, but not the self-cannibalism, and she was under heavy restraint in the intensive-care unit.

In a room that overlooked an avenue of plane trees, Austen visited Carla Salazar, Ana's older sister. Carla had been tested and had shown no sign of Cobra infection, but she had been kept in quarantine. She was frightened, and distraught over the condition of her sister and the death of her sister's little boy.

Austen sat down with her and asked her how she was doing.

In a very small voice she said, "Not good. Not good."

"Do you feel okay?"

"I am okay now. But what about later? I could be like my sister. I can't look at her." She began to cry.

"I want to show you a picture, Mrs. Salazar. Can you look at a picture?"

"I don't know."

Austen handed her the color photocopy of Cope's face, taken from the company card. F.B.I. investigators had earlier showed Carla Salazar the composite image from Nairobi.

She studied the color image for a moment. "Maybe I have seen this man," she said. "Maybe."

Austen's heart turned over. *I wish Hopkins was here, he'd know the right questions to ask.*

"Is this who murdered my sister's son?" Mrs. Salazar asked.

"It is possible. Who is he?"

"I'm trying to think. I seen him a couple times, I think. I'm not sure. I think he's the guy that yelled at some of the kids. He yelled at some of the boys one time. I don't know. I don't know. No, it's not the same guy. . . . You think it's the guy that poisoned Hector? He was real mad at the boys. It was something about a cat."

□

Hopkins got on the telephone to Masaccio. "Frank— listen. We have a possible identification. There's a lady here, one of the Ramirez boy's relatives, who thinks she remembers Cope in the neighborhood."

"How strong is she about it?"

"Weak. But this could be real."

"Will, look. I know it's tough being shut out of the investigation like this. But there's nothing I can do about the White House. You're not a street agent, you're a scientist. We're set up and going to take Cope. My guess is it's going to happen any minute now."

"He could do a lot while you're waiting around there."

"The guy's modus has not been to try destroy a city. He had his chance, and he didn't take out Washington."

"Cope has been in the testing phase," Hopkins said. "What if he's finished with his tests?"

"All right! I'll send someone to run your lead for you. When I get someone available. Calm down, Will."

□

"Let's do the important elements again," Hopkins said to Austen. "Just tell me the details you think are important."

They had been trying to find a pattern, but nothing was coming. She listed the pieces that she thought had meaning. She said: "We have Hector's aunt, who thinks she saw him. That would be around Avenue B. We have Harmonica Man living nearby on Houston Street. We have the black dust in the glue—it's subway dust."

"And there was a pollen grain in the dust, remember? Forsythia."

"We need to go to that part of the city and look in the subway tunnels again," she said.

He stood up and paced, then slammed his hand on the wall. They couldn't go off the island.

Austen turned and headed out of the meeting room. "See you later, Hopkins."

He looked around. Wirtz was off with the communications equipment. Littleberry was still standing out on the deck. Hopkins picked up his gun and holster, which had been sitting next to a Felix. He took a Saber radio—his last voice contact with the federal government. He picked up a hand-held biosensor, programmed to detect Cobra. He took one of the color Xeroxes of Tom Cope's photograph. The mild bespectacled face stared at nothing. Hopkins folded the paper and put it in his pocket.

Mark Littleberry saw what they were doing. "Where are you guys going?" He said he would come, too.

"For once you're not going to go AWOL, Mark. Can you stay here and do the explaining if anyone asks where we've gone?"

Austen and Hopkins walked out of the front door of the hospital and down the long steps. The hospital was quiet now, the Army doctors gathered in the biocontainment suite. They passed down an avenue of plane trees, past abandoned buildings, and they arrived at a pier that stretched into Buttermilk Channel in the direction of Brooklyn. A police launch was tied up, manned by two cops. They were listening to a news-radio station that was carrying sketchy reports of some kind of outbreak of disease in Washington.

"Can you guys give us a lift over to the Battery?" Hopkins asked.

As far as the cops knew, Reachdeep team members still had a priority for anything they wanted, and the two policemen were happy to oblige.

The police launch swung out into Buttermilk Channel, moving fast. The tide was running out to sea, and the boat bucked slightly against the thrust of the East River. Austen and Hopkins looked around: the sun was going down.

On the terrace of the Coast Guard hospital, Mark Littleberry continued his thoughtful vigil. He saw the launch crossing the river. He looked up at the

sky and saw mare's tails fingering in from the south.
The west winds of the past few days had shifted and
then almost died, and the air had gone soft and mild.
He saw from the structure of the sky that an inversion
of the air had occurred over the city, trapping dust
and particles, holding them suspended. The moon
was rising in the late day, and it reminded him of
something he'd seen almost thirty years earlier. He
had not heard the television and radio broadcasts, but
he knew that news of the attack on Washington was
beginning to fill the airwaves. The breaking news and
the structure of the sky would force Thomas Cope to
act. "He'll do it tonight," Littleberry whispered.

Bioprep

The early human trials were finished. A large glass tube with metal ends sat on the lab bench in his Level 3 containment zone. He had filled the tube with hexagons of viral glass. The glass pieces were thin and clear, about the size of quarters. He was wearing a white Tyvek suit with double gloves and a full-face respirator, and he was just filling the tube with the last of the little windowpanes, holding them with tweezers, lifting them out of the drying tray.

He held a piece of viral glass in the last of the day's light, which was shining through a crack in the curtain. The glass refracted all the colors of the rainbow. It reminded him of an opal.

He went to his supply of BX 104 biological detonator. This was one of his little treasures. Biological detonator, or bio-det, is a military low explosive. It is used in biological bomb cores. It's a biological dispersant. One kilogram of viral glass shattered and dispersed in a fine cloud the size of a city block would plume out nicely in the city.

He tucked a lump of bio-det into the large tube full of viral glass, pushing it in with his thumb. The glass cracked and creaked. He added a blasting-cap detonator, with wires attached to it. You wanted to use about one part explosive to three parts dry virus. That was the standard ratio in bomb design of an explosive bioweapon. The explosion would kill some of the virus particles—he knew that, of course—but since each pane of viral glass contained a quadrillion virus particles, it hardly mattered. Plenty of virus would survive the explosion. Many of the particles, embedded and protected in the glass, would merely fly into the air, traveling outward in a fog of viral glass—a viral glass laydown that would grow into a cloud, diffusing like gas.

The blasting cap would set off the bio-det. For a timer, he used a microchip clock. And there was a nine-volt battery. He could set the timer for any length of countdown. It would set off the bio-det, and a kilogram of viral glass would balloon into the air. Three hours was enough time for him to get upwind and well out of the city. New York was about to send a new disease into the world. Of course, it might be two days before the city truly realized that it was sick, and in the meantime perhaps quite a few people who had been in the city would be somewhere else. Including him, Archimedes. He would stay in Washington for a few weeks and observe the situation while considering his next move. Then he would repeat the trouble in Washington. Maybe. It was good to remain unpredictable.

He set the timer, which started to run. He pushed everything into the large glass tube and sealed it with a metal end piece.

He repeated the process with a second large glass tube, so that he had two mother bombs. He would put them in different places. That was a fail-safe.

Next he armed his bio-det grenades. They were smaller than the mother bombs. He had two plastic lab jars, and he filled each of them with a mixture of viral glass and pieces of broken bottle glass. Each grenade contained almost half a pound of explosive. Anyone hit by the shock wave would have a skinful of broken real glass mixed with virus. The grenades operated on a simple push-button timer.

He carried the bombs out of Level 3 into the staging area, where he sprayed his external suit with bleach, and then unzipped his suit and stepped out of it. Deconning was easy. He removed the bombs from the plastic bag and washed them in bleach to sterilize their outside surfaces, and then placed them in a black doctor's bag—my little joke, he thought. I am the greatest public health doctor.

Now he went into his bedroom, carrying the black bag. From his bureau drawer he took out a ten-millimeter Colt Delta Elite semiautomatic handgun. He slid a magazine into it. The Colt Delta Elite was a slim, high-tech version of the classic Army Colt .45. It had a laser-beam sight. The sight threw a spot of red light on the target. That made it extremely accurate. He carried the gun for safety, in case he had to defend himself. Now he was ready to move into the bloodstream of the city.

□

Austen and Hopkins boarded a Lexington Avenue train bound uptown. Austen, reading her subway map, led them off at the Bleecker Street stop. They walked east toward Bowery and over to First Avenue, where they entered the station for the F train on East Houston Street. This led to the tunnel where the homeless victims had lived.

They walked to the eastern end of the platform and down to the tracks, where they picked their way through piles of debris, edging around steel columns that were almost hairy with black steel dust. They went through the hole in the metal wall to the unused tracks, the stub-end tunnel, which extended under Houston Street.

"It smells bad in here," Hopkins said.

Austen didn't say anything.

"I hate tunnels," Hopkins said.

"Some people call them home."

They arrived at Lem's place, the chamber. It had been washed rather casually by a city cleanup crew. Hopkins took out his Mini Maglite, and they looked around. There did not seem to be any way in and out of here, except through the subway station.

They continued walking down the tunnel. They were going deeper into the stub tunnel, farther away from the tracks that were in use.

"We must be almost in the East River," Hopkins remarked.

It grew quieter. The sound of the trains was farther away. They picked their way past a mattress and chair. Finally the tunnel ended with a concrete wall and a steel door. The door was locked. A sign on it said HIGH VOLTAGE — DANGER — NO ENTRY.

Hopkins tried the door. It rattled. "Anyone in there?"

The only sound was a faint humming from electric current.

They retraced their steps and went up onto the street. People were flowing along the sidewalks, crossing the streets. Many of them were young, students or people in their twenties. There were gay men, the occasional homeless man or woman, and there

were people who might be fashion models. Austen
and Hopkins blended into the crowds. They walked
slowly along Houston Street, watching the faces,
studying people. Hopkins pulled the piece of paper
from his pocket and looked again at the face of
Archimedes. It was early evening, and people were
going to restaurants, to movies, or wherever people go
on a Saturday night.

At a small park on Houston Street, Austen sat
on a bench. Hopkins was restless, pacing. He hovered over her. "Are you feeling all right, Alice?"

"Stop staring at my eyes." She looked up at the
buildings, around at the people in the streets, and the
city seemed to dissolve in her imagination. The
buildings became empty bones, like a dead coral
reef. The people vanished. The city had gone stink-
ing and silent.

Hopkins finally sat down next to her. On the adjacent bench a drunk was asleep. Hopkins studied the
color photocopy of Tom Cope's face.

"Did you ever read about Jack the Ripper?"
Austen asked him.

"He was a pathologist, I thought. He cut up
women."

"I don't know what he was," she said. "He
walked to his killings, and he walked away from them.
I think Tom Cope is like that. The guy is a walker."

They kept moving. They headed uptown, into
the East Village. They looked left and right, staring
into people's faces. Occasionally someone would notice Austen and Hopkins staring, and would look annoyed. They walked east until they reached Avenue B,
and they passed the apartment building where Hector

Ramirez's family had been living. They went into a bodega. Hopkins showed the photograph to the grocer; he didn't recognize the face.

"This is hopeless," Hopkins said. "There are nine million people in this city."

"Maybe we should go back into the tunnel," Austen said.

"He's not in a tunnel. He's blending in. Up here is the place to hide."

They searched the East Village in a back-and-forth pattern, walking along numbered streets, turning up avenues. They went past the old Marble Cemetery, where celebrities from the time of Herman Melville are buried, and they crossed through Tompkins Square Park, while Hopkins, the F.B.I. agent, felt an odd pang of envy watching the kids hanging out on the benches with nothing to do but waste time and talk their talk about nothing in particular—it looked like fun. He glanced over at Austen, and he realized that he had stopped thinking of her strictly in professional terms, and it bothered him.

They debated heading into Greenwich Village, but instead walked down the Bowery, past several restaurant-supply stores, most of which were closed. A Chinese man wrestled with a giant used bread-dough mixer that he'd had on display on the sidewalk, trying to move it in through the door of his shop so that he could close. They crossed below Houston Street and started to cruise through SoHo, but the neighborhood seemed too bright and full of tourists from out of town, not really a Cope kind of place. They debated walking around Little Italy, but thought they were moving too far afield, so they turned north and crossed Houston Street again, and found themselves back in the East Village.

It was a transitional moment in the day. A lively Saturday afternoon had tapered off, but the club scene had not gotten going. The people in the street on this spring evening seemed relaxed, their bodies moving gently as they walked, not in much of a hurry to get anywhere. Hopkins and Austen found themselves in the less fashionable part of the East Village, close to avenues C and D, where no trees grew on the streets, giving the neighborhood an empty look. This had always been a poor part of Manhattan, and the residents had never had much heart for planting trees. In the distance they heard the banging of a hammer, and a cat looked at them from a doorway. In a small repair garage, a man lay on a pallet underneath a sports car, and his hand dropped a tool, which clanked beside him. The cross streets were almost deserted; later at night things would be livelier. Hopkins stopped and looked around. "Where are we now?"

"I don't know," Austen said. "We're close to Avenue C."

"Kind of a so-so neighborhood," he said.

"Not so bad."

The area had a funky look. The buildings were mostly nineteenth-century tenements. Some of them had been renovated, and others had been torn down, leaving empty lots where sumac bushes grew around broken-down trucks covered with graffiti. Some of the lots were surrounded by chain-link fences topped with razor wire. Others had been turned into gardens. They passed a fence that opened into a vacant lot where children's play equipment was scattered among raised beds of flowers. The little park extended between two buildings. Hopkins wandered in and sat down on a children's merry-go-round. Austen sat next to him.

"They're going to nail us to the wall for doing this," he said. He scraped his feet in the dirt. A stray cat walked past. It was a dirty brown and white cat, and it had found a can of food someone had left out. It crouched over the food, watching them while it ate. Traffic sounds and flickers of moving cars came through gaps in pieces of plywood that lined one side of the park.

Hopkins planted his feet on the ground and pushed, causing the merry-go-round to turn. It gave off a creak. "Huh," he said, and pushed harder, and he and Austen turned around. *Creeaak!*

"Cut it out, it's bothering me," she said.

Slowly they came to a halt.

Austen found herself facing a row of bushes. They had been recently planted behind a railroad tie. They had yellow horn-shaped flowers, now shriveled and fading with the coming of May.

"See, Will, that's forsythia . . ." She raised her eyes. The back of a brick building rose beyond the flower bed, a four-story building that had been renovated. Fairly new double-paned windows with metal casings had been installed on all the floors. On the third floor, the windows were covered with brilliant white shades, and there was a small, high-tech fan whirring in one of them.

They sat on the merry-go-round, stunned with surprise.

"Oh, my," Hopkins said, "oh, my."

He stood up slowly. "Don't stare. Walk casually."

They walked out of the park, moving like two people with nothing to do. They crossed the street and turned back, and looked at the front of the building. It was a small turn-of-the-century apartment building, faced with yellowish brick, with a heavy cornice running along the top. All the windows on the third floor were covered with white shades. It was a well-kept building, but it did not have an elevator. "You'd have to carry equipment up and down the stairs, but it's doable," Hopkins remarked. "Let's check the buzzer." They went up the steps and looked at names on the buzzer. None of them was Cope. The button for apartment number three said "Vir."

They crossed the street again and stood facing the building. Hopkins put his hands in his pockets and slouched.

"*Vir* means 'man' in Latin," Austen commented.

The front door of the building suddenly opened.

□

Tom Cope was carrying his black leather doctor's bag, his little joke. He saw them as he was going out the front door. A woman and a man standing across the street and staring intently at him. Instantly he changed his mind. He turned around and went back into the hallway. Am I imagining things?

Hopkins saw the door open, and he locked eyes with a modest-looking man wearing eyeglasses, with hair going thin, pale skin, and a face that was burned into his mind. He reached under his jacket for his gun and started to glide for the door, no pause between the identification of the suspect and the movement toward an arrest.

Austen grabbed him. "Dammit. Don't. He was carrying something."

Hopkins stopped. She was right. If a guy has a bomb, you don't just try to arrest him. "Get off to the side," he said to her. He half-pushed her back into a doorway. He pressed her into the corner of the door and kept his body over her, shielding her. "He may be armed," he told her. "It's time for you to leave."

"No."

"Then sit down on the steps, Alice. Keep your body mass close to the wall." He sat down next to her. "Okay. We're waiting for a friend who lives here. We're just sitting on the steps, hanging out, okay? Blah, dee blah, blah, we're talking, okay? Smile. That's it, smile! I need to use my radio." Hopkins twisted his body and hunched over. He switched his Saber radio to the emergency channel and got an F.B.I. dispatcher. "It's Special Agent Will Hopkins. Get me Frank Masaccio! This is extremely urgent!"

Then: "Frank! We're in the East Village, near Houston Street." He looked around, gave the address. "We've got him! Cope. We saw him carrying some kind of bag. We have him under surveillance. He seems to be going under the alias Vir. V-I-R. I need massive backup. Massive! He may have a bomb. I'm sitting in a doorway here with Dr. Austen."

"Hopkins. Number one: you're fired. Number two: you're a better street agent than your old man." Frank Masaccio was standing in the Command Center of the F.B.I. offices in the Federal Building. "I'm sending you everything I've got."

Surveillance

Tom Cope raced up the stairs to his apartment, lugging his bag. He bolted the door and sat down on a couch in the living room, with the bag resting on the couch beside him. *They were staring at me as if they knew. They just* looked *federal. They cannot possibly be the F.B.I. There's no way they can have found me. But why were they staring at me like that?*

He stood up and went over to a shaded window. *Do I dare look?* He pulled back the shade an inch or so and looked out onto the street. *Did they leave?*

He saw them. They were sitting in a doorway across the street. They seemed to be talking.

He returned to the couch. *This is* crazy, he thought. *I'm going crazy. Get ahold of yourself, you're being paranoid.*

Oh, shit. The timers in the bombs were running. He should disarm them. To do that, he had to go back into Level 3. Damn! Several minutes later, inside the hot lab, all suited up, he opened the bombs and removed the timers and disconnected the wires. Then he went out of Level 3, carrying the bombs. He washed his suit and the bombs with the bleach sprayer in the staging-area hallway before he took off the suit and discarded it in a plastic bag.

He sat down again on the couch to try to gather his thoughts. He placed a bomb tube full of viral glass on a coffee table in front of him. He removed the Colt Delta Elite from the bag and placed it where he could reach it in an instant.

Outside, Hopkins and Austen continued to sit in the doorway. A woman came along and had to practically step over them to get inside her building. "Why don't you sit somewhere else," she said.

Hopkins said to Austen, "Don't look at Cope's apartment." It was getting dark.

□

He drew back the shade slightly, and looked up and down the street. He couldn't see the man and the woman now. *Why do I feel so afraid?* He debated whether to make his move downward through the emergency exit. He needed to go to ground. If he could get into the subway system he could disappear.

Still, he couldn't bring himself to move. If he failed, he would fall into the hands of either the F.B.I. or BioArk. He began to hope it was the F.B.I. He would rather go to federal prison than meet some of those people from BioArk. *How can I have allowed myself to be trapped in my building?* he thought. *Am I trapped?* Again he pulled aside a shade, and looked out the window. The man and the woman had moved. They were sitting in a different doorway. *Why wouldn't they leave?*

□

Frank Masaccio had called the Washington headquarters of the F.B.I. He explained that Agent Hopkins had gone AWOL from Governors Island but had apparently found the terrorist. "He and the doctor are on site." He said he was rushing a Surveillance Operations Group into the area. The Reachdeep operations people and additional Hostage Rescue Teams were moving into place. Essentially the entire New York field office was joining the operation, and he called for extra help from Quantico. At the same time, some of his agents were starting to run checks on people who lived in apartments near Cope. The agents were trying to get a sense of who the neighbors were and what the neighborhood was like. "We're going to try to gain access to a common wall with Cope's apartment," Masaccio said to the Washington SIOC group.

A cable television repair van pulled up on the corner of Avenue C. The driver looked straight at Hopkins, and nodded slightly. Hopkins and Austen stood up from the doorway. They walked to the corner, the back of the van opened, and they climbed inside.

Oscar Wirtz was sitting in the back of the van. He was dressed in a gray sweat suit. The van pulled away.

Simultaneously, an old pickup truck full of junk furniture stopped in front of Cope's building and double-parked on the street. A Hispanic man and an African-American woman were sitting in the cab of the pickup. They were shabbily dressed. The woman had something in her ear that looked like a hearing aid. She was talking with Frank Masaccio, and her voice was carrying live into SIOC in Washington. "There's no activity on the third floor," she said.

The cable television van carrying Austen, Hopkins, and Wirtz double-parked on a quiet cross street two blocks from Cope's apartment. Suddenly a large furniture-delivery truck appeared and parked in front of the television van. Hopkins and Austen got out and climbed into the back of the furniture truck. Mark

Littleberry and a number of Oscar Wirtz's people—
the Reachdeep operational squad—were inside.
There were many boxes of biohazard gear in the
truck. For the moment, the furniture truck was a staging and supply area for a biohazard operation.

"Are we going into action?" Austen said.

"Not you, Dr. Austen," Wirtz said to her.

Hopkins was listening to Masaccio on a Saber
radio.

"The lady below him is a shut-in and she has di-
abetes and a heart condition," Masaccio was saying.
"We can't disturb her. We can't get into the apartment above him without risking discovery—he may
notice us going past him. On one side of the building
there's an open lot. It extends around the building
and down to Houston Street. This is bad luck. It's
open ground, and he could see us moving there. The
good news is the building on the other side of him.
This building shares a common wall with his building. So we're going into the building next to him.
We're going to try to get as close to him as we can,
Will Junior. You tell your guy Wirtz to get ready to
move fast in a very hot mess."

The sun had set. It was eight-thirty in the
evening.

□

Before making any move to arrest Cope, they wanted
to learn more about his state of mind and his
weapons, and look at him visually. Another truck
pulled up near Tom Cope's building. It was a Con
Edison repair truck. Three Con Edison employees in
hard hats—one was a woman, the other two were
men—entered the building next to his. When they

got to the third floor, they knocked on an apartment door. A man answered. They pulled out their F.B.I. credentials. It turned out that he was a columnist for a rap music magazine.

The Con Edison woman held up her F.B.I. creds. "My name is Caroline Landau. I'm an agent with the Federal Bureau of Investigation." She introduced her colleagues.

"What do you want with me?" the journalist said.

Landau was firm about needing his help. She explained that there was a killer next door, through the wall. "We think he has a bomb," she said. "This is no joke. We're appealing to you for help."

The man seemed unable to speak. Finally he stammered, "You've got to be kidding."

"I swear to you this is the truth."

"I can't believe this," he said.

"I'm pleading personally with you, sir," Caroline Landau said. "Sir, you are in very great personal danger. We all are."

He had a feeling that he wasn't really being given a choice. He went downstairs with one of the "Con Edison" people, and the truck carried him away. He spent the night at a hotel, courtesy of the F.B.I.

Apartment by apartment, floor by floor, the F.B.I. evacuated the building next to Tom Cope's. They did not dare try to evacuate his building, for fear he would notice—except the first floor, where a single woman was living. They got her out. Debriefing her in the staging truck, they learned from her that the man on the third floor was going under the name of Harald Vir, and that he did not socialize with anyone in the building, although he was very polite. That was Tom Cope.

In the journalist's apartment, Caroline Landau set up her remote sensing gear, working with a group of tech agents. Out of their Con Edison repair boxes they took a silent drilling machine. It could cut through brick and stone without making a sound. They cut through a layer of Sheetrock on the wall, and removed the material in pieces and set it aside. Under it was insulation. They pulled out the insulation. The apartment was getting trashed. Next they came to a brick wall. It was a common wall. On the other side of the brick wall was Cope's apartment.

Caroline Landau set out an array of contact microphones on the brick wall. These microphones were the size of nickels. They picked up sounds in Cope's apartment and fed them into an analyzer. You could listen on headphones and hear everything happening in his apartment, in stereo sound, with a sense of brilliant depth.

The furniture truck containing Hopkins, Austen, Wirtz, Littleberry, and the Reachdeep operational ninjas in it swung around the block and parked on the sidewalk near Cope's building. Under cover of darkness, moving with great speed, they unloaded a series of duffel bags and brought them into the building next to Cope's. They hurried them upstairs to the third floor, where the F.B.I. technical surveillance operation was now getting started.

Special Agent Landau and her crew set up two thermal imaging cameras on tripods. The cameras resembled video cameras, except that the lenses were huge and had gold mirrors in them. The lenses looked like giant golden frog eyes. The cameras could see in infrared light, which is heat. They could see warmth through walls, and see it clearly.

Landau wired the thermal-imaging cameras to display screens. A thermal image of Tom Cope's apartment appeared on the screens. Now they could see Cope walking around. He was in the living room, holding an object in his hands. He moved quickly and smoothly from place to place. He seemed calm, at least from all they could tell by looking at his shape.

They saw a large, warm cylinder in another room, and they thought it might be a bioreactor. To get a better look at it, the tech agents silently drilled a cone-shaped hole in the bricks. It took a while for their cutter to penetrate the brick, and they were fearful that the faint humming noise it made would alert Cope. Eventually the cutter had driven the hole to a point just under the paint surface in Cope's apartment. They were looking at a bit of paint from the back side, from the inner surface of the paint. They broke through the paint with a pin. This made a pinhole in the paint at the point of the cone-shaped hole in the bricks. Then they slid a cone-shaped optical assembly into the hole, so that the point of the assembly just penetrated the pinhole in the paint. The point of the cone was actually a fish-eye lens as small as a pencil point. Everything else in the optical assembly was behind the wall surface and invisible to Cope. Even if Cope had looked directly at the fish-eye lens he might not have noticed it. He might have thought it was a speck of dirt.

"We're a fly on his wall," Caroline Landau remarked.

The optical cone was connected to an electronic
imaging system. On a flat screen appeared a fish-eye
view of Tom Cope's laboratory.

Mark Littleberry recognized a Biozan reactor.
"It's not running. I'd guess he's finished making his
virus stocks. But the liquid in that reactor is probably
hot with Cobra."

They could see Cope's boxes of moths and
caterpillars, and his photograph of the Amazon rain
forest, but they could not see Cope. He remained outside the laboratory, visible in the thermal imagers
only as a ghostly orange figure sitting on the couch
or moving restlessly around the living room, mostly
keeping the long tube-thing in his hands, as if he
couldn't let go of it. In stereo sound, they heard him
talking to himself, saying, "You idiot, you idiot, this
is too important to fail." A fuzzy shape rested on a
table in front of the couch. Hopkins and Austen
thought it was probably the bag he'd been carrying
when they'd seen him. Then he opened it—it *was* the
bag—and he seemed to play with another long tube-
thing and a couple of smaller objects, and then he
pulled out something recognizable.

"He has a gun," Caroline Landau said. "Could
be a .45. Oo-ee, it's got a nifty sight on it."

He placed the gun on the table, and lay back on
the couch not ten feet from a massive F.B.I. surveillance and SWAT group, with no apparent inkling of
the weight of agonized law enforcement that pressed
up against his living-room wall like a flood swelling
behind a dam that was getting ready to burst. They

were fascinated with the large cylinder that he held in his hands: it had to be a biological bomb. They counted possibly two large bombs, they weren't sure, including one that seemed to be in the bag all the time. They debated trying to drill another fish-eye lens through the wall to get a clearer picture of him and his bomb or bombs but decided not to, afraid he might notice. They had been lucky up to now, and the last thing they needed was a surveillance boo-boo, something not unheard of in operations of this type.

□

He sat on the couch. What to do? Were they watching him? Or was he imagining this? He went to the window and peeked out, but he was afraid to stay there for more than a few moments. Soon he would have to make his move. He went back into the living room and picked up one of the small bio-det biological grenades. Despite the fact that the explosive was a low-velocity type, the grenade would be absolutely devastating inside a closed space, such as in a room or a tunnel. The two grenades were both a defense and an offense; he could use them either way.

□

At the F.B.I. Command Center in the Federal Building, Frank Masaccio and his people monitored the situation and stayed in touch with SIOC in Washington, which was in full operation. Masaccio had command: he would call the moves. He was not going to burst in on Tom Cope. Not if the man had a bomb, not if he was barricaded in an apartment. That was far too dangerous. He was going to wait until Cope came out of the building, then swoop on him and make the arrest. The idea was to take him so fast he would not have time to detonate anything.

Snipers with Remington .308 rifles would be standing by on the rooftops. If they received an order to shoot, the snipers would aim for his eyes. This is standard procedure in a sniper takedown. You try to hit a two-inch band around the eyes. The bullet enters through the eyes and explodes the brain stem and sends it out through the exit wound. With the brain stem gone the body relaxes—the muscles don't tense. So if the person is holding a finger on a trigger or on a detonator, the finger relaxes spontaneously.

Masaccio instructed the snipers not to shoot without orders. He didn't know how Cope's bomb worked. It might go off if Cope collapsed. If there were indications that Cope was going to detonate a bomb inside his apartment, then the Reachdeep operations people had orders to move through the wall as quickly as possible and try to stop Cope. The goal was the same as always: not necessarily to kill Cope, but first and foremost to render him harmless.

They needed a man known as a master breacher to prepare the way for them into Cope's apartment. The F.B.I. has several master breachers. They work out of Quantico. While the surveillance operation was getting under way, Oscar Wirtz had called Quantico, and a master breacher named Wilmot Hughes had been put in the air, flying to New York on an F.B.I. plane. He arrived at ten o'clock. Cope was still in his apartment and had not made a move.

Wilmot Hughes was a small, wiry man who had spent a lifetime devising ways of entering secure locations rapidly, often with help from explosives. He could enter airplanes and boats and cars and bunkers.

The master breacher inspected the brick wall, running his hands over it, tapping it lightly. "Fortunately this is trivial," he remarked. He began laying shaped plastic explosive charges in a pattern over the bricks. An oval portion of the brick wall that led to Cope's living room would disappear in a fraction of a second whenever the master breacher wanted it to disappear. He gave instructions to the Reachdeep team to lie flat against the wall on either side of the charges when they went off.

□

Cope seemed indecisive. At one point he went into the bathroom and urinated, and they saw and heard that, and an hour later he urinated in the bathroom again. He seemed increasingly nervous. Every now and then Cope's image—a warm human-shaped form—would cross the living room to a window and peek out. The curtains showed up as black rectangles on the imaging screens.

Masaccio spoke to Wirtz on a headset. He told him to get ready to move, now that the breacher had prepared a way. Wirtz and the Reachdeep ninjas began putting on space suits and body armor.

Littleberry said: "I'm going in. I want to see his lab."

"You're too senior for this kind of action," Hopkins told him.

"You can't deny me." Littleberry turned to Austen. "You comin' too?"

"Sure am, Doctor," she said to Littleberry.

"Hey—" Hopkins said.

He gave orders for the doctors to stay behind him, but he thought he was fighting a losing battle to keep them out of it altogether. Everyone pulled on black Racal biohazard suits, and Wirtz made them wear body armor. They had lightweight radio headsets. Wirtz told Hopkins to stay well back. "You and the doctors come in after we've secured the place."

"I'll be climbing over your back, Oscar," Hopkins said. He buckled a pouch to his waist, which he filled with certain essentials: swabs, his pocket protector full of pens and other junk, his Mini Maglite flashlight, and a Boink biosensor. He strapped on his SIG-Sauer nine-millimeter semi-automatic. He ran his radio headset wire down to a transceiver at his waist, which operated over a wide variety of channels. This piece of equipment made it possible for members of the team to talk with each other and with the command center. Finally he put a Racal hood over his head, running his radio wire under the hood's shoulder shroud. He switched on the battery-powered blower for the Racal filters, and the hood pressurized. The blowers made a low hum. The battery would keep the hood pressurized for up to eight hours. He jumped up and down lightly on the balls of his feet, feeling keyed up and wanting to move.

"Take it down, Will!" Oscar Wirtz said. "You're shaking the floor, man." Wirtz thought: He would not do well in a shooter. But I don't have the heart to tell him.

Hopkins turned off his blowers and removed his Racal hood. There was no sense in wearing it while they were waiting for Tom Cope to make a move.

On the rooftops nearby, the snipers kept the windows of Cope's apartment under surveillance with infrared zoom scopes. They could see Cope occasionally, when he moved close to the metal curtain. They put the crosshairs on his eyes when he peered out, but they couldn't shoot. He always seemed to be carrying the bomb. He moved often and seemed fearful of going near the windows.

A little over a mile away, Frank Masaccio sat in the Federal Building wondering what to do. He had the SIOC in Washington watching his every move, second-guessing him, and the White House seemed ready to have some kind of heart attack. The President had not given the news conference; it had been put on hold while the situation in New York unfolded. Frank Masaccio was pondering his options.

Steven Wyzinski's voice came to him: "Frank? Frank? Do you hear me? The attorney general is here at SIOC."

"Mr. Masaccio." It was the voice of Frank Masaccio's ultimate boss, second only to the President in the chain of authority. "Any decisions you make will be reviewed and cleared by me."

Masaccio continued to recommend that no sudden moves be made. He didn't want to commit his forces to an action or to reveal their presence to Cope. Certainly trying to open negotiations with Cope would be a risky thing to try—it might set him off. It wasn't clear what Cope suspected, but Masaccio planned to wait for him to leave the building, then to take him. Trying to take people inside apartments was a recipe for a shooter gone bad, and if the guy had a weapon of mass destruction in his apartment, you had to suck the egg through a pinhole—so ran Masaccio's thinking.

□

In the apartment, Cope went into the bathroom again, carrying the mother bomb. He placed it on the floor. Then he unraveled a long piece of toilet paper and blew his nose. He wiped his face with more toilet paper. He went over to the sink and rinsed his face with cold water.

The surveillance team knew it was cold water, because they could see the color of the water in the thermal imagers.

He was so nervous that he was trembling. Why am I so afraid? He looked into the mirror. His eyes had a strange color. Was that a golden ring around the pupils? He looked into his pupils reflected in the mirror. His nose was running. His upper lip was glistening wet.

No. It could not be. He knew that brainpox was selective in its infectivity. He knew that it infected only about half of the people exposed to it in low doses. It was like so many virus weapons. He had been around the virus for months and he had not become infected. This was impossible. He wondered if he had made a mistake. Maybe when I did the release in Washington I didn't hold my breath in that subway car for long enough. Maybe some of it stuck to my clothes or my hair. No, that's impossible, I'm immune. I'm imagining things.

There is nothing wrong with my mind, nothing. I don't feel anything. If I was infected with brainpox, my mind would feel different. I am a normal paranoid schizophrenic, he said to himself, and he almost smiled, but he wondered again if he had made a big mistake when he had done the Phase II trial in Washington.

□

Cope had a bioreactor full of liquid Cobra virus. Littleberry believed that the reactor was very hot, and that led to a discussion of what to do if some kind of biological meltdown occurred in the apartment during an action. People from the mayor's Emergency Management Office were in the command center with Masaccio, and they had an idea that sounded as if it might just work. It was to fill some fire-department pumper trucks with disinfectant and spray the entire building if Cope's bioreactor dumped its contents. The fire department found a chemical shipper in Brooklyn who had a lot of sodium hypochlorite on hand—that's common laundry bleach. Several pumper trucks went over to Brooklyn and were filled with bleach and water. They then lined up, as discreetly as possible (which wasn't very discreetly) on a street around the corner from Cope. The fire department also had decontamination trucks, which are used to decontaminate firemen or citizens who have been exposed to chemicals or asbestos, and those trucks were stationed nearby.

It was now one o'clock in the morning. Cope had not been able to fall asleep. He was still indecisive. Part of the reason for that was that he was no longer completely him. The transformation was occurring rapidly now. Crystals were forming in his brain stem.

"Move the fire trucks in as close as possible without making them visible in any of Cope's windows," Hopkins said, speaking to Masaccio. "Get them ready to start spraying bleach into the building if we call for it. Wirtzy is dying to move. If we go through the wall, start the spray. If the bomb goes off, let's hope the spray will decontaminate the building."

"That's a big hope, Hopkins," Masaccio said.

Down

It was now three o'clock in the morning. Alice Austen had been watching Cope on the screens of the thermal imaging cameras. He had not gone to sleep. When he stood up from the couch and began to move across the room, she made a tentative diagnosis. Cope seemed to be making some involuntary gestures. Jerky movements. He was talking to himself. And moaning. "I'm not sick. Not sick."

"Listen, Will. I think he's infected," Austen said.

They studied his body movements, but Austen couldn't be sure.

Then Cope seemed to make up his mind. "Option two," he said.

"What was that?" Hopkins said.

"He's losing it," Littleberry said.

The blurry thermal image showed Cope bent over the object in his hands. They heard a sound. It was the sound of the metal end piece being unscrewed from the glass bomb tube. He fiddled with something. They heard a dry, rustling, cracking sound. It was the sound of wires being pulled through a packed mass of viral hexagons in the tube. He was re-arming the bomb.

Hopkins stood and put his hand up. "Wirtzy! He may blow something! Get ready!"

Everyone put on Racal hoods, which took a few seconds. They zipped up their suits and started their air filters running. If the building goes hot with that bomb, Hopkins thought, it could kill all of us, space suits or not. The air near bioground zero would be so thick with virus, it might overwhelm the suit's protection. Quick as cats, Oscar Wirtz and five Reachdeep operational ninjas positioned themselves against the thinned wall, on either side of the charges. The master breacher, Wilmot Hughes, readied his controls. Everyone was wearing full space-suit battle dress with body armor. The ninjas were carrying flash grenades and Heckler & Koch assault weapons.

In Washington, as it dawned on the SIOC group that Reachdeep was getting itself poised to move, a number of people began shouting contradictory things at the same time.

"What the hell's Hopkins doing?"

"Masaccio! Answer us!"

Cope replaced the cap on the cylinder. The bomb was now armed. He slid it inside the carry-bag.

Hopkins stared at the thermal image, trying to read Cope's body language. Was this a man who was getting ready to blow himself up? Hopkins didn't think so. But what was he doing?

Carrying the bag, Cope walked into the corridor that led to the laboratory. He did not put on a protective suit. He opened the door of the lab. Now, in the fish-eye lens, they saw him clearly for the first time. He stood by the door, looking across the room toward the bioreactor, and suddenly he picked up a heavy glass beaker and hurled it.

The bioreactor, which was itself made largely of glass, exploded, its blood-warm contents splashing through the air in a spray of droplets. The pink contents poured out and flooded across the floor in a warm running meltdown of amplified liquid Cobra virus.

"It's gone hot!" Hopkins yelled.

"Go!" Masaccio responded.

Everyone pressed flat against the wall, and the master breacher detonated the charges.

The wall went down as if it were made of gravel, and an oval hole opened up. Wirtz and the ninjas poured through.

Austen, who was lying on the floor, couldn't look. She tucked her head down under her arm, and her stomach lurched. There were brilliant flashes at her back, from the flash grenades. The flash grenades blinded the thermal cameras.

Wirtz had led his team through the hole. They kept their guns ready but held their fire. Hopkins saw the screens go white when the flash grenades went off. Then the screens came back to normal. He saw Cope's thermal image, running across the field of view.

"Oscar, he's moving to your left!" he shouted over the radio link.

He saw Wirtz and his people moving through the apartment. Two of them detached leftward.

"Wirtzy, he's in the kitchen!" Hopkins shouted. Suddenly he saw the form of Tom Cope curl up in a ball—and, unbelievably, Cope dropped straight down through the floor and out of sight. "He's going down!" Hopkins yelled. They pointed the imagers down through the floor. They saw Cope's form descending straight down through the building, until his image faded away.

□

Tom Cope had smashed the bioreactor, and he had backed out of the room and shut the door. An instant later, the apartment had filled with shocking explosions and flashes of light. He raced into the kitchen. Figures in black space suits were tumbling into his living room.

Many old buildings in New York City have dumbwaiter shafts that are no longer used or are used for trash disposal. The dumbwaiter was Cope's planned escape route. He had not dared to try it because he was afraid they would be in the basement waiting for him. Now he had no choice.

Carrying his doctor's bag, Cope had climbed through an opening in the wall of the kitchen and curled up on the dumbwaiter platform. He let the ropes go and the platform went down fast, the ropes singing in the pulley. He came to a halt with a bang in the basement, inside a closet. He flung himself out the door. No one around. He raced through a heating tunnel and came to a small opening in the brickwork covered with a sheet of plywood. He tore the plywood off. There was his crawl space, his escapeway. He went through it, scraping his knees on broken concrete. He cut his knee, ripping his pants. The crawl space was black with dust. Ahead, he heard the rumble of a subway train.

The F.B.I. Hostage Rescue Team coming in through the front door of the building was in a rush to get to the third floor, and they formed a strung-out deployment, team members stopping on every floor to cover the next wave. They had reached the third floor when they heard on their radio headsets that the suspect had gone down through the building, and was presumed to be hiding in the basement.

□

In the apartment, Oscar Wirtz and some of his team headed for the kitchen, where Hopkins was telling them that Cope had disappeared. In the kitchen they found the dumbwaiter shaft.

Seconds later, Hopkins entered. He was carrying a spray tank full of Envirochem, a powerful antibiological liquid. Austen followed behind him, and Littleberry after that. They headed for the bioreactor room, where Hopkins did his best to spray Envirochem all over the floor and walls, making a mist inside the room. Soon bleach would be pouring into the building from the fire trucks.

On his radio, Hopkins heard Wirtz calling to him. He headed for the kitchen, Austen and Littleberry behind him.

"He's gone down a shaft," Wirtz was saying. "We're heading after him."

They followed Wirtz down the stairs, through tremendous confusion. The other H.R.T. teams in the building were wearing respirators but not space suits, and they were evacuating the building's residents. The elderly woman who lived below Cope had to be gotten out fast now, since the reactor was in a room above her.

Leaving these problems to the other teams, the Reachdeep group focused on getting Cope. Wirtz and his ninjas spearheaded a sweep of the basement, with the scientists hanging back but unable to stay out of the operation. Wirtz was swearing to himself about this, vowing that next time he would make sure the scientists were put in a box. For the moment, he could do nothing about it.

It didn't take him long to find the crawl space and the sheet of plywood lying on the floor. "Cope! Are you in there?" he shouted.

No answer.

Wirtz noticed a spot of blood on the concrete floor of the crawl space, and near it were drops of some kind of moisture that was not blood. Hopkins swabbed the blood and jammed the swab into his Boink. The biosensor beeped. "Cobra," he said.

What now?

They shouted again into the crawl space. Silence.

"Scientists back off," Wirtz said. "Operations people in first." He vaulted up into the crawl space. One by one his people followed him, squirming on their hands and knees, pushing their weapons ahead of them. They barely fit. They did not have flashlights; this was an unforeseen development.

Wirtz, the first in line, came to the end of the crawl space. It opened out into darkness and dropped down into a low, narrow passage running at right angles. He could still see a little.

"What's happening down there?" Frank Masaccio asked. He was sitting at his command post, listening to the audio feed, and he was quietly losing his mind. He did not feel as if he was in control of the team.

"What's happening in New York?" These words were spoken by Steven Wyzinski at SIOC in Washington.

There was a rumbling sound, a roaring, and it grew louder. It was being picked up by Wirtz's mike.

They heard Wirtz's voice over the sound, saying, "That's a subway train you're hearing. We're near the subway. I'm behind some kind of wall here."

Cope had gone into the subway. He had slipped through the grasp of a huge F.B.I. operation, and he was carrying a biological bomb or bombs.

"This is fucking terrible!" Masaccio yelled.

"Maybe we can biocontain him," Hopkins said into his headset.

"What do you mean?" Masaccio asked.

"The subway tunnels are a natural biocontainment area. If he blows a bomb in there, maybe we can seal the tunnels off and stop the trains. Maybe we'd rather have him down there than up in the open air. Let's try to trap him in the tunnels. Frank, you need to shut down the air-circulation fans in the subway. You don't want tunnel air being vented outdoors, and you don't want air being drawn in, either."

Masaccio put through an emergency call to the Transit Authority Operations Control Center on West Fourteenth Street. This is a large control room, manned by dozens of subway system operators. He got a system supervisor on the line. They began stopping the trains. They turned off all the air blowers and fans.

Masaccio went into a flurry of shouting and orders. The bottom line was that F.B.I. agents and New York City police officers were to seal off all the subway entrances in the neighborhood of East Houston Street, and then go down into the subway and sweep the tracks, to find Tom Cope. Almost none of these forces were equipped with any kind of biohazard masks or protection. If Cope's bomb went off, many of them would die. Masaccio was throwing in his reserves, but they were not prepared. He had no choice.

□

Reachdeep team members followed the crawl space that Cope had entered underneath his building. It led to the door at the far end of the Houston Street subway stub tunnel. The door was supposed to be locked, but what appeared to be a secure catch was in fact a mechanism that snapped open if you knew how to operate it. This was Cope's route of escape. The route went directly past the places where Harmonica Man and Lem had lived. They had died because they had seen Cope using the door.

Oscar Wirtz led the way, then five ninjas, and then, bringing up the rear, came Hopkins, Austen, and Littleberry. It is true that Mark Littleberry, or any man his age, did not belong in an operation of this kind, but no one could control Mark Littleberry; the man was fundamentally uncontrollable.

The tunnel was silent. The subway trains had stopped running.

Faintly, they heard Masaccio's voice on their headsets: "What are you doing? Report?"

"I can't hear you, Frank. You're breaking up," Hopkins said. "We're coming into the Second Avenue station. You've got to seal it off."

"We're doing it now, we're sending police into all the stations," Masaccio replied.

They moved forward, running at a jog trot.

F.B.I. communications specialists told the Reach-deep group to switch their radios over to a frequency used by the Transit Authority. This improved the reception, which depended on wires strung inside the subway tunnels. When the Reachdeep people came up onto the Second Avenue platform they found it deserted.

Cutoff

He had come out onto the Second Avenue platform a few minutes ahead of his pursuers. Should he wait for a train? At three in the morning, he might have to wait a long time.

Don't wait for a train, that would be stupid. And the street up there will be crawling with agents. Don't go up to the street here.

Keep moving. He now believed that he might be infected, but he could still move. Perhaps he had developed some kind of resistance to the virus. Perhaps he could survive an infection.

He hurried along the length of the platform, carrying his doctor's bag. He climbed down the stairs at the end of the platform and got back on the tracks, heading west now, following the route of the F train toward the center of Manhattan. His feet pounded along on the ties. He noticed something that he did not like. The tunnels were silent. The power was off in the rails, and he couldn't hear any fans, although the lights in the tunnel were still on. Then he heard a sound behind him. He looked back. He saw five or six people in black space suits moving across the platform of the Second Avenue station, in the distance.

He broke into a run, his feet splashing through puddles, stumbling on the ties. They don't have me yet. He felt a cool determination sweep over him.

Have courage. You will be remembered by future ages as a man of vision and heroic will.

Heading westward through the main subway tunnel, he saw that he was approaching another subway station. He knew it was the Broadway Lafayette stop. He wanted to get out onto the street there. Or did he? What to do?

Set off the bomb right here? He had a better idea.

He had explored this tunnel before, on foot— part of his research into the body of the city, looking for places to do a biological release.

He was looking for a side tunnel that he remembered, a little-used cutoff. He knew that it doubled back. He could circle around his pursuers, if he could just remember where the tunnel was. Here it was: a switch in the tracks, and a single-track tunnel breaking to his left. It headed south, toward the Lower East Side of New York City.

□

At that moment, Frank Masaccio was learning about the side tunnel. He was talking with subway system operators in the control room on Fourteenth Street. Masaccio had sent an F.B.I. team into the Broadway Lafayette subway station, and that team was now moving east toward the Reachdeep team, which was moving west. They were attempting to trap Cope in a pincer between the two stations.

"There's that BJ 1 tunnel," a system operator told Masaccio. "If you're trying to trap the guy, and he finds that BJ 1 tunnel, that will be his only way out."

"Where's it lead?" Masaccio asked.

The BJ 1 tunnel led to a station at the corner of Delancey Street and Essex Street. Masaccio ordered a police or F.B.I. team—whichever was closest—to deploy there fast.

Meanwhile, the Reachdeep team arrived at the entrance of the BJ 1 tunnel. It was a curving tunnel, poorly lit.

"We think he's gone in there," Masaccio told them. His voice was crackly and distant.

"You're breaking up," Wirtz said to him.

"Turn left into that tunnel," Masaccio said.

The Reachdeep team turned into the BJ 1 tunnel, moving quickly. They were in a rarely used tunnel that ran south and east under the Lower East Side. It was illuminated by lightbulbs at intervals, and it was coal black with steel dust. As they went deeper into the BJ 1 tunnel, their radio contact with the F.B.I. Command Center broke up and finally vanished. The team, at this point, consisted of six heavily armed ninjas including Oscar Wirtz, and three scientists—Will Hopkins, Alice Austen, and Mark Littleberry. Reachdeep was on its own.

Essex-Delancey

Tom Cope moved along cautiously but quickly through the BJ 1 tunnel, carrying the black bag with its explosive assemblages of crystallized Cobra virus-dispersal bombs. The Delta Elite handgun was also in his bag. The tunnel stretched out ahead, the single set of tracks gleaming in the occasional lights that burned in niches. He stopped every now and then to listen. At one point he thought he heard them coming behind him, but he wasn't sure.

The tunnel went down a slope, turning south. It passed underneath a parking lot and then underneath Bowery Street, and headed downtown along the Sara Delano Roosevelt Parkway, a strip of greenery and playgrounds on the Lower East Side. It was 3:20 on a Sunday morning, and when police cars and F.B.I. cars suddenly began pouring into the neighborhood, and police teams began running down into subway entrances, there were not too many people around to notice, although patrons of nearby clubs were drawn to the activity and stood out in the street wondering what was going on. Since reporters listen to the police radio, television news trucks soon headed for the Lower East Side, tracking reports of a possible terror incident. The Cobra Event had been kept a secret, but the moment Cope slipped away, and the operation turned into a chase, it started to blow into the media.

The BJ 1 tunnel was going deeper underground, and Cope followed it. At first it headed south, but then it curved eastward, away from the Sara Delano Roosevelt Parkway, and it passed in a swooping curve under the old heart of the Lower East Side, under Forsyth Street, Eldridge Street, Allen Street, under Orchard Street, and then it headed due east under Delancey Street.

Cope knew where he was going, in a general sense. He had explored these tunnels on foot, and he had memorized a variety of routes of escape. This route was perhaps his best bet, he thought. He was heading for the Williamsburg Bridge, which rises from Delancey Street, connecting Manhattan with Brooklyn. He felt that he could hide his explosive devices either somewhere in a tunnel, or perhaps he could leave them in the open air where they would blow and plume into the city. He did not want his pursuers to find the devices. That was the problem. If he left them here in the tunnel, the devices would be found and perhaps disarmed. His leg hurt, and it was slowing him down. He had cut his knee while scrambling out of his building.

The tunnel began to rise, and it curved to the northeast. He saw lights ahead. It was the platform of the Essex–Delancey Street subway station, a complicated station at the foot of the Williamsburg Bridge.

I will get out here, where I don't have to take the stairs up to the street.

The tunnel came out close to the Essex Street platform. A couple of hundred yards past the platform, the tracks headed up onto the Williamsburg Bridge. The platform was deserted. In the distance

Cope could see lights. That was his way out. They wouldn't think to block this way.

Meanwhile, a group of New York City police officers were sweeping a set of stairs to the Essex Street platform.

Cope was hurrying along the tracks by the platform. He heard a sound of running footsteps, voices shouting; he saw movement on the stairs, and he turned around and retreated the way he had come. He faded into a niche in the wall back in the BJ 1 tunnel, listening to their radios crackling. They were searching the platform. It was certain that any moment they would come into the tunnel looking for him. What to do?

He knew that an F.B.I. team was coming down the BJ 1 tunnel behind him. He was trapped between the F.B.I. and the New York City police department.

I should do it here. Set it off. He hesitated. But the issue wasn't so simple. He wasn't absolutely certain he was infected with the virus. Maybe he wasn't infected. It is hard to choose to die. It is easier to choose to be alive, as long as you have life left in you. *There might be a way out.*

He heard the rustling sound of the space suits, the pounding of their light rubber boots. They were coming fast.

He moved out of the niche and crept along the wall, and entered a dark area, some abandoned rooms. Ducking, moving fast, he hurried through the rooms. He was not more than forty feet from the police officers on the platform. He found some old air-blowing equipment, broken and unused machinery. A refrigerator. Where to go? For a moment he thought that he could climb inside the refrigerator. It had been painted black—weird. But it was too small; he couldn't fit in there. He got down on his knees and curled up against the wall, beside the black refrigerator.

He opened his bag and pulled out a bomb full of viral glass. He opened one end of the tube, and tugged out the detonator wires. If he crossed the wires, shorted them out, the bio-det would explode. He would die, but his life-form would live and go into the world.

□

The Essex Street station contains a large abandoned area that was at one time a trolley-car station. The police officers, having swept the platforms, prepared to move out into the trolley area. At that moment, the Reachdeep team arrived at the Essex Street platform. The ninjas had a conference with some of the police officers. Cope seemed to have vanished.

"He could have gone onto the bridge, there," a policeman said. "Either that, or he's in that trolley area." Meanwhile, he was wondering: If these agents are wearing space suits, what am I getting exposed to down here?

"You guys stay back. You don't have protective gear," Wirtz said to the police officers. The F.B.I. people did not have flashlights, while the police officers did. They borrowed the officers' flashlights, and began to sweep through the trolley area, shining the lights left and right, moving among columns. Hopkins, Austen, and Littleberry remained where they were, standing on the subway tracks near the BJ 1 tunnel with no flashlights. In their suits, with the soft, clear helmets around their heads, it was difficult to pick up sounds, but Hopkins thought he heard something at his back. He spun around and found himself facing a group of abandoned rooms heaped with trash. He saw some air blowers and what looked like a black refrigerator. The sound seemed to have come from behind the refrigerator.

Hopkins drew his gun. He circled around the refrigerator. Nothing there. He looked around, and he looked down at the dust. The black subway dust. On the far side of the refrigerator, he found what appeared to be recent scuffmarks. Then he noticed blood. Several fresh drops of blood.

He opened his pouch and pulled out his Boink and a swab. He swabbed the blood and stuck it straight into the sampling port of the Boink. The device gave off its peculiar chime. On the screen it said "COBRA."

Hopkins spoke quietly into his headset. "Breaker. Emergency. It's Hopkins. We're on him. He's near us! Hey!" A veil of silence seemed to have fallen over his radio headset. This was a dead zone. "Frank! Frank, come in!" he hissed. "Anybody hear me? We're tracking on Cope!"

Hopkins heard fragments of Masaccio's voice. He couldn't understand what Masaccio was saying.

"Frank! Come in!"

While he was talking, Hopkins was turning around slowly, trying to see into the darkness. He turned to Austen and Littleberry. "Lie down on the floor, please." He moved forward, inching around some machines. "Dr. Cope! Dr. Cope! Please surrender yourself. You will not be harmed. Please, sir."

There was nobody there.

But on the far side of the machines he found an open doorway leading to an unlit area heaped with trash. Homeless people had been living there. Hopkins moved forward, creeping along the wall in semidarkness, wading through trash, ready to dive for cover. He came to an opening in the wall. It was a low tunnel, about three feet high, full of electrical cables.

Hopkins debated what to do. He could hear snatches of talk on his headset. "Frank! Masaccio! Wirtzy!" he called. No dice. Should he go into the tunnel? He had his Mini Maglite flashlight, but it wasn't exactly useful for night operations. Nevertheless, he switched it on, getting ready to dive if the light drew gunfire.

Nothing happened. He shone the light down the tunnel.

He yelled over his shoulder: "Mark! Alice! Go back and find Wirtz! There's a tunnel."

He bent over and entered the tunnel, shining his minilight along the electrical cables. The tunnel went straight ahead. He moved quickly now, hunched over, concentrating on the problem at hand. Was Cope himself lost, or did he know a way out? He wondered if at any moment a shock wave would ram down the tunnel, from the bomb going off. It seemed pretty clear that Cope had been heading for the Williamsburg Bridge, but that his escape route had been cut off by the police. He had been heading for the open air. He wanted to blow his bomb outdoors at night.

Hopkins had gone an unknown distance down the tunnel when he realized that he was being followed. He stopped. It was Austen, directly behind

him. He turned to face her. "You don't have a gun!
You don't have a light!"

"Get going," she answered.

"You are a pain in the ass."

"Get going, or give me your light."

"Where's Mark?"

"He went back to find Oscar."

Without another word, Hopkins surged forward,
annoyed with Austen, but most of all angry with himself. He felt responsible for having let Cope get
away. If a lot of people die . . . don't think about that.
Keep on Cope. Find him.

Hopkins and Austen moved along through the
tunnel. Sometimes they had to crawl on their hands
and knees. The electrical cables were alive, no doubt,
and Hopkins wondered if he or Austen would wind
up being electrocuted if they touched a broken insu-
lator. The only good thing about these power cables
was that perhaps Cope would fry first.

Then Hopkins noticed something troubling. His
flashlight was becoming fainter. The beam turned a
distinct yellow.

The electrical tunnel led southwest from the
Essex-Delancey Street subway station under the
Lower East Side, heading downtown. Hopkins and
Austen came to a right-angle bend, and then another.
The tunnel continued for several blocks, passing
under Broome Street, under Ludlow Street, under
Grand Street. Hopkins and Austen came to a crossing
point in the tunnels—a choice of three routes to take,
three tunnels.

They stopped. Which way to go? Hopkins got
down on his knees and started searching for blood

on the floor with his minilight. There was no blood. He noticed a puddle of water lying on the floor of the right-hand fork. The puddle had been recently splashed. Cope had gone this way. Hopkins was disoriented. He had lost his sense of direction, and he wasn't quite sure where he and Austen were headed. In fact, they were entering Chinatown.

Now the tunnel narrowed into a crawl space. The going became very difficult. Hopkins got down on his hands and knees and began to crawl forward on his belly, sliding over electrical cables. The cables felt slightly warm, and he could feel them vibrating. As he crawled, he talked with Austen on his radio headset.

"*Dr. Austen.* Will you stop now, please? Just stop. You're going to get yourself hurt."

She did not reply.

They had gone an unknown distance when they came to a steel plate blocking the way. It was a small access hatch. He tapped the hatch lightly with his gloved fingertips. It creaked and began to move.

"What is it?" Austen said behind him. "Move your feet."

"I can't move my feet. Lie down, please, there could be gunfire." He pushed gently on the hatch, his gun ready, and the hatch opened with a drawn-out creak. The sound bounced away into deep echoes and then silence. A vast black space loomed beyond the hatch. Hopkins shone his minilight around the space.

It was an enormous underground tunnel. Where the hell are we? Hopkins thought. What part of the city is this? His flashlight beam did not penetrate far into the tunnel, which seemed to extend a great distance, lost in blackness. It was a double tunnel, with a line of concrete columns marching down the middle of it. Twisted and bent pieces of steel reinforcement bar stuck out of the walls like black thorns. The hatch opened out of a wall about ten feet above the floor of the tunnel.

□

Cope had a flashlight, but he didn't want to use it, because he thought it might give him away. At intervals he flicked it on and off, but mostly he moved through the tunnel with his hand on the wall, going by sense of touch. He had no idea where he was.

When he had arrived at the hatch he had turned on his light and looked around. He lowered himself into the big tunnel, holding the bag in his hand, trying to protect it. He landed hard on the concrete floor, and an ominous cracking sound came from inside his bag. One of the large glass tubes had cracked. That was too bad. Best to leave it here.

He checked to make sure the chip timer was running, and then he placed the glass cylinder in a shadowy corner by a column. It contained some 435 hexagons of viral glass along with bio-det explosive. Then, flicking his light on and off, he moved along up the tunnel, his bag lighter now, but still containing one large bomb, the grenades, and the gun. The tunnel sloped upward, curving gently to the right. He knew where he wanted to be. He wanted to be outdoors. It was a soft gentle night out there, almost windless, a perfect night.

The tunnel was a stretch of unfinished subway running under Chinatown and the Lower East Side. It was one of a number of planned subway routes in New York City that had been partly built but never finished. This was a length of tunnel intended for the never-completed Second Avenue subway line.

□

Hopkins leaned out of the hatch door. What he saw looked like a subway tunnel, but there were no train tracks; the floor was smooth concrete. Hopkins swung himself out of the hatch, hung on the lip, and let go. He landed on his feet. Austen dropped down next to him.

He said: "I'm giving you a direct order to freeze. I am the chief executive—"

She brushed past him.

The unfinished subway tunnel ran from north to south under Chinatown. It headed toward the Manhattan Bridge, which spans the East River. As they proceeded along the tunnel, Hopkins played his light around, holding his gun at the ready. There seemed to be no exits from this tunnel.

Hopkins tried his radio again. "Frank? Wirtzy? Are you there?"

There was no radio service in the tunnel. They kept walking, Hopkins shining his minilight around the columns, until they came to a set of metal stairs leading up to an open doorway. The question was whether Cope had gone up the stairs or had continued to follow the tunnel.

They continued along the tunnel until it ended at a blank concrete wall. Construction of the Second Avenue subway had ended here years earlier. There was no way out from here; it was a dead end. Cope must have gone up the stairs. They hurried back, having lost valuable time, but when they arrived at the stairs, Hopkins hesitated.

"Pull yourself together or give me your gun," Austen said to him quietly.

"That's a bullshit statement! I'm terrified, Alice. You should be, too. He has a bomb and he's armed."

He climbed the stairs, though, and found himself in an empty room. It led to a number of dark, open doorways.

□

In the Command Center, Frank Masaccio was beginning to understand the situation. He had been having great difficulty maintaining contact with Reachdeep on the radio. Wirtz and Littleberry had reported that the team had become separated. Cope had disappeared in the Essex Street subway station. There had been much confusion and delay, with police officers running out onto the Williamsburg Bridge, stopping traffic, and sweeping the bridge. Now it appeared that Cope was still in the subway, still underground. He had apparently disappeared into an electrical service tunnel. Hopkins and Austen had followed him. After a delay, Wirtz and the ninjas had now also entered the service tunnel. As soon as they went in they dropped out of radio contact. Masaccio had lost contact with all elements of Reachdeep.

"Where's Littleberry?" he said to an agent on the radio.

"Dr. Littleberry has gone into the tunnel with Wirtz."

"What? My whole goddamned Reachdeep team has gone down a rat hole!" Masaccio shouted. "Go in there and find them!"

Masaccio got on the telephone with engineers from Con Edison and with the subway system operators, demanding information. Where does that tunnel lead? People were telling him that it ended up in the Second Avenue subway line.

"What Second Avenue subway?" Masaccio yelled. "Do you take me for a fucking idiot? I've lived in New York all my life and you can't tell me there's a *Second Avenue* subway. There isn't!"

But there is, the subway operators insisted. It's an empty tunnel.

"Aw, shit, an empty tunnel!" He turned to his managers. "Send in our Hostage Rescue people. Jesus! How did this happen?"

The subway operators told Masaccio that the best access to the Second Avenue tunnel was a hatchway at the foot of the Manhattan Bridge, in Chinatown.

□

Hopkins had to decide which of the empty doorways to choose. He tried to think the way Cope would think. Cope would be heading up for the street. He would want to get into the open air. Hopkins tried all the doors, and behind one he found a steel ladder leading upward. Hopkins climbed the ladder, with Austen following him. They reached another room. There was a dark open doorway on the far side. Then he heard a sound coming through the doorway—a metallic clink. A light blinked on and off.

He dove for the ground, dragging Austen down with him, and turned off his flashlight. He squirmed forward in the darkness, on his belly. He heard a sharp clattering and a muttered curse. He moved across the floor, gun ready, light off, afraid of dying, if the truth be told, and afraid that Austen might die. He thought to himself: I will never, ever join a Hostage Rescue Team. I don't know how those people do this kind of thing.

He had now arrived at the open, black doorway. He could hear and feel Austen moving behind him. He was so angry at her that he wanted to scream. It would serve her right if she took a gunshot, but he couldn't bear the thought of that happening to her.

He lay behind the edge of the door, for cover, and briefly flicked on his light into the space where the sound had come from.

The light revealed a deep chamber. The floor was twenty feet below the level of the doorway. It seemed to be some sort of air-circulation chamber. There was nobody in it. But on the floor of the chamber lay a flashlight. It was off.

Cope had dropped his flashlight! That was the source of the clattering sound and the reason for the curse.

On the inner faces of the chamber there were small openings, vent tunnels, reachable by ladders that ran vertically up the walls of the chamber. Cope had obviously been climbing on one of the ladders moments before—that was the metallic sound they'd heard, and then he'd dropped his flashlight. He must have gone into one of the vent holes. Which one? There were six holes.

"Dr. Cope! Dr. Cope! Give yourself up!" he shouted.

I have to go down in there, I guess.

He swung out into space and started climbing down a ladder into the chamber, holding his gun. He was going to try climbing up each of the ladders, looking into all the vent tunnels, one by one. What else could he do, except give up? But if Cope got away—. He reached the bottom of the chamber and stood looking up the ladders at the vent holes, pouring with sweat inside his space suit, getting ready to dive and shoot if Cope opened fire on him. He realized he was a vulnerable target, and he began to think that he had just done something stupid, something Wirtzy would never have done.

He was moving to pick up Cope's flashlight when Austen's voice on the radio burst in his ears. "Will! Heads up!"

At the same moment he saw the plastic object. It flew past him. It had been thrown from one of the openings. It bounced at his feet, rolled a short distance, and came to a stop under a ladder. A red light was blinking on it.

Grenade. There was no way he could climb the ladder out of the chamber in time. It was going to explode in the chamber with him.

He heard Austen screaming.

He picked up the grenade and threw it on a hard, flat trajectory into one of the vent openings in the chamber. It disappeared into the opening. He heard it bouncing in there.

That wasn't good enough. He still had to get out of here. The explosion was going to come out of the vent hole.

He leaped for a ladder and climbed it like a chimpanzee being chased by a cloud of hornets from hell, dropping his gun in the process. He was trying to reach another vent hole, to get inside it for cover.

He reached the opening and hurled himself in on his stomach.

There was a yellow-red boom. A thudding shock wave rolled down the tunnel and tugged at his biohazard suit. This was followed by a crunching, creaking sound, and a piece of concrete fell off the roof of his tunnel, trapping him.

He was left lying in total darkness, wedged face-first into a small vent tunnel. There was a whining, pinging sound in his ears, like a jet engine.

"Hello?" he called.

There was no answer.

"Alice?"

He assumed that the grenade had had virus material in it, Cobra crystals.

He shouted, "We're hot! I think we've gone hot in here!"

There was no answer.

He wondered if his suit had been breached. He wondered especially about his air filters, and if his head-bubble had been ripped. The lungs were the most vulnerable part of the body. Struggling against the tight walls of the tunnel, he put his hands up to his soft helmet and pushed on it and felt around. It seemed to be okay. The blowers were still humming. Good.

It was almost totally dark, but not completely. Where was the light coming from? He realized that he was lying on his Mini Maglite. He got a hand under his chest and pulled it out. The light revealed his radio headset lying in front of his face, inside his helmet. He spoke into the mike. "Alice? Are you there?" He waited. "Hello, come in." Nothing but a hiss of dead radio noise.

□

Alice Austen saw Hopkins throw the grenade up into the vent hole and then begin to climb a ladder, heading for another vent hole, trying to get away from the blast. Then she rolled back behind the doorway, to protect herself from the coming explosion. She saw the light, but heard no sound.

The flash died instantly, and now she was lying in total darkness. Hopkins had been carrying the only flashlight.

"Will? Will, are you there?" she called on her headset. She received an answer of white noise. Nothing but the sound of blood rushing in her head and her breath panting.

She did not want Hopkins to be in trouble. She really did not want him to be in trouble.

"Will!" she screamed. "Please talk to me, Will! Will!" Nothing.

Then she thought: I'm making a lot of noise. If Cope is around here, he'll hear me.

She would climb down into the chamber, to help him if she could. She felt around in the darkness. She grasped the ladder that went down into the chamber. It came away in her hand, and leaned crazily away from the wall, or so it seemed from the way it felt in the darkness. The blast had done a number on the ladder, had broken it. There was no way to get down in there. No way to see if Cope's flashlight still worked, which was unlikely anyway.

Now what? She could either stay where she was, lying on the floor, waiting for help to arrive, or she could try to get back to the main tunnel. Soon there would be people and lights in that main tunnel. That was where she wanted to go.

She stood up in pitch darkness. Trying to remember which way she had come, she retraced their route, waving her hands back and forth in the blackness in front of her. She reached a ladder. Yes, we climbed up this ladder to get here. She called softly on her radio again: "Will? Are you all right? Please answer me, Will. Can you hear me?" She inched down the ladder, working by sense of touch. Now she was standing in a room. Which way to go now? Ariadne had had a thread; she had her memory. She began feeling her way along the walls in pitch-darkness.

Austen was playing her hand along the wall when it came into contact with some fabric. Then she felt his arm. It was Cope, and they were inches apart. He had been waiting against the wall.

He fired his gun twice. The muzzle flashes illuminated the two of them, frozen in the light like nocturnal creatures caught in the flash of a naturalist's camera. Both shots went under her arm, missing her by inches.

She dove across the room, howling with terror, and leaped through a doorway into total darkness. Suddenly she was tumbling and falling. She fell down the metal stairs into the main tunnel, gasping with pain. She picked herself up and ran, and collided with something.

She found herself lying on her back in pitch-darkness, weeping with terror. Everything hurt. She wondered if she had broken any bones. Stop it. Stop crying. She rolled over and stood up. Have to move away from here.

It was pitch-dark again, but she knew she must be standing in the main tunnel. She moved off to one side, then crouched by what felt like a wall. She tried desperately to get her breathing under control. Her body ached from falling down the stairs. She could not make a sound. He would target his gun on any sounds. But maybe he was trying to get away. Maybe he was gone. He doesn't have a light. She listened. Heard nothing. She could not hear well, because her head was shrouded in the protective helmet, and her blowers were making a gentle hum.

She waited, straining her ears, in total darkness. She saw sparkles in her eyes—her optic nerves were firing with nothing to see. She heard something—a metallic rattle. Then nothing. Then a faint scraping sound. She waited, absolutely still, trying to avoid the slightest rustle of her suit, but she could not do anything about the hum of the Racal blowers. A great deal of time seemed to pass. Her muscles became stiff and sore. Trapped inside her space suit, she couldn't hear the sounds around her. She was tempted to rip open her hood so that she could hear better. But that grenade he had set off might have been full of Cobra.

Suddenly she noticed a tiny light, a red spot on the wall. She did not know what it was. It moved rapidly, seeming to bounce over coffers and columns. It moved and jumped like a red firefly. She couldn't tell where it came from. It had a life of its own, unconnected to anything else.

It was seeking her.

It was a laser pointer.

She almost screamed. She hunched down.

The red light went bouncing around. She couldn't see Cope, but she realized he was standing in the doorway at the top of the stairs, aiming the laser out into the tunnel, over her.

The dot went down the tunnel. It came back. It went down the tunnel in the other direction.

"I can hear your suit humming," he said. He had a calm voice, rather mild and high-pitched but strangely blurred, as if his mouth were full. "I can't quite locate it. My ears are ringing." The red dot hopped across the floor. "Eventually this will find you," he said.

The red dot hopped across some columns and turned and moved up the floor toward her. It touched her suit.

She screamed and dove sideways. The gun roared, a flat deafening smack in the tunnel, with a bright flash.

She found an opening between two columns, rolled through it, picked herself up, and ran in total darkness. The red dot hopped around, looking for her. She stopped running and crouched down low. She put her fingertips on the floor, in the stance of a runner at a starting block, trying to ready herself to jump in any direction.

His voice came sharply out of the blackness, echoing on the concrete around them. "I am not wearing a mask." The voice was about forty feet away, to her right. "I can hear you better than you can hear me."

On her radio headset she heard Hopkins say: "Hey! Anyone there?" *He's alive,* she thought.

"Ah, your radio," Cope said.

She reached for her belt and ripped the headset out of the jack, then tried to keep herself still.

"The gun is loaded with hollow-point bullets. Each bullet has a viral glass bead in the tip. BioArk is selling this technology, too. I have acquired a great deal of technology from the Concern." His feet clanked down the metal stairs. "You don't understand what I'm doing. I'm not trying to kill too many people. Just some of them."

□

In the F.B.I. Command Center in the Federal Building, Masaccio was talking with the subway system operators. "You've got a lighting system in that tunnel complex? Well, turn on the goddamned lights! I've got people in there! What? What power transformer? Why is it a problem?"

□

In the darkness, she could almost feel the heft of the gun swinging toward her as he focused on the sound coming from her blowers. She tensed herself, preparing to explode from the starting block. She sensed the fragility of her body, the delicacy of her mortal being, and felt the jelly of her mind surrounded by hard bone, that can splinter—

Suddenly, with a humming sound, banks of fluorescent lights clicked on up and down the tunnel, bathing the tunnel in a blue-white glow.

He was holding the gun in a police stance. His face was glistening wet. Fluid was running from his nose and coating his chin. His lips were bloody, his eyeglasses flecked with bloodspatter. He had started chewing. He fired. The bullet splashed on the concrete. She was running fast. The lights went out again.

In total darkness she ran at full speed straight up the tunnel toward the dead end. Suddenly everything exploded. She saw purple flashes and she sprawled on the ground, certain she had been hit. She had tripped over a piece of concrete and was lying behind it. She stayed there, afraid to move.

□

Hopkins had been calling for help on his headset. When he got no answer, he concluded that his radio was broken. He was lying on his stomach in a low horizontal passage. The tunnel was not meant to fit a human body, especially someone wearing a space suit with chest armor. The tunnel went straight ahead into darkness. It was about eighteen inches high and two and a half feet wide. He could not possibly turn around in it. His feet were blocked by the chunk of concrete that had fallen. He had to go forward into the crawlway; he had no choice. He was now beginning to feel the first bad tremors of claustrophobia. If he stayed where he was, he might run out of breathable air. So he crawled forward, occasionally calling on his radio headset. Got to slip this armor off, somehow, that would give me more room in here. He tried. He found that he could undo the Velcro straps, but he couldn't take his arms out of it.

He was coming to a dead end. "Oh, no," he said. Now he would have to back up. But as he reached the end, his fingers felt a lip or corner of some kind. It was a shaft going down. The tunnel went straight downward into darkness. He pushed his face over the lip and pointed his light into a shaft that seemed to be about twenty feet deep. It ended with a flat dead end. A dead-end hole. Just looking at it made him feel sick. What now? I'm going to have to back up, get back to the blockage and wait for help.

He tried to back up. It was more difficult than pushing himself forward.

Then it occurred to him that there might be a way to turn his body around and reverse direction. Then I can maybe get more air, maybe shout around the blockage, and maybe someone will hear me.

It seemed that the vertical shaft, which joined the horizontal shaft at a right angle, might provide enough space in which to turn his body around. He squirmed and twisted and fought against the confinement. He tried every position he could think of, his face suspended over the hole, working his shoulders this way and that. "It's a mathematical problem with no solution," he muttered. The problem was the damned armor vest. Again he struggled to remove his armor. Then a terrible thing happened.

He slipped. He fell headfirst down the hole, a plunge of twenty feet. He whumped to a halt face-down in the bottom of the hole with a sudden wedging jerk. He had almost broken his neck. He was jammed vertically in the shaft, his arms pinned at his sides. And it had gone pitch-dark. He had lost his minilight. He was upside down, face-first in a dead-end hole, with no light and no air. There was no way he could back out.

The roaring in his ears was the sound of his own voice begging for mercy. The panic shook him like a series of electric shocks. He was screaming uncontrollably, howling from pure claustrophobic terror. He struggled, fighting the concrete walls, trying somehow to move up and backward again, but he was jammed face downward at the bottom of the tight, airless shaft. He could not get enough air in his lungs, and he could not force his body upward. He thrashed, moaning, screaming, kicking his feet.

Hopkins took a deep breath and held it. He held it for a while, then let all the breath out of his lungs.

He tried to hold his breath again. He wanted to make himself pass out. If he could pass out, then this would be ended.

He could not pass out, which meant that there was enough air in here to keep him alive.

For a week.

Don't think about that.

I've got to relax. I'm dying. If I'm going to die, I've got to come to some kind of peace.

Think of something. What is that Zen saying? *A wise man can live comfortably in hell.* Forget hell. Think of California. Think of the best beach in California. It might be Malibu Beach. No—those little sculpted coves at Laguna Beach. Yes. He tried to imagine himself lying on his back on the warm sand at Laguna, the smell of the salt air, the cries of the seagulls, the *whush-haaa* of the surf, the sun falling into the Pacific Ocean. . . . So many lost opportunities . . . you geek, if you get out of this alive, you really should ask her out. Strike a blow for geekdom. The air really is depleted in here, it's making me slightly demented.

He realized that something was pressed against his cheek. It felt like—the Mini Maglite. But it was dead. He moved his hand. He got one hand around it, and twisted it, and it came on.

Light. This was progress.

He moved his neck left and right. He saw bare concrete a few inches from his eyes. His face was flushed and sweating, engorged with blood from hanging upside down.

That was when he got a shock. There was something dark and open behind his head. An opening!

Twisting his head as far around as possible, he saw that it was a tight passage that went off into darkness. Wedging his flashlight around, he managed to get a view into the tunnel.

Then he got another shock.

He saw a large glass tube standing upright on the floor of the tunnel at the foot of a ladder. It was packed full of hexagons of viral glass. It was Cope's biological bomb.

It was several feet from his head, and it contained enough viral glass to render areas of New York City and downwind lethally hot.

He would have to try to disarm it. It must have a timer of some kind.

This was going to be difficult, because he was hanging upside down in the shaft. He turned his body and jerked it, and twisted and hunched and struggled. He managed to slowly rotate his body. He was still hanging upside down, but he was facing the bomb. By wrenching his shoulders, he managed to get one hand through the opening. He would try to grab the bomb with his fingers and drag it toward him, where he could work on it. He reached his fingers out for the glass tube . . . it was too far away. It was three feet away from his extended fingertips.

He moved his hand up to his waist, found his Leatherman Super Tool, and unfolded it to the pliers. Tried to grab the thing with his pliers.

Nope. Totally hopeless. I need almost three feet.

Three feet might as well be three light-years.

At his waist he wore a pouch—he had used it to hold his minilight and his pocket protector. He got one hand up to it and unzipped it. The pocket protector fell out, scattering things. He said to himself: Think. *A wise man can build gadgets in hell.*

He looked down at the stuff that had fallen from his pocket protector and he tapped his fingers around, taking inventory, and speaking out loud: "Mechanical pencil. Small box of pencil leads. Goober or Raisinet, not sure which. My Fisher space pen, writes in zero gravity. Swab. Another swab. Another swab. Length of duct tape wrapped around a pencil stub. Ticket stub from a Redskins game. Half an Oreo cookie."

Nobody but a fool goes into a federal counterterrorism operation without duct tape. "To build a sticky probe," he said out loud.

With his head twisted to see what he was doing, and working with one hand only, he pulled a strip of tape from the pencil stub, and he began taping the objects together, trying to make a long stick. He debated trying to remove his glove for better coordination but decided against it; too much virus around here.

With one hand he began stripping small pieces of duct tape off the pencil. He taped the mechanical pencil to the Fisher space pen and the pencil stub, end to end, using strips of duct tape, making a kind of extended stick. A probe. Then he stripped the swabs from their wrapping paper, and taped them together, end to end. That made another stick. Next, he taped the swabs to the pencil-and-pen stick. What he had now was a long probe. The light, flexible, delicate end of the probe consisted of the three medical swabs, taped end to end. They flopped around, but they added length to his probe. He packed a small ball of tape to the soft tip of the leading swab, attaching it firmly to the swab with extra strips of tape. He was running desperately low on tape.

He had built a sticky probe of the classical Caltech design, approximately two feet long, using junk from his pocket protector. Such probes are commonly used to remove nuts and washers and other parts that have gotten loose deep inside tangles of high-tech equipment. He gripped the probe with his Leatherman pliers—that lengthened the probe somewhat more. He reached out toward the bomb. Nope. It wasn't long enough by about five inches.

"Damn, damn!" he said.

Think. Use your God-given brain.

"Jackass—your flashlight!" he blurted. Now he taped his Mini Maglite to the sticky probe, and then held *that* in the Leatherman pliers. He reached out. The tape ball touched the bomb. He let it sit for a moment, to allow the adhesive to bind to the glass of the cylinder. Then he pulled it toward him. The cylinder shifted and toppled over.

It thudded on the concrete with a loud sound, and the glass broke, dumping out hexagons of virus. They poured out in a heap, skittered here and there, gleaming like fire opal in the light of the flashlight.

"Excellent!" he said. The warhead material had spilled out, giving him access to the detonator.

He could see a chunk of explosive in the center of the pile of virus. There was a blasting cap stuck in it, and what looked like a chip timer. He couldn't see the timer. Boy, this was crude. You didn't have to be a rocket scientist to make a virus bomb, as long as you had the virus material.

Then he saw movement and heard a sound. It was a rat, crouched and approaching the viral glass. It appeared to be about to eat some of the glass.

"Get away! Stupid rat!"

The rat looked at him, unafraid.

He found the piece of Oreo cookie. Pushed it at the rat. "Eat that."

The rat took it and waddled away.

Now to disarm the explosive. He could see the chip timer. It was a laboratory timer, not unlike an electronic kitchen timer. He touched the sticky end of the probe to the timer, and it stuck there. Good. He dragged the sticky probe toward him gently, and slowly the timer came along, pulling the blasting cap and the chunk of detonator with it.

He got the chip timer in his hand. Ahh! He sighed. He turned it over and looked at the numbers.

They were running. Currently they said: 00.00.02.

"Yaaaaahhh!" he yelled, and he pulled the blasting cap out of the explosive and flung the cap away, down the tunnel.

Whank!

The cap had gone off somewhere down there.

I wonder if it killed the rat, he thought.

There was still a heap of viral glass lying by his face. But it was underground. It could be dealt with. There would be a biohazard cleanup. It would be a mess, but it might be manageable.

Now I have to get my living body out of here.

He had to rotate his body in the shaft. So he shifted his hips, jamming himself tighter in the shaft, twisting himself, and trying to crunch his body down. He got his head around enough to see into the angle more clearly. Then he got his head into the angle, into the tunnel full of hexagons of viral glass. He took a deep breath and let it out, his blowers still humming, still protecting him, he hoped—and got himself a little farther around the corner. By exhaling and pushing, he could slide along on his back.

"Yes!"

He propelled himself on his back out of the hole, and he stood up, his feet in viral glass. He checked his suit with the minilight. There didn't seem to be any holes or tears, though he wasn't sure. His Racal hood was still pressurized, and his filters were working, it seemed. He hoped he did not have any rips in the suit or cuts in his skin. *I may be a walking dead man,* he thought.

There was a ladder. Cope had climbed down the ladder and left the bomb here. There was also a tunnel leading off horizontally. He had no idea where it led.

Just then he heard gunfire—two shots. Faint. Coming down the tunnel. What was going on? It was a low tunnel. He hurried along it, hunched over, and came to a sheet of plywood across the tunnel. He pushed on it, and it popped and fell away into a large, dark, open space. "Anybody there?" he said. He shone his light around and caught a glimpse of columns, a figure moving. "Alice?" Suddenly a red light appeared on his chest. What was this?

Then he heard Austen scream, "No!"

There was a roar in his ears and something slammed into his chest, driving him backward, with a sensation the likes of which he had never felt before. It was a bullet in his heart, and that was when it came to him that he had been shot and was dying.

□

Austen had heard Hopkins say "Anybody there?" as she was lying in darkness. At the same moment she saw the gleam of his flashlight. He was waving it around, trying to determine where he was, and she saw Cope, fixed, bent, writhing slowly, taking aim at the light. The laser touched Hopkins.

When Cope fired into Hopkins she heard a smacking *oof!* The minilight flew away and rolled across the floor, throwing its beam around crazily. Cope fired again, and again, and again, using the laser to aim.

Shrieking, she got to her feet and raced across the space and fell on Cope, knocking him off balance. She tore at him. She had a glimpse of Cobra's eyes glittering in the light of the minilight. Then she had his gun, and she aimed it at his face, and she shoved the barrel into his mouth. A red laser light reflected out of his mouth, and she saw the blisters. Their faces were inches apart.

There was a clunking sound, and the lights in the tunnel came on.

She was lying across Cope with his gun jammed into his mouth.

He trembled. An arm lashed out, while the other bent suddenly, and his neck arched and lashed around. Lesch-Nyhan writhing. In the light of the fluorescent lamps he looked shrunken, pathetic. "You killed him," she whispered. She stood up slowly, keeping the Colt aimed near those eyes. The red spot trembled on his forehead. Her finger tightened.

"Don't . . . Alice."

She spun around. Hopkins was standing behind her, bent over, the wind knocked out of him. There were two bullet pocks in his armored vest. The other shots had missed him. He was holding what looked like a bunch of junk taped together.

". . . Arrest . . . ," he choked. The bullets had given him a good thump, knocking the wind out of him.

She shook her head.

"You . . . power," Hopkins said, doubled over, looking at her.

To Cope she said, "You're under arrest."

Hopkins tried to straighten up, and coughed. "Need to . . . charge—"

"You are charged with murder," she said.

Cope spoke. "F.B.I. bitch."

"Try again, sir. I'm a public health doctor."

His eyes widened. His lips drew off his teeth, and his face rippled. Something she said may have triggered the seizure.

□

There was a growing chatter of voices on their radio headsets, and then they heard sounds in the air, culminating with a rush of people running up the Second Avenue tunnel. It was Oscar Wirtz with the operational group.

Simultaneously, a SWAT team of New York City police officers wearing respirators was moving down through the street hatch by the Manhattan Bridge, descending the stairs and ladders. You could hear the rattle of feet on steel gratings and the clink of their weapons.

As the operations groups converged on the scene they saw what had happened. The suspect was down in some kind of seizure. Hopkins told them that the tunnel might be biologically hot, because a grenade had gone off, and there was viral glass in the area.

"Where's Mark?" Hopkins asked.

"He was behind us, Will," Wirtz said.

Just then they heard Littleberry. He was coming up the Second Avenue tunnel toward them. His voice sounded crackly on the radio, hard to understand. Then they heard him shout, "Down! Get down! He left one back—" A flash ended his words.

They saw the blast wave come up the tunnel toward them. The wave came from the bomb that Cope had left sitting beside a column near the hatchway. No one had noticed it except Littleberry. He had been trying to warn them when it detonated.

The blast wave took the form of a meniscus, a thin, curved, bubble of powdered viral glass. It moved down the tunnel and passed over them and was gone. For an instant it showed them the face of Cobra virus in fully weaponized form. It filled the tunnel with a gray haze that was alive and aching to find blood.

The echo of the blast died down, leaving the tunnel in complete silence.

Cope turned his head and seemed to gaze down the tunnel.

Hopkins went down on his knees.

Austen knelt beside him. She placed her hand on his back. She saw the tears falling inside his faceplate.

"OUT! EVERYONE, OUT!" Oscar Wirtz was screaming. "WE'VE GONE HOT!"

□

They made their exit through the steel hatch at the foot of the Manhattan Bridge, into a maelstrom of emergency lights near Chatham Square, in Chinatown. Moments earlier, the deep booming thud of the explosion, which had occurred some fifty feet underground, had alerted emergency crews. The streets were jammed with emergency vehicles. There were people wearing Tyvek suits and talking on cell phones—managers from the mayor's Emergency Management Office. Television crews were not being allowed to get anywhere near the action. The area was awash in halogen lights, the air full of the chatter of hand-held radios and the constant deafening flutter of a half-dozen helicopters hovering overhead. Frank Masaccio had called every emergency unit he could think of, and he was still yelling into his headset at the Command Center, calling all units to converge on the hatchway at the Manhattan Bridge.

The Cobra Event had not been lost on New York City residents. Early-morning groups of onlookers were being pushed back by police officers. In the east over Brooklyn, a red thread of a cloud suggested that

dawn was coming. There was no traffic on the Manhattan Bridge—the bridge had been blocked off—
and most of the subway lines in lower Manhattan
were out of service.

At the Command Center in the Federal Building, and at Sɪᴏᴄ in Washington, a feeling was spreading that the situation was still dicey but might
possibly be manageable. Fragmentary reports were
coming in. A bomb had gone off, but the explosion
had occurred underground in an abandoned tunnel,
and an attempt would be made to keep the dust from
the bomb contained in the tunnel. The reports were
broken, confused, sometimes contradictory, coming
from different places, but some things were beginning to emerge. Frank Masaccio listened to his headset. He said: "He's what? The subject is under arrest?
Are you sure? Are you absolutely sure? Who made
the arrest?" He suddenly leaped to his feet. "Austen
made the arrest? Are you kidding me?"

□

Hopkins and Austen stumbled across tangles of fire
hoses. She kept one arm around his waist, almost
holding him up. The two of them were still dressed in
their space suits, but no one paid much attention to
them, because many people were wearing protective
clothing, and no one knew who was who. Fire Department personnel swarmed around, putting on green
chemical-hazard suits, shouting amid a crackle of radios. Crews from the New York City Fire Department
began placing sheets of plastic tarpaulin over a half-
dozen air vents that led to the underground structures
of the Second Avenue tunnel complex. It was presumed that virus particles would even now be flowing

out of these vents. As soon as the tarps were laid down, the emergency crews began piling mats of fiberglass batting on top of them, and then fire trucks began pumping water mixed with bleach onto the batting, soaking the fiberglass with liquids that would kill a virus. Then the Fire Department's HEPA trucks moved in. They would eventually begin pumping air out of the Second Avenue tunnel, passing it through large, truck-sized filters.

Hopkins and Austen made their way over to a Fire Department truck that was bathed in lights. It was the New York City human-decontamination truck.

"Go ahead, Will," Austen said.

He climbed inside the truck and closed the door. He stood in a decon chamber. A chemical spray went on. The chemicals bathed the outside of his suit. Finally the sprays stopped. Then he removed all of his gear, piling the helmet and filters and suit and boots and everything else into a biohazard disposal bag, until he was standing naked in the decon chamber. A water spray went on. It was a hot shower. He washed his body twice, the first time with a bleach solution, the second time with water and disinfecting soap. Whether any particles had been trapped in his lungs during the operation was something that would not be known for several days. He went through a door into the decon truck's change room. There, Fire Department people gave him a blue sweat suit to wear. It was marked with the letters N.Y.F.D.

Austen entered the truck and followed the same procedure.

Cope had been brought up by some of the Reachdeep ninjas. He was tied to a chair they had found in one of the empty rooms. They had lashed him to it with nylon rope, to control the biting and the thrashing. He was lifted up through the hatchway by the Manhattan Bridge. The chair was placed on the ground, the ropes were cut away, and he was lifted onto a gurney under bright lights. He seemed to be conscious but did not speak.

The gurney was loaded into an ambulance that screamed to the Wall Street Heliport, where a medevac helicopter lofted him to Governors Island. On the island, he made no statement to federal investigators. He died in the Medical Management Unit four hours later.

□

In the classified after-action report, the experts generally agreed that New York City had been very lucky. Fire trucks poured chemicals and water into the tunnels all day, and the air vents were piled with batting soaked with chemicals. Meanwhile, the HEPA filter trucks—they were essentially vacuum cleaners on wheels—drew air out of the tunnel system and passed it through filters. The filters accumulated stray particles of Cobra, and the air was discharged into the city.

In the end, fourteen citizens contracted Cobra virus infections at scattered locations around New York, for, inevitably, some particles escaped the chemicals and filters, and ultimately found a human lung. The fourteen cases were scattered across the Lower East Side and into Williamsburg in Brooklyn, and the plume of cases went as far out into Queens as Forest Hills. It created an epidemiological nightmare for the Centers for Disease Control. Almost all of the resources of that agency were used in tracing and managing the fourteen cases of Cobra that occurred following the blast in the tunnel. All active cases of Cobra were flown to Governors Island for treatment in the Army unit.

Five emergency workers who had been at the scene also came down with Cobra virus infection. They were mainly Fire Department people who had worked near the tunnel vents, who had laid down the tarps and fiberglass material, but who, in the chaos, had not had time to put on breathing masks. The number of deaths among emergency workers—just five—was considered miraculous. Many experts had been expecting the city's emergency personnel to be decimated during the Cobra Event.

Captain Dorothy Each, who had been bitten by Hector Ramirez, died on Governors Island. Of a total of nineteen cases of Cobra in New York resulting from the bomb blast, eighteen victims died. One eight-year-old girl survived but ended up with chronic Lesch-Nyhan disease and permanent brain damage. All of the patients were given anticonvulsants and the experimental anti-smallpox drug cidofovir, but the treatments had no effect. The overall toll of infections in the Cobra Event stood at thirty-two cases, including the index case of Harmonica Man, Kate Moran, and many others, and also counting Thomas Cope. Ben Kly did not count as a Cobra case, because he had not been infected, although he died as a result of the Cobra infection of Glenn Dudley. Mark Littleberry counted simply as a man lost in action.

The C.D.C. task force and the city department of health monitored people who had come into contact with active cases of Cobra. The United States

Public Health Service invoked its long-standing legal powers to place people into quarantine. Those quarantined were held in the Coast Guard dormitories on Governors Island. In the nineteenth century, when there had been no cures for most infectious diseases, the only way to prevent the spread of a disease was quarantine. Quarantine is an old practice, and it can sometimes work.

Quarantine

Austen and Hopkins were put in a quarantine unit at New York University Medical Center on the East Side of Manhattan, where they remained in Level 3 biocontainment, under the observation of doctors, for a period of four days. They had done their work and they needed some peace. Frank Masaccio would not allow them to be held on the island. He felt that they had been through enough, and should not have to be kept near people dying of Cobra.

Hopkins called Annie Littleberry in Boston, the widow of Mark Littleberry. He explained to her that Mark had served his country to the end. He told her that in recent weeks Mark had made important contributions to the safety of people everywhere in the world. He had helped develop evidence for the existence of a continuing biological-weapons program in Iraq, a program that had apparently moved into the genetic engineering of viruses, and Mark had helped break open a case of a corporation involved in criminal activity in the United States. "We think that some big prosecutions are going to occur as a result of Mark's work. One or more multinational biotechnology companies based in Switzerland and Russia are likely to end up with their top executives under warrant for arrest in the United States," he said. "It's going to be a nightmare for the diplomats. Mark would be proud, I know he would. It was something

Mark always enjoyed doing—creating extra work for the diplomats, Mrs. Littleberry."

☐

"I'm going nuts in here," Hopkins said to Austen on the afternoon of the fourth day.

They were dressed in bathrobes and hospital pajamas, and they had been pacing in opposite directions across a small recreational room on the twentieth floor of the hospital, which looked out across the East River, where barges churned through the gray tides and traffic murmured along on the East River Drive.

They felt fine. They were the equivalent of the lucky monkeys in the Johnston Atoll tests, the survivors, who might have received one or two particles in the lungs but had remained healthy. It seemed hard to believe that both of them had had no exposure to the Cobra virus, especially Austen. Probably they had received an exposure. On the other hand, perhaps the protective suits had worked.

They had spent the past four days talking on the telephone, it seemed, to every senior official in the United States government. For the moment the news media knew little of the details of the operation: in press conferences, Frank Masaccio's people had been describing Austen and Hopkins merely as nameless "federal agents" who had "arrested the suspect Thomas Cope," and no mention was made of Reachdeep. As far as the public knew, the Cobra Event had been one more brutal act of terrorism, resulting in somewhat more than a dozen fatalities. It had been nowhere near as bad as the bombing of the Murrah federal building in Oklahoma City. Few people understood just how grave the situation had been. Austen and Hopkins were grateful for Masaccio's efforts to protect their privacy.

In the relatively brief meetings they had had with each other, neither of them had mentioned a subject that had become increasingly obvious to both of them during the final days of the investigation and especially at the end.

The telephone rang. Hopkins picked it up. "Supervisory Special Agent Hopkins speaking."

He had a stiff way of answering telephones. It annoyed her, and she wondered if it was part of his Bureau training.

"Yes, Frank, she's here in the room. I don't think she wants to speak with you right now—"

She said: "For the third time, tell him *no.*"

"But he's serious. He says you could rise fast."

"I'm going back to work for Walter Mellis. That's it."

"It's final, Frank. She's going to stay at the C.D.C. Okay, Frank. Okay, yeah, I know, I'm disappointed, too . . ."

He hung up. He threw himself into a chair. "Agh!" he said, apropos of nothing. He was wearing foam slippers, like the kind you get on airplanes, and he tapped them on the floor. Then he stood up, stretched his arms, cracked his knuckles, and walked over to the window. He sighed. "I knew damned well from the moment they put us in here that we weren't going to get sick. It's a law of the universe. When they put you in quarantine, it guarantees your health."

The sky was shining with a clear afternoon brightness that comes when the days are getting long but summer has not quite arrived.

He looked at his watch. "They're letting us out at five. What are you going to do, anyway?"

"I don't know," she said.

He turned and faced her. "Do you like sushi?"

"Yes, I love sushi."

"So do I. You know, there's this incredible sushi place downtown, in an old industrial neighborhood. What do you say we ditch everybody and go eat some sushi?"

That seemed like a fine idea.

The Host

Toward the middle of summer, a three-year-old boy living on the Lower East Side developed Cobra brain virus infection and died at Bellevue Hospital. There was no indication of how he had become infected. It was possible that he had encountered some lingering crystals of virus. It was possible that in spite of days and weeks of treatment with disinfecting chemicals, some corners of the tunnels under the Lower East Side had remained hot. It wasn't clear how long Cobra crystals might survive in the open air, if the place was dark and dry and free of damaging sunlight.

Alice Austen flew up from Atlanta and interviewed the boy's family. She discovered that three days before his death, the boy had been bitten on the foot by a rat while he was asleep.

Then, in early September, a homeless man died of what later turned out to be Cobra infection in Elmhurst Hospital in Queens. He had been living in a subway tunnel under Roosevelt Avenue in Jackson Heights. The abandoned tunnels in that area were vast, and obviously contained rats. The Jackson Heights tunnels connect directly to the east side of Manhattan through a tunnel under the East River. Possibly infected rats had migrated through the tunnel from Manhattan.

The homeless man's body showed no evidence of a rat bite. Nevertheless, investigators from the Centers for Disease Control captured dozens of rats and tested their blood for Cobra. One of the rats tested positive. The rat seemed to have pulled out much of its fur in the belly area. The rat had survived a Cobra infection and had become a carrier of Cobra.

C.D.C. investigators tested more rats from other areas of the city and found that Cobra had entered the rat population, where it could survive without killing its host. Cobra and the rat had made an adjustment with each other. Suzanne Tanaka had first uncovered evidence that Cobra can survive in rodents when her mice became infected but didn't die—and when one of the mice passed the virus to her, she inadvertently showed that transmission of Cobra can go from rodent to human. Viruses jump from one species to another all the time, and some researchers believe they have a tendency to fill ecological niches—habitats for disease. Cobra seemed to have found a niche in the rat population.

It wasn't clear how Cobra had entered the rats. Possibly rats living in the Second Avenue tunnel had become infected when the bomb went off. Alice Austen wondered if the rats that had fed on the body of Lem in Houston Street had been the original source. Probably no one would ever know. In any case, Cobra had entered the ecosystems of the earth, and its future course could not be predicted.

Like all viruses, Cobra had no mind or consciousness, although in a biological sense Cobra was intelligent. Like all viruses, Cobra was nothing more than a program designed to replicate itself. It was an opportunist, and it knew how to wait. Cobra had achieved a kind of stasis in the rat, a point of balance. The rat was a good place to hide for an indefinite time, since the human species would never exterminate the rat. In its new host Cobra would cycle through generations of replication, perhaps changing, taking on new forms and strains, awaiting a chance to make another move, a wider breakthrough.

Glossary

aerobiology. The scientific study of the dispersal characteristics and infectivity of biological weapons in the air.

aerosol, bio-aerosol. A fine powder or liquid-droplet mist dispersed into the air. May be natural or a weapon.

Al Hakam. Biological-weapons facility in Iraq; disclosed by Iraq. Used for manufacturing anthrax up until 1995 or 1996. Destroyed by the United Nations in 1996.

Al Manal. Biological-weapons facility in Iraq; disclosed by Iraq. Produced nine thousand cubic yards of concentrated botulinum toxin ("bot tox") during the Gulf War.

amplification. Multiplication of a virus. Takes place inside cells of a living host or in cells in a test tube or inside a **bioreactor.**

anthrax. Single-celled bacterial organism capable of forming spores. Produces a pneumonia-like fatal illness when used in weaponized form.

Asilomar Conference. A conference held in the spring of 1975 to debate the hazards of genetic engineering. Led to the publication of the Asilomar Safety Guidelines, a set of recommendations governing **genetic-engineering** experiments in the laboratory.

bacterium (pl. bacteria). A single-celled microorganism. The cell has no nucleus and a thick cell wall. The most common life-form on earth.

baculovirus. See **nuclear polyhedrosis virus.**

Biological Toxins and Weapons Convention of 1972. International treaty outlawing the development and use of biological weapons and poisons derived from living organisms. Ratified by 140 nations; increasingly ignored.

biological weapon (bioweapon). A living infectious organism used as a weapon or a nonliving toxin derived from a living organism and used as a weapon.

Biopreparat. A once-secret Soviet biotechnology organization formerly funded largely by the Soviet Ministry of Defense, and devoted largely but not entirely to the research, development, and production of biological weapons.

bioreactor. A tanklike production device designed for **amplification** of a virus.

Biosafety Level 3 Plus. A high level of biocontainment just below Level 4. Requires negative-pressure air with HEPA filtering and safety clothing with respirator masks.

black biology (informal). The clandestine use of biotechnology and **genetic engineering** to create **recombinant** or **chimera** weapons with artificially altered genetic material.

Centers for Disease Control, Atlanta (C.D.C.). The premier U.S. federal agency for epidemiology, disease control, and disease prevention.

chimera. In Greek mythology, a monster with the head of a lion, the body of a goat, and the tail of a dragon. Also a virus made in the laboratory by the mixing (recombination) of genetic material from other viruses. Normally done for peaceful purposes; has obvious military applications.

cloning. The growing of identical copies of an organism that has been genetically altered in the laboratory.

Cobra. A fictional recombinant virus made from the **nuclear polyhedrosis virus,** the **rhinovirus,** and **smallpox.**

Cohen and Boyer experiment. Performed in 1973, when Stanley N. Cohen, Herbert W. Boyer, and others succeeded in putting working foreign genes into the bacterium *E. coli.* It was the first transplantation of a functioning gene, and it ushered in the biotechnology revolution. This experiment is now repeated in high schools.

Corpus One. The main research building at the Obolensk Institute of Applied Microbiology, in Serpukhov, about seventy miles south of Moscow. Biological-weapons inspectors and experts believe that **genetic engineering** of weapons-grade Black Death (*Yersinia pestis*) occurred at the institute over a period of many years.

Corpus Zero. The nickname for a building at the **Koltsovo Institute of Molecular Biology** in Russia where experiments with airborne weaponized Ebola virus and dried weapons-grade **smallpox** virus have been carried out in giant **explosion test chambers,** work that may continue today. The building is described as being off limits to all outsiders. It was visited once by an American-British inspection team, in 1991.

diener. Assistant at an autopsy.

DNA. Deoxyribonucleic acid. An extremely beautiful molecule, in the shape of a ribbon twisted into a double helix. It carries the genetic code in living creatures.

dry-line source. A source of powdered weapons-grade bioparticles that is moving in a line, thus dispersing the particles in a line. The line of particles spreads downwind over a potentially huge area of territory.

Engineering Research Facility (E.R.F.) A building at the F.B.I. Academy at Quantico where supersecret electronic research and development is carried on. Also the present location of the F.B.I.'s **Hazardous Materials Response Unit.**

Epidemic Intelligence Service (E.I.S.). Part of the **Centers for Disease Control** dedicated to investigating outbreaks of disease.

epidemiology. The study of epidemics of disease.

explosion test chamber. A closed steel chamber where aerosolized biological weapons are tested (**aerobiology**) on animals.

Felix. A fictional machine in a briefcase that rapidly sequences or "decodes" the DNA of living organisms.

forensic science. The scientific study of physical evidence at crime scenes.

gene. A length of DNA, generally around 1,500 bases long, that codes for a protein or an enzyme.

genetic engineering. The manipulation of the genetic material of an organism in a laboratory in order to make an organism with different characteristics.

genome. The entire complement of DNA of a living organism.

Hand-held "Boink" biosensor. A partly real, partly fictional biosensor device that can almost instantly detect approximately twenty-five dangerous infective pathogens.

Hazardous Materials Response Unit (H.M.R.U.). The unit of the F.B.I. dedicated to forensic and emergency analysis of nuclear, chemical, and biological substances.

HEPA **filter.** *H*igh-*e*fficiency *p*article-*a*rrestor filter. Used to trap biological particles in the air, thus purifying the air.

hot agent. A lethal biological weapon or naturally lethal infective organism.

Johnston Atoll Field Trials. The large-scale testing of biological weapons done by the U.S. military between 1964 and 1969 in areas of open sea downwind of Johnston Atoll in the Pacific Ocean.

Koltsovo Institute of Molecular Biology. A virology research complex near Novosibirsk, in Russia.

laydown, biological (informal). The release of a biological weapon into the air.

Lesch-Nyhan syndrome. A genetic disease inherited only by boys. Caused by damage to a single gene, it results in a bizarre manifestation of stereotyped self-injury, biting of the lips, fingers, and arms, as well as aggression directed toward other people.

Maalin, Ali Maow. A cook in Somalia. In late October 1977 he had the last case of naturally occurring smallpox on the earth.

midbrain. The top of the brain stem; connects with the underside of the cerebrum. It controls such things as the action of the pupils in the eyes and respiration. It is evidently connected to primitive responses, such as feeding, chewing, and aggression.

nuclear polyhedrosis virus. Also known as the baculovirus. A large, unique insect virus, the genes of which don't seem to be related to any other organism on earth. Has the ability to convert the body of an insect into 40 percent virus material by dry weight. The virus particle has a rodlike shape (*baculum* means "rod" in Latin). The virus particles occur inside large crystals of a protein called polyhedrin.

Office of the Chief Medical Examiner (O.C.M.E.). The medical examiner's office for New York City, situated at 520 First Avenue in Manhattan.

Pasechnik, Vladimir. The first, and by no means the last, major defector from the Soviet (and now Russian) bioweapons program. He was head of the Institute for Ultrapure Preparations in Leningrad (now St. Petersburg).

pathologist, pathology. A doctor who studies diseased tissues and who performs autopsies.

polyhedrin. A crystalline protein manufactured in cell nuclei during infection with **nuclear polyhedrosis virus.**

prosector. The person in charge of an autopsy, who does the dissection.

recombinant virus. A virus made in the laboratory by the mixing (recombination) of genetic material from other viruses. Also known as a **chimera.**

rhinovirus. The common cold virus. Comes in more than one hundred types.

SIOC. Strategic Information Operations Center at F.B.I. headquarters in the J. Edgar Hoover Building in Washington, D.C. SIOC is a radio-secure complex of rooms on the fifth floor, equipped with videoconference capability.

smallpox. Variola virus. Causes blistering and pustules on the face and arms. Is incredibly contagious and highly lethal in human populations that lack immunity to it. One of the scourges of human history.

Snow, Dr. John. An early epidemiologist and London physician who identified a water pump on Broad Street in London as the source of a cholera outbreak in 1853.

strategic weapon. A weapon capable of destroying an army or a city or a nation.

Sverdlovsk accident. An industrial accident resulting in the release of powdered weapons-grade anthrax into the air that occurred during the night of April 3, 1979, in the city of Sverdlovsk (now Yekaterinburg), Russia, causing at least sixty-six deaths.

swab. The central tool in the arsenal of the biological-weapons inspector, used for rubbing and sampling surfaces. Looks like a long Q-Tip, but has a wooden handle and a foam tip. When used with good laboratory backup, can potentially reveal the presence of **black biology.**

tech agent (F.B.I. term). An F.B.I. agent who specializes in the operation of technical equipment, much of it electronic surveillance gear and communications equipment.

transmissible. Contagious.

United States Public Health Service. An *unarmed* branch of the U.S. military services, and one of the oldest. Now a part of the U.S. Department of Health and Human Services. Its responsibilities include the operation of the **Centers for Disease Control (C.D.C.).**

UNSCOM. United Nations Special Commission.

Unsub (F.B.I. term). Unknown subject; unknown perpetrator of a crime.

USAMRIID. United States Army Medical Research Institute of Infectious Diseases at Fort Detrick in Frederick, Maryland. The Army's principal biodefense lab.

viral glass. A term used by the author to describe a glasslike material containing highly concentrated dry virus particles.

virus. A disease-causing parasite smaller than a bacterium, consisting of a shell made of proteins and membranes and a core containing the genetic material DNA or RNA. A virus can replicate only inside living cells.

weaponized, weaponization. A very difficult term to define in the area of biological weapons. Many experts define true weaponization as the act of mass production, preparation, and loading of biological material into a bomb or warhead or other delivery system. In this book, I deliberately use the term "weaponization" to also refer to **genetic engineering** of a microorganism for the purpose of creating a weapon. By my definition, the creation of a recombinant virus for use as a weapon is de facto *weaponization.*

Acknowledgments

The number of people who contributed to this book seems astonishing. It is a reflection of the necessary complexity of any federal bioterror action.

I am profoundly grateful to my editor at Random House, Sharon DeLano. Her editorial judgment went into every detail, from the wording of sentences to the order and structure of scenes, and she contributed some important ideas, especially in the characters of Tom Cope and Alice Austen, and toward some of the twists at the end.

In the **Federal Bureau of Investigation,** Drew Richardson, the head of the Hazardous Materials Response Unit (H.M.R.U.) at Quantico, and Randall S. Murch, chief scientific officer of the F.B.I. laboratory in Washington, provided generous amounts of time and help. Randy Murch invented the term "universal forensics"; Will Hopkins's description of it at the Sioc meeting follows Randy's own words to me, although the angry skepticism voiced by the man at the White House does not exist in reality. Other H.M.R.U. people at Quantico gave help, especially David Wilson and Anne Keleher, and I owe thanks to Bruce Budowle, Cyrus Grover, Keith Monson, Kenneth Nimmich, and John Podlesny for their time. At the New York field office, Joseph Valiquette showed me around and gave me a lot of his time. At the F.B.I. laboratory in Washington, thanks to William Bodziak, F. Samuel Baechtel, Jennifer A. L. Smith, and

Deborah Wang. I am also very grateful for the cooperation and assistance of the staff of the F.B.I.'s Public Affairs Office.

At the **Federal Centers for Disease Control and Prevention** in Atlanta, Richard Goodman, Stephen Ostroff, and Ruth Berkelman have been supportive friends and helpful minds. I spent many pleasant days interviewing officers of the Epidemic Intelligence Service: Frederick Angulo, Lennox Archibald, Susan Cookson, Marc Fischer, Cindy Friedman, Jo Hofmann, Daniel Jernigan, Elise Jochimsen, David Kim, Orin Levine, Arthur Marx, Paul Mead, Jonathan Mermin, John Moroney, Don Noah, Pekka Nuorti, Nancy Rosenstein, Jeremy Sobel, and Joel Williams. Others at C.D.C. generously gave their time: Dan Colley, Marty Favero, Randy Hanzlick, Brian Holloway, Robert Howard, James Hughes, Rima Khabbaz, Scott Lillebridge, William Martone, Joseph McDade, Bradley Perkins, C. J. Peters, Robert Pinner, and C.D.C. director David Satcher.

Dr. Frank J. Malinoski encouraged me from the very start of this project. As an eyewitness and participant in several sensitive visits to Russian biowarfare facilities, he provided me with key insights into the reality of biological weapons in Russia. Many thanks also to Judy Malinoski for her personal support.

At the **U.S. Army Medical Research Institute of Infectious Diseases (USAMRIID)** at Fort Detrick, Maryland, Peter Jahrling provided extremely valuable insights, and thanks to USAMRIID commander David Franz. At the **U.S. Navy Biological Defense**

Research Program, in Bethesda, James Burans provided a great deal of supportive friendship, not to mention unmeasurable hours of answers to my questions; and many thanks to William Nelson, David Frank, Gary Long, Beverly Mangold, and Farrell McAfee. Former undersecretary of the Navy Richard Danzig encouraged me in a literary sense: he helped me believe that the subject was important and that words could be found. Many thanks also to Pamela Berkowski.

At the **Office of Chief Medical Examiner** of the City of New York, many thanks to Ellen Borakove, David Schomburg, and Robert Shaler. At the **Medical Center at Princeton** (New Jersey), I am indebted to pathologists Elliot Krauss and Thamarai Saminathan and to diener Daniel Britt for allowing me to participate in a human autopsy. My notebook from that day is stained with blood and cerebral fluid, for they permitted me to have a hands-on experience as a reporter. And many thanks to Daniel Shapiro.

The New York subway historian and expert Joe Cunningham helped me with the final chase scenes in the subway, and we spent many happy days tramping all over the city, especially above and below ground on the Lower East Side, inspecting tunnels, pacing out distances, mapping action. Robert Lobenstein of the New York Transit Authority gave generously of his time, and I am also grateful to Roxanne Robertson for her help and supportive friendship.

For expertise with the virus, I am especially grateful to Malcolm J. Fraser of Notre Dame University. Whatever scientific follies exist here are my fault and certainly not Mac Fraser's.

At the Chelsea Garden Center in New York City I had valuable help from Betsy Smith and Nina Humphrey—it was Nina's idea to use forsythia as the plant that produced the grain of pollen in the story. At the New York Botanical Garden, many thanks to Kevin Indoe for help with the pollen grain.

Other experts gave interviews and time: Lowell T. Anderson, Anthony Carrano, William E. Clark, Sr. Frances de la Chapelle, Freeman Dyson, D. A. Henderson, Stephen S. Morse, Michael T. Osterholm, Marie Pizzorno, David Relman, Barbara Hatch Rosenberg, H. R. "Shep" Shepherd of the Albert B. Sabin Vaccine Foundation, Jonathan Weiner, and Frank E. Young.

Some of my most important sources did not wish to be named. I hope they will accept my profound thanks here. They know who they are.

A number of people gave help under trying circumstances as this book was being published. At **Random House,** special thanks to Joanne Barracca, Pamela Cannon, Andy Carpenter, Carole Lowenstein, Lesley Oelsner, Sybil Pincus, and Webb Younce. Also at Random House, Harold Evans, Ann Godoff, and Carol Schneider deserve thanks for their early enthusiastic support. At **Janklow & Nesbit,** special thanks to Lynn Nesbit, Cynthia Cannell, Eric Simonoff, and Tina Bennett. I am very grateful for the heroic work of the staff of North Market Street Graphics, especially Vicky Dawes, Lynn Duncan, Jim Fogel, Steve McCreary, and Cindy Szili. Nicole LaPorte, Matt Lane, and Harold Ambler gave emergency assistance.

Many thanks to copy editor Bonnie Thompson, and thanks to my personal assistant Cheryl Wagaman for her deft work.

Above all, loving thanks to my wife, Michelle, ever my guide star.

ABOUT THE AUTHOR

RICHARD PRESTON is the author of *The Hot Zone* (about the Ebola virus), *American Steel* (about a revolutionary steel mill), and *First Light* (about modern astronomy). He is a contributor to *The New Yorker* and has won numerous awards, including the McDermott Award in the Arts from MIT, the American Institute of Physics Award in science writing, and the Overseas Press Club of America Whitman Basso Award for best reporting in any medium on environmental issues.

LARGE PRINT EDITIONS

Look for these at your local bookstore

American Heart Association, *American Heart Association
  Cookbook, 5th Edition Abridged*
Ben Artzi-Pelossof, Noa, *In the Name of Sorrow and Hope*
Benchley, Peter, *White Shark*
Berendt, John, *Midnight in the Garden of Good and Evil*
Brando, Marlon with Robert Lindsey, *Brando:
  Songs My Mother Taught Me*
Brinkley, David, *David Brinkley*
Brinkley, David, *Everyone Is Entitled to My Opinion*
Byatt, A. S., *Babel Tower*
Carter, Jimmy, *Living Faith*
Chopra, Deepak, *The Path to Love*
Ciaro, Joe, editor, *The Random House Large Print Book
  of Jokes and Anecdotes*
Crichton, Michael, *Disclosure*
Crichton, Michael, *Airframe*
Crichton, Michael, *The Lost World*
Cronkite, Walter, *A Reporter's Life*
Cruz Smith, Martin, *Rose*
Daley, Rosie, *In the Kitchen with Rosie*
Dunne, Dominick, *A Season in Purgatory*
Flagg, Fannie, *Daisy Fay and the Miracle Man*
Flagg, Fannie, *Fried Green Tomatoes at the
  Whistle Stop Cafe*
Fulghum, Robert, *Maybe (Maybe Not): Second Thoughts
  from a Secret Life*
García Márquez, Gabriel, *Of Love and Other Demons*
Gilman, Dorothy, *Mrs. Pollifax and the Lion Killer*
Gilman, Dorothy, *Mrs. Pollifax, Innocent Tourist*
Grimes, Martha, *Hotel Paradise*

(continued)

Guest, Judith, *Errands*
Hailey, Arthur, *Detective*
Halberstam, David, *The Fifties* (2 volumes)
Hepburn, Katharine, *Me*
James, P. D., *The Children of Men*
Koontz, Dean, *Dark Rivers of the Heart*
Koontz, Dean, *Icebound*
Koontz, Dean, *Intensity*
Koontz, Dean, *Sole Survivor*
Koontz, Dean, *Ticktock*
Krantz, Judith, *Lovers*
Krantz, Judith, *Scruples Two*
Krantz, Judith, *Spring Collection*
Landers, Ann, *Wake Up and Smell the Coffee!*
le Carré, John, *Our Game*
le Carré, John, *The Tailor of Panama*
Lindbergh, Anne Morrow, *Gift from the Sea*
Ludlum, Robert, *The Road to Omaha*
Mayle, Peter, *Anything Considered*
Mayle, Peter, *Chasing Cezanne*
McCarthy, Cormac, *The Crossing*
Meadows, Audrey with Joe Daley, *Love, Alice*
Michaels, Judith, *Acts of Love*
Michener, James A., *Mexico*
Mother Teresa, *A Simple Path*
Patterson, Richard North, *Eyes of a Child*
Patterson, Richard North, *The Final Judgment*
Patterson, Richard North, *Silent Witness*
Peck, M. Scott, M.D., *Denial of the Soul*
Phillips, Louis, editor, *The Random House Large Print Treasury of Best-Loved Poems*
Pope John Paul II, *Crossing the Threshold of Hope*
Pope John Paul II, *The Gospel of Life*
Powell, Colin with Joseph E. Persico, *My American Journey*

(continued)

Puzo, Mario, *The Last Don*
Rampersad, Arnold, *Jackie Robinson*
Rendell, Ruth, *The Keys to the Street*
Rice, Anne, *Servant of the Bones*
Riva, Maria, *Marlene Dietrich* (2 volumes)
Salamon, Julie and Jill Weber, *The Christmas Tree*
Shaara, Jeff, *Gods and Generals*
Snead, Sam with Fran Pirozzolo, *The Game I Love*
Truman, Margaret, *Murder at the National Gallery*
Truman, Margaret, *Murder on the Potomac*
Truman, Margaret, *Murder in the House*
Tyler, Anne, *Ladder of Years*
Tyler, Anne, *Saint Maybe*
Updike, John, *Rabbit at Rest*
Updike, John, *Golf Dreams*
Whitney, Phyllis A., *Amethyst Dreams*